Lost in

BARKERVILLE

Lost in
BARKERVILLE

BITTEN ACHERMAN

RONSDALE PRESS

LOST IN BARKERVILLE
Copyright © 2020 Bitten Acherman

RONSDALE PRESS
3350 West 21st Avenue, Vancouver, B.C. Canada V6S 1G7
www.ronsdalepress.com

Typesetting: Julie Cochrane, in Minion 12 pt on 16
Cover Art & Design: Nancy de Brouwer, Massive Graphic Design
Paper: 100 Edition, 55 lb. Antique Cream (FSC) — 100% post-consumer
    waste, totally chlorine-free and acid-free

Ronsdale Press wishes to thank the following for their support of its
publishing program: the Canada Council for the Arts, the Government of
Canada, the British Columbia Arts Council, and the Province of British
Columbia through the British Columbia Book Publishing Tax Credit program.

Library and Archives Canada Cataloguing in Publication

Title: Lost in Barkerville / Bitten Acherman.
Names: Acherman, Bitten, author.
Identifiers: Canadiana (print) 20200288660 | Canadiana (ebook)
    20200288679 | ISBN 9781553806110 (softcover) | ISBN 9781553806127
    (ebook) | ISBN 9781553806134 (PDF)
Subjects: LCSH: Murder — Investigation — British Columbia — Cariboo
    Regional District — Juvenile fiction. | LCSH: Cariboo Regional District
    (B.C.) — Gold discoveries — Juvenile fiction. | LCSH: Barkerville
    (B.C.) —History — Juvenile fiction.
Classification: LCC PS8601.A435 L67 2020 | DDC jC813/.6–dc23

At Ronsdale Press we are committed to protecting the environment. To this
end we are working with Canopy and printers to phase out our use of paper
produced from ancient forests. This book is one step towards that goal.

Printed in Canada by Marquis Book Printing, Quebec

to my husband, Andrew,
for always believing
in my writing

ACKNOWLEDGEMENTS

Thank you to the dedicated manuscript group
at the Shadbolt Centre, Burnaby, BC, who throughout
the years helped me to become a better writer.
A special thank you goes to my editor Ronald B. Hatch
whose guidance and sharp eye for details were
immensely helpful.

Last but not least I want to acknowledge
my eldest son, Marc, for being my sounding board
when it came to plot outlines and ideas for new
characters and also my youngest son, Zach, who once
asked me when I was going to write a story for him.

Well, Zach, here it is.

Lost in
BARKERVILLE

Chapter 1

ZACH PUT HIS BACKPACK down at his feet and zippered up his dark-blue down jacket. Even though it was only the end of April, the air still carried a chill.

"Are you expecting a snow storm?" Derek, one of his classmates, asked as he sauntered up to him with his usual officious expression. With his round freckled face, upturned nose, and small pale blue eyes Derek resembled a pig. Zach groaned inwardly when Derek dropped his pack down next to his. Just great. Now he would probably be saddled with this moron for the field trip.

"Did you finish the quiz?" Derek cleared his sinuses and spat the results on the ground, barely missing their packs.

With disgust, Zach bent over and snatched his pack from the ground. "What quiz?" He pulled the straps of the pack over his shoulders.

"The history one that Youtz assigned us." Derek shook his head when he saw Zach's confusion. "He told us yesterday that he was going to collect them when we got on the bus."

"I didn't hear him say that," Zach protested.

"Well, he did at the end of class." Derek leaned close to Zach, who recoiled when he got a whiff of Derek's nasty morning breath.

"Youtz is going to eat you for lunch, you know."

Eat you for lunch, Zach mused. Now that sounded like something his dad would say. He looked around, desperate for a way to escape Derek, and he noticed that other tenth graders had now assembled in front of the school. He spotted Eric and Ryan, two classmates that he often hung out with. Ryan, noticing him, waved him over.

"I think I'll go . . ." Zach let out a gasp mid-sentence when Derek poked him hard in the ribs with his elbow.

"There's Kyle," Derek said.

Zach watched Kyle strolling down the sidewalk towards them, his hands buried in the pockets of the black leather jacket he always wore. A pair of scuffed Doc Martens peeked out from beneath loose-fitting blue jeans. Kyle, a tall lanky youth, had transferred to Zach's Burnaby area high school early in the year and was still an enigma to his fellow class-mates. He had so far pretty much kept to himself and mostly regarded the other students with a mixture of amusement and irritation.

"I seriously can't stand that guy." Derek said, very much expressing a popular sentiment regarding this newcomer.

"I kind of like him," Zach said, partly because it was true, but also to be contrary to what his classmate thought.

Derek scratched nervously at a zit on his forehead. "Jeez, he's headed over here." He glanced at Zach. "You know him?"

Zach shrugged. "No, not really." Which was true, since he had hardly ever exchanged more than two words with Kyle.

Derek did some more excavation of the zit. "He's not even supposed to be on this field trip."

Zach glanced curiously at him. "Why is that?"

"Because he told Mr. Anderson to get lost."

Zach gaped at Derek. "The gym teacher?" Mr. Anderson was over two-hundred and fifty pounds of pure muscle and no one, as far as Zach knew, had ever dared mouth off to him.

Derek gave up on the zit. "Yeah, he got detention for a week." He looked at Zach. "You didn't know?"

"He really said that to Anderson!" Zach watched Kyle with new respect as he covered the last distance between them.

Kyle's long dark hair had that disheveled look, which was usually achievable only if you had just rolled out of bed. He gave Derek a sour look. "Beat it," he told him.

Stunned by his directness, all Derek could do was stare at him.

Kyle leaned close to him. "I told you to beat it, you little midget."

Derek stirred into action, quickly grabbing his pack, and scurried over to a nearby group of classmates.

Kyle stared darkly after him. "I hate that pygmy." He kicked the toe of his boot into an old dried glob of chewing gum sticking to the cement. It dislodged and sailed out in the street.

Zach wasn't quite sure if he should feel awed, or amused as he stole a glance at Kyle's hawkish profile. "I didn't think you were allowed on this field trip?"

"Oh, because of what I said to that Neanderthal, Anderson." Kyle turned his head and regarded Zach with a look that wasn't unfriendly at all. "The principal figured it might be enlightening for me to go on this trip." He shook his head. "Enlightening! Give me a break," he snorted as he buried his hands even deeper into his pockets. "I sure as hell didn't wanna go. I hate field trips."

"This one might be interesting since it has to do with the gold rush." Zach grinned at him. "At least we won't have to go to class today."

Kyle acknowledged his remark with a reluctant smile. "Yeah, school sucks."

They both turned when they heard an engine struggle up the steep road towards the school. Soon Zach glimpsed the nose of the yellow school bus. It came to a screeching halt in front of him and Kyle. The doors hissed open.

"Better get going," he said to Kyle, who trailed reluctantly after him.

Mr. Youtz, their Social Studies teacher, had already placed himself next to the entrance of the bus. He was a slim man, Zach's father's age, with a crew cut and piercing blue eyes. Despite the chilly morning he wore no jacket. His tight navy-blue T-shirt drew attention to muscular shoulders and chest area, and a stomach like a washboard.

Mr. Youtz fixed his gaze on Zach and stretched his hand out towards him. "Quiz?"

"Eh, was that due today?" Zach asked, all innocence.

"Yeah, I thought you wanted it on Monday," Kyle said behind Zach.

Mr. Youtz gave them both the once-over with his humourless gaze. "My directions were clear as to when this assignment was due, so spare me your feeble claptrap." He squared his shoulders. "On my desk, first thing tomorrow, together with a minimum five-hundred-word essay explaining why you enjoyed this field trip so immensely." He nodded up towards the open doors to the bus. "Now get going. You're holding up the line."

With cheeks burning, Zach scrambled up the steps and found an empty seat in the middle of the bus.

Kyle slumped down next to him. "I never heard him say it was due today, did you?"

Zach shook his head and looked out the window at the students, crowding in front of the bus to get inside. He noticed Miss Reid, their English teacher, among them. At close to six feet she was towering over a lot of the tenth grade students. She had absolutely no fashion sense and always dressed in ill-fitting clothes with colour combinations that made people's eyes spin. Today she was wearing orange pants and a Kelly-green fleece jacket. A small bright red backpack topped off the ensemble.

Zach felt warm breath tickle his neck. Kyle was leaning over his shoulder to take a look out the window.

"Don't tell me that she's coming too?" he said with a groan when he spotted Miss Reid.

Zach turned to Kyle. "Yeah, she's one of the chaperones. You didn't know?"

Kyle slumped back in his seat. "Of all the teachers I hate her the most. Hell, she doesn't even look like a woman. More like an ostrich." He closed his eyes with a deep sigh. "This is going to be one lame trip."

Chapter 2

"LISTEN UP," Mr. Youtz yelled as he clapped his hands.

The din of voices subsided. All the students had found seats. Up front Miss Reid sat together with the two parent chaperones. She smiled warmly back at Zach. For some odd reason she had chosen him as one of the favourites in her English class, which was an honour he could have done without.

Mr. Youtz held up a hand to hush the last voices coming from the back. "Quiet!" He waited for total silence before he went on. "Miss Reid and I will be in charge. That means what we say goes. Understood?"

The students nodded. Mr. Youtz turned to the bus driver. "Mr. Jennings here will be our trusted driver."

Mr. Jennings, who reminded Zach of Gollum from *The Lord of the Rings*, grinned broadly, exposing tobacco-stained teeth. "I'll make sure we all make it in one piece."

Mr. Youtz pointed to a short wiry Chinese guy and a chubby woman with very blonde hair, sitting in tentative closeness on the narrow seat behind the bus driver. "Mr. Chan and Mrs. Oberon here have kindly agreed to go with us today to act as extra chaperones. Don't give them any grief." Mrs. Oberon smiled timidly as she waved a plump hand at them. In the back someone snickered, drawing a scathing look from Mr. Youtz.

"The driv . . ." The bus started up so suddenly that the teacher had to grab onto the seats on either side of the aisle so he wouldn't fall.

"Sorry." Mr. Jennings flashed a sheepish grin at Mr. Youtz. "Cranky old bus."

"The drive," Mr. Youtz repeated as he turned his attention to the students again, "will take about two and a half hours. We'll make a pit stop at Bridal Falls before we continue to the town of Yale."

"Mr. Youtz." Susan, a short girl with long red hair, who was sitting across the aisle from Zach and Kyle, eagerly thrust her arm in the air. "Mr. Youtz."

"Yes, Susan."

"Were we supposed to read the chapter about the Cariboo Wagon Road too?"

The teacher shook his head. "No, only the chapter covering the first part of the gold rush. That includes the info on Fort Langley and Fort Yale, of course."

Susan looked triumphantly at Derek who was sitting next to her. "See. I told you."

"Maybe you can tell us a little bit about Yale's early history, Derek?" Mr. Youtz had to grab onto the seats again when the bus lurched around a corner.

Face ablaze, Derek sank down in his seat.

Susan got up. "Yale was once called Fort Yale and it was founded in 1848 by the Hudson's Bay Company." She turned to the students in the back of the bus. "When the Cariboo gold rush was at its height in the 1860s it was the largest city west of Chicago and north of San Francisco. It was . . ."

Kyle leaned forward in his seat, looking at her. "Excuse me, is your name, Derek?" he asked.

Two bright red spots showed on Susan's cheeks. "No, but he wasn't going to answer anyways."

"It's okay, Susan," Mr. Youtz said with a sharp look at Kyle. "Since you obviously know so much about this subject, you can continue."

Kyle snorted. "Oh jeez." He dug his hand into his jacket pocket and brought out his cellphone. "Tell me when birdbrain is done," he told Zach as he stuck the attached ear buds in his ears. Listening to the music, he leaned back in his seat and closed his eyes.

Chapter 3

∽

WHEN THEIR BUS HAD arrived in the town of Yale in the late morning, the class had first visited the Creighton House, a small museum displaying artifacts and photographs from the Cariboo gold rush period. Afterwards they had gone on to explore the museum's adjoining outdoor area where a tent city had been erected, which showed what life was like for miners in 1858. Zach had found this part of the field trip the most interesting, but he would have enjoyed it more had Kyle not constantly commented on how pointless it all was. The only activity Kyle had liked was trying his hand at gold panning.

They had now moved on to the small Church of St. John the Divine where a young woman in a period costume stood waiting for them outside the church.

"This is your guide," Mr. Youtz told the class. "Her name is Sarah and she's going to give you a tour inside the church." He looked sternly at them. "Needless to say, I expect best behaviour so that means keeping quiet and listening carefully to what Sarah has to tell you."

"I like your costume," Susan told Sarah admiring her long white and blue checkered dress. "Especially the shawl. It's very 1860s."

Some of the other students moaned. "Shut up, Susan," Derek said, a remark that drew an instant reprimanding look from Miss Reid.

"Well, let's get started, guys," Mr. Youtz said clapping his hands. "We still have a lot to see and do today."

The students followed Sarah up the steps to the open door into the church. They first filed into a small room before they continued through the door leading into the Sanctuary of the church itself. At first, the class heeded Mr. Youtz' admonition about being quiet, but as Sarah walked up the middle aisle between the rows of pews, a group of guys started poking each other, which in turn sent some girls into a fit of giggling, and soon everyone was talking and laughing. When the guide stopped in front of the chancel and began speaking, the din of voices drowned out most of her words.

"Be quiet!" Mr. Youtz yelled at the students from the back

of the church where he stood together with Miss Reid and the two chaperones. "Didn't you hear? Quiet, I said."

The voices gradually died down.

Sarah cleared her throat nervously. "The church of St. John the Divine," she said as she looked out over the students, "was built in 1863 by the Royal Engineers and is one of the oldest surviving churches in BC." She turned and looked up at the altar. "Some of the altar pieces within this church are originals from the 1860s, and . . ."

Zach's attention was diverted from what the guide was saying when Kyle, who was standing right next to him, prodded him in the ribs with his elbow. "Let's go outside," he said. "This is boring."

Zach cast a glance over his shoulder toward the back of the church where the teachers and chaperones still stood in the same spot close to the entrance. "That won't be easy without Youtz spotting us."

Together with the rest of the students, they followed Sarah up the few steps leading to the altar of the church. Kyle pointed out a closed door to their left. "We can go out that way."

"It's probably locked."

"Or maybe not." Kyle seized Zach by the arm and pulled him over to the door. Letting go of Zach, he reached out his hand and pushed the handle down. The door slid open and Kyle peeked around it. "It looks like a furnace room," he said with a glance back at Zach. "And there's another door leading to the outside." Before Zach had time to respond, Kyle had disappeared entirely from view.

Zach looked across the church to where the teachers were standing and found Miss Reid staring at him. She gestured at him to come over. Just then Kyle's arm shot out from behind the door and took hold of Zach's sleeve, pulling him through the doorway.

"Miss Reid saw us," Zach whispered as Kyle closed the door firmly behind them.

"So what's she going to do? Send us home?" Kyle pushed the door to the outside open. Bright sunshine blinded Zach. When his eyes had readjusted, he saw Kyle saunter over to the whitewashed wall of the church and lean his back up against it. He fished a pack of cigarettes out from an inside pocket in his jacket, pulled a cigarette from it, and put it between his narrow lips.

Zach closed the door softly behind him. "I didn't know you smoked."

Kyle pulled a yellow plastic disposable lighter from the same pocket and lit the cigarette, shielding the lighter's flame between his hands. He blew smoke out through his nose as he dropped the lighter back into the pocket. "You want one?" he stretched out his hand, offering Zach his pack of Pall Mall.

Zach shook his head. "I don't smoke." He came over to Kyle, and placed himself next to him. He looked at the small wooden house just across from where he and Kyle were standing. It had a wide porch and on top of the roof a weather vane shaped like a rooster made a slow turn and pointed its arrow straight at them. "Well, that's weird."

Kyle picked a piece of tobacco from the tip of his tongue with two fingers. "What's weird?"

Zach nodded at the house. "I don't remember seeing that house when we walked over here."

Kyle glanced at him. "Well, obviously it must have been. It's not like houses shoot up from the ground, or drop from . . ." He stopped in mid-sentence when the door into the furnace room was opened, and quickly tossed the cigarette on the ground, planting the sole of his heavy boot over it. He was grinding it into the dirt just as Miss Reid filled the door-opening.

"You two are not supposed to be out here." Her attention was drawn to Kyle's boot. "Were you smoking?"

He shook his head. "Nope."

Face flushed, she marched over to him. "Don't you dare lie to me, Kyle."

The sun moved behind a cloud at the same time as the door to furnace room banged shut.

"Lift your foot," Miss Reid ordered Kyle, who raised his boot, so she could have a good look at the half-smoked flattened cigarette.

"It was not like I was smoking inside," he said.

Miss Reid fixed him with a hard gaze. "You're not supposed to smoke — anywhere." She turned her attention to Zach, making a brisk gesture with her hand towards the closed door to the furnace room. "Inside now, Zachary." She was one of the few people who used his full first name.

With a glance at Kyle, who was viewing the teacher with open dislike, Zach walked up to the closed door and reached out his hand, turning the handle. He pushed. The door didn't budge. Figuring it was just stuck, he pressed his shoulder against the door and leaned in, but nothing happened. Zach turned to the others. "I think someone must have locked it from the inside."

Miss Reid came over to him. "Here let me." Zach stepped aside so she could try, but she had no better luck. She lifted her hand and knocked on the door. "Open the door," she yelled. They waited, but no one responded. "Let's walk around to the front," Miss Reid said at last. "They probably can't hear me."

Zach nodded and followed her around the corner of the church. Kyle trudged after him, the hard soles of his boots sounding hollow across the pathway. When they reached the front of the building they saw that the heavy door to the church was closed.

"Wait here," Miss Reid told Zach and Kyle. She resolutely walked up the wooden staircase and stopped in front of the closed door. She tried the handle but the door was locked.

In the distance, Zach heard the crunching sound of wheels driving over gravel and turned to have a look. Behind a line of trees he saw a horse-drawn carriage moving swiftly along. Kyle was too busy watching Miss Reid banging on the door of the church with her fist to notice the carriage.

"Open up," Miss Reid yelled. "Open up."

A dark pall had descended. Looking up, Zach saw that the sky was now covered with low-hanging, grey clouds that promised rain. The weather had sure changed fast. He turned his attention to Miss Reid again when he heard her come down the stairs.

"No one's responding," she said as she walked over to them. "They must already have left."

An uneasy feeling made Zach's stomach contract. "But we would have heard them leave. I mean with all those people."

Miss Reid slipped off her red backpack, unzipped one of its pockets and pulled out her cellphone. "I'll give Mr. Youtz a call to find out where they are." She punched in some numbers and looked at the screen. Frowning, she pressed the phone to her ear. "Well, that's odd." She glanced at the screen again. "My phone has no signal."

"Where's the class supposed to go after the church?" Kyle's question was directed at Miss Reid.

She tore herself out of her reflections. "Down to the Fraser River," she answered as she tightened the straps of her pack. "Mr. Youtz wanted to show the class where the steamships used to dock back in the gold rush days and, of course, where the Cariboo Road had its starting point." She bit her lip nervously. "Zachary is right. We would surely have heard something if so many people left at once."

"Why don't we just go down to the river and check it out,"

Kyle said. "We'll probably find them there." He turned around and sauntered down the pathway leading from the church to the road. "Let's go," he yelled over his shoulder when he realized the two others had remained behind.

Kyle stopped at the low gate in the fence surrounding the church property. The hinges squeaked as he opened the gate and walked through. Zach and Miss Reid followed him, with Miss Reid closing the gate after them.

Doubts were weighing Zach down. From what he knew about Mr. Youtz, he was a perfectionist. No way would he have left the church before everyone had been accounted for. Especially he would have noticed if Miss Reid was missing. "This road should be paved," Zach said as the three of them stopped at the edge of a dirt road filled with wheel tracks and potholes.

"No kidding." Kyle grinned at him as he kicked a small rock across the road. "These small hick towns never wanna spend the money."

Zach shook his head. "No, you don't understand." He could feel the stomach acid burn in his throat as he looked from Kyle to Miss Reid. "This road was asphalted when we drove here on the bus."

"Well, obviously it can't be the same road then," Miss Reid said. "Come on now, let's go and find the class," she added impatiently as she turned and began walking alongside the road. Zach and Kyle trudged after her.

They all stopped when a horse-drawn wagon pulled out

from a side street a little further down the road. The sturdy work horse pulling the wagon turned and trotted in their direction.

"They sure take this heritage stuff seriously around here," Kyle said as the three of them stepped aside to give the wagon enough space to pass by them.

The small wiry man who was driving pushed his broad-rimmed hat back on his head and gaped openly at them as he rolled by.

"Look out," Miss Reid yelled after him as the wagon veered from the road, its wheels coming dangerously close to the ditch.

The man gave a start, yanked at the reins, and at the last second managed to turn the horse back towards the middle of the road. He continued sending bewildered glances back at them as he drove on.

Kyle looked down at himself. "Did I leave my fly open? I mean, the way that guy gawked at us." He glanced up at Miss Reid. "Maybe it's your jacket. Did anyone ever tell you that it sort of makes you look like Kermit the Frog?"

Flustered, Miss Reid's hand went to the zipper of her jacket.

"It's okay," Kyle told her, clearly enjoying her befuddle-ment. "I totally dig Kermit — and Miss Piggy too," he added. "She's the most misunderstood of all the Muppets. She's basically just a lonely pig who wants to be loved."

Miss Reid's face reddened. "That's quite enough from you." She turned her back to him and started marching down the road. "Let's move on, you two," she yelled back at them.

"You probably shouldn't be talking to her that way," Zach told Kyle as they trailed after her.

"Why? Because she's a teacher?" Kyle cried out in surprise when his boot caught in one of the many potholes in the road. Had Zach not been next to him and managed to grab hold of his arm, Kyle would have fallen flat on his face, instead of just falling to his knees. Zach helped him up. "Oh jeez," Kyle exclaimed.

Miss Reid, alerted by Kyle's outburst, turned around and walked back to them. She looked at Kyle's dirty pants legs. "Oh, very unfortunate," she said with a certain satisfaction in her voice. She was obviously still sore at Kyle because of his Kermit remark.

Kyle ignored her as he wiped at his pants with his hand, which only made it worse. He finally gave up and rolled his eyes towards the sky. "I hate this freaking place."

They went on their way again with Kyle complaining bitterly.

"Git out of the way," someone yelled at one point behind them. They all jumped aside to make room for a fast-approaching wagon. The driver, a portly middle-aged man with a handlebar moustache, gave them a dour look as he drove by. "Folks might have more sense than walkin' in the middle of the road," he barked.

"Scumbag!" Kyle yelled after him and gave him the finger.

Miss Reid turned angrily on him. "That was unnecessary."

Kyle pulled angrily at the sleeves of his jacket. "Well, he *is* a scumbag."

Zach watched as the man in the wagon, pulled hard at the horses' reins and turned left, rounding the corner of a building.

"You know what's weird," Kyle told Zach as they again trudged side by side after Miss Reid. "We haven't seen a single car drive by."

"Well, that's true," Zach said.

Miss Reid crossed the road where the wagon had turned a moment earlier, then stopped abruptly. When Zach and Kyle came up next to her, they saw why. Below them, down a steep embankment, flowed the Fraser River, its green waters lapping at the sandy shore.

"Wow, I didn't know they had a steamship here." Zach told Miss Reid as he stared curiously at the large vessel, which lay moored at the nearest bank. It had a single smokestack that rose almost two storeys high from the deck to the small wheelhouse on the very top. A large wooden paddle wheel was attached to the stern. Strong looking men, laden down with goods, balanced precariously from the ship's hold down a narrow wooden ramp to the shore where empty wagons drawn by sturdy workhorses stood waiting to be loaded.

"It's called a sternwheeler," Miss Reid told Zach, nodding at the steamship. "It must belong to the museum." Her face took on a puzzled expression. "Strange that they didn't tell me about the steamship when I called for our reservations."

The three of them stood watching as yet two more empty wagons pulled up next to the ship to be loaded.

Zach felt a nudge in the side. "Look behind you," Kyle said, pointing to a long row of one-and two-storey clapboard houses, which lined the other side of the street. Clearly it was some sort of business district, considering all the signs mounted there, the most prominent reading The Yale Hotel, smaller ones were for McKenzie's General Store, Laura's Eatery, and Angus' Apothecary.

The majority of the people milling in and out, and between the buildings were men, most of them dressed in work pants, collarless long-sleeved shirts and sturdy leather boots. The few women Zach saw were clad in ankle-length dresses with tight-fitting, long-sleeved tops and long billowing skirts. Some of them also wore bonnets. A handful of men looked quite gentlemanlike in long jackets, white shirts and neckties.

Miss Reid too was watching the going-ons across the street with great interest. "Strange," she commented. "When I did my research to prepare for this field trip, I saw a drawing similar to this, in one of the books I was reading."

Zach glanced at her. "Why is that so strange?"

"Because it was a drawing from the 1860s." She bit her lip. "I have visited Yale only once before, a long time ago when I was a child, and I'm quite sure that those buildings weren't there then."

"It must be part of some heritage stuff they're doing." Zach continued watching the people. They seemed so full of purpose and unbelievably well-adjusted in their roles from this by-gone era.

"I'll try to get hold of Mr. Youtz again." Zach turned to see Miss Reid pull her cellphone out of her pack and push a button. She held the phone to her ear, then shook her head in frustration. "Still nothing!" The teacher glared at the phone in her hand as if she thought she could will it to work. "Nothing at all," she reiterated after having put it to her ear again.

Kyle reached into his jeans pocket. "Maybe it's just your phone that isn't working. Try mine." He pulled the earphones out of his cellphone and handed it to the teacher.

With unease, Zach noticed that a small group of scruffy-looking men, standing nearby, had started taking an interest in them. He kept a wary eye on the men while the teacher tried Kyle's phone. She soon handed it back to Kyle. "It doesn't work with your phone either."

The group of men were still staring at them. "Are you from the actin' troupe that just came to town?" a big burly guy with a broad pock-marked face, sporting impressive whiskers, asked.

Miss Reid shook her head. "No, why would you think that?"

"Because of them costumes you have on, of cours'."

Kyle dropped his cellphone down in his pocket. "That's a little rich coming from you guys, since you're the ones wearing the costumes." Confused, the men looked down at their checkered shirts, and woollen pants.

Zach looked up into the grey sky when a fat drop of rain hit him on the nose. "Great, just what we needed."

"And I didn't bring my umbrella, since the weather report said it would be sunshine all day," Miss Reid said as more drops fell around them. The men who had stood next to them were hotfooting it across the street. Zach saw them pull open the door and rush into the Yale Hotel.

Kyle pulled his jacket collar up around his ear. "What are we standing around here for?" he asked. "Let's go."

Chapter 4

∽

THE THREE OF THEM dashed through the rain to the Yale Hotel, where Kyle pulled the heavy front door open and held it for the others. Miss Reid said something when they were inside, but the din of voices from all the people around them as well as the loud piano music coming from the far end of the lobby drowned out her words. Zach shook his head at her. "What?"

"Some kind of hotel this is," she yelled. A long polished counter in the back of the lobby ran the length of the room. Behind it a tall wiry man with a handlebar moustache was busy pouring drinks to the men crowding around the counter. Numerous liquor bottles filled the shelves on the wall behind him. Every available space in the rest of the lobby was filled with tables, around which people sat smoking and playing cards.

Suddenly three men sitting at a table next to one of the lobby's windows, shot up from their seats. "Let's go and git them," one of them yelled. The three of them headed for the door. Before Zach had time to get out of their way, the man in front, a tall young guy with long blond hair, shoved him aside so hard that Zach slammed his shoulder and the side of his face against the wall.

"What's goin' on, Hugo?" a man, sitting at a table close by the door yelled as the young man struggled with the door to the hotel.

"We just saw Stuart and those cheatin' brothers of his out-side," Hugo answered. "We'll make sure they've played their last game of poker." His two friends rushed outside with him.

"Are you all right?" Miss Reid asked Zach, who sat slumped against the wall. With two fingers he wiggled his nose, which presently hurt the most. Tears of pain blurred the teacher's form in front of him.

"Is it broken, do you think?" she asked anxiously.

"I don't think so." Zach let go of his nose and looked at his fingers. At least he wasn't bleeding.

Miss Reid leaned towards him, her fingers hovering above his nose. "Here, I better check?"

He tilted his head away from her. "No thanks."

From the street came sounds of fighting: grunting and

hollering and outbursts of pain when a punch hit its target. With his hand covering his throbbing nose, Zach got up and tried to sneak a peek around all the people crowding the doorway. He heard a commotion behind him, and turned around. The man Zach had just seen serving drinks behind the counter, grabbed him by the arm and pulled him aside. "Git away from that door." He thrust aside the rest of the men clogging the doorway in a similar brusque fashion. Finally, he slammed the door shut with his foot.

"Can't abide a little blood, Sam!" A sharp voice yelled from further back in the lobby.

The voice, it turned out, belonged to a woman, standing on a narrow staircase leading up to the hotel's second storey. She was dressed in a short black frilly skirt and a tight, low-cut top that gave an alluring view of cleavage. Leaning against the bannister, she flicked her long red hair over her shoulders and folded her arms over her chest while viewing Sam with an impertinent look.

Sam scowled up at her. "Blazes, Rosie, shut your yap and get back to work." Amidst boisterous laughter and hooting from the people in the lobby, he returned to his place behind the counter.

"Boy, is she ever hot," Kyle said with an admiring look at Rosie, who was wiggling her backside provocatively as she took the last few steps up to the second-storey landing.

Zach, turning to Miss Reid, saw that the teacher's attention was caught by one of the men standing at the counter. "What's up?" he asked.

She squinted her eyes to get a better look. "Isn't that Mr. Youtz?" she asked, pointing.

Zach, whose nose was still hurting, blinked tears of pain from his eyes and tried focusing on the man Miss Reid had pointed out. "It sort of looks like him," he said, wondering why Mr. Youtz would have changed into a white and red checkered shirt.

"If that's Youtz where's the rest of the class?" Kyle asked exchanging a puzzled glance with Zach. Miss Reid headed for the counter, making her way between the tables and chairs in the lobby. "Well, we better go after her," Kyle added.

When they reached her, she just stood there staring, her arms hanging limply by her sides. "Miss Reid?" Zach asked.

She turned to them with a look of disappointment on her face. "It isn't Mr. Youtz after all."

Zach leaned forward and glanced at the man in question. Up close he didn't even look like their Social Studies teacher. He hadn't noticed them staring, as he was busy watching the bartender called Sam putting weights on a small balance scale on the counter.

When Sam was finished with the weights, he did a quick mental calculation. "That's fifty-seven dollars worth, Frank," he said, looking up at the tall man, dressed in a long dust-covered coat, standing on the other side of the counter.

The light from the oil lamp hanging overhead flickered across Frank's chiselled face. "That's a fair price for a nugget that size," he said with satisfaction.

"Where are you prospectin', Frank?" asked the guy Miss

Reid had thought was Mr. Youtz, as he stared at the gold nugget on the scale with a greedy look.

Frank viewed the man from underneath hooded eyes. "Wouldn't you just like to know, Robert."

A thin smile stretched Robert's lips. "Last I heard you was snipin' at a place called Lightnin' Creek." He nodded at the scale. "Perchance that's where that there gold came from."

The bartender cleared his voice. "Well, this here piece, Frank." He picked up the gold nugget from the scale, "will buy you my best room, some grub, a dip in the tub, and the services of any of my girls." He winked at Frank. "Or maybe you'll want all of them?"

Frank snatched the gold nugget from Sam's hand and dropped it into his coat pocket. "No offence, Sam, but I'll be lookin' for another place to stay tonight." With one last sharp look at Robert, he turned and left.

Sam gave Robert a sour look. "You're bad for business, you know."

Robert shrugged, then slammed a coin down on the counter. "Keep the change." He too left.

"Good riddance," Sam grumbled as he pocketed the coin, took the scale and placed it on one of shelves behind him.

"Sir ... Mr ..." Miss Reid waved at him to get his attention.

Sam straightened up and spotted the teacher. "What do you want, eh ...?" He looked at her green fleece jacket and her short brown hair with a frown. "Eh Sir? ... Ma'am?" He kept staring at her.

Miss Reid, feeling flustered by his scrutiny, nervously brushed a lock of hair away from her forehead. "Yes, could I please borrow your phone?"

"My what?" he asked.

People standing close enough to hear the exchange turned silent.

Miss Reid cleared her throat. "Your phone. If you have a landline phone, could I please use it?"

Sam added a few more furrows to his forehead. "A phone? What the blazes are you blatherin' about?"

Kyle raised his eyebrows at him. "It's this thing you call people up on, so you can talk to them."

Sam viewed him with mistrust. "Are you playin' me for a fool?"

Kyle fixed Sam with a glare. "Okay, you've had your fun now." He indicated Miss Reid with a motion of his head. "Let her just use your phone, okay?"

Sam's eyebrows had knitted together. "You askin' for trouble?"

"She only wants to use your damn phone." Kyle leaned in over the counter. "Why are you giving her grief about it?"

With lightning speed, Sam's hand shot over the counter, and grabbed the front of Kyle's T-shirt. He pulled Kyle so close they were face to face. "Git out of here," he hissed.

"What's wrong with you?" Kyle tried to pry Sam's fingers from his T-shirt, but Sam held on. "This is assault. Plain and simple."

Miss Reid placed a hand on Sam's arm. "Really, there's no need for this," she said. "We'll leave peacefully." Zach had to admire the way she kept it together, her voice firm and her gaze unfaltering. He didn't know how she managed it, because his own legs were trembling so much he had trouble standing.

After some hesitation, Sam finally decided to release Kyle from his grip.

Kyle turned around and looked across the many faces in the room. "You're all my witnesses to what this jackass did to me," he yelled as he pointed at Sam. "This was an unprovoked attack."

The piano player, a stooped old man with white hair and sweat stains around the armpits of his dirty white shirt, stopped playing. He turned and viewed Kyle with a stunned look. A wave of silence swept across the room. Everyone stared at Kyle. The animosity surrounding the three of them made Zach break out in goose bumps. Everywhere he looked he saw hostile faces.

A thickset guy with broad shoulders, sitting at a table in the middle of the room with three other guys, put his cards down, and got up. "These folks givin' you bother, Sam?" He came out from behind the table, his surly gaze fixed on Kyle.

"Come now, Charlie," a tall slim man, dressed in a dark-grey suit got up from a chair in the far end of the room. A black hat pushed back on his head, which very much resembled a bowler, gave him a jaunty appearance. "I'm certain these folks meant no harm," he said when he reached Charlie. "They're clearly from out of town, so let's give them the benefit of doubt."

Charlie kept glaring at Kyle. "Theo, this upstart called Sam a jackass."

The man called Theo put a hand on Charlie's shoulder. "Most likely, he was just nervous. I'm sure he didn't mean it." Theo looked over at Kyle. "Only a lapsus linguae, wasn't it?" There was a clear warning tone behind his affable words.

"Lapsus what?" Kyle shook his head at Zach. "What the heck's he talking about?"

Before Theo had time to explain, Charlie was on the move again, his face red and his eyes narrowed. "There goes this upstart again, openin' that foul trap of his."

Miss Reid quickly stepped in front of Kyle, holding out her arms in a protective gesture. "Sir, you have to calm down," she said, bravely staring Charlie down. "Clearly, he's feeling intimidated by you, and is therefore acting in a way very unusual for him, since he's normally such a sweet boy."

"I'm what?" Kyle seethed behind her.

"Kyle, shut up!" Zach warned. As he had already discovered, his classmate was a hothead who was now about to land them all in a heap of trouble. He swallowed hard and turned to Charlie, with what he thought was a contrite expression. "I'm so sorry about my friend." His eyes pleaded with Charlie's. "He has a tendency to shoot his mouth off, but he means no harm, he really doesn't."

Charlie's rigid stance began to relax, his fists unclenching. "Go back to your cards," Theo told him casually. "I'll handle this."

Charlie swore something behind his thick beard, and then, still grumbling, he did a turnabout and walked back to his table, where he sank down on his chair with a loud grunt.

Sam came out from behind the counter and walked up to Theo. "Git them plonkers out of here."

Theo gave Miss Reid a quick apologetic smile. "Ma'am, it might be best if we take our leave from these premises."

"It can't be soon enough," Sam said, while scowling at Kyle.

Theo ignored Sam and gallantly offered his arm to Miss Reid. "May I escort you outside, Ma'am?"

With a pointed look at Sam, Miss Reid hooked her arm through Theo's. "Yes, thank you so much."

Cold stares and insults from the tables followed them as they made their way through the lobby to the front door.

Kyle shot Zach an incensed look. "Do they have anyone here in Yale who isn't an absolute jerk?" he whispered.

Zach shrugged. "Well, at least *he* seems all right." He nodded at Theo who was presently holding the door for Miss Reid.

Kyle shrugged. "Yeah, he seems okay," he admitted reluctantly.

Theo closed the door firmly behind him when they were all outside the hotel. It had fortunately stopped raining. The men who had been fighting were all gone. Either they had grown tired of fighting, or someone, maybe the police, had dispersed them. Most likely the latter.

Theo shrugged at Miss Reid. "Sorry about this little unfortunate incident." He gallantly held her by the elbow as they walked down the few steps to the street, which felt strangely empty now. He let go of Miss Reid and turned to her. "We've had a large influx of miners from California lured here by the promise of Cariboo gold," he told her, "and they're, what shall we say, somewhat crude in their manner."

Kyle leaned towards Zach. "What's he on about?" he whispered.

Zach shrugged. "Beats me."

Miss Reid shook her head at him. "I don't understand. Gold? What gold?"

Theo seemed surprised by her question. "Well, you must surely know . . . I mean, isn't that why you're here too?"

"I assure you, that we're not here for any gold." Miss Reid looked closely at him. "Is this just a part you play in whatever all this is, because I would really like to know?"

For a moment Theo was at a loss for words. "Ma'am, I'm not sure what you're implying?" he said at last, staring at her in confusion.

With her hand she made a sweeping gesture of their surrounding area. "Are you an actor, a participant, in this . . ." She glanced up and down the street. "This re-enactment."

"Ma'am, I . . ." Theo stalled hopelessly.

"Miss Reid here is our English teacher, and we're not

here for any gold," Zach explained. "We're on a field trip."

Kyle sighed as he buried his hands in his jacket pockets. "Well, this is obviously a waste of time."

Miss Reid turned to him, her eyes narrowed. "Kyle, don't be rude."

Kyle pulled his phone out of his pocket again. "Let's try calling Youtz again."

"Maybe we should just look for the class at the river and if we don't find them there, come back to the bus for lunch," Zach said.

Kyle nodded eagerly at the suggestion. "Yeah, it's almost lunchtime and I'm starving." He glanced at Miss Reid. "Okay with you?"

After some hesitation, she nodded and extended her hand to Theo, who couldn't seem to tear his eyes away from the cellphone in Kyle's hand "Thank you so much for all your help."

It was only when Kyle dropped his cellphone into his pocket again that Theo managed to pull himself together and take Miss Reid's proffered hand. To Kyle's great amusement, Theo lifted the teacher's hand to his lips and kissed it, which in turn made her blush deeply. "Ma'am, if you need my assistance, don't hesitate to seek me out," Theo said as he let go of her hand.

"Assistance!" Kyle sputtered. Zach, too, had a hard time keeping a straight face.

"You'll most likely find me at Laura's Eatery," Theo added

as he pointed to the building a couple of doors down from the Yale Hotel. "I usually eat my lunch there."

"Thank you very much," Miss Reid said, scowling at Kyle, who had a hard time containing his laughter.

"Did you see how he stared at Kyle's phone?" Zach asked as the three of them walked away from Theo. "Honestly, you would think he had never seen one before."

"Jeez, Miss Reid, he kissed your hand," Kyle could finally give vent to the laughter, which had built up inside him. "What a dinosaur."

"He at least has manners," Miss Reid snapped at Kyle. "Which is more than I can say for some people." She turned to Zach. "Yeah, now you mention it, he did seem rather taken with that phone."

Zach looked behind him just before they turned a corner of a building. Theo was still standing there watching them keenly.

Chapter 5

❧

THE EXERTION WALKING up the hill from the river had made Zach sweat underneath his down jacket. "I could sure use something to drink," he said as he unzipped it.

"Me too." Kyle gave him a hopeful look. "You don't by any chance have some food to spare? I just remembered that I didn't bring anything."

Not that he had, but since Zach didn't feel particularly hungry, he nodded. "I'll share my lunch with you."

Miss Reid, who was walking just in front of them, stopped so abruptly, Zach and Kyle bumped into her. "I don't see the bus anywhere." She turned to look at them. "And the parking lot is gone."

Zach walked around her. She was correct. All he saw was grass, bushes and a couple of trees instead of the parking lot. He looked behind him. It didn't make sense, because they had just passed by the church of St. John the Divine, so they were definitely in the right place.

Miss Reid took a couple of steps forward. "And where's the museum?"

Zach was staring at the spot where the museum was supposed to be. He felt bewildered as he looked around. This was all wrong. The building with the toilets the class had made use of before they went down to the church and the outdoor museum were also missing.

"There has to be some logical explanation." Shaking her head, Miss Reid waded through knee-high grass and around the shrubs to where the museum was supposed to be. Zach was following her. She turned to him, giving him a searching look. "What in the world's going on?" she asked him as if she thought he somehow knew the answer.

Since he didn't, he just shrugged. His attention was drawn to the road when he heard the sound of wheels rattling across potholes and spotted the back of another horse-drawn wagon as it turned towards the river.

Kyle, who had been wandering the perimeter where Zach and Miss Reid were standing, came over to them. "This is just plain weird."

"There simply has to be a logical explanation," Miss Reid repeated as she kept staring at Zach.

Kyle gave the teacher a crooked grin. "If I didn't know any better I would say we have suddenly gone back in time." He sounded as if he himself didn't know if he was joking, or being serious.

"The church!" Zach blurted out. Without explaining to the others, he turned and hurried across the field towards St. John the Divine. "Come on," he yelled over his shoulder when the others just kept standing there, watching.

Kyle finally took off after him. "Why do you wanna go to the church?" he asked as he caught up with Zach.

"Because I think all this has to do with the church." Zach cast a glance behind him to see whether Miss Reid was following them. She was. He turned his attention to Kyle again. "Am I the only one who has noticed it?"

Kyle, his face looking like a big question mark, shook his head.

"When we walked through that door from the furnace room everything had changed," he said. "There was a building where there was not supposed to be one. Suddenly it was all cloudy when the sky had been clear before."

Kyle shrugged, a wary look on his hawkish face. "Well, that in itself is not really unusual. Weather can change fast."

"Yeah, but not that fast." Zach thought for a moment, his mind working at high gear now. "Have you . . . have you ever read about portals . . . like entries into alternate worlds?"

"Alternate worlds?" Kyle shook his head at him. "What the heck are you on about?" He was beginning to sound angry.

"I just read a novel where this type of thing happened to someone," Zach explained.

Miss Reid, who had finally caught up with them, heard that last part of their exchange. "Yes, but that's fiction, Zachary, not real life."

Zach was beginning to lose his patience with both of them, his gaze flitting from one skeptical face to the other. "Well, personally, I can't see what we have to lose by going inside the church again and see if everything reverts to normal."

"Well, if it'll put your mind at ease," Miss Reid said exchanging a dubious look with Kyle, who just gave a resigned shrug in answer.

. . .

They saw that the front door to the church was no longer closed, when they walked through the gate. Reaching the base of the stairs, they heard voices from the inside drift out through the open doors.

Miss Reid's eyes lit up. "That must be Mr. Youtz and the class." She ran up the steps with Kyle following her closely. Troubled by a strange foreboding, Zach trudged after them.

When he stepped inside the church, he saw Miss Reid and Kyle stop abruptly midway through the aisle. A couple of boys, about nine or ten years of age, sitting in a back pew had noticed their entrance, and were gawking at Miss Reid with fascination.

"She has on trousers," one of them said out loud. The boys put their blond heads together and snickered.

Zach walked up next to Miss Reid, and saw for himself what she and Kyle were staring at. There was no sign of Mr. Youtz, their chaperones, or their classmates. Instead, there was a group of strangers, three women and a man, who sat huddled together in the front pew, all of them dressed in old-fashioned clothes.

"I think this would be a good hymn to use on Sunday," one of the women, who had on a green bonnet, said, while pointing into a book. "I can play that by heart, and it fits your sermon so well, Reverend," she added.

The man, the woman had addressed as Reverend, glanced up and caught sight of Miss Reid, Zach and Kyle. He got up from the pew and marched down the middle of the aisle toward them. He was a gaunt-looking stooped man with wispy grey hair and thick glasses. He stopped in front of them, smiling uncertainly at Miss Reid as he took in her short hair, and outfit. "We always welcome new members to the flock, but I'm rather busy right now with the women's auxiliary group," he said. "We have our service on Sunday morning at ten. You're welcome to attend then."

A young woman, in her early teens, wearing a long blue and white-striped dress with a matching bonnet, smiled shyly at Zach from a nearby pew, where she sat reading in a thick book, probably the Bible considering where they were. He timidly returned her smile. His attention was brought back to Miss Reid when with a small cry, she spun around, pushed past him and Kyle, nearly knocking them over, and rushed out of the church.

"Miss Reid!" Kyle yelled as he and Zach took off after her. They found her standing at the base of the steps holding onto the banister while pressing a hand to her chest.

"Are you okay?" Zach asked.

Miss Reid's gaze jumped to his face. She was deadly pale. "No, I don't think so," she said, her other hand clutching the wooden bannister. The teacher turned her head and looked up towards the church. "Those people in there . . ." she was unable to finish the sentence.

Kyle shook his head. "Yeah, I agree, they have gone way overboard."

"What do you mean by that?" Zach asked him.

"This whole reenactment, of course." He seemed irritated with Zach.

Miss Reid looked up at the church. "So you think that in there is still part of a reenactment?"

"Of course it is." Kyle eyed her suspiciously. "What did you think it was?"

Miss Reid rubbed her forehead with her hand. "Oh, I don't know anymore. I just don't."

"Let's just keep looking for Youtz," Kyle said.

Zach found that to be a complete head-in-the-sand suggestion. When he saw Miss Reid nod as if this seemed to be a totally reasonable next step, he had had enough. "Sure we can continue searching for him and the class, but since we haven't found them yet, chances are we won't."

Kyle pointed angrily at him. "Don't start that portal thing again, because I won't listen to it."

Miss Reid let go of the bannister. "Obviously, they have to be around here. It's just that we've already looked pretty much everywhere." She bit her lower lip for a moment. "A big class like that . . . well, they can't hide that easily."

Zach watched Kyle reach for the cigarettes in his jacket pocket. He was about to shake one of the cigarettes out of the pack when he caught sight of Zach's warning look as he nodded at Miss Reid. With a roll of his eyes, Kyle slid the cigarette back in the pack and pocketed it again.

Miss Reid gazed at Zach. "Have you any ideas where to search?"

He decided to deflect the question by instead making a suggestion. "Why don't we go and find this guy, Theo, we met at the hotel?"

Kyle shook his head. "What for?"

Zach shrugged. "I've no idea, but he did say that if we needed help we could come to him."

"And what exactly is he supposed to do?" Miss Reid was clearly annoyed with him, even though he was not sure why.

Kyle buttoned his leather jacket against the cool wind, which had started blowing down from the mountains. "Come on, Teach, don't be a-stick-in-the-mud. After all, what do we have to lose by talking to him?"

Chapter 6

LAURA'S EATERY WAS what Zach's grandfather would have called a homey place with its lace curtains and tables covered in red and white checkered tablecloths. On each of the tables stood a small vase with yellow and white spring flowers and a strand of garlic was strung across the wall behind a counter. The smell of meat roasting, which wafted through the open door from the kitchen, made Zach's mouth water.

"Hello there," Miss Reid said when she spotted Theo sitting at a table by one of the windows. She waved, and hurriedly approached him.

Looking surprised, Theo quickly got up from his chair, pulled the napkin from the collar of his shirt, putting it down next to his plate. "Mrs ... Miss ..." He became flustered when he suddenly realized he had never learned their names.

"Eliza Reid, and it's *Miss*," she said, as she stopped short of his table, somewhat hesitant now. "You did tell us that if we needed help we would find you here."

"Of course. Of course." Theo rushed to the other side of the table and pulled out a chair. "Please take a seat, Ma'am."

Miss Reid pulled her backpack off, placing it next to her chair as she seated herself. "Thank you so much," she said with a grateful smile at him.

"My name is Theo Cox by the way," he said. He turned to Zach and Kyle. "I don't believe you told me your names either."

"The tall one in the leather jacket is Kyle," Miss Reid said before either of them had time to answer. "The other one is Zachary."

Great, Zach thought with some resentment. I've now been reduced to *the other one*. "I prefer Zach," he told Theo with a pointed look at the teacher.

Theo viewed them curiously as he shook hands with them. He had remarkable eyes, Zach noticed, dark blue with specks of luminescent yellow and green. With a sweep of his hand, Theo indicated the two remaining chairs at the table. "Please, sit down." Theo himself went around the table and reclaimed his own seat.

Zach chose the chair beside Theo. After a sharp glance at the teacher, Kyle pulled his chair away from hers, and slumped down on it with a grunt.

Theo stroked his goatee as he contemplated Miss Reid across the table. "I hope you don't mind me saying this, Ma'am," he said, "but it struck me from the beginning that — how do I put this best — that you seem so out of place here."

Well, that might just be the understatement of all times, Zach thought. "What year is this?" he blurted out, drawing startled looks from Kyle and Miss Reid.

Theo turned to Zach with a puzzled expression. "Year? Well, it's 1866, of course."

There was a sharp sound as Miss Reid's breath caught in her throat. The colour had drained from Kyle's face. Seeing how stunned the other two were by Theo's revelation, Zach wondered why he wasn't feeling the same way, until he realized that he had already anticipated an answer like this, that they had inexplicably left their own century and stepped into another.

Kyle's Adam's Apple bobbed up and down as he swallowed hard. "1866?" he asked in a drawn-out whisper.

With a puzzled expression, Theo viewed them all in turn. "How could you not know what year it is?"

Zach certainly had no idea how to answer him. The truth was too implausible for words. Kyle and Miss Reid didn't respond to the question either. A long, and what certainly had to be an awkward silence for Theo, followed. He was the one to finally break it. "So where do you all hail from?"

Kyle, finally recovering from his initial shock, glanced uncertainly at Zach. They were not going to get any help from

Miss Reid, who still sat staring in front of her in disbelief.

"I . . . We . . ." Zach began, then stopped again, not sure how to proceed.

"I don't aim to be disrespectful," Theo continued, "but your dress . . . your manners — not that anything is wrong with your manners —" he quickly corrected himself, "I just never saw clothes like that before." He was looking at Zach's puffer jacket.

Theo's attention was caught by the door to the restaurant opening. A group of three: two men and a young lady walked inside, their voices filling the room.

A short rotund woman came rushing out from the kitchen, and with a big smile, showed the newcomers to a table in a corner. The older one of the two men, sporting impressive whiskers, nodded at Theo as he sat down. "Greetings, Theo." He removed his hat and placed it at the far end of the table. "How's your poker playin' comin' along these days?" he asked.

Theo nodded. "Fine Neil. I have a game going on later today at the Yale Hotel in case you're interested." He smiled at the young lady, who had viewed him with great interest ever since she arrived. "I don't think I've ever had the pleasure of making your acquaintance," he said.

Smooth guy, Zach thought.

"This is my daughter, Evelyn." With pride in his eyes, Neil grinned broadly at Theo. "Hands off, she's spoken for."

Only now, did Zach have time to pay any mind to the second man. He had been too busy looking at the young woman, who had impish blue eyes, and the cutest upturned nose. Zach took an instant dislike to the guy, who was short and pudgy with a receding hairline. Possessively, he put his plump hand over the young woman's. What the heck was she doing with an ugly guy like that, Zach thought. She didn't look a day over eighteen and he was old enough to be her father.

"The gentleman sitting next to my daughter is Rudy Harris, my future son-in-law," Neil said, introducing the other man.

Harris' small eyes, buried in craters of fat, shot daggers at Theo. "Pleasure," he snorted.

The rotund woman, who had stood sentinel at the table while everyone settled in, discreetly cleared her throat to draw attention to her presence. "Ah Laura, my little gem," Neil said as he turned to her. "What do you recommend for us today?"

While Laura listed all of the culinary delights the restaurant had to offer, Theo turned to Miss Reid again. "You're a teacher?" he asked.

"I am?" She blushed when she realized her blunder. "Oh yes, of course, I am. I teach high school English. I've worked at the same school in ... in ..." Her voice broke and she looked away.

Theo pushed his plate aside and leaned forward, folding his hands on the table. "So where do you teach English, Ma'am?"

Miss Reid opened and closed her mouth a couple of times. "Teach? I ..." She was unable to continue.

Zach, who had sat there watching as the tears slowly welled up in Miss Reid's eyes, answered hurriedly for her. "She teaches up north."

Theo frowned. "Funny with your accents, I would have placed you maybe in Minnesota or even New York. I've travelled far and wide, including up north," he explained as he turned to Zach. "What area are you actually talking about?" he asked him.

"Believe me, Mr. Cox, you wouldn't have heard of the place." Zach tried to sound nonchalant. He even managed a smile.

Theo draped his arm over the back of his chair. "Try me. As I said I've travelled extensively."

Zach was hoping to get help from Kyle, who had given him the impression that he was a quick thinker, but all he got from him, when he looked across the table, was a shrug.

"Springfield." The word escaped Zach before he had time to think. His favourite show was *The Simpsons* and the name of their hometown sprang right to his mind.

Kyle stared at him. Springfield! he mouthed.

Theo shook his head in wonder. "Springfield? Up north you say? The Springfields I know are located down in the States."

"Well, now there's a Springfield up north too." Zach was feeling ruffled. He wasn't used to thinking so fast on his feet.

Theo nodded. "These days towns spring up in the middle of fields everywhere." He chuckled at his own joke. "It's hard to keep up. So what are you doing here in Fort Yale?"

Miss Reid had at last regained some of her composure. "We're ehum . . . visiting relatives. An uncle of mine. Unfortunately . . ." She averted her eyes from Theo, and instead looked down at her hands, which lay folded in her lap. "Unfortunately, he died a short while ago." She grabbed hold of a silver ring with a turquoise stone she was wearing and began twirling it around her finger.

Across the table, Zach caught the reluctant look of awe in Kyle's eyes. Turned out their teacher could think fast on her feet too.

Theo nodded at Kyle and Zach. "So will you and your sons be heading back to Springfield?"

Disgust was written all over Kyle's face. "I'm not her son!"

Miss Reid let go of the ring. "They're my nephews," she added quickly.

They were saved from further interrogation when Laura trundled up to their table. "Anything else, Theo?" Her cheeks reddened as she spoke to him.

Theo gazed across the table at Miss Reid. "You look like you could use a cup of coffee. It so happens that Laura here makes the best coffee in town." He winked at Laura. "Isn't that so?"

Laura, clearly pleased with his assessment, blushed even deeper. "People have been known to say that. Coffee for two then?"

Miss Reid nodded gratefully at her. "Coffee would be wonderful."

"What about you, lads? What would you like?" Theo asked.

"A Coke," Kyle answered. With fingers that were none too clean anymore, he played absentmindedly with the fringe of the table cloth, which drew a disapproving look from the otherwise affable Laura.

Zach kicked at his leg under the table. "They don't have Coke," he whispered.

Startled, Kyle abandoned his assault on the table cloth. "How do you know?"

"Because this is 1866, you idiot."

Understanding flooded Kyle's eyes. "Oh yeah, I forgot." He smiled up at Laura. "A 7up will be fine."

Zach closed his eyes in exasperation.

When he opened them again, Laura was shaking her head. "I don't think I've ever heard of such a drink."

"We'll also have coffee," Zach intervened, before Kyle had time to come up with some other inane request.

"Anything else?" Laura asked, her heavy eyebrows lifted in expectation.

"Yes, could you please add four pieces of your excellent apple pie to that order." Theo pushed his plate towards her. "And if you would, please take this."

Laura glanced at the plate. "Are you sure? You still have food left."

"It's cold now. Anyhow, I feel more like apple pie."

Zach whose stomach was now growling with hunger was tempted to tell Laura that he would eat the left-over food, cold or not. His eyes followed the plate with longing as she picked it up and whisked it away.

Chapter 7

THEO HELD THE DOOR for the three of them. Zach felt much better now his stomach was full of Laura's apple pie. The piece he had devoured in record time was huge and the best pie he had ever tasted.

"Bye, Laura," Theo yelled into the restaurant before he closed the door firmly behind him. They began walking in the direction of the Yale Hotel.

"So why *did* you come to see me?" Theo asked with a side-long glance at Miss Reid, who was walking next to him.

The teacher fidgeted anxiously with the straps on her backpack as she tried to come up with an answer. "We . . ." she began, then with a deep sigh, stopped, and faced Theo.

"It really wasn't anything important." She managed a smile, even though it looked more like she was close to tears again. "I want to thank you so very much for the coffee and pie."

"You're very welcome, Ma'am." Theo seemed uncertain about what to do next. "Can I walk you back to your place of residence, at least?" he asked.

Miss Reid shook her head. "No, that won't be necessary. We can manage from here."

Zach had been listening to their conversation in disbelief. What did Miss Reid think she was doing dismissing Theo like this? Hadn't it occurred to her that he was the only person who could help them? At the very least, they needed a place to stay tonight until they figured out what to do next.

Kyle cleared his throat. "So where exactly are we supposed to go, Teach?" Obviously, his thoughts had moved along the same lines as Zach's.

Theo looked at Miss Reid in surprise. "You won't be going back to your uncle's residence?"

"See, the thing is, we really don't have a place to stay," Zach interjected before Miss Reid had time to harm their cause any further. "Our . . . her uncle," he nodded at Miss Reid, "well, when he died, his landlord didn't want us living at the house anymore, so he threw us out this morning."

Miss Reid gaped at him. "Zachary, that's not at all how . . ." She shook her head at him.

Kyle gave her a wry smile. "You do seem to have a short memory, Auntie."

Theo removed his hat, and smoothed his dark hair with

his hand. "Well, I can talk to the landlord." He replaced the hat and pulled the brim down over his forehead. "Yes, that's what I'll do," he said with conviction. "To think that he would throw a defenceless woman out on the street like that." He was beginning to look rather upset on their behalf.

"No, no don't do that," Miss Reid blurted out.

Theo straightened his shoulders. "Ma'am, I'm sure he'll listen to reason. Furthermore, you'll need to get your things."

She gave him a bewildered look. "What things?"

The door to the Yale Hotel burst open and a heavy set guy was unceremoniously tossed outside. He tumbled down the steps and landed on all fours in a puddle. Swearing, with his pants all muddy, he struggled to get up. The door to the hotel slammed shut. "Damn you, Sam," he hollered and shook his fist at the closed door. "Jackass!" he cursed as he swung around in their direction. A broad smile crossed his lips. "Damnation if it isn't you, Theo." He came swaying towards Theo, who marched resolutely up to him.

"Time to go home, Ellis."

Miss Reid shook her head at Zach. "I don't understand. What things was he talking about?"

Zach thought she was being rather dense. "Normally, when people travel they carry around clothes and tooth-brushes and stuff."

"Oh yeah," Kyle said. "That's only logical." His classmate was obviously dense too. Just Zach's luck to be stuck here with these two!

Theo returned to them after having sent Ellis reeling down

the road towards his home. "So where does this landlord live?" he asked Miss Reid. He obviously was not about to let go of his cause.

"Not here in town . . . not anymore at least," she answered. "He . . . he went away just after he threw us out. We don't know when he'll be back, and we don't have anything of ours to pick up. It was . . ." She stalled hopelessly.

Zach quickly picked up the thread, since he was after all getting some practice in lying. "We were robbed this morning," he informed Theo. He looked at Kyle for help, but again all he got was a shrug. "We were . . . we were walking through this dark alley," he continued. "Suddenly, from behind, some barrels came these three mean-looking guys. One had a gun and . . . and the two others carried machetes." He saw Kyle hide a smile. "The guy with the gun asked us to hand over our valuables. We were all scared shit . . . I mean we were all really scared."

"Oh, yeah, we sure were," Kyle said with a serious expression.

Miss Reid stood frowning at Zach, but he ignored her as he kept going with his narrative. "We, of course, didn't want them to kill us, so we gave them everything we had: suitcases, money, credit cards. Everything! The men took off, and now we have nothing."

At first Theo appeared to be astounded by Zach's dramatic account of events, and for a while he just stood staring at him, but then his expression became one of determination again. "You've certainly had some bad luck." His face bright-ened. "I, however, have some good news. Judge Begbie is coming to Fort Yale next week." He looked excitedly at them. "Since the Yankees began mining up here, lawless conditions have taken hold of the gold country, and he's trying to imple-ment some order. He should truly hear about your appalling experience."

"No, no, that won't be necessary," Miss Reid said hurriedly.

Theo's face showed obvious disappointment by their lack-lustre reaction, but to his credit he didn't take the matter further. Instead he pushed his hat back on his head, and crossed his arms over his chest. "So what do you plan to do, Ma'am?" he asked of Miss Reid.

"Well . . . go back home, I guess, to . . . to Springfield."

Theo gave her a piercing look. "Without clothes, provi-sions, or money?" He stepped up to her. "Ma'am, I don't think that's wise." His voice fell to a whisper, but it wasn't low enough for Zach not to hear. "You do have your nephews to think about."

She nodded. "I know." Her face took on a burdened look. "Don't I know it."

"Travelling north is an arduous and dangerous trek for even the most experienced and well-equipped of travellers. You won't last a day out there on that road alone." Theo stood lost in thought for a while, staring in front of him.

At last he lifted his gaze to meet Miss Reid's. "Tell you what," he said. "My brother, Enos, will be taking freight up to

Barkerville. Actually, he's leaving tomorrow and I'm going with him." He flashed a smile back at Kyle and Zach. "I'm a gambler, you see, and there's always a game of poker to be had up there."

"Mr. Cox, I don't see what this . . ." Miss Reid began, but was interrupted by Zach.

"Sure, we'll go with you and your brother," he told Theo.

"To where?" Kyle asked.

Zach turned to him. "To Barkerville, of course."

"But what about Mr. Youtz?" Miss Reid protested. "We can't just take off like this."

Zach gave Theo an apologetic look. "Sorry, she's a little confused." He turned to Miss Reid and pointed down the street. "Can I talk to you in private, Miss Reid . . . I mean Aunt?" he quickly corrected himself.

"You don't mind, do you?" Miss Reid asked Theo.

He shrugged. "By all means."

"I'm coming with you guys," Kyle said, trailing after them until they were out of Theo's earshot.

"What do you think you're doing?" Miss Reid asked Zach. She sounded none too happy with him. "Why would we want to string along with him and his brother to Barkerville?"

"You have a better idea, Miss Reid?" Zach turned to Kyle who stood just behind them. "Either of you for that matter?" He got no answer from them. "I don't know how, or why, but the fact is that we're now stranded in this place and it's freaking 1866, and we have no idea how we're going to get back home again. Since our money and our credit cards, for that matter, are worthless here, we don't know where our next meal is coming from, or where we're going to stay tonight." He glared at them in turn. "If we don't take him up on his offer what do you suggest we do instead? You tell me, because I certainly don't know."

His gaze wandered in Theo's direction. He was busy talking to an older man with a droopy moustache, who had come up to him. Zach took a deep breath and turned to Miss Reid. "If we go with him, at least we have someone looking out for us."

The teacher bit her lip uncertainly. "That might be, but I would still prefer to stay here and wait."

Zach recognized that there was more fear than stubbornness in her voice, so he decided to play on that fear. "For what, Miss Reid?" He deliberately made his voice soft and steadfast. "We'll most likely end up sleeping in the gutter and eating scraps of food out of garbage cans."

With trembling hands, Kyle patted his pockets, located his pack of cigarettes and pulled it out. "I have to say I'm with Zach," he told Miss Reid. "I think our only choice is to go with him and his brother." His hands shook so much he dropped the cigarettes on the ground. "Damn." He bent over and fished the pack out of a puddle.

Miss Reid zippered her fleece jacket all the way up to her chin. "Maybe we should just tell him the truth," she said.

Zach shook his head at her. "Oh yeah, that's really going to go over well if we walk up to him and say, Mr. Cox, by the way we're from the twenty-first century, and how's your day going? He's definitely not going to help us then."

Miss Reid shrugged. "Okay, I see your point." She sighed. "I guess, the best cause of action is to go with him then."

"And no more talk about Mr. Youtz," Zach added.

Kyle finally managed to dislodge a cigarette from his pack and was about to stick it between his lips, when Miss Reid turned ferociously on him. "What part of no smoking didn't you get?"

Chapter 8

THEO STOPPED IN FRONT of a big rectangular log building with a peaked wood-shingle roof. M. W. Anderson, General Merchandise it read in tall white letters on a sign, dangling on two chains above a shaded porch.

A covered wagon drawn by six sturdy horses was waiting in front of the steps, leading up to open double doors of the establishment. Zach could hear loud quarrelling voices coming from inside the store, one deep and insistent, the other high pitched and whiny.

Theo chuckled as he shook his head. "My brother and Mr. Anderson, the proprietor, they're forever haggling over prices. It sounds far worse than it is."

As they passed by the restless horses, Zach jumped when one of them nipped at his backside. Theo, as always the gentleman, helped Miss Reid up the steps to the porch.

"What — are you tryin' to drive me out of business, you little muck-worm?" the deep voice boomed through the open doors.

Zach and Kyle followed Theo and Miss Reid into a huge room covered from floor to ceiling with shelves that were filled to capacity with packages, sacks, clothes, footwear, bottles and jars. Open barrels overflowing with potatoes, onions and other produce were lined up against a rough-hewn wooden counter which ran the length of the room. Behind the counter stood a fat, short, red-faced man in a dirty white apron that barely covered his protruding stomach. Aside from a few strands of hair, which had carefully and strategically been plastered across his shiny dome, he was as bald as a cue ball.

Ignoring the newcomers, he glared at a tall broad-shouldered red-haired man, dressed in a black and yellow-checkered shirt and stained, grey pants held up by green suspenders. He was standing next to the large black stove, which figured prominently in middle of the room. "Crikey, Enos, you know you can sell a pound of coffee for well over a dollar up in Barkerville."

Enos' features hardened. "You just go right ahead and chat all this out. Bottom line is, if you charge me seventy cents a pound, my profit will probably be less than fifty cents and for that I have to plod through god-forsaken country." He took a deep breath to get himself under control. "You're such a miser."

Anderson shook his sausage finger at him. "I've listened enough to your insults, Enos Cox. You get your sorry ass out of my store and . . . and I dare you to find another place in Fort Yale that will sell you coffee for less than I charge." Perspiration ran down Anderson's meaty forehead. Zach was half expecting him to keel over from a heart attack.

Theo marched across the plank flooring, which creaked at his every step. "Gentlemen, gentlemen, I'm sure this whole matter can be settled in a civilized manner."

Enos shot him an angry glance. "Theo, where in Sam Hill have you been?"

Theo smiled disarmingly at his brother. "I was off rescuing a damsel in distress, dear brother."

This statement only produced a derisive snort from Enos. Theo ignored it and turned to Anderson. "Schliemann, I heard, sells coffee for sixty cents a pound."

"That's not true," Anderson sputtered. "Seventy cents is what everyone's askin'."

Theo shook his head, his expression calm. "Not so. As I just said, Schliemann's selling for sixty."

Anderson was about to protest again, but then suddenly deflated, his shoulders drooped and his face fell. "The pox on Schliemann!" he hissed. "You can't trust anyone to keep their word."

Enos hitched up his pants and readjusted his suspenders. "Well, I guess I'll be paying Schliemann a visit then." With a nod in the direction of the door, he signalled to his brother to leave. "Come on, Theo." He ambled across the wooden floor, a thumb wedged behind each suspender.

"Now you wait just one minute," Anderson yelled after him. "Let's talk about this. Since you're orderin' such a large quantity, I'll sell it to you for sixty-five cents a pound." It was easy to see how hard those words were to utter by the way Anderson's whole face clenched.

Enos turned to Anderson, his eyes taunting him. "Anderson, are you deaf? Didn't you hear my brother? Schliemann sells his for sixty."

The skin puffed up around Anderson's small eyes. "It would surprise me greatly if Schliemann's coffee has much more than fifty percent real coffee beans in it. They don't call him the Ersatz King around here for nothin', you know." He grabbed the edge of the counter with both hands to steady himself, and glared at Enos. "All right, sixty cents it is."

Enos exchanged a quick pleased glance with his brother. "It's a deal."

Anderson grumbled an angry reply as he leaned over the counter and pulled a slate tablet toward himself. He picked up a piece of chalk and quickly scribbled something on the tablet. It was only when he looked up again that he finally took notice of the newcomers. With open dislike, his gaze wandered over Zach, Kyle and Miss Reid. "Why are you dragging these ragbags into my store, Theo?"

Kyle's eyes narrowed, and he took a threatening step towards the counter. "That's rude, man."

Anderson puffed himself up. "Out!" he yelled at Kyle. "You git out of here." He glared at Miss Reid and Zach. "All of you."

"Do as he says," Enos hissed at them.

Zach grabbed hold of Kyle's arm when he saw he was about to object. "Let's just go."

Kyle, however, wasn't leaving before he had his parting shot at Anderson. "You bristly little pork butt," he yelled over his shoulder, while Zach pulled him across the floor and out the door.

Chapter 9

ZACH ONLY LET GO of Kyle when they had made it down the steps. He was furious with him. "We can't go and piss people off like this," he said through clenched teeth. "Not when we need their help."

Kyle spat on the ground. "Fatso in there had no right to dis us like that." He kicked angrily into the dirt with the toe of his boot.

Miss Reid came rushing outside, nearly stumbling over her own feet down the steps. She stopped short of Kyle. "You have to learn how to show restraint. This is a different kind of society, and we don't know the rules yet."

"Thanks for the lecture, Teach!" Kyle scoffed.

Zach saw Theo and his brother come out of the store. When they reached the street, Theo could no longer hide the merriment that showed in his eyes. He burst out laughing and slapped his brother on the back. Enos allowed himself a gruff smile.

"Cheapest coffee in Fort Yale," Theo said, wiping his eyes with the back of his hand.

Enos peered at his brother through narrowed eyes. "You never did speak with Schliemann, did you?"

Theo shook his head, still sputtering with laughter. "No, I sure didn't."

Enos nodded up at the store. "So that in there was just a cock-and-bull story?" .

Theo slapped his brother on the back again. "You got it."

Together they walked up to Miss Reid. "Allow me to introduce you to my brother, Enos," Theo said, while he affectionately put an arm around Enos' broad shoulders.

Miss Reid smiled at Enos. "Pleased to meet you."

"Likewise Ma'am." Enos didn't pay her much heed. Instead his gaze fell on Kyle. "You surely have a mouth on you, lad."

"And he does apologize for that," Miss Reid said quickly as she sent Kyle a warning glance.

Theo squeezed his brother's shoulders. "Come now, there was no harm done."

Reluctantly, Enos nodded. "Well, I suppose not."

"These are some folks I ran into here in town, Enos. They're from up north." He let go of his brother. "This lady's name is Miss Eliza Reid. She's a teacher. The two lads there are her nephews. The tall one is Kyle and the other one, Zachary."

"I do prefer Zach," Zach said with a sharp look at Miss Reid.

They were interrupted when a short wiry man, dodging the many puddles on the dirt road, came hurrying toward them. "Enos," he yelled as he waved. "When you fixin' to leave?"

It was rare that Zach took an instant dislike to a person. This was one of those occasions. The newcomer had a pointy face much like a rat. The stubble, which grew prickly and sparsely on his sunburned face, only enhanced this image. He had a sullen, unfriendly expression and his eyes were small, dark and shifty. His matted brown hair stuck out from underneath a dirty, grey hat with a narrow brim. He reeked from old sweat and beer.

Miss Reid made a face when she got a whiff of the newcomer and quickly turned her head away.

Enos looked at the man with annoyance. "I was beginnin' to wonder if you were goin' to show up, Jackson. There's a second wagon that needs loadin'."

"I had a fallin' out with my brother-in-law." Jackson hawked and landed a big glob of phlegm on the ground, which barely missed Zach's feet. Zach stepped back in disgust. "He's an ongoin' pain in the arse." Jackson peered at Miss Reid. "Who's she? One of Sam's new cracks?"

"Cracks?" Miss Reid inquired.

"Yeah, woman of the town, a pully-hawly girl, a doxy."

Miss Reid showed remarkable restraint. True enough, her hands clenched tightly, knuckles showing white through the skin, but all Jackson got was a pinched smile. "Since I recognize you as a person with limited social skills, I'll forgive you for that remark," she said with great dignity.

Jackson gaped at Enos. "What's she prattlin' on about?" A suspicious look came into his small eyes. "Is she mockin' me?"

Theo hid a smile. "Jackson, may I introduce you to Miss Reid who, by the way, is not one of Sam's new acquisitions." He turned his attention to his brother. "They have to travel up north too, Enos, so I figured we could just as well keep company until we reach Barkerville."

"I don't want them three stragglin' along," Jackson shuddered. "They don't look like normal folk to me."

"Shut up, Jackson," Enos snapped. He viewed his brother with irritation. "Theo, you know well what I feel about strangers travellin' with us."

Zach's hopes sank when he heard the tone in Enos' voice.

Theo nodded. "I'm well aware, but I think . . ."

"You heard your brother," Jackson interrupted him. "What we don't need right now are some foot-draggers taggin' along." Jackson shot Zach and Kyle a spiteful look.

Zach clenched his teeth. "What a jerk!"

Jackson's small shrewd eyes moved to Miss Reid. "And we

certainly don't need the distraction of women folk." He scratched his groin area through his dirty pants.

Her face reddened. "Don't be insulting, Mr. Jackson."

He showed his rotting teeth in a smirk. "I don't aim to." He turned to Enos. "Let's get that last wagon loaded." Enos nodded and followed Jackson.

"Now just wait a moment." Theo grabbed his brother by the arm. "We could surely use a cook."

Enos smiled wryly. "I don't think we'll need a cook to make the grub we usually eat."

To Miss Reid's credit she right away saw an opportunity. "I'm very creative with food. I know a great deal about wild herbs, and . . ."

Jackson cut her off. "She wants to poison us," he said.

"The lads here are strong," Theo pointed out to his brother. "They could be of great help on the trip."

"We'll do anything." Zach meant what he said. He was desperate not to be left behind in Yale and the uncertainty they would face there. "Your brother is right, we're both strong." He didn't even know why he bothered. The answer could already be read in Enos' eyes.

"My answer is still no." Enos tried to free his arm from his brother's grasp, but Theo held on tight.

"Why not do it?" he said with a beseeching look. "The road is long and tedious and some company would certainly be welcome."

Enos' lips tightened into a stubborn line. "I would have

three more mouths to feed, Theo. Who's goin' to pay for all that extra grub, not to mention the passage on the steamer from Soda Creek to Quesnellemouth?"

Theo let go of Enos' arm. He shook his head in frustration. "For heaven's sake, Enos, have some compassion. They haven't got a place to stay, and they were robbed of most of what they own. They just need a way to get back home." Theo dug into his pants pockets and brought out a wad of bills. "I'll pay you all the money I won in poker games this morning."

Enos waved the money away. "That won't even cover a small part of the expenses and you know it." He shook his head. "Why are you so hellbent on helpin' them?"

Theo shrugged. "Maybe, because it's the right thing to do. Have you forgotten what our mother always taught us about compassion?"

Enos shook a finger at him. "You've some nerve bringing our mother into this."

"Why shouldn't I. She was, after all, the kindest person I ever knew." He stared into his brother's face. "Without a moment's hesitation she would have helped these good folks, and you know it."

The brothers stood across from each other, Enos with his hands clenched. "You'll be responsible for them," Enos finally told Theo. He looked ticked off as he turned on his heels.

Zach let out the breath he had been holding.

"You can't be serious," Jackson yelled as he ran after Enos, who was hurrying up the stairs to the store.

Chapter 10

∞

ZACH STRETCHED OUT on his back. It took a while before the various aches and pains he had woken up with went away. It was a result of having only a blanket between himself and the cold hard ground. He had always hated Hans Christian Andersen's lame story, "The Princess and the Pea". Lately though, he had to admit he was beginning to relate to the overly sensitive princess when he hunted for the offending pieces of gravel and twigs underneath the blanket that prevented him from going to sleep at night.

After a week on the road, a soft bed was on the top of his wish list, right after food. Not that he ever went hungry. Meals were hearty and filling, but most of them consisted of bacon and beans, Cariboo turkey and Cariboo strawberries as the men called them and, on occasions that were far too rare, they had fried potatoes.

The beans, Zach had found, had unfortunate after-effects. His innards rumbled constantly and the farting was relentless, which was difficult when he was around Miss Reid, who would reprimand him for his bad manners when he broke wind. Kyle on the other hand didn't care what she thought and consequently let go whenever he felt like it.

"That was a big one," he would say and give the teacher a broad grin as if he really enjoyed aggravating her, which he most certainly did. "Come on, Teach, don't tell me you don't fart."

Miss Reid blushed. "At least I don't do it in front of everyone."

Miss Reid and Kyle drove Zach crazy with their constant bickering, mostly about what she considered Kyle's rude manners and laziness. More often than not, the two of them got on Enos' nerves, and he would holler at them that he regretted the day he agreed to let them come along on the trip.

Zach had come to dislike Jackson so intensely he could barely stand the sound of his squeaky voice. The only one Jackson talked to was Enos. He was like a pesky little fly in Enos' ear, going on about this and that. His bellyaching, Zach suspected, was mostly about their presence. He had picked up little snippets of conversation: how inept the three of them were, how they slowed everyone down, their incessant quarrelling.

Zach hoped Enos wasn't listening too closely to Jackson's

complaining, but with increasing unease he noticed that Enos grew more and more sullen towards all three of them. Zach was reasonably sure by now that Theo was the only one who prevented his brother from dumping them at the roadside. Thank God for Theo who was always nice to the three of them and treated them with a warm, courteous manner that Jackson completely lacked. It was clear that Enos was only occasionally interested in their welfare.

With a deep sigh, Zach pushed aside the blanket that covered him. He began to shiver in the frigid morning air and quickly grabbed his jacket. Since it was totally unsuitable for this kind of travel, it was a sorry sight. Sharp rocks and low hanging branches had torn into the outer shell. More goose down was by now littering the Cariboo Road behind him than was inside the jacket. The left sleeve was completely empty, while the right still had retained its fullness. If the jacket had been white, he would have looked sort of like a lopsided Michelin Man. He put his arms into the sleeves, pulled it over his shoulders and zippered the jacket all the way to his chin.

Theo, who had the last watch of the night, and was sitting at the fire sipping coffee from his mug, turned to Zach when he walked by, "Coffee, lad?"

"In a moment," he answered and made a beeline for some nearby bushes. The beans had another side effect. They made him very regular, morning, noon and night. When he was finished, he wiped himself with some leaves. By now, his anus was as tender as a sore thumb. He added another item to his wish list, soft toilet paper.

When he straightened up and hitched up his pants, the first rays of the sun made it above the mountaintops and coloured the grey canvas, covering the two wagons, orange.

Zach hurried over to Kyle. With an anxious glance at the still-sleeping Enos and Jackson, he bent over and shook Kyle's shoulder. "The sun is up. We have to get the horses ready."

Kyle grumbled in his sleep and curled himself into a ball. Zach shook him again.

"Did you hear me?"

Kyle pushed his hand away. "Leave me alone."

Zach leaned over him and spoke sternly in his ear. "Listen, you feeb, we can't be late getting the horses ready again. Enos was mad at us all day yesterday."

"What the hell is a feeb?" Kyle muttered without opening his eyes.

"A feeble person just like you."

Kyle peered up at Zach through two narrow slits in his eyelids. "Man, I can't wait until we don't have to look at Enos and that rat Jackson again."

Zach watched as his friend sat up, grabbed his jacket and patted its pockets. Kyle finally found his cigarettes. He looked dismally inside the wrinkled pack. "Only one left." He scratched his hair that was stiff from dust and sweat, and pulled out the cigarette.

"No smoking," Zach said, nodding towards the sleeping men.

"I have a right to a smoke." Kyle put the cigarette between his cracked lips.

"Enos is going to have a fit. He's afraid you'll start a fire. You heard him yesterday."

"I don't care what that dumbass says." Kyle dug through his pockets for the lighter. He finally found it in his jeans. "This is so unfair, Cox smokes cigars all the time so why can't I have a lousy smoke once in a while." He lit the cigarette and blew smoke into the frigid air. It hung suspended for a while before dissipating. A blissful expression crossed over his face. "Jeez, this feels great." He looked at Zach. "I had eight cigarettes left in the pack when we started on this trip and I've smoked one each day." He held up the burning cigarette. "This is the last, which means we've been on the road for over a week." He shook his head. "It feels a helluva lot longer, that's for sure."

Zach thought back over the last week. It had already been an arduous journey, and had been quite scary in places, especially that first part from Yale through Spuzzum and Boston Bar where engineers in some places had had to blast through rock walls to make space for the road. He shuddered as he recalled the huge drops down toward the churning, rushing Fraser river. Theo had told them that one misstep could mean death and that many had died on that stretch, both men and animals.

Kyle looked at the disposable lighter in his hand. "I guess I'll give this to Theo since he likes it so much." He emitted a deep sigh. "I certainly have no use for it now."

Theo was the only one who had taken any interest in the items they had brought with them from the twenty-first century. Zach had demonstrated to him several times how the zippers in his pants and jacket worked, explained how cellphones functioned, when they worked. His nail clipper, however, had been the greatest source of amazement to Theo. By now, the gambler had the most well groomed nails in camp.

Zach was startled when Kyle crumpled the empty cigarette packet in his hand and threw it angrily on the ground. "I don't know how much longer I can stand this." He glared at Zach. "I mean it. I've had it with their garbage food and sucky attitude and . . ."

"Would you keep it down," Zach hissed with a quick nod in Theo's direction. Miss Reid, he noticed, was stirring underneath her blanket next to Kyle.

"I wanna go home, Zach." Kyle bit his lower lip to keep the tears at bay. "I don't belong in this place."

"None of us do." He was shocked to see Kyle so emotional all of a sudden. As soon as the three of them had settled into their routine on the road, he had seemed the least affected by their circumstances. "So what exactly do you suggest we do?" he asked Kyle.

His friend shrugged. "If I knew that, do you think I would

still be here?" He inhaled deeply from the cigarette again.

"Is everything okay?" Miss Reid propped herself up on her elbow and gave them a sleepy look.

"We're fine." Zach got up. "I'll start rounding up the horses," he told Kyle.

Kyle blew out another cloud of smoke. "Okay," he said with a gloomy expression.

Theo looked up as Zach passed by the fire. "The horses are down by the river. I checked on them a little while ago."

Zach nodded. They had camped close to the river so Miss Reid would finally have a chance to wash their clothes. It was high time. Zach's jeans were stiff from sweat and the dust, which was their constant companion on the dirt road. He had taken to wearing a kerchief over his mouth and nose to protect his airways, just as Theo, Enos and Jackson did. Miss Reid and Kyle hadn't yet picked up this habit, and the two were often plagued by a wracking, dry cough.

They're both too stubborn for their own good, he thought, as he slid down the embankment to the river in a cascade of rolling rocks.

He stopped abruptly when he saw a group of people on the riverbank. Natives! He had seen others before. Theo had explained that they often continued prospecting for gold in places abandoned by the white miners, who had gone in search of richer pickings in the Cariboo creeks. The Natives had the patience to methodically pan for the gold dust that the white miners had left behind.

A teenager, his age, who was trying to lift a big rock with his shovel looked startled when he saw Zach. The teen reminded him of someone he knew. With a pang he suddenly remembered. Matt from his science class. He had the same dark hair, eyes and nose as his classmate. Zach debated if he should return to camp, but the other Natives, five women and a man, looked peaceful, and seemed more interested in their work than him. They were all dressed in western clothes, the man and teen in pants, shirts and broad-rimmed hats, the women in long skirts, blouses and colourful woollen shawls.

He spotted the horses further down the riverbank and started walking toward them. He looked curiously at the man, who was standing in front of a rocker, a box-like contraption, which Theo had told him separated the gold from gravel. He stopped for a moment to look as the man pulled back and forth on a long handle attached to the box. It created a rocking motion and Zach could hear the water swish forth and back inside the box.

Theo said that this rocking motion caused the lighter material to be washed out of the box, while the heavier gold sank and was trapped in the bottom. The man looked up at him, a cautious, apprehensive look in his eyes. Zach smiled uncertainly at him, but the man quickly averted his gaze and poured more water and gravel into the rocker.

He continued along the riverbank and whistled when he spotted the horses. They raised their heads and turned them in his direction. "Rudolph, Prancer," he called. He had given some of the twelve horses, six for each wagon, reindeer names.

When he had run out of those, he had given the rest of them names of their teachers. Youtz was a sturdy brown horse with small intelligent eyes. He was the lead horse pulling Enos' wagon. The second lead horse, pulling Jackson's wagon, he called Blodell after his science teacher, because the animal's magnificent grey mane reminded Zach of Mr. Blodell's hair.

Youtz came up to him and nuzzled his hand with his soft nose. "You want your oats, big guy," he said as he stroked Youtz's neck. The fear he had always had for horses had almost disappeared now. The exception was when he and Kyle had to remove pebbles and sharp rocks from their hooves. He dreaded that because the animals became unpredictable and cranky during this procedure and would suddenly kick out their hind legs in protest. Zach had learned early on to stay clear of the horses' hind hooves. Nothing hurt more than a horse's kick. He still had a huge black mark on his thigh where Vixen had gotten him good. He grabbed Youtz's rein and led him up toward camp. He hoped Kyle would feel more upbeat by now.

The camp was busy when he returned. Miss Reid was bent over a heavy skillet, placed over the flames on an iron grill. She flipped the bacon pieces with a long fork, while blowing stray locks of hair away from her face. Theo had lent her one of his shirts and a pair of his pants, which she had tied around her waist with a rope since Theo had no extra belt to lend her. The smell of bacon wafted across the camp, making Zach's stomach growl.

Theo was busy shaving in front of a small mirror he had propped on the side of the Enos' wagon. Zach didn't know how he always managed to maintain such a well-groomed appearance. The two other men by now looked scruffy, but not him. His shirt looked as if it had just been ironed and his dark pants were free of dirt and grease spots.

Jackson, who was leaning his back against the other wagon, a mug of steaming hot coffee in his hand, gave Zach a sullen look. "How come you always tend to Enos' horses first?" He nodded at Youtz.

Zach shrugged nonchalantly, determined not to be drawn into one of Jackson's petty little quarrels.

"If I take Youtz first, it's because he is Enos' lead horse, and then the other horses follow faster."

Jackson snorted to show his disdain for Zach's reasoning.

Enos came out from behind the wagon where his brother was shaving. "Actually the lad has a good point there." He pulled his suspenders over his broad shoulders. The long-sleeved woollen undershirt he wore was supposed to be white, but was by now dark grey with brown stains around the armpits.

Jackson laughed derisively. "That boy doesn't know his backside from a hole in the ground if you ask me." He tossed the rest of the coffee from his mug on the ground. "The brew that woman makes ain't fit for drinkin.'"

Theo wiped the shaving blade on a piece of cloth. "Yet you keep drinking it," he said with a wry smile.

Jackson snorted again as he angrily walked over to the fire. "Is that grub ready, woman?" he barked over Miss Reid's head.

She looked up at him, not even trying to hide her loathing. "Instead of constantly complaining, why don't you make the coffee yourself?"

Theo chuckled. "Please don't let him. Jackson's coffee is the worst."

Enos nodded. "That's true enough," he said with a grin.

Jackson shot the two men a scathing look over his shoulder. "You two never complained before."

"Well, we do now that we've had better." Theo dabbed at his face with the cloth. He turned and smiled at Miss Reid while wiping his hands. "Please continue making the coffee, Miss Reid. We'd rather live."

She gave Jackson a keen look. "I promise, I will."

"Where's Kyle?" Zach asked.

Theo pointed to the bushes where Zach had taken care of his business before. "Over there. Stayed for a while, he has. Hope he's all right."

Zach pulled Youtz over to Enos' wagon and tied the reins to the side of it. He went to the back of the wagon, stepped up on a wooden board and retrieved one of the small bags of oats he had refilled the night before. He jumped down again and went over to Youtz, tying the bag under his muzzle. "Go ahead and eat," he said, and walked over to the bushes pointed out to him by Theo.

"Kyle, I need your help with the horses," he called out.

"Can't people have some privacy around here?" came Kyle's answer. "I hate those damn beans. Just the smell of them makes me wanna hurl."

"Those horses have to be ready soon."

"It's not like I have a choice, man," Kyle hissed. "Do you think I wanna sit here and crap my insides out? Jeez, leave me alone."

Zach sighed. It sounded like he would have to do most of the work himself.

"Remember, I have to wash your clothes," Miss Reid said, when he passed by her at the fire.

He stopped and turned to her. "There are Natives down there."

She gave him a blank look.

"Indians. Down at the river." He pointed. He thought he better warn her, so they didn't surprise her.

Jackson's head shot up. "Injuns! Jesus Christ Almighty. Why didn't you say somethin' before? They might steal our horses." He jumped up and stormed toward the wagons. "I'll show them not to hang around decent folks."

"They're harmless," Zach yelled after him. He gave Miss Reid a helpless look. "They were just mining for gold."

She wiped the perspiration from her forehead with the back of her hand. "It's best to let the men take care of this."

Jackson came charging back with his rifle and quickly loaded it. "I'll show those good for nothin' heathens," he said, his finger on the trigger.

"Where are you off to with that gun?" Enos yelled after him.

Jackson stopped in his tracks and spun around. "You heard the boy, there are Injuns down there."

"I also heard him say, they appeared to be harmless."

"Appear doesn't mean . . ." Jackson started protesting.

"I want no needless strife." Enos strode toward Jackson holding out his hand. "Give me that gun."

"It's not like I'm going to shoot them, Enos. I'll just give them a scare."

Zach didn't like the look in Jackson's eyes.

Enos reached for him, grabbing for the rifle. It startled Jackson so much that his finger must have pulled on the trigger, for a bullet whizzed by Zach's head and blew a hole in the wooden side of Enos' wagon.

Enos' face turned red. He tore the rifle out of Jackson's hands. "You idiot," he yelled. "Now look what you've gone and done. When are you ever goin' to learn to control yourself? You nearly killed the lad and you shot a damn hole in my wagon."

Jackson opened his mouth as if he was about to say something, then clamped it shut.

Miss Reid had come rushing over to Zach. "He could have killed him," she yelled back at the men, her voice shrill.

Zach felt dazed and grabbed hold of her for support.

Theo hurried over to them. "I think the lad might need to sit down." He put an arm around Zach's shoulders and guided him over to the fire where he helped him sit on one of the rocks placed around it.

"You damn moron," Enos yelled again at Jackson.

Theo produced a small silver flask from his pocket. "Here Zach, this will help steady your nerves."

He accepted the flask and brought it to his lips with a trembling hand. The liquid started a fire inside him. He coughed, eliciting an alarmed outcry from Miss Reid. "Are you okay?"

"I'm fine." He coughed again, then took another gulp from the flask. It wasn't so bad, he found, after you got used to the burning, and it did settle his nerves. His hands had stopped shaking. He even managed a smile as he returned the flask to Theo.

"Man that was close." Kyle seated himself next to Zach. He looked pale underneath the mixture of suntan and dirt, which had now become his complexion.

Zach took a deep breath as he nodded, feeling he would be okay if he could just get his heart to beat at a normal rate again. But no, it kept pounding away in his chest. He looked at Theo and Miss Reid's concerned faces. "I'll be fine." His gaze wandered to Enos and Jackson. Enos was pushing Jackson toward the wagon, which had the bullet hole.

"You start unloadin' now so we can find out what damage you've done, you jackass."

Jackson scowled at Enos. "I said sorry. There's no need to

continue bustin' your sides about it."

It was exactly the wrong thing to say. Enos exploded in a rage, grabbing Jackson by his shirtfront and pushing him up against the side of the wagon. Jackson's legs kicked about as he was lifted up in the air. He tried frantically to scratch Enos' face.

"You don't go tell me when I ought to bust my sides," he yelled into Jackson's face.

Theo jumped up. "Enos be careful," he yelled. "You might kill him."

Enos spat on the ground as he let Jackson go. "Your foolishness is going to cost me hours of delay, so yes I'll bust my sides if I damn well feel like it."

Theo came over to his brother and handed him the flask.

"Thanks." Enos threw his head back and drank. He held the flask out to Jackson who was sitting on the ground massaging his neck. "Git yourself a dram?"

"I don't want it," Jackson croaked.

Enos wiped his mouth with the back of his hand. "Suit yourself." He returned the flask to his brother.

"Come now, Jackson," Theo said. "Have a dram with us."

"I'm not drinking with the likes of you."

Theo chuckled. "I guess our booze isn't good enough for the almighty Jackson," he said to his brother.

"Shut up, Theo," Jackson hollered. His outburst only made the gambler laugh even harder. "Shut the hell up, you hear!" His hate-filled eyes were trained on Theo.

Chapter 11

IT TURNED OUT THAT the bullet from Jackson's gun went through two sacks of sugar before it lodged in a third. The two first sacks Enos managed to patch up before too much of the sugar had leaked out. The third they had to open so they could sift through the sugar to collect the bullet.

"Why even bother?" Kyle asked Theo.

"Because if someone broke their tooth on that bullet, the merchant who sold it would be blamed, and he in turn would blame his supplier. Enos can lose customers that way."

As the men were cleaning up the mess, Miss Reid took the opportunity to wash their clothes down by the river. "The

Natives have left," she told Zach, when she came back after having spread the newly washed clothes out on rocks to dry in the sun. Zach figured the Natives had been scared away by the errant shot.

Since he and Kyle didn't have an extra change of clothes, it meant wrapping themselves in blankets and enduring countless jokes from Enos, who found the whole thing terribly amusing.

Theo finally pulled the boys aside. "Don't mind him. Enos has a somewhat skewed sense of humour."

Strange word choice, Zach had thought. Personally, he would have liked to skewer Enos with something sharp.

Jackson's mood hadn't improved as the morning wore on. He went silently about his chores. Now and then, he would snarl at Theo, the boys, or Miss Reid if they were in his way.

Zach stayed clear of him. He did not at all like the look in Jackson's eyes, and sensed that if he said, or did the wrong thing he might very well see his last day as he had almost done earlier. He shuddered every time he thought about that bullet whizzing by his head.

"You seem out of it," Kyle said when they were sitting across from each other at the fire eating their breakfast. "Are you sure you're okay, man?"

"I'm fine."

"He's being a jerk." Kyle shot Jackson a resentful look. "He's acting like it's all your fault that he discharged that rifle."

Zach had finally had enough. "I wish everyone would just stop going on about this. It was an accident."

"No need to snap at me," Kyle said and got up. He walked over to the bucket of water where Miss Reid had washed their dishes earlier. To Zach's surprise Kyle bent over and cleaned his dish himself. That was something he had never seen him do before. Miracles never cease to happen, Zach thought wryly, as he closed his eyes and let the sun warm his face. It was shaping up to be a hot afternoon, maybe even hotter than yesterday where the heat had radiated from the road through the thin soles of his Nikes.

"Here Zachary. Get dressed."

He blinked and looked up at Miss Reid. She was holding their clothes in her arms.

"Thanks." Zach accepted his clothes. They were still damp to the touch, especially the jeans.

"There was no time to dry them completely," she said. "Mr. Cox told me I had to hurry up, because Enos wants to be on the road again." She shook her head. "It's hard to be a woman in this time and age, that's for sure."

Kyle came over to her. She handed him his clothes with a sigh. "What I wouldn't give for some Cold Water Tide. That brown stuff that they pass off as detergent is an absolute joke." She cast a glance towards the river. "Well, I guess I better check on the men's clothes." She wrinkled her nose. "Jackson's stank like there was no tomorrow. God knows what he does in them."

Zach watched Miss Reid hurry down toward the river again. He felt sorry for her. True, his and Kyle's work was not always easy or pleasant. Horses could be stubborn and single-minded, but her tasks were mostly dirty and monotonous, and she was treated no better than a slave by Enos and Jackson. To her credit she didn't complain much. The frustration she had just vented was a rarity. Zach was not sure he would have been able to handle the constant verbal abuse had it been him.

Giving no thoughts to modesty, Kyle dropped his blanket on the ground so he could dress. Zach was far more self-conscious and carefully put his clothes on underneath his blanket, which took a lot longer. When he was finished, he found Kyle staring at him with an amused expression.

"Jeez, what a pain it must be to be so modest."

"Well, at least I don't flaunt everything I have, or don't have," Zach retorted. "Besides, someone might pass by on the road."

Kyle grinned. "I would just moon the suckers."

• • •

It was nearly noon before they were back on the road again. Enos kept complaining about the time they had to make up until Theo told him to stop his griping. They were all getting sick and tired of listening to him, and it only helped to put Jackson in an even fouler mood.

Zach wished he could ride on one of the horses, but only Jackson and Enos were allowed that privilege. They each sat astride the left back horse of the wagon they drove. The men controlled the other animals in their team with a so-called jerk-line. This name had elicited endless jokes from Kyle, until Enos yelled at him to shut the hell up.

The jerk-lines were tied to each wagon's lead horse, in this case Youtz and Blodell. These two horses knew what to do by the number of jerks Enos and Jackson gave the line.

As Zach trudged behind the wagons, next to Kyle, he wished Enos would teach him how to use the jerk-line. He quickly dismissed the idea before it became a possibility in his mind. There was no way Enos was going to relinquish his ride and entrust his horses to him.

Zach removed the kerchief Theo had lent him from around his neck, and tied it over his nose and mouth. The clouds of dust kicked up by the horses and wagons on the bone-dry road made visibility poor. The sky, which had been a bright blue before, was now obscured by grey. Grit had already made it into his mouth, and with a sickening feeling he felt it crunch between his teeth.

He watched Miss Reid walk in front of him, involved in an animated discussion with Theo. Those two always seemed to have something to talk about. He overheard only snippets of their conversations, mostly because he was not really interested. Once it had been about delicate eco-systems, the phrase she had used. Another time she had promoted the virtues of total equality between women and men. Zach had noticed that Theo had looked rather uncomfortable during that conversation.

"Why should women be able to vote?" He had asked. "They know nothing about politics."

"And why is that?" Her voice was shrill with indignation.

"Maybe because they don't have a head for such complicated matters." Theo was beginning to sound hesitant.

Miss Reid stopped and glared at him. "That is such male chauvinistic nonsense."

"That's possible." At this point Theo had looked so miserable Zach had felt sorry for him.

"Why don't those two just jump each other and get it over with," Kyle said.

Zach's initial reaction was to laugh out loud. "She's old!"

Kyle snorted. "You think her plumbing stops working after a certain age?"

Zach swatted irritably at a pesky fly. "How old do you think she is?"

Kyle shrugged. "Forty at least. I heard rumours that Mr. Blodell was sweet on her, but apparently she turned him down. I think she might be picky." He grinned at Zach. "Looks to me like she picked Cox, even though he doesn't look like he's much more than thirty. Maybe she has something for younger men."

Zach was about to answer when he felt a drop of water on his head, then another.

"Damn, if it isn't raining," Kyle said in disgust.

At first when the rain started pouring, Zach was glad because it killed the dust, but after about fifteen minutes of a relentless downpour he wasn't quite as happy about it, since the road was quickly turning into a muddy mess.

Finally, Enos and Jackson gave up driving the wagons. They jumped down from their horses, Enos straight into a big puddle. Swearing, he waded through the mud and water, giving Kyle, who stood sputtering with laughter next to Zach, a withering look.

Once they were stopped, Zach and Kyle found themselves scrambling to find shelter, any kind of shelter. At first, they crept in underneath Enos' wagon, but sitting in the mud soon became intolerable. They finally ended up standing underneath the same tree as Miss Reid and Theo. Not that the tree provided much shelter, but at least it gave the illusion of it. Enos and Jackson had to stay with the horses because thunder had rolled in and was spooking the animals.

The three men were donning oversized brown coats. Theo offered Miss Reid the use of his coat. After some half-hearted protesting, she accepted it.

"This sucks big time," Kyle said, pretty much expressing in his own terms the sentiments of everyone else standing underneath the tree. When the rain tapered off about half an hour later, Zach was soaked to the skin. The storm had brought a raw wind in its wake, and he could not remember having ever been this cold before.

Enos sauntered over to them, while Jackson stayed where he was. He pulled his wide-brimmed hat off and wiped his forehead with his forearm. "How are you all doin'?" he asked.

"Aside from freezing our asses off, we're just hunky-dory." Kyle's teeth were clattering in his mouth.

"We should start a fire, Enos, so we can dry our clothes," Theo suggested. "Otherwise we're all going to catch our death."

Enos put his hat back on and pushed it down over his head. "When has a little rain ever stopped us before?"

Theo stepped close to his brother and lowered his voice, but not enough for Zach not to overhear what was said. "May I remind you that we have a woman with us now."

"And whose idea was that?" Enos snapped.

"Some consideration might be in place."

"Damnation, Theo." Enos didn't make an effort to keep his voice low. "I can't allow myself to be slowed down by some persnickety woman."

"I'll be fine," Miss Reid said with a pointed look at Enos. "I've no intention of slowing anyone down."

Enos grumbled something none of them could make out, and turned angrily on his heels. "Let's git goin'," he hollered at Jackson.

Theo turned to her. "I'm sorry, Ma'am. Tact was never my brother's strong suit."

She removed Theo's coat from around her shoulders and handed it to him. "It's not your fault that your brother's rude and inconsiderate," she said loudly, making sure Enos overheard.

As it turned out, they had to stop anyway when one of the wheels on Jackson's wagon became stuck in the mud. Locating the jack used to ease the wagons out of holes proved to be difficult, since Jackson, who carried the jack in his wagon, seems to have forgotten where he had put it. They went through most of his load before finally the jack was located underneath a sack of dry beans. By that time Enos was seething.

"Why didn't you make sure the jack was put back in its place?" he yelled at Jackson.

"I guess I didn't think about it." Jackson's small dark eyes flashed at Enos. "It probably slipped underneath the sack when we reloaded this morning."

Enos tore the jack out of Jackson's hands. "Here, help me with the jack."

After a while the men managed to work the jack and lift the wheel out of the mud hole. By that time, the horses were stamping impatiently, ready to move on.

Theo ran his hand over one of the big-rimmed wooden wheels. "Enos, we need to find a tire shrinker soon."

Enos nodded. "I know. This wretched road seems to get worse and worse each time I travel it. In some places there are more potholes than road."

"What's a tire shrinker?" Zach asked. He had a vision of a big muscular man with tattoos dressed in leather pants and vest, who squeezed the wheels between his enormous hands.

"It's a contraption that heats and folds in the iron rims," Enos explained.

"Look, a camel," Miss Reid yelled from up ahead.

Zach spun around, thinking he must have heard wrong, but sure enough further up the road he spotted what was unmistakably a camel trudging toward them.

Miss Reid shrieked when the camel veered a little to the right, heading straight toward her. Theo hurried up to her side and pulled her away from the camel. The animal passed by them acting as if they weren't even there.

Kyle gaped after the lumbering animal. "Did he escape from a zoo?"

Did they even have zoos in 1866, Zach wondered as he watched the camel disappear down the road.

Kyle wrinkled his nose. "Jeez, did he ever stink."

"That must be one of Frank Laumeister's camels," Theo said.

Zach turned to him. "Who's Frank Laumeister?"

Theo grinned at his brother. "You want to tell the story?"

"No, you go ahead, but make it quick. I wanna be on my way again."

"Frank Laumeister got this brilliant idea." Theo underscored the word *brilliant,* "to buy camels in order to carry freight to the gold country. He had heard each animal would carry about eight hundred pounds and could go days without food or water. Furthermore, they travelled up to thirty or forty miles a day. In their infinite wisdom, Frank Laumeister and his partners figured that with twenty-three camels they might net an easy sixty thousand dollars the first year."

Enos shook his head in disdain at their folly.

"Where did they find twenty-three camels?" Miss Reid looked doubtful. Zach could understand why. One camel was hard enough to fathom, but twenty-three!

"They had actually been used as pack animals by the United States army in Texas at one point," Theo explained.

"Oh, I see." She nodded as if using camels in the United States army was the most natural thing.

"And where did the army get them from?" Zach asked.

Theo shrugged. "Who knows? They're always enterprising down there."

Zach pointed in the direction the camel had just disappeared. "So why is that camel running around loose?"

Theo looked at his brother. "Some of them were taken to a ranch, I heard."

Enos nodded. "That's what I heard too."

"As for the rest of them." Theo shrugged. "Maybe they just turned them loose."

"Why don't they use the camels anymore?" Zach asked.

Theo grinned. "Well, apparently Laumeister had not been told that camels are highly odorous animals, very bad-tempered and easily excited. These camels were no exception."

Enos nodded again. "When I last talked to Jack Hume in

Soda Creek he was still upset about how those camels had kicked and bit his horses. And some years ago Henry Collins almost lost his load when he met the camels on the road, and their stench alone made his horses shy and bolt."

"So this Frank Laumeister just turned some of them loose?" By the tone of Miss Reid's voice she was clearly not approving.

Theo shrugged. "Well, I guess. After all, the animals were no use to him anymore."

"Yes, that might very well be true, but camels are not used to harsh winters. What a cruel thing to do."

Theo gave her an amused look. "Are you suggesting that he should have shipped all the animals back to the Sahara, or wherever they came from?"

"No, I'm just saying that he could have contacted some animal rescue centre, or what about the SPCA?"

"SPCA?" Theo asked puzzled. "I'm not sure I understand."

"Those poor camels." There were tears in Miss Reid's eyes now.

"Why would you care?" Enos asked, genuinely surprised.

"I love animals," Miss Reid answered.

Enos shook his head. "I understand lovin' your horse or dog for that matter but who, in their right mind, can love a camel?"

Jackson, for a moment forgetting his animosity towards the brothers, nodded fervently, a mocking look in his eyes.

Miss Reid shook her head in exasperation. "You people! Backward is what you are. I'm sick and tired of all this. The dust. The heat. The rain." Tears were now running down her cheeks. "My feet are all blisters from walking. My hair is dry as straw, because I don't have any decent shampoo and conditioner." She wiped angrily at her tears with the back of her hand. "What I wouldn't give for some strawberry yogurt, or a smoked chicken sandwich and . . . and bottled water." She sank to the ground right into a mud hole, her face buried in her hands. "I hate this place. I hate it so much. I want toilet paper." Her shoulders started to shake.

"Miss Reid," Zach said in shock. "Get a grip."

Kyle shook his head. "Now she has really lost it."

Zach pulled at her arm. "Miss Reid, get up."

Enos shot his brother an annoyed look. "Didn't I tell you it was a bad idea to bring a woman along? They just don't have the grit for this. And this one is especially high-strung."

"Rubbish, Enos." Theo walked over to Miss Reid. "She's just feeling a bit overwhelmed. It happens to the best of us." He waved Zach away and put an arm around the teacher, helping her up.

Enos shook his head. "Well, at least I don't squat down in a mud hole and snivel."

"We don't need this kind of stress." Jackson's eyes glinted. "Why don't we just leave them behind?"

Theo shot him a blistering look. "How can you even suggest leaving a defenceless woman in the middle of nowhere?"

Sobbing even harder, Miss Reid buried her face against Theo's shoulder.

Jackson jutted out his unshaven jaw. "This is not exactly

the middle of nowhere. There are wagons and stagecoaches comin' through here all the time. Let someone else take care of them."

"Jackson has a point, Theo," Enos said. "Let someone else deal with this. Don't forget she has the lads helpin' her out."

Theo's features were taut as he glared at his brother. "Our mother often told me she was concerned about the tendency to cruelty that she saw in you. I'm just grateful that she's not here right now to witness your shameful behaviour. You disappoint me gravely, Enos Cox."

Enos' gaze faltered. "I wish you would't keep bringin' our mother into this." He straightened his shoulders. "Okay, they can stay, but this is the last warnin'. I'm not puttin' up with anymore of her batty behavior." He looked at Theo. "You've been forewarned, Theo." He turned on his heels. "And now let's get a move on. Enough time has been wasted," he yelled over his shoulder.

Soon they were on their way again. Miss Reid had recovered from her nervous breakdown, even though that's not what she called it. A vulnerable moment in my life was her term as she apologized profusely to Theo. Her apologies to Enos made no difference. He still called her a madwoman.

Chapter 12

ENOS WAS DETERMINED to make up for lost time, and he pushed everyone to their limit. When Theo finally convinced his brother that they were all exhausted and needed their rest, the sun had dipped well below the tree-covered hills. Their surroundings submerged into dark shadows as Theo got the fire going. Zach sank down in front of it and turned his palms toward the flames. When the sun went down it always grew cold. He had to get himself a new jacket when he reached Barkerville. His spirits sank when he realized he had no money to buy one.

He watched as Miss Reid first made coffee and then began

to prepare their dinner. Her movements were beginning to look slow and uncoordinated. She was as exhausted as the rest of them. The handle of the cast iron pan she was holding slipped out of her hand and fell into the fire.

"Watch the handle," Enos yelled at her, "or the wood'll burn."

Silently, a grim expression on her face, she grabbed a cloth and quickly extracted the pan from the flames. She smiled wryly at Zach. "What would you like for dinner tonight?"

He returned her smile even though it was an effort. "Hamburger and fries with ketchup."

Kyle sat down next to Zach. "Steak, baked potato and sour cream for me, Miss E." Since her first name was Eliza, he had recently started calling her Miss E, which, surprisingly enough, she didn't seem to mind.

"Will baked beans and slightly rancid bacon do?" She sounded as if she was about to cry.

Please don't have a nervous breakdown, Zach prayed.

"Yeah, what the heck, we haven't had that for a while." Kyle made a face and fell into silence, staring into the dancing flames.

Zach's eyes were smarting from the smoke and he closed them. Soon he dozed off.

He was startled awake when he heard a commotion around him. Turning his head, he saw Theo and Enos approach a tall man clad in an oversized grey coat. He was leading a mule behind him. The hat he wore was pointy with a broad rim, and it reminded Zach of the one his former cub-leader had always favoured. He watched as the stranger shook hands first with Enos and then Theo.

Jackson wandered over and also shook the man's hand. Leaving the mule tied to the branch of a small tree, the men headed to the campfire.

With his elbow Zach poked at Kyle, who sat snoozing next to him. "We have a visitor."

"He must have smelled the coffee I just made," Miss Reid said with a wry smile as she watched the men's approach.

When the men reached the fire, the stranger lifted his hat at her in greeting, revealing a bald dome. "Hello there, Ma'am. Name's Dan McKenna."

"Hello, Mr. McKenna." She pushed some stray locks away from her face with the back of her hand.

"This is Miss Eliza Reid," Theo said. "And those lads sitting over there are her nephews, Zach and Kyle." He pointed at each of them in turn.

McKenna nodded at them. "Nice meeting you." He had an open friendly face.

"All we can offer you, I'm afraid, are bacon and beans," Enos told the stranger as he sat down in front of the fire, gesturing with his hand at McKenna to do the same.

"Well, I never tire of that, especially if it's made by a purty lady." McKenna smiled at Miss Reid, revealing gaps where teeth were missing.

His compliment brought a flush to her cheeks. "Well,

thank you, Mr. McKenna." She gave him a quick smile. "I just made coffee. Would you like some?"

McKenna replaced the hat on his head. "Sounds most welcome, Ma'am."

"I'll take care of it," Theo said to Miss Reid. "You just go ahead and finish dinner."

Miss Reid nodded. "We still have a sack of potatoes left. I'll fry some of them up for tonight." She turned and headed for the wagons where the potatoes were kept.

While Theo poured a steaming mug of coffee for their guest, McKenna pulled his coat off and seated himself next to Enos.

"Careful, it's very hot," Theo said as he came over and handed the mug to him. "So where are you headed, Mr. McKenna?"

McKenna blew on the hot liquid and sniffed it with obvious relish. "I'm on my way to Victoria. I wintered around the creeks." He shook his head and sipped from his coffee. "Hard winter it was too. Thirty below in January." He took another sip. "Together with my partner, Vernon, I sank a shaft at the end of September, and we worked it through the winter. I've never been so cold in my life." He shuddered at the memory.

Jackson sat down directly across from McKenna. "So did you strike gold?" His eyes gleamed in the firelight.

McKenna's jovial smile faded, and his expression became guarded. "Some."

Jackson acted as if he didn't notice the other's change of demeanour. "How much?"

McKenna took another sip of his coffee. "Enough to break even on expenses and some extra for our efforts."

Zach thought there was a challenge in the look McKenna gave Jackson, but apparently Jackson had decided to drop his line of inquiry. The silence that followed became a little awkward.

It was Theo who broke it with a grin at his brother. "Enos, maybe you should get yourself a claim, strike it rich."

McKenna's tense shoulders relaxed. "I'm afraid that's too late now. Last I checked, all claims were taken around the creeks."

"So how come you're here and not workin' on your claim?" Enos asked.

McKenna's eyes became moist, and he blinked a couple of times before he answered. "Unfortunately, Vernon caught the Mountain Fever and died about a month ago. I just didn't have the stomach to continue. I sold the claim to some Yankees. After I've been to Victoria, I'm coming back to Barkerville one last time to sign the papers."

"Mountain Fever. What's that?" Zach asked.

Self-consciously, McKenna wiped a tear from the corner of his eye with his big work-worn hand. "Oh, it's a terrible sickness to be sure." He took another sip of his coffee.

"So what does it do, the Mountain Fever?" Zach asked, his tiredness gone. He loved all the medical shows on TV, especially reruns of *House* with all those mysterious diseases.

Kyle inched closer to Zach. "Yes, what does it do?"

McKenna sighed. "It's an illness that fools you, that's for

certain. First we thought it was the influenza: the malaise, the headache." He shrugged, his eyes again welling with tears. "What else were we to think? People are always sick in the camps with colds, earaches and stomach pains. Doc Healy told us that Vernon's nosebleeds should've alerted us to the fact that this was more serious, but how were we to know, when Vernon was so prone to frequent nosebleeds." He took another swallow of coffee and wiped his mouth in his coat sleeve. "Then the high fever started. Real bad it was. Vernon was delirious most of the time."

Theo sat down next to McKenna. "Patrick McAllen, who was a blacksmith back in Fort Yale, died from it last fall. He suffered greatly, I heard."

"The fever kills you then?" Zach looked inquiringly first at Theo, then McKenna when he didn't get an answer from him.

McKenna nodded. "Yeah, that and the bloody diarrhea. Doc Healy says the illness fills your insides with sores and pus."

"Wow!" Kyle stared at McKenna in awe.

Zach couldn't help thinking of his own frequent bouts with the runs. Was he going to end up filled with sores and pus? "How do you get it?"

McKenna shrugged. "No one knows for certain. Doc Healy thinks it might come from the food or water."

Zach swallowed hard. "Like beans?"

Theo gave a chuckle. "If it was from the beans I reckon all of us would be sick with the Mountain Fever right now." The chuckle turned to a hearty laughter. Enos and McKenna joined in.

Jackson had been listening impatiently to McKenna's description. Finally, he couldn't keep quiet any longer and pointed toward McKenna's mule, standing there patiently waiting. "What's in those packs? Gold?"

Abruptly, Theo stopped laughing and viewed Jackson with annoyance. "He's our guest. Stop bothering him with all those types of questions."

Jackson's expression soured. "Well, I was just inquirin' is all. Can't blame a man for bein' curious."

"Shut up, Jackson," Theo said firmly as he got up and held out his hand to McKenna. "More coffee?"

The miner nodded. "Sure, wouldn't mind." He handed his mug to Theo.

Kyle poked Zach in the side. "Can you imagine if he's carrying gold in those bags?" he whispered to him.

Zach stared at McKenna's mule. In addition to the big bundle tied on top of the mule's back, the animal also carried two bulging leather bags, one hanging down each flank.

Theo came over to McKenna with the refilled mug. "Here you go Mr. McKenna," he said handing it to him.

McKenna smiled up at him. "Please, why don't you just call me Dan." He smiled at Miss Reid as she returned from the wagons carrying a small sack with potatoes. "All of you call me Dan. I'm not much for formality."

Chapter 13

AFTER DINNER, WITH fried potatoes for a change, and once the cleanup was finished, McKenna unloaded the bundle containing his belongings from the mule's back and brought it over to the fire.

"What about the rest of it?" Jackson asked, nodding at the saddlebags still strapped to the mule.

McKenna shrugged as he looked toward the mule, which stood peacefully nibbling at the grass around the tree. "I'll deal with that before I go to sleep."

Enos held up a clear bottle containing a yellow-ish liquid. "Anyone for firin' a slug?" he asked with a wink.

McKenna smiled broadly at the prospect. "I sure wouldn't mind. The road gets mighty dusty at times."

Enos uncorked the bottle with his teeth, poured a generous amount of liquid into McKenna's empty coffee mug, and returned it to him. "For your continued safe journey to Victoria, Mr . . . I mean Dan."

McKenna held up the mug. "To my continued safe journey to Victoria."

Zach was surprised to see Miss Reid accept some of the drink too. Somehow he didn't see her as someone who boozed it up. When he noticed the exhaustion etched into her features, he figured she probably needed something strong.

Kyle looked expectantly at Enos. "May I have some too?"

"Sure, lad," Enos said, and he grabbed a mug from behind him and poured a goodly amount into it.

"What is it?" Zach asked Enos.

Enos nodded. "It's real Scotch," he answered. "Hails all the way from Scotland where they know how to make a right good spirit."

Full of hope, Zach regarded the bottle Enos was holding in his hand. "Does it help against the Mountain Fever?"

Amused glances passed between Enos, Theo and McKenna. Enos held up the bottle. "If this doesn't kill it, lad, I don't know what will." Once again, he poured a generous amount of Scotch into another mug and gave it to Theo, who came over and handed it to Zach. "Enjoy."

Zach took a sip of the Scotch. As he expected, the liquid burned its way down to his stomach. He couldn't help gasping and tears came to his eyes. The men laughed out loud.

Kyle drank from his mug. He wiped his mouth with the back of his hand and gave Zach a grin. "Great stuff, huh?"

Zach shrugged and turned his attention to Miss Reid again. "Are you going to be okay?"

She sighed as she tucked her hair behind her ears. "Aside from burnin' my hand on the frying pan, I'm just hunky dory." She looked down at the big blister, which had formed on the side of her thumb. "When it bursts it's going to really hurt." Miss Reid took a sip of her drink and grimaced. "Oh, this stuff is truly awful."

Zach, agreeing with her, put his own mug down on the ground.

The men continued drinking and toasting each other, except for Jackson. He had moved over next to McKenna, where he now sat nursing his mug of Scotch. Zach noticed Jackson's gaze make several cursory sweeps of McKenna's mule.

"Are you going to drink the rest of your Scotch?" Kyle asked Zach, nodding at his mug.

Zach shook his head. "No, you can have it if you want."

Miss Reid got up. "You must all excuse me," she said with a yawn, "but I'm exhausted. It's time for me to go to bed."

McKenna smiled at her. "I sure appreciate the meal, Ma'am, especially the potatoes. It was all very good."

"Thank you Mr. McKenna." She went over and put her

mug down next to a stack of cleaned plates. She nodded at the men. "Well, good night, gentlemen."

"Night, Ma'am," McKenna said.

While Theo went with her to help spread out her blankets on the ground, McKenna extracted a big pocket watch from his vest and flipped it open. "My word, it's gettin' late, nearly ten, and I need an early start tomorrow." His voice was beginning to slur.

"That's a fine watch you have there," Enos complimented him.

McKenna smiled at him as he snapped the watch closed. "It was my father's. He gave it to me when I left the old country. See, his initials are right here, W. M. William McKenna." He turned the watch over and showed first Enos, then Jackson, the etched letters on the smooth silver surface.

Zach got up and walked over to McKenna to have a look too. The miner let Zach hold the watch in his hand so he could feel how heavy it was. "Way cool," he said to McKenna.

Zach's grandfather had a similar watch to McKenna's, also with a chain you could attach to a pocket so you wouldn't lose it. The watch had been in the family for generations and had the initials of Zach's great-great grandfather, and one day he was going to inherit it.

Theo, who had finished helping Miss Reid, also came over to McKenna to have a look at the watch. "Clearly, a very fine and skilled watchmaker made this piece," he said smiling at McKenna.

McKenna nodded proudly. "This watch is very dear to me

and I guard it with my life," he said as he pocketed the watch again. "It's my great hope that my father is still alive." McKenna slapped the front of his thighs with the palms of his hands. "When my business in Barkerville is finally concluded, I'm going back to the old country, England that is, to see for myself."

Enos held up the half-empty bottle of Scotch. "Well, let's drink to that."

When Zach made it back to Kyle, he found him asleep where he had left him next to the fire. "Come on, time to hit the sack," he said as he shook Kyle's shoulder.

Kyle's head jerked in his direction. "What?"

"We're going to bed."

"Oh, okay." Kyle said, promptly nodding off again, his chin sinking down on his chest.

Leaning over, Zach grabbed Kyle by the arm, trying to pull him up, but he was too heavy. "Come on, Kyle." He shook him awake again. "Get a move on."

Mumbling something incoherent, Kyle finally obeyed. "I . . . I must be back home by August," he said as Zach put Kyle's arm around his neck and half-dragged him toward their sleeping spot next to Miss Reid.

"Why?"

Kyle nearly took Zach down in a fall as he tripped over a rock and dropped to his knees. Zach helped him up again.

"Because . . . because I'm supposed to go to a Nickelback concert in Vancouver." His eyes had trouble focusing on

Zach. "We . . . we absolutely have to get back home, do you understand?" He burped. "Jeez, I don't feel so hot."

Zach put an arm around his shoulders. "You need to go to bed, man."

None of the men, except Jackson, had noticed they were leaving the circle around the fire. Zach felt his small alert eyes follow him and Kyle. He was the only one of the men not drinking, which he found odd. Jackson usually didn't hold back when he and Enos "fired a slug".

Zach's head hardly hit the ground before his eyes closed. The last thing he heard was the men's laughter and animated talk.

Chapter 14

⌘

IT WAS STILL DARK when Zach woke up. He lifted his head and looked toward the fire, which burned strong. Two figures sat huddled together, arguing in low, heated voices. Enos and Jackson.

Miss Reid was snoring loudly next to him. Maybe that was what had woken him up. He turned his back to her and closed his eyes. Soon he drifted off to sleep again. When he woke up this time, the sun was peeking over the hills. Loud quarrelling voices could be heard from the campfire. "His mule is gone too," Zach heard Theo say. He propped himself up on his elbow to have a look at what was going on.

Theo was standing over Jackson, who was sitting on a rock

warming his hands over the flames. "Why would he just up and leave in the dark?"

Jackson cast a sullen glance up at Theo. "I reckon he didn't want to wake anyone. Anyway, why are you bustin' my sides about it? I'm not the man's keeper."

Theo shook his head. "This doesn't make sense at all. Had he waited an hour or two he would have had daylight, and a full stomach."

Yawning, Enos came out from behind his wagon. He scratched his chest through the woollen undershirt. "Where's Dan?" he asked as he looked around.

Theo turned to him. "Jackson told me that he has left." His forehead creased as he looked down at Jackson again. "Did you say something to cause him offence?"

Jackson jumped up, an indignant expression on his face. "Now why would I go and do that?"

Theo shrugged. "You might inadvertently have said something that made him angry." The antagonism was gone from his voice. "You know how your mouth has a tendency to run away with you, especially when you're drinking."

Jackson's face reddened. "Well, I didn't say anythin' to annoy him. I don't know why you're makin' such a goddamn fuss over this." He turned his head and spat on the ground. "He just up and left, I told you." Jackson looked over to where Zach was lying and he fixed him with his stare. "Wake that darn woman up, so she can make me some grub. I'm hungry."

Zach leaned over Miss Reid, who was still sleeping, and

shook her shoulder. She opened her eyes, giving him a groggy look. "What?"

"The men want their breakfast," he whispered. "I warn you, Jackson's in a foul mood," he quickly added, thinking it was better to let Miss Reid know, so she didn't say something that would further antagonize him.

Miss Reid sat up and yawned, stretching her arms over her head. "I feel like I hardly slept at all."

"Dan McKenna apparently left," he told her.

She lowered her arms. "I thought he would stay for breakfast."

Zach shrugged. "So did I, but according to Jackson, he changed his mind."

"Well, I find that rather odd." Miss Reid pushed her blanket aside. "Why in the world would he . . ." Her eyes narrowed. "I bet it was Jackson who said something stupid to him."

"Most likely." Zach watched as Miss Reid got up and in vain tried to smooth down her hair, which stuck out in all directions. She finally admitted defeat and sighed. "Well, better get to it." Yawning again, she drifted over to the fire.

Zach crept out from underneath his blanket. It was time he started seeing to the horses.

Fortunately, he found all the horses gathered in the same spot where the grass grew tall. He had just reached out his hand to pat Youtz on the neck when his stomach began cramping. Zach made a beeline for some nearby bushes. Here he had thought that deciding not eating the beans last night would make a difference, but his bowels seemed to be in a constant state of rebellion.

He was pushing branches aside after taking care of business when he saw something glint on the ground in the early morning sunlight. He bent over to get a better look and saw a pocket watch. Puzzled, he picked it up and turned it over in his hand. The initials W.M. jumped out at him. He looked up and spotted Theo standing by Enos' wagon combing his hair. Zach ran through the grass and reached him. "Look what I found," he said, startling Theo so much he dropped the comb. He forgot all about the comb when he saw the watch dangling from Zach's hand. "It's Dan McKenna's," he said with instant recognition.

Zach nodded, his throat dry as he turned the watch over to show Theo the engraved initials. "Where did you find this?" Theo asked.

Zach turned and pointed the cluster of bushes out to him. "It was just lying on the ground over there."

Theo took the watch from Zach's hand and held it up in front of him. "Look, the chain is broken," he said, fingering the break. "McKenna must surely have noticed by now that it's gone, and must be looking for it." Theo glanced toward the fire. No one was there. Just then Miss Reid came around Jackson's wagon carrying a bucket of water in her hand. "Where did my brother and Jackson go?" Theo asked her.

She stopped and put the bucket down on the ground. "I have no idea." She wiped her hand across her brow as she looked toward the fire. "They certainly were there when I went to get water. Wonder where they might have gone to?"

Theo leaned over and picked up his jacket from the driver's seat of the wagon. Pulling it on, he turned to Miss Reid. "Mr. McKenna mislaid his pocket watch." He held the watch up for a moment for Miss Reid to see before he dropped it into his jacket pocket. "When you see my brother tell him that I've taken one of the horses and gone looking for Mr. McKenna. I'll be back soon."

"Okay," Miss Reid said as she watched him head over to where the horses were grazing. With a deep sigh, she bent over and picked up the bucket again.

"Here let me," Zach said as he hurried over to her and took the bucket from her hand. "Where's Kyle?" he asked as they walked to the fire.

"Still sleeping," she said. "He complained of a headache when I tried to wake him up. Hangover, if you ask me."

Zach nodded and put the bucket down on the ground next to the fire. "I'll go and check on him," he said to Miss Reid and continued over to the spot where he, Kyle and Miss Reid had slept last night. Kyle lay curled up underneath his blanket with his eyes closed. Zach nudged him awake with his foot. "Dan McKenna lost his watch," he said when Kyle looked bleary-eyed up at him. "Theo's riding out to try find him so he can give it back to him," Zach added.

"What the heck are you babbling about?" Kyle groaned, closing his eyes against the bright daylight.

Zach remembered that Kyle didn't even know yet that the

miner had left. "McKenna took off early this morning, before any of us were awake, and he dropped his pocket watch, so Theo is trying to locate him to return it."

"Okay." Kyle said without much interest as he rubbed the heel of his hand against one of his eyes. "Jeez, my head hurts."

"It's most likely a hangover," Zach said with a measure of glee. Served Kyle right. "You were pretty wasted last night."

Kyle stopped rubbing his eye, and peered up at him. "I was? I don't remember." He pushed the blanket covering him aside and tried to get up, but finally gave up and fell back on the blankets again. "I feel like crap." He held the palm of his hand against his forehead. "Can you take care of the horses this morning?"

Zach was about to protest but then reconsidered. After all, what did it really matter? He was usually the one who did most of the work anyway, and this morning Kyle would definitely be more of a bother than a help.

He headed out to bring in the horses. He stopped when he saw Enos and Jackson come toward him. They were arguing again. "Jackson, I can't . . ." Enos abruptly shut up when he saw Zach.

"What do you want, you little runt?" Jackson sneered.

Zach ignored him and instead turned his attention to Enos. "Your brother has taken one of the horses to go look for Mr. McKenna." Enos' look turned dark. "Mr. McKenna dropped his watch," Zach added quickly. "And he wants to return it to him."

. . .

Enos put his empty coffee mug down on the ground and stared at Zach who was sitting across from him at the fire, eating leftover potatoes from the dinner last night. "How long did my brother say he would be away?" He was red-faced and clearly upset over the delay.

Zach swallowed his mouthful. "All he said was that he would be back soon."

"Well, it's over an hour now." He glanced at Jackson who was sitting next to him eating the last of his beans. "Why don't we just take our leave? Theo can find us later."

With his dirty finger nail, Jackson dug out some food from between his teeth. "You'll need the horse that he took, Enos. You can't pull your wagon with five horses." He picked up his now empty plate with both hands and licked it, a habit that was always a sure fire way to infuriate Miss Reid.

This time was no exception as she stormed over to where he was sitting and tore the plate out of his grimy hands. "Do you know anything else but disgusting habits?" she snapped.

Jackson's eyes narrowed. "Did you see that, Enos? She's a menace."

Enos threw up his hands. "Just shut your yaps," he shouted. "All of you."

Zach wondered from his tone and voice if something else was bothering him.

Chapter 15

∽

NEARLY TWO HOURS after he had set off, Theo finally made it back to camp. The horse he had ridden sounded winded and its flanks were glistening with sweat. Zach saw it was Rudolph, a good-natured animal, rarely causing trouble.

Enos crossed his arms over his chest and viewed his brother angrily. "What are you tryin' to do, kill a good horse?"

Theo dismounted, and removed the kerchief covering his nose and mouth. He took off his hat and slapped it against his thigh to get rid of the dust. His hair, damp from perspiration stuck out in all directions. He did not at all look like the well-groomed man Zach was so used to seeing. "I couldn't find Dan McKenna." Theo's voice was hoarse, and he had to cough before he could continue. "People I met on the way hadn't seen him either. I did, however, notice a mule running loose, but it was too skittish to catch." He bit his lip. "I can't help thinking something must have happened to him."

Enos' tense muscles slackened. "Yeah, that is mighty odd," he agreed.

Theo wiped perspiration from his forehead with the kerchief. "I do feel, Enos, that we should continue searching for him," he said as he stuffed the kerchief into his jacket pocket. "We owe McKenna that much, especially if he's in some sort of trouble."

Enos shook his head, his eyes darkening again. "Absolutely not. We've already wasted enough time as it is and now we also have to wait for the horse you took to rest up."

"But, I think . . ." Theo began protesting, but his brother quickly cut him off.

"No Theo, and that's final," Enos said firmly. "We're not the man's keeper."

Theo watched his brother with disappointment, then gave a deep sigh as he fished McKenna's watch out of his vest pocket, turned it over in his hand, and viewed its initials again. "I guess, all I can do then is to keep this until McKenna returns to Barkerville again as he said he would."

"Seems to me that's the prudent thing to do." Enos watched his brother keenly as he pocketed the watch again.

Theo went over to Miss Reid, and with a tired smile at her, picked up his mug from the stack of dishes she had just washed. He sauntered back to Zach, and held out the mug. "Do me a favour and get me some water. I'm parched from the long ride."

Zach took the mug and hurried off to Jackson's wagon, where the camp's water was stored. Jackson was there, busy hitching the horses to the wagon. "What did Theo have to say?" he asked with a sidelong glance at Zach.

"That he couldn't find Mr. McKenna," Zach answered him. Jackson's hands tightened hard around the harness on one of the horses. He had been jumpy all morning. Zach looked towards the wooden barrel hanging on the side of the wagon. "Theo sent me here to get him some water." He wasn't sure why he felt the need to inform Jackson, since it really didn't involve him.

Jackson nodded absentmindedly, his thoughts clearly focused on something else.

Zach walked up to the water barrel, lifted the hinged lid and dipped the mug inside to fill it, only to discover that the barrel was empty. He turned to Jackson. "There's no water left," he said holding up the mug.

Jackson's unfriendly gaze met his. "What am I, your hired help?" he snapped. "There are other barrels inside the wagon. Quit pesterin' me, you little toad eater."

"No need to be rude," Zach retorted. "All I did was ask." Jackson spat on the ground and turned his attention to the horses again.

Fuming, Zach went to the back of the wagon, and climbed

up on the step. He loosened the flap of the canvas cover and looked inside. He quickly located two water barrels in the corner of the wagon and crawled inside, mug in hand. As he was reaching out to lift the lid off the nearest barrel, his eyes fell on a shovel. He recognized it as the one used to dig dirt from around the wheels of the wagons when they got stuck and the ground wasn't stable enough to use the jack.

Wet soil was clinging to the blade, which was strange since he knew the shovel hadn't been used for days. Something was smeared on the wooden handle. He touched the smear with his index finger and his heartbeat quickened when he studied the sticky substance clinging to his finger. He had no doubt that it was blood.

Thoughts swirled through Zach's mind. First there was McKenna's disappearance this morning, then the watch Zach had found, and now blood. He also thought about how odd Jackson had been acting the night before. First of all, not drinking the Scotch, when he usually didn't hold back, and his gaze had kept wandering to those saddlebags that McKenna had brought with him.

Had Jackson been sitting there all night at the fire, planning to kill McKenna and bury him somewhere? It sure would explain both the blood and the wet soil on that shovel. Goose bumps had erupted all over his body, as Zach quickly pulled the lid away from the barrel, and filled the mug with water.

The sound of Zach getting down from the wagon made

Jackson turn around. He eyed him suspiciously. "You surely took your time."

At a loss for words, Zach just nodded. His hand was shaking so much, water spilled over the side of the mug

"Cat got your tongue, lad?" Jackson asked.

Zach could no longer bear to be in close proximity to him. "Have to go," he croaked. He felt Jackson's eyes bore into his back as he hurried away.

The discovery Zach had just made was far too important to keep to himself. Should he tell Kyle? No he was always shooting off his mouth without thinking. Miss Reid then? That wouldn't work either, since she would probably panic and fret to no end. He needed someone level-headed — like Theo, of course.

Zach spotted the gambler, who was in the middle of kicking soil over the campfire to extinguish the flames. Miss Reid was busy packing their plates, utensils and pots into their boxes. Kyle was nowhere in sight. Zach stopped next to Theo and held out the mug. It was only half-full now but that couldn't be helped. "Here's your water."

Theo stopped what he was doing and turned to Zach. With a grateful smile, he took the mug from Zach's hand and greedily downed its content. He wiped his mouth on his shirt sleeve. "Is something the matter?" he asked. "You look like you saw a ghost."

Zach eyed Miss Reid, but she was too busy with her tasks to pay them any attention. "I need to speak with you alone for a moment," he told Theo. "Somewhere more private," he added quickly when he noticed Enos come out from behind his wagon and head towards them.

Theo nodded and waved at his brother. "Just a moment," he yelled as he walked away with Zach. Enos nodded sullenly and headed over to Miss Reid, no doubt to complain. Zach and Theo stopped when they were well out of earshot of Enos and Miss Reid. Zach faced the gambler. "It concerns Mr. McKenna."

Theo showed immediate interest. "About his disappearance? Did you discover something?"

Zach nodded. "Actually, I did. The water barrel on the side of the wagon was empty so I went inside Jackson's wagon to get some water there instead." Zach lowered his voice. "There was a shovel right next to the water barrels, the one you use to dig the wagons out when the wheels get stuck in mud," he added as an explanation. His hands still trembled and he clasped them in front of him to keep them from doing so. "The shovel had fresh dirt on it, and . . . and on the handle some blood."

"Blood?"

Zach glanced in Jackson's direction. He was nowhere to be seen. "Yeah, it's definitely blood. Something is just not right, and Mr. McKenna . . ." He stopped abruptly when he saw Jackson come around the wagon. The horses were scraping the ground with their hooves, impatient to get going. "Cut it out," Jackson yelled at the animals.

Theo's gaze had moved to Jackson too.

"Mr. McKenna said last night that he would have breakfast with us," Zach continued. "Why then did he sneak off in the dark without as much as a goodbye to anyone?" He bit his lip. "This thing with his watch." He shook his head at Theo. "You must admit that doesn't compute . . . I mean . . . make sense," he quickly corrected himself.

Theo gave Zach a penetrating look. "Are you suggesting that Jackson might be a cold-blooded murderer?"

Zach took a deep breath. "Yes."

Disbelief was written all over Theo's face. "He's a disagreeable sort, no doubt, but a murderer!" He shook his head. "No, I don't believe that."

"I absolutely think he's capable." The gambler's reluctance to come around to Zach's thinking frustrated him. "You must have noticed how Jackson kept looking at Mr. McKenna's saddlebags last night, and how he kept asking questions about how much gold he had taken out of his mine," he continued. "He figured that Mr. McKenna had gold in those saddle bags, and then decided to kill him, bury his body and keep the gold for himself."

Theo put a hand on Zach's shoulder. "Listen, lad, I think your imagination is running away with you."

Zach felt the frustration build inside him. "You said yourself that something might've happened to him, and besides you also saw his mule running loose." Zach held Theo's gaze. "Were the saddlebags still there?"

Theo hesitated, then shook his head. "No, but then again, I don't know for certain if it was indeed his mule."

"Of course it was." The more Zach talked about it, the more he was convinced he was right. "You have to admit that there's at least a good reason to be suspicious."

Theo thought about what Zach had said. "If you're right," he said after a while. "And I'm by no means saying you are," he added quickly with a glance at Zach. "If Jackson did indeed kill Dan McKenna for his gold, then the only place he could have hidden it without anyone noticing would be in the wagon he's driving."

Zach nodded eagerly. "I bet you the gold is there."

Theo straightened his shoulders and nodded, a determined look on his face. "All right then, I'll go and check inside the wagon, if only to put your mind at ease, because I'm still certain you must be wrong."

Before Zach had time to respond, Theo brushed past him and was on his way to where Jackson was standing, his cup in hand.

With his heart pounding in his chest, Zach followed him.

Theo held up his cup when he reached Jackson. "I'm going to get some more water from the wagon."

"Since when do you need my permission to git water?" Jackson asked him sourly.

Theo ignored the barb. Giving Zach a quick nod, he turned and went around the wagon, where Zach saw him climb inside.

Jackson's gaze dug into Zach. "What are you standin' around here for?"

Swallowing hard, Zach stood his ground. "Just waiting for Theo to come back." He jumped when he heard something heavy topple over inside the wagon.

Jackson hurried to the back of the wagon. "Theo!" he yelled as he removed his dirty hat and wiped the sweat from his brow with the back of his hand. "Are you all right in there?"

"I'm fine," Theo responded. "Something fell over. No harm done." He appeared through the opening in the canvas cover and jumped down on the ground.

Zach nearly choked when he saw that Theo was holding the shovel in his hand. He showed it to Jackson. "You know that Enos is going to have your hide for not cleaning the shovel after you used it."

Jackson didn't blink an eye. "I was goin' to." Angrily, he pressed his hat down over his head again. "But I can't very well do everythin' at once, can I now. I'll git to it."

Theo's brow furrowed as he examined the handle of the shovel. He pointed to the dark smear that Zach had identified as blood. "Did you kill someone with this?" His voice was good-natured.

Jackson's eyes narrowed as he appraised Theo. "What kind of bosh is this?"

Theo's finger stayed next to the smear on the handle. "Well, this sure looks like blood."

Jackson came close and made a show of examining the handle. "So it does." He looked up at Theo. "Probably from the damned racoon I found goin' through our provisions last night. I bashed him over the head and buried him, is what I did."

Zach gaped at him. A racoon! That was sure a convenient explanation. "I haven't seen a single racoon in all the time we've been on the road," he blurted out.

Jackson turned to Zach with a venomous look. "That don't mean there wasn't one, and if I hadn't done away with him you would have gone without grub this mornin.'"

Theo smiled broadly at Zach, relief written all over his face. "See I told you there would be a simple explanation." Obviously, he was buying Jackson's excuse hook, line and sinker.

"Simple explanation for what?" Jackson asked Theo.

Zach desperately shook his head at Theo. The last thing he needed was for him to tell Jackson about Zach's suspicions.

Theo shrugged. "I'll tell you another time. It will be good for a laugh over a campfire one evening."

Jackson shook his head. "You're plum crazy. Both of you," he said.

"You didn't find the bags, did you?" Zach whispered as he and Theo approached Enos, who was waving impatiently at them to hurry up, so they could leave camp.

Theo shook his head. "No, Dan McKenna's bags weren't there. Believe me, I looked." He sighed. "You heard Jackson's explanation for the blood and dirt found on that shovel, and I believe him."

"Well, I don't," Zach said.

Chapter 16

ZACH FOUND HIMSELF unable to breathe and clawed frantically at the hands pushing down on his throat. He jerked awake. The dream had been so real that his heart was racing.

Kyle stirred next to him. "What's going on?" he asked. "You're thrashing around like nobody's business." He had his eyelids cracked open just enough to give Zach an annoyed look.

"It was a nightmare." Zach sat up and massaged his neck, which hurt from sleeping on his folded up jacket. "I'm okay." He breathed deeply from the cool night air. "Go back to sleep."

Kyle murmured something before he turned his back to him. Soon his breathing became even.

This was the second time during the night that Zach had woken up, the first time because Jackson was about to hit him over the head with a shovel, and now because he was about to strangle him. His gaze wandered to Theo, who had guard duty. He sat with his back turned to Zach, staring into the flames, a coffee mug in his hands. Jackson and Enos were sleeping soundly nearby, Enos' loud snoring echoing through the still night.

Zach sank back on his makeshift bed and pulled the blanket over him. With his hands folded under his head, he stared up into the starry sky. He was afraid of going to sleep again, dreading more nightmares. Those first days after McKenna's disappearance, Zach wasn't sure how to proceed, especially knowing that he was alone in his suspicions about Jackson killing McKenna.

A couple of times he had seized upon the opportunity to go through Jackson's wagon when he wasn't around. McKenna's gold had to be there somewhere, but so far Zach hadn't found a single nugget. What he did discover, however, was that the shovel was now gone. He had looked in Enos' wagon to make sure, but it was nowhere to be found.

At that point he had cornered Theo. "The shovel has disappeared?" he had breathlessly told him.

"Shovel?" Theo's expression had clearly conveyed the fact that he had no idea what Zach was talking about.

Zach couldn't help rolling his eyes even though he knew it was rude, but he found it hard to believe that Theo had already forgotten. "The shovel with the blood on it." He tried hard to suppress his irritation, which was no use either.

Theo either ignored his impoliteness, or didn't notice. "Oh, that shovel." He shrugged. "Jackson probably lost it."

"Well, that's really convenient. He just tossed away the evidence." Zach had paused as Enos passed by them, carrying a bucket.

Theo removed his hat and smoothed his hair while he watched his brother walk up to the fire and put the bucket down next to Miss Reid, who was doing the cooking. She said something to him, one eyebrow raised disapprovingly. Shaking his head, Enos moved the bucket to the other side of the fire. Theo had turned his attention to Zach again. "You must realize that there's no way to prove anything untoward happened based on that shovel."

Zach shook his head in exasperation. "Are you kidding me? They can match the DNA from the blood on the shovel to Mr. McKenna's when they find his body. They'll know it's the murder weapon then."

Theo had given him a mystified look. "DNA?"

Realizing his blunder, Zach was thrown off balance. "Match the blood," he had corrected himself.

Theo replaced his hat on his head, pulling the brim down to shield his eyes from the sun. "How could they possibly do that? All blood looks the same."

"Oh, just forget what I said . . . I . . . I don't know what I'm talking about," Zach made a show of slapping himself on his forehead. "I'm being stupid, okay."

Their conversation had ended abruptly when Jackson walked by, giving them both a wary look from underneath his wide-brimmed hat.

Zach was now convinced that Jackson must have overheard part of that conversation between him and Theo because after that Jackson had kept a sharp eye on both of them.

. . .

The sun was at its highest when they reached the small hamlet of Soda Creek, where they were going to board a steamship, which would take them up the Fraser River to the town of Quesnellemouth. From there they would then embark by road on the last stretch of their long journey to Barkerville. Zach was looking forward to sailing. It would be a welcome break in the monotony of the constant road travel.

Enos and Jackson stopped the wagons in front of a broad two-storey log building. Zach looked up at the big wooden sign mounted above the wide porch. The name Colonial Hotel was hard to miss with its tall white capital letters. Men were lounging on the porch in chairs, enjoying the warm sun. A short wiry man in his thirties, who stood leaning up against one of the posts supporting the roof, waved at them. He was dressed in an old grey duster and the rim on his worn

hat was all frayed as if some sort of animal had chewed on it.
"Theo, thought you'd be in Barkerville already?" He walked
over to Theo and greeted him with a hearty handshake.

Theo smiled broadly at him. "How's it going, Harry? I had
a late start from Victoria this year."

Chuckling in his beard, Harry let go of Theo's hand.
"Poker games and women folk kept you busy, ain't that so!"

Harry turned to Enos who was dismounting his horse.
"Well, Enos, you old dog, how you doin'? Only this mornin'
Robert McLeese said, 'I wonder where Enos might be? Bet he
got hisself hitched to some unsuspectin' woman, or mayhap
he be settlin' down to open up that general store he keeps
talkin' about'." Harry held out his hand to Enos. "Now I'll tell
Robert that you be still up to your old tricks."

"As my brother just said, we all got a late start, that's all,"
Enos grumbled, ignoring Harry's extended hand. "Where's
Robert anyways? I need the use of his tire shrinker."

"He ain't fixin' wheels no more, Enos. This new hotel of
his is keepin' him busy."

"Damnation!" Enos said with feeling.

"Well Enos. Finally!" A heavyset balding man with a long
flowing beard had come out of the double doors leading into
the hotel. He hurried over to greet Enos. Delight had replaced the expression of annoyance Enos had shown toward
Harry.

"Robert." Enos slapped the man on the back and grabbed
his hand, shaking it hard.

Robert McLeese was a cheerful man, and Zach liked him right away. He seemed taller than he really was, maybe because he carried himself straight without the hunched shoulders Zach saw on so many of the other men. He obviously took great pride in his clothes, judging from his starched white shirt and pressed grey pants. Zach felt dirty and grubby next to him.

McLeese let go of Enos' hand and pointed down toward the river where a large sternwheeler lay moored at the nearest bank. "You're in rare luck. The *Enterprise* leaves at five this afternoon. The captain, Mr. Doane, is inside the hotel." He gave Enos a wink. "He's presently fortifyin' himself for the strenuous journey ahead."

Enos laughed, so genuine and joyful, it took Zach by surprise. It was hard to connect that kind of laughter to the gruff, direct Enos he had come to know.

Stretching his hand out, McLeese turned to Theo. "Been a while, Theo. About time you decided to turn your nose toward Barkerville again. Some of the miners are becomin' rich and have nothin' to spend their newfound fortune on, except women and gamblin'. You're sure to make a killin' up there."

Theo nodded with a pleased smile. "So I've heard."

"Speakin' of miners, did you run into someone called Dan McKenna?" McLeese asked Theo. "He stayed one night at the hotel a while ago, but took off the next morning at daybreak before I had a chance to say goodbye."

Theo exchanged a quick glance with Enos. "Dan McKenna

did stop at our camp," he said. "In fact, he forgot his watch, so if he comes through here again will you tell him I have it?"

"Will do." McLeese looked around. "Where did that weasel, Jackson, go?"

Miss Reid nodded up at the hotel. "He went looking for a washroom."

McLeese turned to Enos, shaking his head. "Never understood why you hired such a disagreeable sort of feller." Enos only gave a shrug in answer.

"Here comes Mr. Piss-ant," Kyle, who stood next to Zach, whispered in his ear. Sure enough, Jackson came out the front door of the hotel, hitching up his pants.

"Hopefully, the privy's still standin'," McLeese joked.

With a cross look at the hotel owner, Jackson walked to his wagon and disappeared behind it.

McLeese turned to Enos, and put his arm around his shoulders. "Come inside. Join me for a dram. It'll be on the house."

McLeese, together with Enos, Harry and Theo, walked the few steps to the porch.

Zach viewed Miss Reid, who stood absentmindedly stroking the neck of one of the horses. "Do we go with them?" he asked her.

"Of course we do," Kyle said before Miss Reid had time to answer. Without waiting for the others, he hurried off.

"I guess we can just as well tag along," Miss Reid told Zach. Together they followed after Kyle.

"What a racket," Kyle yelled over his shoulder at Zach and Miss Reid when he opened the door to the hotel.

The racket he referred to, grating tinny-sounding music, came from a piano that played all by itself, the keys moving up and down as if a mischievous ghost was amusing himself on it.

The lobby of the hotel was filled to capacity. At most of the tables men were playing card games. Their loud swearing and boisterous talk was now and then heard over the music.

McLeese and the other men had stopped at a table in a corner, where a lone occupant, a portly man with chin whiskers and a moustache, dressed in a blue uniform, was busy polishing off a bottle of bourbon by himself. So this must be Captain Doane, Zach thought, as he Miss Reid and Kyle approached the table.

Captain Doane pushed the bottle across the table. "Here Robert, Enos, help me drink this wee bottle," he yelled over the music.

"Don't tell me that's the man who's in charge of our steamship," Miss Reid said, horror written all over her face.

"Afraid so." Kyle didn't seem too bothered by that prospect.

As an afterthought, Captain Doane, pushed his chair back and stood up. He saluted the men smartly with his fingers touching his cap, even though for a moment it looked as if he was going to take out one of his own eyes. "How's my ship farin'?"

"Just fine, from the looks of it." McLeese nodded at the half-empty bottle. "You're not plannin' on runnin' it aground, I hope."

Captain Doane slumped down in his seat. "You work up quite the thirst runnin' a steamer up and down that hellish river." He leaned forward, seized the bottle and poured himself another drink. With his large hand, covered with red hair on the back, he gestured at the men to sit down at the table. "Now, dammit, sit down and join me."

Theo, Enos and Harry each pulled out a chair.

"I'll get us some more glasses," McLeese said and headed to the counter located at the far end of the lobby.

Upon seeing Miss Reid and the boys, Theo quickly got up from the table and offered Miss Reid his chair. "Here, take a seat, Miss Reid. Captain Doane won't mind."

"No, of cours' not." Captain Doane stumbled to his feet and nearly fell against her when he attempted a bow. "Make yourself com . . . comfortable, Ma'am," he croaked as he fell back in his seat again.

Apprehensively, Miss Reid seated herself on the very edge of the offered chair. Zach and Kyle each pulled over chairs from a nearby table and sat down.

Captain Doane smiled at Enos and Miss Reid in turn, merriment in his watery eyes. "You old poky, when did you go and git yourself hitched?"

Enos turned red. "She ain't no wife of mine."

Captain Doane looked up at Theo. "I guess she's yours

then, Theo, and here I had picked you for a lifelon' bachelor."

"You're being rather presumptuous, Captain Doane," Miss Reid said with great dignity. "I'm just along as their cook and general caretaker."

She looked surprised when this statement sent Captain Doane into spasms of laughter.

Chapter 17

ZACH LOOKED DOWN at the churning water as the *Enterprise* strained against the powerful current of the Fraser River. They would probably only cover about ten miles before nightfall, Captain Doane had told them, and then they would anchor and overnight until daybreak. The captain figured they were going to reach Quesnellemouth at about six o'clock the following evening. Apparently, it took only ten hours to return from Quesnellemouth to Soda Creek because the current then worked in the steamer's favour.

Zach heard laughter and lively banter from the wheel-house. Captain Doane, Enos and Theo were in there, still drinking. He was surprised the captain was able to navigate the ship as well as he did.

Miss Reid and Kyle were sound asleep in the cabin, kindly offered to them by Captain Doane. Zach, despite being exhausted, had found himself unable to do the same. His mind was too preoccupied to give him the rest his body craved. Every time he had started to drift off, Jackson's rat-face encroached on his thoughts and startled him awake. Finally, having had enough of all the tossing and turning, he had decided to step outside.

Zach looked over the railing down to the lower deck of the steamship, where the animals and freight were kept. He wondered where Jackson was now? He hadn't seen him since they embarked on the trip. When the steamer reached Quesnellemouth it would be about sixty miles until they reached Barkerville, he reminded himself. What a relief that would be.

The door to the wheelhouse jerked open. Enos' face, red from booze, peered out at Zach. "Go down to the lower deck and make sure the horses have settled for the night."

Before Zach could answer, he slammed the door shut again.

The men's laughter followed Zach as he made his way down the ladder to the lower deck. He walked inside the storeroom, weaving his way between barrels and sacks of goods to the back where the horses were kept. The animals were restless and constantly whinnying and scraping their hooves into the wooden planks. Most likely they were spooked by the crashing sound coming from the water wheel straining to move passengers, animals and goods up the river and the hissing and whining from the boiler engine that powered the wheel.

Youtz was shaking his mane and looking anxiously around. Zach went over to him and stroked his neck. "Settle down now, Youtz," he said. "We'll be back on the road soon."

Youtz finally relaxed enough for Zach to do an inspection of the other horses. When he was about to stroke the mane of Prancer, a loud bang from the other side of the wall startled him so much he jumped. Prancer snorted and rose on his rear legs, his front hooves kicking wildly.

Zach dropped to the floor and rolled quickly across the deck just as Prancer's hooves came down right next to his head. The other horses went into a full-blown panic. Dazed and frightened, Zach scurried up against the wall and huddled, protecting his head with his arms. Was he screaming? The horses made so much noise, he didn't even know. Through the pandemonium he heard someone yell. He didn't dare look up. The voice came closer. "Where are you, lad?"

Zach lowered his arms. "I'm over here," he croaked, and saw Theo approach the nearest horse, grabbing it by the lead rope. Theo managed to calm the animal down by stroking its neck and speaking gently to it. He moved from one horse to the next until they had all settled down. Only then did Zach dare to sit up.

Theo hurried over to him, his face pale. "Are you okay?"

Zach nodded, his mouth dry. "Someone shot off a gun on the other side of the wall." His voice shook so much he had trouble getting the words out. He grabbed the hand Theo had extended to him and stood up, legs shaking. The sound of the horses' hooves stomping on the wooden planks still echoed in his ears.

Theo's expression turned from fear to anger. "Who in blazes would be so stupid to discharge a gun so close to the horses?" He put a hand on Zach's shoulder in a gesture of reassurance. "I aim to find out, so I can give him a piece of my mind."

Zach wrapped his arms around himself. "It was Jackson, I've no doubt." He couldn't stop himself from shaking.

Theo removed his hand from his shoulder. "Jackson!"

"He's been waiting for his chance to kill me, and I know he's going to try to make it look like an accident." Zach bit his lower lip to keep the tears from flowing.

"I doubt that's the case. He's a scoundrel all right, but a cold-blooded killer..." Theo shook his head. "No, I still don't believe that." He viewed Zach with concern. "This whole business with Dan McKenna's disappearance has really spooked you, hasn't it?"

Zach nodded. Theo gave him a reassuring smile. "You really needn't worry. Most likely McKenna's in Victoria as we speak."

Zach doubted that very much.

Chapter 18

QUESNELLEMOUTH, A BUSTLING and rapidly growing town, was located at the confluence of the Fraser and Quesnel Rivers. Since it was late in the day when the *Enterprise* docked, Enos, who was in a rare good mood after his enjoyable time with Captain Doane, had bragged that he was in tight with one of the two owners of the town's Occidental Hotel, and was certain he could get rooms there at a deep discount. Zach had been excited at the prospect of finally sleeping in a bed again, but the excitement had been short-lived since it turned out that Enos' friend, Hugh Gillis, had headed to Victoria on the stagecoach the week before, and the other owner of the hotel, Thomas Brown, had not at all been in a generous mood. To Zach's great disappointment, they had all ended up camping just outside town.

Once they were underway the next morning, Zach found the route through to Cottonwood not to be too challenging since they had mostly sunny weather, but from there to Barkerville it was gruelling. The wheels from all the previous pack trains had carved deep grooves into the dirt, which was slippery as soap from the frequent downpours they had encountered. Zach had often slipped and fallen headfirst into the mud. Miss Reid and Kyle fared no better. The three of them were now once again learning to live with layers of caked mud on their clothes.

. . .

The Barkerville of 1866 looked nothing like the quaint orderly twenty-first-century tourist spot Zach had once visited as a boy. First of all, it was larger. The main road, which Theo told them was called "Main Street", seemed much narrower than he remembered and was a sludgy, murky mess from recent spring freshets. The buildings erected on log posts were jammed together making use of every last square inch of space. They were randomly set at different levels, making the raised wooden boardwalks that ran in front of the buildings uneven.

"Watch out!"

Zach turned just in time to see a herd of cattle bear down on their wagons. Enos and Jackson quickly moved the wagons to one side of the road. The sound of the herd's hooves thundered in Zach's ears as they passed by, spraying mud everywhere. "Where are they headed?" he asked Theo, who had stopped next to him.

"The slaughter house in Richfield." Theo waved at a man who was riding on horseback behind the herd, shooing stray animals away from the boardwalk with a long stick.

The man returned the gesture. "Haven't seen you for a while, Theo. How are you?" he yelled.

"Just fine," Theo answered.

"Well, I'll probably see you at the Parlour Saloon tonight," the man yelled in parting. "Billy Barker will be there too."

Billy Barker! Now where had Zach heard that name before? Oh yeah, now he remembered. He turned to Kyle. "They talked about Billy Barker when I visited here with my parents. He was . . . I mean is a famous guy."

Kyle glanced briefly at him. "Huh?"

"This guy Billy Barker is the reason Barkerville exists at all. He found gold right here in the middle of town and became very rich."

Now he had Kyle's undivided attention. "Gold. Where?"

Zach looked down the road toward the centre of town. "I'm not sure. Everything looks so different from what I remember. We had a guide who showed us around and explained everything. You know that this place burned, I mean will burn down at one point. The Great Fire the guide called it."

Kyle didn't seem particularly impressed with this part of Zach's knowledge. "So you don't even know where this Barker found his gold?" He sounded deeply disappointed.

Zach shrugged at him. "Even if I did, and even if we found the place, what good is that going to do us? It's after all his claim."

"Claim?" Kyle asked.

"Yeah, Theo told me how it works. To mine for gold you have to buy yourself a miner's certificate. It's required before you can stake out a claim."

"So let's get one." The excitement was putting a new spring in Kyle's steps. "Don't you see if we find ourselves some gold, we won't have to work." He had been in a foul mood ever since Miss Reid had told him a couple of days earlier that they would probably all have to look for a job when they arrived in Barkerville.

"Remember what Mr. McKenna told us," Zach said. "All claims around here are already taken." He couldn't help feeling some smugness when he saw Kyle's disappointment. He had resented the fact that he had been the one doing most of the chores on the trail. He was convinced Kyle was the laziest person alive.

Kyle's face suddenly lit up. "Heck, we can just grab some gold from Barker's claim then. If he has so much he won't miss a few handfuls."

"You can't just do that." Zach nearly bumped into Kyle when he tried to skirt another pothole. "They would probably have you arrested."

Kyle gave a dejected sigh. "Why does everything always have to be so complicated?"

The cattle herd had finally disappeared down the street and the wagons were moving out into the road again. The wheels turned painstakingly through the mud-soup. Zach tried hard to walk on whatever dry ground he could find, but he soon gave up. To heck with it, he thought as he trudged through the mud in his Nikes, which by now were in tatters anyway.

"Do you mind if we use the boardwalk instead?" Miss Reid asked Theo.

Theo nodded. "I was thinking of doing that myself. This street is much worse than last year. Too many people now." He led the way up to some crude steps leading to the front of a building that housed a brewery. Although the boardwalk had plenty of boards with loose nails, which had worked themselves out of the wood by all the bouncing, it was considerably easier to walk on than the street. The sheer volume of people created the greatest hazard. Zach constantly had to watch that he wasn't pushed off, especially by the drunken miners of which Barkerville seemed to have plenty.

He soon figured out that walking right behind Theo was his safest course of action. The gambler strode purposefully over the planks, nudging aside people who were in his way with an "Excuse me, Sir," or, as often was the case, addressing them by their names. Zach soon realized that Theo knew an awful lot of people in town.

They passed by all sorts of businesses: restaurants, bakeries, stables, a fruit store, something called a Tin Shop, black-smiths, hotels and saloons with names like The Gazelle, El Dorado, Go-At-Em, and The Fashion.

At one point, Theo stretched his neck and waved. "Billy Barker," he yelled.

So this is the famous Barker, Zach thought, curiously studying the grinning, slightly bow-legged man with the huge beard, who staggered out from the entrance of a saloon toward them.

"Damn if ain't Theo Cox," Barker yelled at people around him. He staggered over to Theo and grabbed onto his shoulder.

Kyle, wondering what all the fuss was about, came up to Zach. "He looks like he's three sheets to the wind," he said as he watched Barker with amusement.

He was right. Barker's red-rimmed eyes were unfocused and the left side of his mouth drooped. Swaying, he held onto Theo's shoulder for dear life.

Theo smiled fondly down at the much shorter man. "I thought you went back to Victoria."

Barker chuckled in his beard, and moved his face close to Theo's shirt. Zach saw him wipe his nose on it. "Yuck," Kyle said.

"I figured once there, I would only long for this darn place again, so I decided to stay on here." Barker hung his head. "I so miss my dear departed wife." He blinked tears from his eyes. "Elizabeth was a fine lady from London in England from where the Queen hails, she was."

Theo patted him on the shoulder. "I heard about her passing, Billy, and I'm so very sorry for your loss."

"Billy! Where's English Bill?" someone yelled from inside the saloon.

Barker let go of Theo. "Guess, those toss pots want me in there. I'll see you around."

Theo nodded. "Tonight at the Parlour, Thomas told me."

Barker lurched back into the saloon, his hand waving goodbyes. Loud, drunken voices greeted him from the inside.

"They're turning left. The wagons!" Miss Reid yelled from up front, and pointed. She had been waiting impatiently for Theo and Barker to end their conversation.

Zach saw a glimpse of the back of Jackson's wagon as it quickly turned the corner of a building. They all hurried forward, pushing their way through the throng of people.

Theo glanced back at Zach, who was still right behind him again. "Don't worry, Enos is most likely headed to the back of W. Davison's Grocery Store. Davison usually buys a good part of Enos' goods."

They rounded the corner of the street and saw the rear of Jackson's wagon disappear to the left again. Sure enough, they soon discovered, both wagons had stopped behind the grocery store.

A man of medium build in a dirty white apron came rushing out of the door and hurried down the steps. His hair stuck out in all directions, giving him a kind of mad scientist look. He approached Enos, who was getting off his horse. "Enos Cox, you're certainly a sight for sore eyes. I expected you here a couple of weeks ago." There was rebuke in the man's voice as he shook Enos' hand.

"We ran into difficulties on the way, Davison." Enos let go of the man's hand. "The road is gettin' worse and worse. The governor needs to do something about it soon. The potholes are so deep that if a wheel gets stuck it takes forever to get it out again."

Davison nodded, looking somewhat appeased. "Yeah, Rich Patterson, who drove his wagon in yesterday, said it was quite bad. Do you have the coffee I wanted?"

"Sure do," Enos said and nodded at Jackson. "We'll get it unloaded right now. As you can see, I got myself some extra hands." He waved Kyle and Zach over. "Come on, let's get to work."

. . .

In less than an hour, the goods had been moved from the wagons into Davison's store, a room no more than twenty by fifteen feet, which was stuffed so full of packages, barrels and sacks it was hard to move around. The place was ruled by a stern-looking grey-haired woman with small calculating eyes. Davison referred to her as Dear Mother in a constant refrain. "Dear Mother, don't hurt your back now. Oh, thank you so much, Dear Mother. You're much too kind, Dear Mother."

"If he doesn't stop that soon, I'm going to hurl," Kyle said with a dark look at him. At that point, Zach was beginning to think he would too.

When something displeased Mrs. Davison in the way they handled the merchandise, she didn't mince words.

"Not there, you heavy-thumbed numbskull."

"Have you no brains, you beetle-headed idiot."

"Watch the merchandise, you randy rascal."

"Stay away from there, you little squeeze-crap."

"You're pissin' me off, cork-brain."

"Move those trotters."

"You must excuse my mother," Davison told them outside, smiling apologetically when they had finished unloading. "A cast iron pot fell on her head a while ago. Since then," he shrugged, "she can on occasion become somewhat direct."

"Where's your Missus?" Enos asked. "She's usually the one helpin' out in the store."

Davison sighed. "She's unfortunately been ailin' as of late so that's why my mother kindly stepped in to help out until my wife's better."

Enos shot the old woman a withering look as she walked up the stairs and disappeared into the store. "You sure as hell haven't done yourself any favours keepin' her on, Davison."

Zach wasn't sure if Davison was blushing from embarrassment or displeasure with Enos' remark. His gaze didn't indicate one way or the other as he brought out a big worn leather wallet from his jacket pocket and flipped it open. He licked the tips of his index-finger and thumb and meticulously went through a wad of bills, counting out a bunch of them. He handed them to Enos. "I'll need some flour on your next trip. Stocks will be running low soon." He smacked the wallet closed. "Have a pleasant journey back, Enos."

"Will do," Enos said, and watched Davison return to the store, closing the door firmly after himself.

Miss Reid cleared her throat and stretched out her hand to Theo. "Thank you so much, Mr. Cox, for all your help and kindness." She quickly blinked away the tears, which had risen to her eyes. "We're now in Barkerville," she reminded him when she noticed his confusion. "It's time we part ways."

"So you'll be continuing up to Springfield?" Theo looked at her with concern. "You'll have to find someone you can trust to take you up north. Let me help you with that," he added readily.

Miss Reid fidgeted, her hands busying themselves with brushing off caked mud from her pants. "Well, I don't know. Barkerville looks like an enterprising place. I think we'll stay on for a while." She smiled bravely at Theo. "I did waitressing when I was younger. I also can cook, so maybe I can work in one of the restaurants."

Theo nodded. "It's true that there might be plenty of work here for someone with your skills, Ma'am, but . . ." He hesitated for a moment before he at last blurted out: "How do you expect someone to hire you looking like that?" Miss Reid blushed as she glanced down at her muddy torn clothes.

Enos, who was standing by his wagon, stuffing bills into his oversized wallet, gave his brother an irritable look. "Let them go on their way, Theo. We've done enough. You don't owe them anythin.'"

Theo turned to his brother. "I'm not asking you to help, am I?" he said sharply.

Enos shrugged. "Suit yourself then." He glanced over at Jackson. "Come on, let's move on to the next customer. Let my do-gooder brother deal with this."

Her lips set tight, Miss Reid strode over to Enos and extended her hand. "Thank you for bringing us up here. It was very solicitous of you."

Uncertainty showed in Enos' eyes. "You're welcome," he finally said and shook her hand tentatively. She turned to Zach and Kyle. "Come and show your respect."

"When hell freezes over," Kyle muttered.

Zach walked over to Enos and shook his hand "Thanks, for everything," he said and meant it. After all, Enos might very well have saved their lives when he agreed to bring them along to Barkerville.

Something in Enos' eyes softened. "I was only glad I could help. Take care of yourself and your aunt." He lowered his voice. "And give Kyle a good kick in the arse from me."

Zach had to smile. "Will do." He ignored Jackson altogether.

Only after a lot of prompting from Miss Reid did Kyle finally walk over to Enos and shake his hand.

. . .

Zach stood watching as the two wagons rumbled down the road, and disappeared around a corner.

With a somewhat shamefaced expression, Theo turned to Miss Reid. "I know I might have expressed myself rather awkwardly before, but it doesn't alter the fact that no one will give you work looking like a . . . a . . ." He was searching desperately for a word that was not going to come across as insulting. Zach felt sorry for him. Being a gentleman clearly came with disadvantages.

"Mess," Zach said in effort to be helpful. "She looks a mess," he added, when Theo gave him a blank look.

"Disgusting," Kyle piped in. "Nasty, and . . ."

"Well, thank you so very much, Kyle," Miss Reid interrupted him. "Too bad, you can't show as much creativity in English class."

"The terms Zach and Kyle just used," Theo stammered, looking horrified, "was not at all what I meant."

Miss Reid sighed. "I know that, Mr. Cox, because you're a gentleman, which is more than can be said of these two goofs." She glared at Kyle and Zach in turn.

"Why don't you just wear your old clothes," Kyle said. Enos had handed Miss Reid a bundle, containing her twenty-first-century clothes and her backpack just before he had left. "If that colour combination doesn't give you a competitive edge, I don't know what would."

"Why don't I set you three up for the night in one of the hotels, and tomorrow we'll look at how to get you and the lads some new clothes," Theo suggested quickly.

"Sounds good," Zach said when Miss Reid didn't respond right away. She was too busy giving Kyle the evil eye.

Miss Reid finally acknowledged Theo with a grateful smile. "That's a very kind offer, Mr. Cox, and I accept, even though I've no idea how we're ever going to repay you for all you've done for us."

Chapter 19

⤔

THEO HAD TOLD THEM that he knew the two proprietors of the hotel he was taking them to and that it was clean and respectable with reasonable rates. It had the very distinguished name of Hôtel de France and was a two-storey building with a big second-storey balcony jutting out over the boardwalk. Inside, it was indeed clean and orderly. It turned out that the woman who was usually in charge of housekeeping was at present also overseeing the daily running of the hotel. "Messieurs De Lecuyer and Brun are visiting family in Quebec," she informed Theo. Her name was Madame Isabelle Pond, and she was a middle-aged, slender woman who was also from Quebec.

Zach, who had been a French immersion student in elementary school, instantly endeared himself when he responded to her French greeting in what she described as flawless French with an impressive rolling of the 'R's.

"So Monsieur Cox, how can I help you?" she asked with what Miss Reid later described, with some resentment in her voice, as coquettish.

"I'm hoping you have a room available for this lady and the lads."

Zach looked at the men, sitting at the tables in the lobby. Everything seemed so much more controlled here than in the hotels in both Fort Yale and Soda Creek. No grating music, no loud voices, no drunken singing. The business of poker playing was conducted in a manner that could make any retirement home proud. Sudden laughter from a card player resulted in an instant look of reprimand from Madame Pond.

She turned her attention to Theo again. "Pardon, Monsieur. You've seen the town. It's literally bursting at the seams. Too many to accommodate. All the rooms here, *toutes les chambres*, they're booked for weeks to come." She looked at Zach. "*Je regrette, mon petit.* You look like you really could use a bath and a bed." She pinched his cheek, a gesture which drew a disgusted look from Kyle.

"We thank you, Madame Pond," Miss Reid said as she turned and began pushing Zach and Kyle toward the door.

"Come back here, please," Theo told them.

Miss Reid turned reluctantly around.

He took Madame Pond's hands in his. "Madame, we've been on the road for weeks. I'm not asking for any accommodations for myself, but this lady and her nephews urgently need a place to stay. Nothing fancy."

Zach felt encouraged when he saw Madame Pond hesitate, but then she quickly withdrew her hands from Theo's. "I would dearly love to help, Monsieur Cox, but I can't."

"It's all right. We'll go to another hotel," Miss Reid said.

Madame Pond looked at her with regret. "Oh, *Chérie*, I doubt you'll find any place to stay in Barkerville. Of course you can try Richfield or Camerontown, but . . ." She shook her head with a sigh.

"That sign you have in the window," Theo said quickly. "It says you're looking for someone to clean and wash?" There was an apologetic look in his eyes when he turned to Miss Reid. "You don't mind, do you?"

"I still haven't found anyone," Madame Pond said before Miss Reid had time to answer. "*Mon Dieu*, the last woman who worked here was useless, absolutely useless. And I told her so, and she just up and left." Madame Pond looked offended. "Last I heard, she's now living with some miner in Camerontown."

Theo exchanged a glance with Miss Reid. She nodded her agreement. "Miss Reid would like to apply for this position. It does come with room and board, I take it."

"*Mais certainement.*" Madame Pond studied Miss Reid,

who, of course, didn't make a very good first impression with her torn muddy clothes, worn boots and dirty, stringy hair. "You have any experience with cleaning and washing?" she asked.

Miss Reid nodded eagerly. "I do. I clean my own apartment at home. I'm sure I can do a good job for you."

"So would you be interested in hiring her, Madame Pond?" Theo asked.

Madame Pond hesitated for a moment. "Oh, why not," she finally agreed. "I need someone urgently, and hardworking. Honest women are a rarity around here." She gave Miss Reid the once over. "If you're as good as you say, *Chérie*, I would be foolish not to take a chance on you." She turned to a tall man who had just entered through the door in the back of the lobby, and now stood behind the hotel counter.

"You can take care of things here, Monsieur Sinclair, so I can show Madame Reid . . ."

"Mademoiselle," Miss Reid corrected her.

"*Ah oui*, Mademoiselle Reid her room. No rowdiness among the men, Monsieur Sinclair. Keep an eye on how much they drink."

Sinclair nodded and folded his arms over his chest while surveying the room with a scowl.

Madame Pond took all three of them through the same back door from which Sinclair had just come. Behind it were a series of rooms: a fairly big kitchen with a gleaming wood stove as the most prominent fixture, and next to the kitchen a smaller room with shelves, covering the walls from ceiling to floor, stocked with goods. "Pantry," Madame Pond informed them. Right across from the pantry was a bigger room with a small window near the ceiling and gleaming, whitewashed walls. Madame Pond strode inside. "This is the laundry room," she announced. "Part of your duties will be to wash the linen."

Miss Reid looked discouraged as she took in the wooden barrels and washing boards. "Tell me that there's running water," she said.

Madame Pond nodded. "*Oui*, we're lucky to have the Barkerville flume." She seemed quite proud of this fact. "It brings the water in from the goldfields."

"Flume?" Miss Reid asked.

Madame Pond gave her a peculiar look. "*Oui*, the Barkerville flume. We all use it."

"What's a flume?" Zach decided to be the one to ask.

Theo cleared his throat. "It's a channel made of lumber that transports water to where you want it to go."

Miss Reid walked up to a big iron pot, standing on a stove and looked inside. She glanced back at Madame Pond. "I take it that this is where you heat the water?"

The hotelkeeper nodded. "Yes, it's a wash boiler." She was beginning to look like she was regretting hiring her new maid.

Miss Reid sighed. "Do you at least have a wringer?"

Madame Pond's face brightened. "I've heard about those.

Invention magnifique." She shook her head. "I don't have one yet, but I plan on buying one next year."

"Wonderful," Miss Reid muttered.

"We wash the bed clothes in this hotel every week, after each guest leaves or by request," Madame Pond told her. "The cook, Mademoiselle Combs, will help you hang the larger and heavier items on the clotheslines." Her back became ramrod straight, and her eyes shone with self-satisfaction. "I have the cleanest hotel in Barkerville, Camerontown and Richfield." For some reason she fixed Zach with her stare. "I do not tolerate lice, or bed bugs on the premises."

Zach had a sudden image of her chasing giant-sized bugs out of the hotel with a broom while yelling, *"Sors d'ici, je ne le tolère pas!"* He scratched discreetly in his hair, already suspecting he had a lice infestation.

They all followed Madame Pond out of the laundry room. Across from it was a second door, which Madame Pond opened with one of the keys attached to her belt. Zach peeked inside. It was a tiny bedroom with a single bed, a desk and a tall wardrobe. "And this will be your room, Mademoiselle Reid."

"What about Zachary and Kyle?" Miss Reid asked Theo, who stood leaning up against the doorjamb, taking in the room with a critical look.

"We'll get a couple of mattresses so they can sleep on the floor." Theo eyed Madame Pond. "Would that be possible?"

"Les garçons, ici?" She shook her head in regret. "I'm afraid

you'll have to find other accommodations for them."

"We can work for you," Zach said quickly. He looked at Kyle, who nodded reluctantly.

"I can't have them stay here," Madame Pond pointed a defiant chin at Theo. "*Non, c'est impossible.* They would only be in the way."

Theo went to Miss Reid and placed his hand on her arm. "You stay here, where I know you'll be safe and dry," he told her firmly. "I'll find another place for your nephews." He let go of her arm and turned to Madame Pond. "I think Miss Reid would appreciate the use of a bathtub and if you have some clothes to spare, that would be most welcome too." He gave Miss Reid a reassuring smile. "I'll get the lads settled in somewhere else, and later I'll come by and fetch you so we can all go out for dinner." He gestured at Zach and Kyle to follow him. "Let's leave."

Zach gave Miss Reid a thumbs up. "We'll be fine." He knew Theo was right when he said the teacher would be safe here in the hotel. "See you later, Miss Reid," he said and followed Theo and Kyle out of the room.

Chapter 20

FINDING A PLACE where Zach and Kyle could stay proved to be impossible. Madame Pond was right. Barkerville was bursting at the seams. Everything was occupied down to the smallest mouse hole. Theo looked up people he knew in Barkerville to find a place for them, but everywhere it was the same answer. "Sorry Theo, I wish I could help."

After hours spent in a futile search even the usually cheerful Theo looked dejected. They finally went into a small eatery called the Wake Up Jake Bakeshop, Coffee Saloon, and Lunch House where Theo pointed to a small table by the window. "Sit down, lads. I'll order you some grub. I'm going to have a word with the proprietor, Mr. Kelly, for a moment."

Zach and Kyle went over to the table and flopped down in chairs across from each other. "This sucks big time!" Kyle said. For once, Zach couldn't agree with him more.

Kyle turned his head and looked out the window. "It's great that Miss Reid found a place to sleep, but what about us?"

"I guess all we can do right now is place our trust in Theo." Zach was so exhausted he felt like putting his head down on the table and going to sleep.

Kyle's sullen gaze targeted Zach. "So how long do you think it'll take before he gets sick and tired of dragging us around?"

Zach turned his attention to Theo, who stood leaning up against a counter talking to a tall lanky man. He couldn't imagine that Theo would leave them in the lurch.

"I sure hope they hurry up with that grub. I'm starving."

Lately Kyle had taken up using 1866 terms, and it was irritating Zach to no end. "It's food, not grub," he snapped.

"Hey man, I'm just trying to fit in. Jeez. Are you touchy!" Kyle turned his attention to the street outside again.

Zach did the same. It was getting dark now, and dirty, sweaty miners were straggling back to town from a hard day of prospecting for gold. The days of easy gold panning on Williams Creek were long over, Theo had told him. Most mining now took place underground in narrow, cold, and wet shafts with the help of pickaxes and, hopefully, Lady Luck as a companion. Most miners found hardly enough gold to meet daily living expenses, but still carried on, for who knew, maybe they would be some of the few who eventually hit a major strike. Major strike was the term Theo used. He also called gold, colour. Zach gave a start and ducked down.

Kyle looked over at him in surprise. "What's wrong?"

"Jackson is across the street." His heart was racing. "Wasn't he supposed to leave today?"

Kyle gave a shake of his head. "No, Enos told me they were leaving tomorrow." He looked strangely at Zach. "Why are you so freaked out over that idiot all the time?"

Zach still hadn't told Kyle about the bloody shovel he had seen in the wagon, and his suspicion that Jackson had used it to kill McKenna and the fear he had that Jackson was going to kill him too.

Theo had confronted Jackson about the shot fired on the *Enterprise* right next to the horses, which had nearly caused Zach to be trampled to death. Jackson, of course, had denied having anything to do with it.

Zach peered out the window again. Jackson was gone.

The smell of fried bacon filled his nostrils. He turned his head and saw a young guy, probably no older than him, place a plate first in front of Kyle then himself. Without looking at them, he hurried away.

"Look at that grub." Kyle rubbed his hands together. "I think I've died and gone to heaven."

Zach forgot all about Jackson as he looked down at the

plate in front of him. True, it displayed the usual bacon and beans, but also eggs, sunny-side up, fried potatoes and, he could hardly believe his eyes, fresh strawberries, five of them lying there on the edge of the plate, stems still attached. Carefully he held one of them between his thumb and index-finger and studied it for a while, then closing his eyes, he bit down into the sweetness.

He heard someone pull a chair up to their table and opened his eyes. Theo looked more cheerful than before. "They had already closed the kitchen for the day, but Mrs. Kelly was still around. She was kind enough to put something together for you two," he said as he nodded at the plates.

"That was really nice of her," Zach said as he picked up his fork.

"I've good and bad news," Theo said with a smile as he watched them eat.

"Give us the good news," Kyle said between mouthfuls of egg.

"Mr. Kelly just told me that a carpenter I know, by the name of Johnny Knott, is looking for a strong, hard-working lad to help him. He'll take care of room and board. This place, as you can see, is booming, so Johnny has more work presently than he can handle."

Kyle knitted his eyebrows together. "Now that Miss E. has a good job why would we have to work?"

"Of course you have to work," Theo said. "Your aunt will

make very little money at the hotel and definitely not enough to feed, clothe and house you two. If you want to eat, you better work." Theo sounded as if it was the most natural thing in the world for a fifteen-year-old to work for his keep.

Kyle turned to Zach. "I'm sure he knows more about wood than I do."

Zach couldn't hide his gleeful smile. "I have two left hands when it comes to woodworking. Mr. Franks, the shop teacher, told me so, but I did overhear him say that you had a real knack for it." He was determined that Kyle was not going to squirm out of this one. After having been a witness to his laziness on the trip to Barkerville, there was nothing he would love better than to watch Kyle get up early in the morning to go to work.

Theo nodded, his expression brightening. "I'll talk to Johnny about it. Maybe he can make use of you too, Zach, helping him clean up around his workshop. As soon as you two have finished eating we'll go and see him."

Chapter 21

THE WOOD SHAVINGS covering the floor of Johnny Knott's shop were ankle-deep. Zach, who entered last, couldn't resist kicking through them, sending up a spray that covered the back of Kyle's leather jacket.

Kyle turned his head and gave him a cross look. "Watch it."

A broad-shouldered man stood bent over a long workbench, where he was busy planing a piece of wood. The workbench, Zach noticed, was not unlike the one his grandfather used, with a place to tighten the wood down so it could be worked on. Tools were hanging on the walls and there were shelves filled to capacity with smaller pieces of wood.

Bright daylight illuminated the interior through two narrow windows above the workbench.

Theo cleared his throat to get the carpenter's attention.

Johnny let go of the plane and turned quickly, breathing a sigh of relief when he saw who it was. "Theo, you gave me quite the scare." He spat out the toothpick he had been chewing on.

"Sorry, to startle you, Johnny," Theo said with a good-humoured smile.

The carpenter came over and shook his hand firmly. "It's good to see you again."

"Likewise," Theo said. "I heard from Mr. Kelly that you were looking for a hard-working lad to help you out." He waved Kyle forward. "Well, I brought you one here that you might consider," he said as he put a hand on Kyle's shoulder.

Johnny smoothed his handlebar moustache as he gave Kyle the once over from underneath heavy eyebrows. "Are these boys relations of yours, Theo?"

Theo shook his head. "No, I'm their friend."

The carpenter walked up to Kyle and checked him out further. "You look strong enough. How old are you?"

"Fifteen," Kyle informed him glumly. He had hardly spoken since they left the restaurant.

"If you're willing to work hard, I'll give you a try. The pay is room and board and ten dollars a week, payable on Thursdays."

"Jeez thanks," Kyle muttered.

Theo looked expectantly at the carpenter. "I was hoping he could start right away."

Johnny grinned broadly at Kyle. "The sooner the better. I've more work than I can presently handle."

Zach liked the carpenter. There was an irrepressible energy about him that was quite engaging.

Theo pulled Zach forward. "I was hoping, Johnny, that you could also find something for this lad to do. He's hard-working. I know that for a fact." His gaze made a cursory sweep of the messy workshop. "Looks like you could use a pair of extra hands to help clean up here and maybe run errands."

Johnny fished a fresh toothpick out of the breast pocket of his shirt and put it in his mouth while he appraised Zach. "So would you like to work for me too?" he finally asked.

Zach nodded. His fingers formed a hopeful cross behind his back as he awaited the carpenter's answer.

"Well, I guess that's settled then." Johnny chewed on the toothpick for a few seconds as he viewed Zach's torn down jacket and mud-caked jeans. He turned to Theo. "They'll need proper work clothes."

"I'll bring some over for both of them tomorrow," Theo promised.

The carpenter put an arm around each of the boys' shoulders. "It'll be dark soon, so what do you say we head for my cabin?" He glanced back at Theo as he led Kyle and Zach to the door. "It's located above Camerontown. Everyone knows the place, if you need to get hold of me, that is."

"Work hard, lads. Don't disappoint Mr. Knott," Theo said. Zach was the only one who nodded. An acute longing for his old life filled him. Had he been at home he would right now be finishing his homework and would go on to surf the net. Here in 1866's Barkerville he was preparing for his first real workday. On the road there hadn't been much time to think about family and friends, but now tears stung his eyes at the thought of his parents. His sudden longing for them was so acute that he had a hard time breathing. How devastated they must be, not knowing what had happened to him. How he wished there was some way to send them a message, so he could tell them that he was okay.

· · ·

"I'm not sure about this." Those were the first words out of Kyle's mouth when the two of them were alone together in Johnny's small one-room log cabin after he had left to get water.

"About what?" Zach asked.

"Working for this carpenter."

Zach shrugged. "I don't see that we have much of a choice. You heard Theo. We have to work since Miss Reid won't make enough money to support us, and honestly, why should she? It's not like we're her kids or anything, only fake nephews." He didn't understand what Kyle was so upset about. Johnny seemed a nice-enough guy, who had even offered to share his living quarters with them. He looked around the room. Obviously it was not luxury, but it was a friendly-enough place with two beds, a table, some chairs and a pot-bellied stove that radiated a comfortable heat.

"It's not that I don't wanna to do my part, but I would like it to be on my terms."

Exhausted, Zach sank down on one of the sturdy dining chairs and folded his hands on the table. "What do you mean when you say, my terms?"

Kyle tossed his jacket on one of the beds. "I wanna make money playing poker, like Cox does."

"Don't forget, he's a professional gambler and has a lot of experience." Zach watched a mouse scurry along one of the log walls. He was glad Miss Reid wasn't here. She would probably have freaked.

"I bet you it wouldn't take me long to learn to play like him."

Zach sat back in the chair and viewed Kyle with annoyance as he flopped down on the bed. "So what would you use for money?"

Kyle turned his head, giving him a puzzled look. "Money?"

"Yeah Kyle. Money to play with."

Kyle sat up in bed, looking deflated. "Oh yeah, money." Suddenly he perked up again. "I'll just ask Cox to lend me some."

Zach wanted to laugh out loud but was too tired. "And you think he would wanna finance his competition? He's not stupid, you know. Probably, you also have to be at least eighteen to play," he added as an afterthought.

Kyle shook his head at him in irritation. "Have I ever told you what a downer you are?"

Zach lifted an eyebrow at him. "Oh, once or twice," he answered. "Listen, if you really wanna play poker save the money you make."

The door opened and Johnny came inside, carrying two buckets filled with water. Whistling, he slammed the door shut with his foot and brought the buckets over to the stove where he put them down next to it. "Time to get some grub started, lads, so we can call it a night. Mornin' comes bright and early."

Chapter 22

❧

ZACH WATCHED MISS REID from the doorway as she stretched the sheet across the bed and deftly tucked it underneath the mattress, finishing off with neat hospital corners. She was dressed in a white, ruffled long-sleeved blouse and a billowing calico skirt that rustled when she moved.

"So how is it going, Miss Reid?" he asked as he stepped inside the room.

She straightened up and turned to him, a joyful expression replacing the fatigue on her face. "Zachary, how good it is to see you. Have you and Kyle settled in okay? Do you get enough to eat?" She appraised his appearance. "At least the clothes we got you fit fairly well."

He viewed himself in the small mirror above the washstand. He looked like so many other men walking around Barkerville with his yellow and white checkered shirt and grey pants. The pants were a little loose, but Johnny had lent him a leather belt, which Zach had strapped around his waist, using the extra hole the carpenter had punched in it.

Zach turned to her and smiled. "We're both doing fine and the food's okay." He made a face. "Just too much bacon and beans still."

Miss Reid looked at the knee-high leather boots which had replaced his rundown Nikes. She nodded at them. "What about the boots?"

He shrugged. "A couple of blisters, that's all." Theo had told him that he had bought the boots off the estate of an unlucky miner who had died during a cave-in. Zach tried not to think about that.

She blew a lock of hair away from her face. "It was nice of Theo to lend us the money for your and Kyle's clothes."

So now it was Theo instead of Mr. Cox, Zach thought. "Yeah, it was," he agreed.

Miss Reid pointed at the big bulky comforter draped over a couple of chairs. "Could you help me with that? It's so heavy."

He walked over and grabbed one end of the comforter and helped her cover the bed with it. She smoothed it out, then straightened up and wiped her forehead with the back of her hand. "I already feel beat, and the day has barely started. I hardly got a wink of sleep last night because of some miners who made a racket out in the street with their drunken brawls and carrying on." She placed her hands on her hips and arched her back, her face taking on a pained expression from the movement. "Do you have time for a sarsaparilla? Madame Pond had several cases delivered to the hotel this morning."

Zach nodded eagerly. He had been running errands for Johnny all morning and had worked up quite a thirst. "Sounds great. Whatever it is." He followed Miss Reid as she hurried out of the room and down the stairs. In the kitchen, she opened a wall cupboard next to the stove and brought out a couple of glasses.

"Where's everyone?" Zach asked.

"Madame Pond is out on errands. Miss Combs, that's the cook, went to Davison's for some supplies, and Mr. Sinclair," she added as she pushed some bowls aside on the table and put the glasses down, "he's presently relocating a guest to another room." She went over to a wooden box, standing on the floor next to the door, and pulled out a bottle. "Here we go," she said holding it up for Zach to see. "The best sarsaparilla money can buy, at least according to Miss Combs."

Miss Reid came over and put the bottle down on the table next to the glasses. She sank down in one of the chairs, leaned over the table and pushed the bottle towards Zach. "Could you open that?"

He took the bottle, sat down across from Miss Reid and carefully opened it. He poured an equal amount of sarsaparilla in each of the two glasses, carefully replacing the cork in the bottle after he was done. He pushed one glass towards Miss Reid, and then raised his own. "Here's mud in your eye," he said to her.

She lifted hers. "Cheers."

Glass in hand, Zach slumped back in his chair, and drank from the cool amber liquid. "This is good. Almost like root beer."

Miss Reid nodded. Exhausted lines furrowed her face but there was a special glow in her eyes he hadn't seen there before.

"So how do you like working here?" he asked.

She swallowed the rest of the sarsaparilla. "It's hard physically. Harder than anything I've ever done before." Miss Reid put her empty glass down on the table and pushed it towards Zach, who pulled the cork out and refilled it. "Yesterday was washing day," she said with a sigh. "I honestly didn't think I was going to survive. I had to carry the water inside in buckets; and those washboards!" She winced as she rolled her shoulders. "Everything hurts today." She smiled wistfully. "What I wouldn't give to have my washer and dryer here."

Miss Reid picked up her glass again and leaned back in the chair. "We're getting three new guests today, Madame Pond said, and their rooms have to be ready by noon-time."

Zach poured more sarsaparilla in his own glass. "Is Madame Pond okay to work for? I mean she's not nasty, or anything?"

Miss Reid smoothed her skirt. The skin of her hand was

still red from yesterday's washing. "She's somewhat of a slave driver. 'Please do this. Would you be so kind as to straighten that out', blah, blah, blah. Always very polite, mind you, but she works all of us to the bone."

She took another sip from her glass. "Miss Combs is constantly complaining about the workload, but then of course she's at least three hundred pounds, so it's hard for her to move about." Miss Reid glanced around the kitchen to make sure they were alone. "She doesn't walk, she waddles just like a duck, and sounds like one, quack, quack, quack."

Zach laughed. It was great to see Miss Reid, who was normally so serious, loosen up for once. He felt a sudden desire to compliment her. "That dress doesn't look too bad on you."

She smiled wryly. "Well, I guess I'll take that as a compliment." Miss Reid looked down at herself. "I guess I'll eventually get used to these kinds of clothes, and it was certainly nice of Madame Pond to give me this outfit for free. "That *vieille* thing." She mimicked Madame Pond to perfection. "You can have that, *Chérie*."

Zach fingered his glass. "Has Mr. Cox come by here lately?" He and Kyle hadn't seen the gambler since he came to Johnny's workshop with their new clothes. That was five days ago. He noticed the glow intensify in Miss Reid's eyes.

"Don't tell me you're falling for the guy?" he blurted out before he could stop himself.

A flush spread over Miss Reid's cheeks. She shook her head fervently. "No, of course not. I'm just enjoying his company, that's all. He's a very interesting man. I'm . . ." She hesitated.

Again Zach was unable to stop himself even though it was really none of his business. "When we go back to Vancouver you'll have to leave him behind. You do realize that, don't you?"

Miss Reid looked down at her hands, which she had wrapped around her glass.

"What if . . ." She paused and then looked up at him with unease. "What if we never return home? Hasn't that thought crossed your mind? It must, because I think about it all the time myself."

Of course, Zach had thought about it, but it still jarred him to hear his worst fears spoken out loud. "I refuse to believe that, because . . . because I just can't."

"It's unfortunately a possibility we have to accept," she said softly. "Life goes on no matter where we are, or what situation we find ourselves in, and as long as we're here . . ."

Zach fixed her gaze with his. "If there's one piece of advice I can give you, don't go and fall in love with Mr. Cox." He didn't know why he felt so strongly about it. After all it was no skin of his nose if Miss Reid fell in love with someone from 1866, but to him it felt like a line crossed that shouldn't be.

She leaned over and patted his hand. "Of course, I won't."

He didn't believe her.

The door to the kitchen flew open and Miss Combs sailed

into the room. "Oh, here you are, Miss Reid. Madame Pond is back, and she's lookin' for you." Miss Combs didn't even acknowledge Zach's presence as she plopped a couple of paper-wrapped packages on the counter. She wrestled her arms out of her black coat and hung it on a knob next to the door. Her dress looked like it was busting at the seams, and her round glistening face was red from exertion.

Miss Reid got up from the chair. "I better get busy."

Zach drained the rest of his glass and followed her out of the kitchen.

At the bottom of the stairs leading up to the second floor, she turned to him. "Guess who I saw last night?" She looked expectantly at him. "That annoying weasel, Jackson," she added, when he didn't answer right away.

"I thought he had already left."

Miss Reid shrugged. "He told Theo that he had decided to stay in Barkerville. Apparently, a friend of his has a claim up here, and he is going to help him prospect."

Chapter 23

✌

ZACH WAS SO PREOCCUPIED with what Miss Reid had just
told him about Jackson still being in Barkerville that he
didn't even notice he was walking in the opposite direction
from Johnny Knott's workshop, toward the town of Richfield. He felt tense and his jaw was clenched so hard it hurt.
Now he had to live in fear for his life again, constantly looking over his shoulder.

Finally becoming aware that he was in unknown surroundings, he stopped abruptly. The wooden boardwalk had
ended, and he had been so lost in thought, he hadn't even
noticed walking down the wooden steps to the muddy street,

where he was now standing. Zach looked down at his feet and saw that his new boots were all covered in caked dirt. A filthy-looking pig was grunting at his feet, rooting around one of the boot soles to see if it was hiding some edible treasure. The pig protested loudly when he nudged it aside with the toe of his boot and moved to drier ground.

Zach turned and was heading for the boardwalk when he saw something glint on the ground in the bright sunlight. He bent over, picking it up. A small round gold pendant dangled from a chain. He straightened up and wiped the dirt from the surface of it with his thumb. There was some kind of symbol on the pendant. He turned it toward the sun and studied it in more detail. It looked like a Chinese character.

Zach cast a glance across the street at a two-storey building with a sign posted above the door. Chinese Masonic Hall it read, followed by a lot of Chinese characters. This was the part of Barkerville where the Chinese lived. He had heard Johnny talk about it once.

"It's the place where the Celestials live," he had informed Zach and Kyle as they sat outside his workshop, eating their lunch of ham sandwiches.

"You mean extra-terrestrials?" Kyle had asked doubtfully around his mouthful of food.

Frowning, the carpenter had shaken his head. "No Celestials. Chinese," he had said.

Zach checked his surroundings. The street was empty, except for a young guy dressed in grey pants and a white shirt, and a broad-rimmed hat on his head, who was walking further down the street. Maybe he was the one who had lost the pendant, or if not, he might, at least, know who it belonged to.

"Hey, did you lose this?" Zach yelled after him, holding up the pendant.

The guy didn't hear him. Instead he crossed the road and stepped up on a low boardwalk fronting a narrow building where he pulled a door open and disappeared inside.

Zach closed his hand around the pendant and ran after him. The building the young guy had entered turned out to be a store called Lung Sing's General Merchandise. Zach looked through a small window in the door. The young guy was standing in front of a counter quarrelling, it seemed, with the tall man behind it.

Zach hesitated. Maybe this was not a good time to interrupt the two. He sighed. No, better get it over with. The pendant looked valuable and he didn't want to carry it around.

There was a jingle of bells as he opened the door. The smell of incense and exotic spices in the store was overwhelming and made his eyes water. The exchange between the two at the counter stopped abruptly. The man, clad in a kimono-like black garment and a matching skull cap, eyed Zach suspiciously as he closed the door behind him.

Zach was caught off guard when the guy he had been following spun around and turned out to be a young woman instead. She bore an uncanny resemblance to Cynthia, a

Chinese girl from his French class back home that Zach had developed a crush on.

That resemblance alone made him blush deeply. "Ump . . . eh . . ." he stammered.

"What do you want?" the young woman asked in perfect English. Not only her voice was impatient, her whole being exuded it, including her hands that kept clenching and unclenching, and a twitching in the corners of her mouth that made her lips purse.

Zach held up the chain with the pendant. "I . . ." He took a deep breath. "I was wondering if this might be yours."

The young woman's hand flew to her neck. "How did you get that?"

He resented her accusatory tone. "I didn't steal it if that's what you think. It was lying in the street."

She rushed over to him, the hard soles of her boots pounding across the wooden boards.

He liked the way she smelled as she stood there in front of him, a mixture of incense and something minty. A sudden bright smile chased her reproachful expression away. It was a smile that made his heart flutter, because she now looked even more like Cynthia. He handed her the pendant with a trembling hand.

The man behind the counter, who had been glaring at them during their exchange, barked something in Chinese at the young woman.

She turned around and stamped her foot so hard into the

floor that a clay jar from a nearby shelf fell to the ground. It broke and something that looked like tea leaves spread over the rough-hewn planks.

The man rushed around the counter while pointing at the broken jar, then stormed up to the young woman, yelling something at her. Spinning around, he returned to the counter, grabbed something behind it and slapped it down on the top. It was a photograph. With a rigid index finger, the man pointed first at the photograph, then at Zach while he continued yelling. The chickens held in a cage that was standing in front of the counter started clucking furiously.

The young woman yelled back at him in Chinese, then seized Zach's arm, dragging him to the door. She tore it open with such force that the door bounced against the wall.

When they were outside, Zach turned his head and saw that the man had followed them and was now standing in the doorway, shouting and waving at them to come back. Zach tried to yank his arm free from her grasp, but she held tight. "What the hell's going on?" he asked while she kept dragging him through the mud. He dug his heels in. "Would you stop already."

She let go and turned to him, her face flushed from anger. "Oh, he makes me so angry."

"Well, I get that. Who is he?"

"My father, of course. He doesn't like the way I dress, or that I'm out on my own, but I don't want to stay in the house with my aunt all the time." The young woman tore off her broad-rimmed hat, and her long black hair cascaded down her shoulders. "My aunt constantly wants me to cook and clean and do stupid sewing, so I escape every time I have a chance." She bit her lip for a moment. "I'm sorry to bother you about all this. Thanks for finding my pendant. It means a lot to me." Tears welled up in her eyes. Oh no, Zach thought with dread, she's going to cry now. To his relief she quickly blinked the tears away. "The pendant belonged to my mother," she explained softly. "She passed away last summer."

He didn't know where to look. "I'm sorry," he mumbled.

"What's you name?" the young woman asked.

"Zach," he answered. "And yours?"

"Su-Li."

"That photograph your father was showing you. What was that all about?" Zach asked.

Su-Li's face darkened. "It's a picture of the man I'm betrothed to back in China. My father constantly tells me how much he would disapprove of the way I behave."

Zach gave her a surprised look. "Betrothed. You don't look like you're old enough to marry."

Su-Li wrapped the chain of her pendant around her neck and squinted down as she fastened the clasp on it. "Well I am." She let go of the chain, and the pendant slid behind the neckline of her shirt. "I just turned fifteen. It was all arranged when I was five."

"Jeez." Zach was offended on her behalf. "How old is this guy?"

"Oh, he's very old," Su-Li said. "Thirty-six."

"And he has waited all this time for you to turn fifteen . . . that's ten years."

Su-Li looked insulted. "You don't think I'm worth waiting for?"

"I didn't mean it that way," Zach said flustered. "It's just, how can a man look at a little five-year-old girl and say that he wants to marry her."

"It's an arranged marriage, of course. It was all done through correspondence." He could hear Su-Li was getting annoyed with him.

He shrugged. "Why don't you just tell your father you don't wanna marry the guy."

Su-Li snorted. "I can't do that. He promised Ling Wu I would be his wife and that's the way it's going to be." She looked down the street. "Listen I have to go." She turned to him. "Why don't you come back tomorrow, and I'll show you my strawberries."

He was confused. Was this slang for something sexual? "Your what?"

"Strawberries." Su-Li gave him an enquiring look. "The ones you grow," she added. "What did you think I meant?" Shaking her head, Su-li turned around and walked away.

Zach felt rather stupid as he stood there in the middle of the road, watching her leave.

Chapter 24

SU-LI CROUCHED DOWN and picked a handful of strawberries. "Here try them," she said as she straightened up.

Zach took one of the berries from the palm of her hand and put it into his mouth. He had to admit that it was the sweetest strawberry he had ever tasted. "Very good." He looked around. The slope behind the Chinese Masonic Hall had been terraced and was lush with vegetables and fruit bushes. "All this is yours?"

Su-Li laughed at him. "No, of course not. We all share. The Chinese, that is. I have only this plot." With her finger in the air, she outlined the piece that was hers. "Here you take the rest." She gave him her strawberries and headed down the terraced slope toward the street.

Zach followed her while eating the rest of the berries. His hand was covered in strawberry juice. Since he didn't want to wipe it on his pants, he just licked it off instead.

Su-Li turned to him when they reached the street. "Do you really have to leave right now?"

He was gratified to see disappointment in her eyes. They had had a great time together laughing and talking, and Zach didn't want it to end either. "I'm not even supposed to be here right now. Johnny Knott, my boss, sent me out on an errand. By now, he's most likely wondering where I am."

"Why do you keep looking over your shoulders all the time?" Her dark eyes scrutinized him. "It's as if you're expecting someone to jump at you. Who are you afraid of?"

Was it really that obvious? The fact that Jackson was still in Barkerville had been constantly on his mind since Miss Reid told him yesterday. He shrugged. "I'm not afraid of anyone." Zach tried to make his voice sound nonchalant, but knew he wasn't succeeding very well.

With a sigh, Su-Li hooked her arm through his. "It's okay if you don't wanna tell me about it right now," she said.

Obviously, he hadn't fooled her. Maybe later when he had more time to tell her the whole story about Jackson and McKenna he would. He gave a start and quickly pulled his arm from Su-Li's when, across the road, he saw her father come out of his store.

"What's going on?" Su-Li asked Zach.

"Your father," he warned, nodding at the tall Chinese who, pulling up his long garment so as not to get the hem muddy, came hurrying towards them across the street. Zach felt her body stiffen next to him.

Su-Li's father came to an abrupt halt in front of them. "Go to your home," he hissed at Zach as he pointed down the street. "Leave Su-Li alone."

"You better go," Su-Li told Zach.

He was reluctant to leave her but considering how irate her father looked, he figured he would only make the whole situation worse by staying. "See you later," he murmured, hoping that would be the case, and left. Now and again as he walked down the road, he would glance over his shoulder to see what was happening. At first, Su-Li and her father argued, but eventually she gave a shrug and trudged after him to the store. Standing in front of the door, she turned and waved at Zach. He waved back.

The rest of the day the taste of sweet strawberries lingered in his mouth.

Chapter 25

THE NEXT DAY IT WAS raining hard, and Zach borrowed a jacket and a broad-rimmed hat from Johnny that had clearly seen better days as he set out on an errand for the carpenter.

"No need to hurry," Johnny Knott yelled after him as he stood leaning up against one of the door jambs into his workshop, smoking a pipe.

The errand was to a blacksmith located near the Chinese section, Chinatown, as he had decided to call it. He hoped to find Su-Li there.

Zach didn't think it likely she would be working in her garden in this weather, but he still slipped behind the Masonic hall just in case. She wasn't there, of course. When he stepped out onto the street again he looked with trepidation toward Lung Sing's General Merchandise. No matter how much he wanted to see Su-Li, he didn't feel up to a confrontation with her father.

Resigning himself to the fact that he probably wouldn't see Su-Li today, he pulled the jacket collar up around his ears and began trudging in the direction of the blacksmith where he was going to pick up the hinges Johnny had asked for.

Zach was passing by the open door to a small one-storey building, when he thought he heard Su-Li's voice come from the inside. He looked up. Lee Wah Laundry it said on the wooden sign above him. The doorframe was so low, Zach had to duck to get inside, and his head was nearly touching the ceiling of the small room he found himself in. A veil of steam from water boiling in huge washing kettles obscured the bent forms of the women working. He squinted and made out Su-Li sitting on a bench in the back of the room. She was leaning forward, hands on her knees, while chatting with the women in Chinese.

She laughed, then saw Zach standing there in the room and jumped up and ran over to him. "I was afraid you wouldn't come after what happened yesterday."

"So what did happen?" he asked.

"Not here," Su-Li told him. "Let's talk somewhere else." She turned and waved at the women, yelling something in Chinese and then motioned at Zach to go outside. He ducked through the door opening again.

"You're going to get wet," he said when they stood outside and he saw that she only had on her usual shirt and pants. "Here take this," he said and began removing his jacket

She put a hand on his arm to stop him. "No, keep the jacket on. I like the rain."

"Well, I can't say I do," he said. "Is there a place we can talk where we're not going to get totally soaked?"

"There's a small shed behind my father's store," she said. "We can go there."

Zach hesitated. He preferred to stay as far away from Su-Li's father as possible.

"He rarely goes back there," she said, noticing his reluctance. Before he had time to protest, she was already darting across the street.

With his heart in his throat, Zach hurried after her while casting tentative glances up at the storefront of Lung Sing's General Merchandise. He followed Su-Li around the corner of the building.

When they reached the courtyard behind the store, she pointed to a small shed in the very back. "Over there."

Inside, the shed was stocked with barrels and wooden crates. As was the case inside the store itself, the air in the shed was also heavy with the smell of exotic spices and incense. They each found an overturned crate to sit on.

Su-Li looked around. "When I was a little girl I loved to play in here," she said. "I would imagine I was inside the hull of a ship, held captive by a pirate captain or that I was a princess trapped by an ogre, who couldn't bear the thought of my marrying the handsome prince I was in love with."

"Sounds like fun," Zach said, not knowing how else to respond to her revelation. Casting a sidelong glance at her, he cleared his throat. "So what happened yesterday?" he asked.

She gave a long sigh. "My father told me I couldn't leave the house anymore."

"You mean like a house arrest?"

"More like a room arrest. He locked me in my room." When Zach had done something wrong, he had been told plenty of times to go to his room by his parents, but no one had ever locked him in there. "That's terrible," he said.

They sat in silence for a while. "I escaped this morning," Su-Li finally told him. "While my aunt was playing Mahjong in the living room with her friends, I crawled out the window."

"Well, your father obviously can't keep you in your room forever," Zach said, looking at her hands clasping the edge of the crate she was sitting on. "Or can he?" he asked, not knowing what fathers in the 1860s were allowed to do.

"He's talking about sending me away." Her lips trembled. "I just can't even imagine . . ." She didn't have time to finish the sentence when the door to the shed was torn open. In the doorway loomed her father.

"Su-Li," he roared. They both jumped up from the crates. "You!" Su-Li's father moved toward Zach, hands clenched into fists. "You again."

Su-Li quickly placed herself between her father and Zach. "He's leaving now, okay." She held her father's gaze. "Right now." She glanced quickly at Zach. "Go."

"But what about ..."

"Go, I said," she yelled at him.

Zach slipped past Su-Li and her father. Only now did he notice the rotund woman, dressed in a long embroidered green and black striped skirt with a matching jacket, who had accompanied Su-Li's father. She was holding a blue umbrella over her head, while she anxiously listened to what was going on inside the shed. Her nose was swollen and red as if she had been crying a lot. Probably Su-Li's aunt, Zach figured. "Hello," he greeted her, feeling stupid afterwards for doing so as he hurried out of the courtyard.

Chapter 26

❧

SINCE JOHNNY KEPT Zach busy during the following week, it was only sporadically that he found the opportunity to go to Chinatown. Every time he managed to go there, he hoped that he would run into Su-Li but was always disappointed. Finally in frustration, he went inside the Lee Wah Laundry. The women, who had seemed very affable towards him during his last visit, were now outright hostile. "Su-Li not come here no more," one of them told him.

"You know where she is?" Zach asked.

The women looked at each other. One of them nodded and then turned to him. "At house. Green house, not far from Lung Sing store." At that point all of them turned their backs to him and resumed their work, clearly conveying to him that no more information was forthcoming.

Zach found Su-Li's home easily enough, since it was the only green building close to the store. It was a one-storey small square house, newly painted and meticulously kept up with a row of neatly spaced yellow and red flowers growing along the foundation. He placed himself across the street where he had a clear view of the front door to Su-Li's house.

The place was eerily quiet and the curtains in the two windows were drawn closed. He wondered where Su-Li's room was. If he knew that he could maybe knock on the window, so he could at least make sure she was okay.

After about an hour he gave up, mainly because he was beginning to attract attention from the neighbours in nearby businesses and houses, but also because it was becoming clear that the green house was empty.

. . .

Zach hesitated when he stood in front of the closed door into Lung Sing's General Merchandise, trying to work up enough courage to go inside. He squared his shoulders. No, he wanted to know what had happened to Su-Li, and her father was the one with the answers. He pushed the door open.

Su-Li's father was busy pushing some crates into place behind the counter. When he turned and saw who stood in the store, his amiable smile disappeared.

"Where's Su-Li?" Zach asked with his heart in his throat.

"Su-Li San Francisco with uncle."

Zach took a deep breath ignoring the other man's dark look. "When will she be back?"

"Su-Li no come back. Marry husband." Su-Li's father began coming around the counter. "Now go home. No welcome here."

"Don't worry, I'm leaving." Zach turned and stormed out of the store, slamming the door after himself. Dejectedly, he headed toward town. He had already passed by Hôtel de France, when he reconsidered and returned. The last thing he felt like right now was going back to the workshop. He pushed the heavy door into the hotel lobby open.

"Ah, *Chéri*," Madame Pond exclaimed cheerfully from the first floor landing when she saw him walk into the lobby. She breezed down the stairs amid the rustling of her skirt and stopped in front of him. "So glum you look."

"Where's Miss Reid . . . I mean my aunt?"

Giving him a curious look, Madame Pond pointed up the stairs. "*Chambre neuf.*"

"Thanks." He walked heavily up the stairs and continued down the hallway to room nine, where he pushed on the door, which was ajar. Inside Miss Reid, cloth in hand, was busy wiping down the washstand.

He cleared his throat when she didn't notice him.

She turned quickly. "Zachary!" The look on his face, made her put the cloth down. "What's wrong?" she asked. "Is it Kyle?"

He shook his head. "No."

Miss Reid went to the still unmade bed and sat down. She patted the space next to her. "Let's have a talk."

Zach came over to the bed, where he sank down next to her.

Miss Reid put her hand over his. "So what's going on?"

"I . . . I met this girl," he said.

"Well, tell me about her," Miss Reid said, squeezing his hand.

He told her about how he had met Su-Li, about her inflexible father and her impending marriage to a man she had never met. Miss Reid listened carefully. "I feel so bad for her," he ended his story. "It's just not right that she should be treated like someone's possession."

"Su-Li is from another culture," Miss Reid said, "and don't forget another time." She patted his hand and let go of it. "Her father probably realized how close you two were becoming, and he became nervous and sent her away to stay with relatives in San Francisco until it's time for her to go to China and marry the man her family has picked for her." Miss Reid got up from the bed and contemplated Zach. "She would shame her father if she didn't marry him. Family honour is something the Chinese take very seriously."

Zach sank back on the bed and stared up in the ceiling. "This really truly sucks."

"Listen, I have to get this room ready before the guest returns," Miss Reid said. "Come back later, and we'll talk some more."

Zach scooted off the bed and walked across the creaking floor boards. In the doorway, he turned around. Miss Reid was already busy straightening out the bed. "When will be a good time to come back?"

She straightened up and looked at him. "In a couple of hours, okay?"

He nodded and left.

Chapter 27

ᥱᴏ

KYLE TURNED AROUND when Zach walked into the workshop. "Where were you, man? Johnny's looking for you." Kyle had started to call the carpenter by his first name, probably because he now felt they were more like colleagues, having worked as a carpenter for all of three weeks. "Why the gloomy look?"

Zach just shrugged in answer.

"Guess who I ran into this morning?" Kyle raised an eyebrow at him. "Jackson," he said when Zach didn't respond right away. "He didn't go back to Yale with Enos after all."

"I already know." Zach didn't really feel like talking to Kyle about Jackson.

"Well, he's working a claim with a friend." Kyle grinned at Zach. "Man, I'm surprised he even has friends. I guess we didn't get rid of Mr. Piss-ant after all."

"Guess not." Zach turned his head when he heard heavy footfalls outside. Through the doorway he saw Johnny come down the walkway leading to the workshop.

The carpenter stopped in the doorway while wiping his hands in a piece of cloth. "Finally you're here, Zach."

His gaze moved to Kyle. "Are you finished with that piece of wood?" He nodded at the plank Kyle had been working on.

"No, not yet," Kyle answered.

"Well, anytime now." Johnny's dig was a good-natured one, but judging from Kyle's expression it didn't sit well with him.

"I'm working as fast as I can," he told the carpenter.

Johnny ignored his remark, and turned his attention to Zach again. "Where did you put the hinges?"

Zach stared at him. "Hinges?"

The carpenter nodded. "Yeah, the ones I sent you out to pick up."

Zach's cheeks burned. "Oh, I forgot."

Johnny wedged the piece of cloth that he had been wiping his hands on, behind his belt. "How can that be! It was the only errand I sent you on."

Zach thought fast. "My aunt distracted me when I passed by the hotel. I'll go and get the hinges right now." He had expected the carpenter to move away from the doorway so he could leave, but he didn't. Instead he pulled out a pocket watch, flipped it open and glanced at it.

"No, it's close to lunch time. You can get the hinges in the afternoon." He shook his head at them in frustration. "What is it with you two lately? All of sudden you both seem so absentminded, especially you Kyle." Johnny turned and left the workshop. Whistling, he walked down the pathway and rounded the corner of the building.

"I've had it up to here with all his crap!"

Zach turned his head just in time to see his friend throw the plane he was holding in his hand across the workbench. It bounced against the wall and landed on the floor. "What the heck did you do that for?"

"He's constantly telling me what I can and cannot do." Kyle crossed his arms over his chest and leaned back against the workbench. "No one would dare dis me like this back home."

"I hate to break it to you, Kyle, but this is not back home." Zach shook his head in exasperation when he saw that Kyle's disgruntled expression didn't change. "It's not about you all the time. Grow up already," he said and walked outside.

He found Johnny around the corner of the building, busy inspecting some wooden boards, which stood leaning against the wall. "Sorry about forgetting the hinges," Zach told him.

"Hinges? Oh yes the hinges." Preoccupied, Johnny removed his cap and scratched his hair with his index finger.

"Too many knots in this wood." He replaced the cap and pointed at the planks. "Look here, it's beginning to crack. This wood is of such poor quality." He let out a deep sigh. "Oh, it's truly a curse to be a craftsman in this place."

Only now did the carpenter really pay attention to Zach. "You look off-colour. I hope you haven't gone and picked up one of the maladies goin' around. Davison is laid up with some stomach ailment." He grinned. "Unfortunately, his mother isn't."

Johnny stuck his hand in one of his jacket pockets and extracted a wad of bills. "Here." He peeled a bill from the wad. "I know you're only supposed to get room and board, but here's a fiver for all your hard work. You do keep the workshop spotless and that's appreciated."

Zach accepted the bill. "Thank you."

Johnny peeled some more bills from the wad. "Why don't you go to the Wake Up Jake and buy us some roast beef sandwiches for lunch." He gave Zach the money.

"Will do." As Zach walked away he thought about how elated he would have been had Johnny given him a fiver a week ago. It was after all the first money that was his, since his mother had given him his last allowance, but now he didn't really care.

• • •

Kyle leaned over the edge of the bed and looked down at Zach who was lying on a mattress on the floor. The light from the lantern standing on the table cast shadows over

Kyle's face, making his features look leaner and sharper. "Sorry about earlier at the workshop. I'm just frustrated."

"Heck, so am I," Zach said. "We shouldn't really be complaining. Mr. Knott has been nothing but nice to us, and he gave me five bucks even though he didn't have to." He pulled the blanket he covered himself with at night up to his chin. "Things could be much worse, you know."

"I'm not saying he isn't an okay guy. It's only . . ." Kyle cast a quick glance at the closed door. Johnny was outside visiting the privy. "I really don't wanna work as a carpenter anymore."

"So what would you rather do?" Zach was beat and wished Kyle would just shut up so he could go to sleep. "Look at Miss Reid. She has to clean up after people all day," he added.

Kyle's teeth glistened in the lantern light as he smiled broadly. "I've already told you that there are much easier ways of making money."

Zach squeezed his eyes shut in exasperation. "Don't start that poker talk again. I'm sick of hearing about it."

"Well, you don't see Cox swinging a hammer to make a living."

Zach propped himself up on his elbow. "It's a stupid idea, Kyle!"

"I work my butt off all week, and for what?" Kyle said. "A lousy ten bucks, that's what."

"I'm going to sleep." Zach turned his back to him.

"Gee-whiz, some friend you are." Kyle flopped back down in his bed.

Zach closed his eyes and fell instantly asleep.

Chapter 28

ZACH WAS ALONE in the cabin. Johnny Knott had given him and Kyle an unexpected day off. The carpenter had left earlier in the day to see the owner of one of Barkerville's many saloons, who needed an addition built. Zach didn't know where Kyle had gone. His friend had been silent and strangely nervous all day. The silence had suited Zach just fine since he didn't feel much like talking himself.

Outside the cabin, miners yelled and gave orders as they wound down the day's activities. Soon the creaking of the waterwheels and the sound of water rushing through the flumes would cease. The day's haul of gold dust and nuggets would be taken into Barkerville to be spent, put in the bank or, since a lot of the miners didn't trust authorities, hidden under their mattresses. Some even carried the gold on their bodies at all times.

He lit the lantern, and bringing it with him, sat down at the table. He pulled the only book in the cabin, an old tattered Bible, toward him. Johnny read a passage from it before breakfast every morning, his lips moving silently around the words. Zach didn't know where to look during this show of worship. His family was not religious. True, his parents would take him to church at Christmas and Easter, but even to them, he suspected it was more a social thing, an excuse to catch up on community gossip.

When he randomly opened the Bible to a page, he found a folded piece of paper. Knowing he shouldn't really snoop, he still opened it. Something was written on the paper in a meticulous handwriting. He pulled the lantern closer, and read what looked like a poem to Johnny:

> *See yonder shanty on the hill?*
> *'Tis but an humble biggin',*
> *Some ten by six within the wa's —*
> *Your head may touch the riggin'.*
>
> *The door stands open to the south,*
> *The fire, outside the door;*
> *The logs are chinket close wi' fog —*
> *And nocht but mud the floor.*

A knife an' fork, a pewter plate,
An' cup o' the same metal,
A teaspoon an' a sugar bowl,
A frying pan an' kettle;

The bakin' board hangs on the wa',
Its purposes are twa-fold —
For mixing bread wi' yeast or dough,
Or panning oot the braw gold!

A log or twa in place o' stools,
A ned withoot a hangin',
Are feckly a' the furnishings
This little house belangin'.

The laird and tenant o' this sty,
I canna name it finer,
Lives free an' easy as a lord,
Tho' but an honest miner.

See you on your name day so we
can celebrate in style.
James

Zach folded the paper again, and put it back between the pages of the Bible. Name day? That probably meant birthday. The word triggered something in his mind. He thought hard and finally remembered that on their way to Barkerville, he and Kyle had been discussing how much nicer it was to have a birthday that fell during the summer vacation. Miss Reid had then mentioned that her birthday was on the 24th of June. He looked up. What was the date today? Last Thursday was the 18th of June. He remembered Johnny mentioning that when he had been talking to a customer. Today was Tuesday the 23rd, so tomorrow was her birthday. He should do something for her, he decided.

Zach thought of the five bucks Johnny had given him. He would buy her a gift with the money. Maybe candy, or a hairbrush. She complained about not having one. He could also get her some perfume.

Zach got up from the chair and went to where his old down jacket was hanging on one of the pegs next to the door. Since it was in tatters now, he really should throw it away, but every time he was about to do it he always ended up reconsidering. Probably because of nostalgia. It was after all the last piece of clothing that was left from his old life. He had hidden his five dollars in the inside pocket of the jacket, but when he flipped the jacket open and reached inside, the pocket it was empty. He quickly went through the other pockets, just in case, but came up empty-handed.

Zach hadn't worn the jacket since he had put the money there, so he couldn't have dropped the bill outside. The cabin was locked when they were not there, which meant that only Kyle or Johnny could have taken it, and it sure as hell wasn't the carpenter. Zach's jaw tightened as he let go of the jacket.

"You jerk!" he yelled out loud. Time to find Kyle and get his money back.

When he leaned over the table to blow out the lantern, the door to the cabin opened. Zach spun around just as Kyle slammed the door shut behind him. He was pale and out of breath.

Zach's hands clenched. "Where's my money, Kyle?"

"I'm going to pay you back." Kyle slumped down on his bed, making the springs creak.

"You better." Zach was so infuriated with Kyle that he wanted to punch him. Only the miserable look on his friend's face held him back. "What going on?"

"I'm afraid we've gotten ourselves into a bit of trouble." This was certainly not the usually cocky Kyle that he was used to.

"What do you mean we?" Zach asked. "I haven't done anything wrong, except for not hiding my money in a safer place."

Kyle pulled nervously at the sleeve of his shirt. "Sorry. I just happened to see you sneak that money into your jacket pocket when you thought I was asleep."

"So what did you do with it?"

"I took it, and whatever I had myself, and went to a saloon in Camerontown to play poker," he replied.

Zach's heart sank. "You lost my five bucks, didn't you?"

"Afraid so." He shrugged. "I lost all the money." He gave Zach a glum look. "I really . . . really thought I could win. I mean, a lot of people in this place are such hicks, and after all I played against that dumb-ass, Jackson."

Zach felt the blood drain from his face. "You what?" It had been nearly two weeks since Miss Reid had told him that Jackson was in Barkerville. He hadn't seen neither hide nor hair of him since that time. Now the mention of the hated name brought all his old anxieties back full force.

Kyle began pulling at his earlobe. "Heck, you know Jackson. He's not the brightest, and his friends, they're morons." He heaved a deep sigh. "I really thought I could double my money, and then pay you back. No harm done."

That Kyle now looked like the personification of an injured party only helped increase Zach's outrage. "I can't believe you played poker with Jackson!"

"Unfortunately, my losing that money is not all that happened." Kyle picked up his pillow and threw it hard on the ground, barely missing the water bucket next to the stove. "I had some good hands. I should have won."

Zach came over to the bed and sank down on it next to Kyle. "You owe him money, too, don't you?" He gave Kyle a sidelong glance, and could see from his expression he was right. "How much?"

Kyle's hands closed around the wooden edge of the bed, knuckles showing white. "Actually, Jackson didn't want to play for money." His voice trembled when he continued. "If I won the game, he told me, I would get all my money back, plus an extra twenty. If I lost . . ." He paused.

"What?" Zach asked, feeling as if the walls of the cabin were closing in on him.

Kyle's words stumbled over each other when he continued. "If . . . if I lost, me and you would have to work in his mine for the next two weeks."

Zach jumped up from the bed. "Me! You can't promise him that, you moron."

Kyle got up from the bed, and edged away from Zach. "I signed a promissory note on your behalf. Jackson said it was a binding document, and his friends were all witnesses. We'll have to start working for him tomorrow."

"When did I become your slave?" Zach yelled at him.

Kyle scratched at the day-old stubble on his chin. "Jeez man, I really . . . really need your help on this one." He stopped scratching and gave Zach a pleading look. "Jackson told me that him and his buddies, who by the way are the meanest looking bunch of guys you can even imagine, will break every bone in my body if we don't honour that contract."

Zach was breaking out in cold sweat. "Boy, if you only knew what you have done."

Kyle looked uncertainly at Zach. "It'll only be for two weeks. Johnny is a nice guy, so I'm sure he'll understand."

Disgusted, Zach stormed over to the door and tore it open.

"Where are you going?" Kyle yelled after him.

"None of your damn business." He slammed the door shut and hurried into the goldfields. He zigzagged his way between the flumes and water wheels as he headed toward the noise of Barkerville. He hoped Theo could help him undo what Kyle had just done.

When Zach reached town, he began working his way through the saloons one by one, asking people if they had seen Mr. Theodore Cox, the gambler.

A miner well on his way into an alcoholic stupor, pointed in the general vicinity of the Eldorado Saloon, its name emblazoned on a sign hanging from a building further down the street. "In ther' with Billy Barker," he hiccuped.

"Thank you." Zach hurried toward the saloon. From the inside, he heard someone singing in a hoarse voice:

"I'm English Bill,
Never worked, an' never will
Get away girls,
Or I'll tousle your curls."

The door stood open and he slipped inside the Eldorado. The room was filled to capacity with loud, rowdy miners. When a large group of men headed for the door, pushing Zach aside, he spotted Barker, sitting on a chair close to the window. A scantily dressed woman perched on his knee was nuzzling her nose into his beard. Zach dived into the crowd, making his apologies on the way, when he bumped into someone. Barker was the one he had heard singing, because he decided on an encore just as Zach reached him.

"I'm English Bill,
Never worked an' —"

Zach tapped him on the shoulder, interrupting his ditty. "Sir, Mr. Barker, can I talk to you for a moment."

Barker looked up at him with glazed eyes. "Who might you be, lad?" He burped. "Oops." He held a hand over his mouth. "Can't do that in front of the lady." He winked at the woman, sitting on his knee. She gave such an unladylike chortle that the men standing close to Barker broke into uproarious laughter.

"I'm a friend of Mr. Cox," Zach said to Barker when the men's laughter finally died down. "I'm looking for him right now, and was hoping that you might know where he is."

"Mr. Cox?" Barker's face lit up. "Oh yeah, tall feller. Handsome."

"So you know where he is?"

Barker nodded. "He only just left for the Fashion Saloon down the street. He was meetin' up with his lady friend, Miss . . ." He thought so hard he added deep furrows to his forehead.

The woman in his lap leaned over and whispered something in his ear. "You have a rare good memory, Lucy," he said with admiration. He turned to Zach. "Lucy here says that Theo's lady friend is called Miss Mulligan."

"Thank you," Zach said and headed towards the exit.

The Fashion Saloon was not quite as full as the Eldorado had been, and Zach right away spotted Theo, who was sitting next to a young woman at a small table in the back. They were leaning toward each other, heads close together, talking.

Zach walked over to them. The two of them were so absorbed in their conversation that they didn't notice him stop at their table. He had to clear his throat a couple of times to get their attention.

Theo gave him a startled look. "Zach, what are you doing here?"

"Who's this?" the young woman asked. She was pretty with her heart-shaped face, thick blonde hair and large grey eyes.

"A friend of mine," Theo told her.

"Mr. Cox, I really need to talk to you," Zach said. "In private," he added with an apologetic look at Theo's companion.

Theo nodded and turned the young woman. "Do you mind, Charlotte?" he asked.

She shook her head even though it was plain to see that she wasn't happy about the interruption.

Theo squeezed her hand quickly and got up from his chair.

"Is your aunt all right?" he asked Zach right away when they stood outside the saloon.

"Yeah, she's fine," Zach said. "It's about Kyle." He swallowed the lump in his throat. "Without me knowing, he went and played poker with Jackson and some of his friends. He lost all his money, and mine too, and . . . and . . ."

Theo squeezed his shoulder and looked into his eyes. "Slow down."

Zach's heart felt as if it was beating its way out of his chest, and he took a deep breath to calm himself. "Jackson gave Kyle a chance to win his money back. If he lost, Kyle agreed that we, both me and him, would work in Jackson's mine." His voice began trembling. "Of course, he lost. Mr. Cox if I go to that mine I'm toast."

Theo frowned. "Toast?"

"Yeah, as in Jackson's going to kill me. He knows that I suspect him of murdering McKenna." Zach felt like stamping his foot when he saw the doubt in Theo's eyes. "Argh, Mr. Cox why can't you just believe me?"

Theo let go of Zach's shoulder. "Seems to me this is Kyle's problem, not yours."

"Jackson told him that if we didn't both show up for work, his friends would break every bone in Kyle's body. They even had him sign a promissory note." He gave Theo a dejected look. "I know that Kyle did a stupid thing, but he's still my friend, and I don't want to see him hurt."

"I understand, you want to protect Kyle, but . . ." Theo paused. "Okay, I'll talk to Jackson tomorrow."

"Afraid that'll be too late," Zach told him. "Jackson wants us to show up at the mine early tomorrow morning."

"That soon. I guess that means I'll have to talk to him to-night." Theo gave a sigh as he cast a regretful glance toward the open door into the saloon. He looked at Zach. "Go home," he said. "I'll come by the cabin later to tell you how it went."

Zach grabbed Theo's hand and shook it hard. "Oh, thank you so much, Mr. Cox." True, there were still no guarantees, because Jackson was as underhanded as they came, but there was at least hope.

Chapter 29

ZACH WAS WAITING nervously by the cabin door for Theo's arrival. Johnny Knott had come home early, and was doing his best to lighten the tense atmosphere in the room, but he soon realized it was a lost cause, and settled down at the table where he began whittling another playing piece for the chess set he was making.

After a while he stopped the whittling, and looked first at Zach, and then Kyle, who was sitting on his bed, staring gloomily in front of him. "Whatever is between you two, I hope you work it out. It's downright chilly in here, and that's despite the fire I just lit in the stove."

Zach stopped biting his nails and looked at Johnny. His

legs were beginning to ache from having stood next to the door for so long. "Sorry," he said.

Kyle's gaze tentatively sought Zach, who ignored him as he had done ever since he returned from his meeting with Theo.

"Johnny, me and Zach have decided to help an old friend at his gold mine." Kyle couldn't even look at the carpenter. "We start tomorrow morning. It'll only be for a couple weeks," he added quickly.

Johnny put the knife and unfinished playing piece down on the table. "A couple of weeks!" He shook his head at him. "You work for me, Kyle. You gave me your word."

Kyle's gaze kept avoiding the carpenter. "My friend really needs our help."

"And who, may I ask, is this friend?"

Kyle pulled nervously at his shirt sleeve. "One we travelled with from Fort Yale. His name is Jackson."

Johnny leaned back in the chair and wedged his thumbs behind his suspenders. "Isn't he the one you despised? If I remember correctly, you called him a dirty rat."

Kyle shrugged, trying to appear nonchalant. "You know how it is between friends."

"No, I surely don't." There was an edge to Johnny's voice now. "Enlighten me, please?"

They were interrupted by a knock on the door. "I'll get it." Zach ran to the door and opened it. Outside on the stoop stood Theo, an angry scowl on his face.

"Who is it, Zach?" Johnny asked.

Zach glanced back at the carpenter. "It's Mr. Cox."

Johnny pushed his chair back, got up from the table and walked up behind Zach, who was standing in the door opening. The carpenter smiled at Theo. "Come inside. Have a dram with me."

Theo shook his head. "I appreciate the offer, Johnny, but I have to be back in town shortly. I just need a few words in private with the lad here." He nodded at Zach, who stepped outside.

"Certainly." Johnny's gaze passed curiously between the two, but he didn't inquire.

Zach followed Theo down the slope from the cabin to where the gold fields started. The last rays of the sun bathed the flumes and water wheels in a soft golden light.

"It's gettin' dark." the carpenter yelled after them. "Do you need a lantern?"

"No, we'll be fine," Theo answered. Johnny lingered for a moment in the doorway, before he went inside the cabin again, closing the door after himself.

"So what happened?" Zach asked in breathless anticipation as Theo stopped and turned to him.

Theo gritted his teeth. "I had a good mind to punch Jackson." He removed his hat and wiped perspiration from his brow with the back of his hand. "When he realized that he wasn't going to outwit me, he began with his insults." Theo slapped his hat angrily against his thigh. "Why Enos ever took him on as a driver is beyond me." He put his hat on again, pulling the rim down. "Anyways, the contract has been torn up. You and Kyle don't have to go to his mine."

Zach's tense muscles relaxed. It was as if a physical burden had taken off his shoulders. "Oh, thank you so much. How did you make Jackson change his mind?"

Theo smiled wryly. "It was rather simple actually. I consulted with a friend well-versed in legal matters, and he told me that since Kyle is not yet sixteen and therefore not of legal age the contract he signed was null and void." He fished a cigar out of his jacket pocket and bit the tip of. "In truth," he said as he spat on the ground, "the law around here already views gambling as a nuisance, so they don't look lightly at underage gambling. I told Jackson that if I took that contract to a constable, he and his friends would most likely end up in jail for trying to take advantage of a minor." He gazed into the shadows of the goldfield as he wedged the cigar between his teeth. "Jackson, of course, was furious." Theo patted his pockets looking for matches. "He took to threatening me."

"With what?" Zach asked with unease.

Theo finally gave up looking for matches and pocketed the cigar again. "Oh, nothing specific. Just that I would be sorry."

"I would take his threat seriously."

"If I had to take serious every threat directed at me, I would forever have to watch over my shoulder. Who wants to live that way?" Theo reached into his vest pocket with his index and middle finger and brought out a wad of bills. "I nearly forgot. Here's the money Kyle lost in the game." He pressed the bills into Zach's hand.

Zach raised his eyebrows in surprise. "How did you manage that?"

"Ill-gotten gains," Theo told him with a wry smile. "Since it's illegal to gamble with someone under the age of sixteen, it's also illegal to keep the spoils from such an unlawful endeavour."

Zach closed his fingers around the money. "I'm sorry that we continue to cause you so much trouble, Mr. Cox. I guess we're like unwanted relatives, who refuse to leave." He had heard his mother use that term. He turned around when he heard steps behind him.

Johnny was coming toward them with a lit lantern in his hand. "It was takin' so long," he said as he stopped next to Zach, "that I took to wonderin' if everythin' was all right."

Theo gave him a nod. "Everything's fine, Johnny. Zach and I, we just finished our little talk."

"So, you're quite certain that you don't have time for a dram?" the carpenter asked. "I have this bottle of good Scotch that's beggin' to be drunk."

Theo gave him a regretful shrug. "Sorry, but I have a high-stakes game going on tonight."

"Another time then," the carpenter said.

Theo gave him the thumbs up. "Wouldn't miss it, Johnny." He turned to Zach. "You take care of yourself now, lad." He touched a hand to his hat as a farewell.

Johnny watched with Zach as Theo negotiated his way across the goldfield towards Barkerville. "Honourable man, if I ever saw one," he said. "So unlike his brother."

Zach was surprised by the statement. "Why do you say that?"

"Enos is an even better poker player than Theo, but he got caught cheatin'. He shrugged. "Theo had a hard go at pickin' up games just after it happened, and of course Enos was banned permanently from the tables. People figured that if Enos cheated, so did his brother." He shook his head. "Theo's not that kind of man," he said with conviction.

Zach stood staring after the gambler until he disappeared into shadows. Things weren't as easy for the confident Theo after all.

Johnny put a hand on Zach's shoulder. "Come inside. It's time we called it a night."

Kyle's anxious gaze met them as soon as they walked inside the cabin. Zach cleared his throat as he closed the door firmly behind him. "Mr. Knott, we don't have to go and work at Jackson's gold mine after all," he told the carpenter. "That's what Mr. Cox came to tell me. It turns out Jackson doesn't need our help."

Kyle's tense features relaxed. "Phew, that's a load off."

Zach avoided looking at him. He was still so angry with Kyle that he could barely stand being in the same room with him.

"I'm quite relieved to hear that," Johnny said from the

stove where he was throwing more wood in the fire. "I would've had a hard time gettin' by right now without your help, Kyle, since I just picked up a new building contract."

Kyle got up from the bed and came up to Zach. "Thank you, man, for taking care of this."

"Don't ever do this to me again, you jerk," Zach said, eyes blazing.

Chapter 30

MISS REID UNFOLDED the fan and held it up in front of her. "It's exquisite," she said as she took in the fan's delicately painted landscape of rolling hills dotted with exotic looking trees. "To think you would remember my birthday, when I myself had completely forgotten." She lowered the fan. "How did you even know?"

"You mentioned it on our trip up here." Zach had spent the better part of his morning hunting for a birthday gift, finally finding the fan in a small obscure store, catering to frills rather than practical goods. He was glad his effort had paid off, since Miss Reid was obviously delighted with his gift.

"So what is this then?" Miss Reid carefully put the fan down on the kitchen table and picked up the small wooden box that was Zach's second birthday gift for her. Curiously, she lifted the lid.

"Candied fruit," he said, watching for her reaction.

Wheezing, the cook waddled from the tub where she had been peeling potatoes over to the table and gave the box a cursory glance. "Candied fruit sticks to your teeth and rots them until nothing is left, e'cept your gums."

"I'm sure it's not as bad as that." For Zach's benefit, Miss Reid rolled her eyes towards the ceiling. More often than not, the two women got on each other's nerves.

"You only wait." Miss Combs waddled to the stove where a beef stew was bubbling ferociously in a big pot.

"We could go out for dinner tonight to celebrate." Zach suggested to Miss Reid.

"If you don't mind, could we make it tomorrow instead?" There was a flush to Miss Reid's cheeks. "Theo invited me out for dinner tonight."

After Theo had left Johnny's cabin last night, and Zach's anxiety had abated, he had thought about the encounter with Theo and Miss Mulligan at the Fashion Saloon. The way Theo had leaned over and squeezed the young woman's hand before he left the saloon had seemed intimate somehow. If he was interested in Miss Reid, what was he doing with another woman? Zach studied the teacher's face: the glow in her eyes, her flushed cheeks, and decided he was not going to let what he had seen ruin her birthday. "Sure, we can make it tomorrow," he told her. "Hope you have a great time tonight."

She smiled at him. "Thanks, and thank you so much for the wonderful gifts."

• • •

When Zach stepped out of the Hôtel de France, another cattle run was underway down the main street. This time instead of trampling through a muddy mess, the cattle were running along a bone-dry road, the result of nearly a week of no rain. The dirt they kicked up created a cloud of dust so thick it choked Zach's airways. People on the boardwalks were quickly heading inside the nearest saloons and stores to escape. He did the same and found himself inside a barbershop. Only one of the two chairs in the room was occupied. The barber, a wiry black guy, with a mass of black curls, was busy slapping shaving cream on his customer's face. He glanced over at Zach. "Vile out, ain't it?"

Zach nodded. "Is it okay if I stay in here for a moment?"

"Be my guest." The barber leaned over and put the mug with shaving cream, and brush down on a small wall shelf.

"Is that you, Zach?" He heard Theo ask from underneath all the shaving cream.

"Would you kindly keep that potato trap shut, Theo?" The barber had unfolded a straight razor, and was holding the sharp blade against the gambler's neck. "I don't much like to cut you by accident." The razor blade scraped down Theo's throat. The barber gave Zach another quick glance. "If you want, you can sit in the other chair, while I finish here." The barber pointed to the chair with the razor, flinging flecks of shaving cream on the floor.

"So how are things, Zach?" Theo asked.

The barber grabbed Theo by the chin to keep him still. "What did I just say about talkin' when I'm shavin' you?"

"I'm doing fine," Zach answered as he went over to the chair pointed out to him and sat down on the worn leather seat. He looked into the small mirror in front of him. Was that really his reflection? He turned his head in different directions, studying himself as if he were a stranger. His hair, which had by now grown well below his ears, looked stiff and dirty. He thought back. How long was it since he had had a bath, or washed himself for that matter? With horror he realized he couldn't remember. Did a dip in the cold water of the creek about a week ago count?

Zach leaned closer to the mirror. His cheeks, he noticed, had lost some of their fullness and his face now looked more angular than round. The peach fuzz on his chin was also getting coarser. He fell back in the chair. Soon, he would have to start shaving. Zach turned his head and looked at Theo, who sat there trapped in his chair, while the razor blade scraped across his face. Imagine shaving with a straight razor like that? Since he was not likely to find triple blade Schicks around here there wasn't really much of a choice unless he wanted to grow a beard. Zach's gaze wandered above the mirror, where there was a sign posted to the wall.

NEW HAIR INVIGORATOR
Prevent baldness, restore hair that has
fallen out or become thin and brittle.
Will relieve headaches, cure dandruff and
give your hair a darker and glossy colour.
You'll find this hair invigorator quite agreeable
and a great addition to your toiletries.
Safe if used on children's heads.

"Thank you, Moses," Zach heard Theo say, and turned his head just in time to see the barber remove a steaming hot cloth from the gambler's face. "What about a haircut, Theo?" Moses asked.

"Next time." Theo pushed himself out of the chair, reached in his pocket and gave the barber some money. He smiled at Zach. "You could, however, give this lad a trim, Moses. He looks like he's in need of one."

• • •

Forty-five minutes later they left the barbershop, Zach feeling renewed and a lot cleaner. Moses had washed his hair out behind the store with buckets of the coldest water ever to have touched Zach's skin. Afterwards, still shaking from the cold, he had sat in the same chair Theo had occupied earlier, and Moses had cut his hair with an enormous pair of scissors. Zach thought the result had a kind of Theo effect, which wasn't exactly his style.

The dust outside had settled now, and people had again taken to the boardwalks. Barkerville was back to its usual hustle and bustle.

Theo smiled at him as they walked down the boardwalk. "What about something to drink?"

Zach nodded eagerly. "Sounds real good."

Soon they were seated at a table in the Wake Up Jake, Zach with a cold sarsaparilla, the gambler with a beer. Zach's throat was parched and he took a long grateful sip of his drink.

Theo leaned back in the chair and studied him, his thumbs wedged behind his belt. "Any more trouble from Jackson?"

Zach shook his head. "No, but I sure wish he had gone back to Fort Yale with your brother. I'm tired of looking over my shoulder." Leaning over the table, he lowered his voice so people at nearby tables wouldn't hear him. "I noticed how Jackson kept looking at those saddle bags all night," he said. "At one point he must have checked out what was inside them and when he saw the gold, he decided to kill McKenna."

Theo took a long swallow of his beer and wiped the foam off his moustache with the back of his hand. "The goldmine he's working on would be the perfect ruse, I grant you that," he said after a while.

Zach stared at Theo. "So you do believe Jackson killed Mr. McKenna, after all?" It felt so good to finally have someone share in his suspicion. "I'm so . . ."

Theo held up his hand to stop Zach. "No, no that's not at

all what I'm saying. It was only pure conjecture on my part." He slumped back in his chair. "The reason I said the gold-mine was the perfect ruse is because everyone knows a hired wagon driver doesn't make much in wages, so consequently, it would be hard to exchange a large amount of gold without arousing suspicion." He paused as he thought about what he had just said.

"So Jackson decides to stay here in Barkerville and help his friend prospect," Zach quickly chipped in. "They haven't yet found gold, but I predict that they soon will." He looked triumphantly at Theo. "No one would be able to prove that he didn't mine that gold himself. Maybe he'll even kill his friend. Make it look like an accident."

Theo gave a chuckle. "Do away with Archie! I doubt it. He's the meanest old dog you could ever encounter." He drained the rest of his beer and looked at the grandfather clock standing in a corner of the restaurant. "Listen, I have a poker game in the Parlour soon, so I better be on my way."

Zach watched him as he got up from the chair. "You're taking my aunt to dinner tonight, she told me."

The gambler pushed the chair up against the table. "That's right."

"She likes you a lot."

"As I her." He buttoned his jacket and pulled at the sleeves. "I find her very refreshing to talk to. I think you can say we've become good friends."

"She's hoping for more than a friendship, you know." Zach

hesitated before he continued. "That woman you were with in the saloon, Miss Mulligan . . . is she your girlfriend?"

Theo pulled the chair out again, and sank back down on it with a sigh. "I never let your aunt believe I carried romantic feelings for her. I'm truly sorry if she has misinterpreted our relationship."

"So Miss Mulligan is . . ." Zach paused.

Theo nodded. "Charlotte is someone I've known for a while now. I meet up with her when I'm in Barkerville. And yes, we . . . we're involved, but not planning on getting married. At least not anytime soon."

Zach watched the special gleam that had come into Theo's eyes as he talked about his Miss Mulligan and he felt sorry for Miss Reid. "It's just that I don't wanna see her hurt. I've come to like her a lot."

Theo gave him a strange look. "Of course you care for your aunt. Just as you care for your brother."

Zach gave him a blank look. "Huh?"

"Kyle, your brother," Theo explained.

"Oh yeah," Zach said quickly.

Theo folded his hands on the table as he contemplated Zach. "I would never make your aunt believe I was romantically inclined toward her, if I wasn't." There was sadness in his gaze.

"Then promise me, that you'll tell her about Miss Mulligan at dinner tonight."

Theo nodded. "I will."

Chapter 31

ZACH WAS IN THE middle of sweeping wood shavings from the floor and collecting them in a big pile outside the workshop, when he saw Kyle rounding the corner of the building, all agitated and out of breath.

"They arrested Cox."

The broom made a clatter as Zach in his surprise dropped it on the ground. "What?"

"About an hour ago. Davison told me." Kyle could hardly stand still. "He saw Cox being taken away in handcuffs right outside the store."

Zach still couldn't believe his ears. "Is it because of the gambling?"

"I have no idea," Kyle said. "Davison told me that he would probably be taken to the jail here in Barkerville."

Zach picked up the broom. "I know where the jail is." He leaned the broom against a wall and took off. "Tell Mr. Knott I'm going over there, will you?" Zach yelled over his shoulder. He was still sore at Kyle for the Jackson incident and didn't want him tagging along.

Right away Zach felt the excitement on the street. People were drawn into groups, shock and puzzlement on their faces. Some of them were shaking their heads. Agitated, shrill voices rose above the buzz of the conversation. Zach caught fragments of sentences as he hurried down the boardwalk toward the jail.

"Why Theo?"

"Too much of the law around here."

"If you ask me, that Jackson . . ."

Zach stopped in his tracks and turned to the pot-bellied man in the stained white shirt, who had spoken the hated name. "Why did you mention Jackson?" he asked him.

"Because he was with the constable when they took Theo in, that's why." The pot-bellied man looked at the faces around him with an expression of great importance. "I saw the whole thing, I did. Saw him marched off to jail by the constable, and with that bloody Jackson in tow."

With dread Zach realized Theo's arrest might not have anything to do with gambling after all, but then what?

He was out of breath when he reached the jail, which was

located in the lower level of a narrow two-storey building. A wooden sign posted over the door read Barkerville Jail. Property of British Columbia.

Zach burst through the door, startling the tall broad-shouldered man in his mid-thirties, who was napping in a chair, behind a desk.

The man snatched a shotgun from the table and pointed it straight at Zach's forehead. His heart jumped to his throat as he stared down the barrel. It looked enormous, as if it could swallow him up whole. "What do you want?" the man barked, and expertly aimed a jet black stream of chewing tobacco into a spittoon, standing next to the desk.

"Crissake, Constable Stevenson, put that gun down. He's my friend," Zach heard Theo say.

Only when Stevenson had put the gun down, did Zach dare turn his head. Theo occupied one of the two small cells in the jail. He was standing at the cell door, staring at Zach, his hands wrapped around the iron bars.

Theo's gaze still bore traces of disbelief. "Let me talk to him," Theo said to the constable, who had reclined in his chair and folded his hands over his lean stomach.

"You were told, no visitors today." Stevenson was watching Zach with suspicion.

"Listen, you and I go back a long time," Theo said. "He's only a lad. What's he going to do? Break me out of jail?"

Stevenson grumbled something underneath his breath. "Five minutes," he said out loud. "No more."

Zach's legs felt like rubber, when he walked over to the cell. He too wrapped his hands around the bars, and looked closely at Theo. "Why have they arrested you?" he whispered.

Theo cast a glance toward Stevenson, who kept watching them keenly. "They think I killed someone," he whispered back.

Zach squeezed the bars so hard, his fingers hurt. "Killed someone!"

Theo nodded. "Dan McKenna's body was found in a shallow grave not too far from where we all camped that night." His face filled with anguish. "I should have listened to you." He took a moment to collect himself. "The authorities were alerted, and they began asking around. Jackson got wind of it and . . ." He looked away.

"And what?" Zach asked breathlessly.

Theo met his gaze again. "He told the authorities about McKenna's visit to our camp, and how he left early the next morning without a word to anyone, and that I was in possession of his watch."

"Which I found and gave to you." Zach's jaw tightened with resolve. "I'm going to tell the constable about what really happened, and also about the shovel I found."

"You'll do no such thing." Theo's voice had risen. "Jackson already has it in for you. If you get involved in this it'll only embolden him further."

"But Jackson did this, not you." Zach was livid with the injustice of the whole thing.

Stevenson got up from the chair and walked over to them. "Is everything all right?" he asked.

Zach made a quick decision, and turned to the constable. "Jackson is trying to frame Mr. Cox. He was the one who killed Dan McKenna," he said firmly. "I was the one who found that watch on the ground, and I gave it to Mr. Cox for safekeeping." With a sinking heart, he saw skepticism mixed with a good dose of hostility in the constable's gaze.

"I know you wanna help your friend here," Stevenson nodded at Theo, "but lyin' on his behalf ain't goin' help matters."

"I'm not lying!" Zach yelled. "Jackson's the one who's lying. He's had it in for Mr. Cox for a long time."

Stevenson's eyes narrowed. "Are you quite finished?"

Theo grabbed Zach's arm through the bars. "Yes, he is," he said giving the constable a quick smile. "Certainly, you can understand how upset he is about all this?"

Stevenson's tense expression softened somewhat. "Well, don't get me wrong," he said to Zach. "I understand that you want to save your friend from the gallows, but this is not the way to go about it."

Zach gaped at the constable. "Gallows?" He swallowed hard. "They hang people!"

Stevenson gave him a strange look. "Of course they do."

"But that's horrible!" Zach turned to Theo in alarm. "Is this true? You could hang for this?"

"I think it's best you take your leave," Stevenson told Zach as he walked over to the door and opened it.

Zach turned to Theo. "Where are you staying?" He whispered. "I'll get rid of McKenna's watch. That way all evidence pointing to you is gone and it'll be Jackson's word against yours."

Theo let go of the bars. "The constabulary are already in possession of the watch," he said. "I always carried it around in my pocket, so I could give it back to McKenna when he showed up." The exhaustion and despair were etched into his face now. "Why do you think they arrested me on the spot?"

Zach gave a frustrated sigh. "You should've left it under a mattress, or something."

"Theo, I said he had to leave," Stevenson said.

"Better go now, lad," Theo said hurriedly. "Don't worry, this will all be sorted out somehow." He fixed Zach's gaze with his. "Stay away from Jackson, and promise me that you won't say anything to anyone about your suspicions."

Zach nodded reluctantly and left. Stevenson slammed the door shut behind Zach as soon as he was outside.

Chapter 32

MISS REID SAT WRINGING her hands at the table in Hôtel de France's kitchen. "I was waiting and waiting for Theo to show up here at the hotel so we could go out for our dinner when I heard about his arrest." She blinked tears from her eyes. "Oh, this is absolutely dreadful." Her face looked haggard as she viewed Zach across the table. "They must know that he could never do a thing like that. He's the kindest, sweetest, most honourable person I've ever known."

A loud snort came from the stove, where Miss Combs was dropping chunks of carrot into a big cast iron soup pot, simmering on the stove. "All gamblers are deceitful, selfish creatures."

Miss Reid turned around on her chair and frowned at the cook. "That's not at all true."

Miss Combs rubbed her plump hands over the soup. "Like I wouldn't know. My sister was married to a Faro player who never worked an honest day in his life. Had a woman in each town, the scoundrel." Her ruddy fleshy nose wrinkled in disapproval. "Gamblers! They're like leeches, sucking money from honest, hardworkin' people. My brother-in-law was shot one day by someone who claimed that he was cheatin', and he probably was too. Good riddance that was."

"Certainly not all gamblers are like that!" Miss Reid's voice was shrill from indignation.

The cook waddled to a wooden cutting board lying on the kitchen counter and came back with a handful of cut potatoes that she dumped unceremoniously into the pot. She gave Miss Reid a piercing look. "Oh, they are. Every single one of them."

The chair scraped across the floor as Miss Reid got up. She grabbed hold of the edge of the table and leaned towards Zach. "That woman gets on my nerves," she said through clenched teeth. Miss Reid turned to the cook. "Tell Madame Pond that I've gone to the jail to let them know that they have the wrong man in custody."

Miss Combs chuckled, her eyes disappearing into craters of fat. "You're truly gullible if you think they're goin' to listen to a woman." She shook her head at Miss Reid as she returned to the cutting board.

The teacher's hand closed tightly around the top of the chair. "I'll make them listen. Tell them that Jackson is a cheat and a liar, who's only trying to get poor Theo into trouble."

Zach seized her arm to get her attention.

Her head snapped in his direction. "What?"

"Miss Combs has a point. They most likely won't listen to you — not because you're a woman," he interjected quickly when he saw she was about to voice her objection, "but because they simply don't care how honourable or wonderful you think Mr. Cox is. All they're interested in is evidence and he happened to be in possession of McKenna's watch."

Miss Reid came around the chair and sank back down on the seat, a dejected expression on her face. He felt sorry for her. The feelings she had for Theo were genuine and heart-felt, and she happened to be right. He was a great guy. Zach put a hand over hers. "Don't worry, Mr. Cox told me every-thing would be sorted out."

The door slammed against the wall as Kyle burst into the kitchen, red-faced and agitated.

Miss Combs spun around. "Watch it, you scoundrel," she yelled holding up her thumb. "Look, you gave me such a fright that I cut myself." She put her thumb in her mouth.

"Sorry." Unconcerned, Kyle made for the kitchen table and pulled out a chair, which he slumped into. "They'll prob-ably hang Cox!"

Miss Reid's face turned ashen, her eyes wide with horror.

"It's true," Kyle told her breathlessly.

This was the one piece of information Zach hadn't yet relayed to Miss Reid, and now he wished he had. That way he could've broken it to her gently instead of having Kyle springing it on her like this.

Kyle leaned back in the chair and wedged his hands behind his belt. "It's all they're talking about in town." He shook his head, his expression one of disbelief. "I didn't know that they just go and hang people like that."

Miss Reid picked anxiously at the lace edging on one of her dress sleeves. "They must surely have a trial." Her voice shook as much as her hand.

"Of cours' there'll be a trial," Miss Combs said from the stove where she was busy tossing onions into the pot. "After all, we ain't barbarians."

Zach's gaze moved to Miss Reid again. It was time he told both her and Kyle about what he knew regarding McKenna's disappearance. He leaned over the table toward the teacher. "Is there somewhere private we can talk?" he whispered, with a knowing glance at Miss Combs, who was stirring the contents of the pot with great gusto.

Miss Reid got up from the chair. "We can go out back." She turned to Miss Combs. "I'm not visiting Theo in jail after all. Tell Madame Pond I went out for some fresh air."

"Good, I'm sure a little sunshine and fresh air will help clear your mind," came the cook's laconic reply.

Zach and Kyle got up from their chairs and followed Miss Reid into the hallway and through the back door. Zach, who was last, pulled the door closed behind them. They walked away from the hotel. Glancing around, Zach quickly ascertained that there was no one in sight who might overhear what he had to say. "It wasn't Mr. Cox who found McKenna's watch." Kyle and Miss Reid stopped abruptly and turned to him. "I was the one who spotted it lying on the ground . . . The chain was broken," he added quickly.

"You mean the chain on the watch was broken?" Kyle asked.

"Of course, Kyle, what other chain would he be talking about?" Miss Reid shook her head impatiently at him, before she turned her attention to Zach again. "What are you trying to tell us?"

Zach saw an old man with a cane approach and waited until he had hobbled by, lifting his hat at them in greeting. "That the chain must have broken during McKenna's struggle with his killer," he answered when the old man was out of earshot. "I also found a bloody shovel in Jackson's wagon the day after McKenna disappeared, so I'm sure Jackson's the one who murdered him. Of course he lied to Mr. Cox when he confronted him about the shovel, telling him he killed a racoon with it, and Mr. Cox believed him even though I told him not to. Now he's . . ."

"Wait . . . wait, this is all very confusing," Miss Reid interrupted him.

"So why the heck is Cox the one sitting in the jail, when it's Jackson who did it?" Kyle asked.

"Because, damn it, I can't prove it." Zach shot Miss Reid a warning glance. "And don't you start in on me about finger prints and DNA because obviously that's not even an option, and besides, the shovel is gone now."

Miss Reid cupped her face in her hands. "Please, my head is spinning. Could you two just slow down for a moment." She took a deep breath. "Zachary did you tell anyone about this?"

He nodded. "Yes, I told Constable Stevenson who was guarding the jail, but he was convinced that I was lying to get Mr. Cox off the hook."

Miss Reid dropped her hands to her sides. "Why on earth didn't you tell me about all this before?" She sounded deeply disappointed.

"I can understand you didn't wanna tell Miss E.," Kyle said. "But, I'm your friend."

Zach didn't much care if Kyle was sore at him, but he now felt some remorse about not telling Miss Reid. "At the time, I didn't see a reason to," he excused himself. "I handed the watch over to Mr. Cox, and he went in search of McKenna, but then, as you already know, he couldn't find him."

Miss Reid crossed her arms over her chest. Her expression told him that she wasn't buying his excuse. "You've no idea how hurtful this is to me. After all our time together I thought we had built some trust."

Since she obviously remained upset with him, he saw no reason to hide the truth. "With all due respect, Miss Reid, at times you do tend to overreact. I was afraid you would confront Jackson, and who knows what might have happened then."

Her cheeks reddened. "So that's what you think of me, an hysterical woman, who's incapable of showing any tact or common sense?"

"And I couldn't be trusted either, is that what you're saying?" Kyle asked him with his eyes narrowed.

Zach was now beginning to wonder if he should have told them at all. "I was only trying to keep you and Kyle safe, okay." He looked at each of them in turn. "Okay?"

Miss Reid relaxed her shoulders. "I guess I can be a little impetuous at times," she admitted. "The important question really is, what do we do now?"

Kyle still bore a disgruntled look on his face. Obviously, he was in a far less forgiving mood than Miss Reid.

"The problem is that with no evidence, it's my word against Jackson's." Zach paused when the back door to the hotel opened. Miss Combs came outside with a pail and tossed the contents into the yard. She eyed them curiously before she went inside again, but to Zach's relief didn't ask questions. He waited until she had closed the door again. "Most likely they're going to believe Jackson over me, since he was the one who came forward and told them who had McKenna's watch. Mr. Cox says that all I'm going to accomplish is antagonizing Jackson even further."

"What do you mean further?" Miss Reid asked. "Did you say something to him before?"

"Jackson happened to overhear a conversation I had with Mr. Cox about my suspicions concerning his involvement in McKenna's disappearance." Zach gave her resigned smile. "Ever since he's had it in for me, and has already tried to kill me once."

Kyle gaped at him. "When? How?"

"On the steamboat from Soda Creek, Jackson shot off a gun when I was with the horses. Well, I actually didn't see him do it, but I know it was him." He glanced at Miss Reid, who was as stunned as Kyle by his admission. "If it wasn't for Mr. Cox coming to my aid, I would probably have been trampled to death."

Miss Reid was the first to speak. "But why did Jackson kill McKenna to begin with? He seemed such a nice harmless guy."

"Because he was bringing gold with him down to Victoria, that's why," Zach answered. "He kept it in the two saddlebags he brought along."

"What a fool!" Miss Reid said. "Travelling alone with gold in this uncivilized place."

Chapter 33

AT THE END OF THE WEEK Theo was transferred to the Richfield jail, which was situated close to the courthouse a little less than a kilometre down the road from Barkerville. The Honourable Matthew Baillie Begbie, who was coming to Richfield to review the case against Theo, had a reputation as a fearless, outspoken judge. A flyer currently circulating in Barkerville said he was a Tireless Advocate of Just Law in the Gold Country. The flyer also stated that Theodore Joseph Cox was suspected of having willfully murdered another human being, Dan Philip McKenna, and attempted to cover his crime by burying the remains of said Dan Philip McKenna.

Zach read the sentence on the flyer again: A Tireless Advocate for Just Law in the Gold Country. He thought that sounded promising. Judge Begbie would surely be able to view the case against Theo for what it was, a gross miscarriage of justice. Zach had heard that phrase on the show *Law & Order* once, and thought it sounded cool.

He folded the flyer and stuffed it into his pants pocket. Barkerville was still buzzing as it had been ever since Theo's arrest: even more so now, of course, with the news of Judge Begbie's arrival. People were very excited about attending a possible trial.

Zach gave a start when he saw Jackson walk into The Parlour with Archie in tow. It was the first time he had seen Jackson's partner in his goldmine venture, and he had to admit he was one of the meanest looking guys he had ever seen, big and brawny with a pock-marked face that carried a permanent scowl. Zach had made a solemn promise to Theo to stay clear of Jackson, but it had proved to be more difficult than expected, since Jackson had become somewhat of a celebrity in town. The man who turned over the gambler Mr. Theodore Joseph Cox to the Authorities — as it also said on the flyer now in Zach's pocket.

Zach was hurrying past The Parlour when he heard a peal of laughter from inside. Through the open door, he caught a quick glimpse of Jackson standing at the bar, a woman sidling up to him. How any woman could even look at him was beyond Zach.

When he passed the Hôtel de France, he heard Miss Reid

call to him from above. He stopped, turned around, and saw she was on the balcony, shaking a feather duster over the railing.

"Are you going to visit Theo?" she asked.

He nodded.

"Can you bring him something from me." With the feather duster, she signalled at him to come inside. "Go to the kitchen," she yelled.

Madame Pond, who was standing at the hotel counter, talking to Mr. Sinclair when Zach came through the door, turned to him. "Ah, *Chéri*, here to visit your aunt?"

Zach closed the door behind him. He never knew what Madame Pond was going to do, whether she would come over and pinch his cheek, or admonish him because his boots were dirty. Miss Pond's starched skirt rustled as she hurried over to him and pinched his cheek. "I like your new coiffure." To Zach's horror she lifted her hand and tousled his hair. Mortified, he glanced at a group of men, sitting at one of the tables, but fortunately they were far too absorbed in their card game, and didn't notice his humiliation. Madame Pond turned to Sinclair. "He looks handsome, *n'est-ce pas*, Monsieur Sinclair?"

Clearly uninterested in Zach's new hairdo, Sinclair grumbled something unintelligible in answer.

Miss Reid came rushing down the stairs from the second floor, the heels of her boots making a clickety-clack sound as they hit the wooden steps. "Madame Pond, is it all right if I give my nephew one of those meat pies Miss Combs just made, so he can bring it to Mr. Cox in the jail?" She stopped at the base of the stairs and looked eagerly at Madame Pond. "Just subtract the cost of the pie from my pay," she added quickly. "The food he gets in jail is probably dreadful."

"I don't think that would be a good idea," Zach said in alarm. He didn't exactly relish the idea of walking all the way to Richfield, lugging a pie.

"Excellent!" Madame Pond exclaimed. "Monsieur Cox will appreciate such a gesture. Pick any pie you want, Mademoiselle Reid."

Five minutes later, Zach was pushed out the door of the hotel by both Miss Reid and Madame Pond, carrying a still warm pie wrapped in cloth. At that point he wanted to wring both women's necks, but settled on unkind thoughts as he started the trek toward Richfield.

At long last, he spotted a large cluster of buildings on top of a hill. That had to be where the courthouse was located. The pie felt as if it had doubled in weight as he carried it with him on the long steady climb. When he finally made it, sweat was pouring off him and his arms ached unbearably.

The courthouse, it turned out, was a large log cabin. A tall flagpole out front was the only testament to the fact that this was an official building. He walked up the few steps to the door and tried the handle. It was locked. He stepped back, wondering where the jail might be. He crossed to the one-storey building that was located across from the courthouse, and knocked on the door.

"Enter," a brusque voice ordered.

Zach pushed the door open and stepped inside. It was no longer constable Stevenson, guarding Theo, but a man with a long dark beard and moustache, who was sitting behind an old worn desk, cleaning a gun. Behind him, in the back of the room were two jail cells. Theo, occupying one of them, looked up from the cot he sat slumped on, and greeted Zach with a weary smile.

"What's that?" The constable nodded at the pie in Zach's hand. There was a definite lisp to the man's brusque voice.

Bet he got teased as a boy, Zach thought as he closed the door behind him with his foot. "A pie," he answered, deciding to be just as surly.

The constable put the gun down and waved him over. "Bring it over here."

Zach approached him apprehensively.

The constable tapped with his finger on the desk top. "Put it there."

Zach placed the pie on the desk. It was a huge relief to finally be rid of the weight. He stretched his arms in front of him to get some feeling back in them.

The constable leaned over and flipped the checkered cloth away from the pie. He eyed it suspiciously, then looked up at Zach, an accusing look in his small unfriendly eyes. "You're not supposed to bring food to the prisoner." The word "supposed" sounded like "suppothed".

Zach had a hard time keeping a straight face. "Well, I didn't know."

"Oh, come on now, Constable Beedy, are you afraid he baked a file in it?" Theo asked with a wry smile.

"One never knowth." Beedy pulled out a drawer in the desk and rummaged through it for a while. At long last he brought out a knife, and promptly plunged its blade into the crust of the pie, working through it with short little thrusts.

"Jeez!" Zach couldn't help exclaiming as he watched this senseless assault on the pie.

Beedy looked up at him with his pinprick eyes. "What did you thay?"

"Nothing." He glanced back at Theo, who only shrugged. "Can I talk to Mr. Cox for a moment?" he asked Beedy.

Finding nothing in the pie except for meat and an assortment of cooked vegetables, and clearly disappointed by this fact, Beedy cleaned the knife blade on his pants, and dropped the knife back in the drawer. "Why do you wanna talk to him?" He pushed the pie away from him in disgust.

None of your business, was what Zach felt like saying, but of course he didn't. "I just wanna visit with him." He made his voice sound nonchalant.

"Empty your pocketh here." Beedy's index finger tapped in front of him on the marred surface of the desk.

"What! Why?" Zach was confused.

Beedy smiled slyly up at him. "You think I'll let you go over there with a knife, or file in your pocketh?"

"I don't have any of those things."

"Empty your pocketh, or leave," Beedy barked.

Zach put his hands in his pockets and placed their contents on the desk in front of Beedy: the folded flyer, a crumbled one-dollar note, a small roll of string, a couple of nails, a few small nuggets from Williams Creek that might be, but most likely were not gold, and his nail clipper.

"Whath that?" Beedy asked, fingering the last item.

"A nail clipper." Zach was taking a certain satisfaction in knowledge that the constable had no idea what he was talking about.

Beedy snatched the nail clipper from the pile and turned it over in his hand. "Looks like a potenthial weapon." With dread he saw Beedy drop the nail clipper down into the open drawer of his desk. Since his plastic comb broke, it was pretty much the only thing Zach had left from his old life, and it was a luxury he didn't want to be without.

"That nail clipper's mine," he said, angrily pointing at the drawer.

"You'll git it back when you're done talkin' to the prithoner," Beedy answered. He grabbed a toothpick from the same drawer and began excavating his teeth with it.

Zach counted to ten, something his Dad had always told him to do when he was close to losing it. Beedy's eyes didn't leave his face for a moment. "Okay," Zach finally said. "Can I talk to Mr. Cox now?"

Beedy motioned him towards the cell. "Go on."

Zach walked over to Theo, who got up from the cot, smiling apologetically. "Sorry about that," he said. "How's everyone?"

"Well, of course, Miss . . . I mean my aunt is still very upset, and worried about you. The pie is from her." He glanced back at Beedy's desk where the vandalized pie stood. "Whatever is left of it, that is." He hesitated as he turned to Theo again. "It turns out you have a few enemies here in town. I'm surprised, because I thought everyone liked you, but I think mostly it has to do with what your brother did . . . Mr. Knott told me about the cheating," he added quickly when he saw Theo's surprised look. "It's just not fair that they blame you for what he did."

There was bitterness in Theo's eyes now. "I guess some people smell blood. That it's my blood and not Enos' apparently doesn't matter to them."

"Well, it's not like you don't have a lot of supporters, but Jackson is spending a lot of time in town, and Mr. Knott told me that he's stirring the pot, as he put it."

Theo sank down on the cot again. "Billy already told me when he came to visit me at the jail in Barkerville." He folded his hands in his lap and stared in front of him. "Well, at least now I know who my true friends are," he said with a sigh. His expression had brightened when he looked up at Zach again. "I have one piece of good news. I've acquired a barrister."

"Barrister?" Zach wrapped his hands around two bars, looking at Theo. "Oh, you mean a lawyer, but they cost a lot of money, don't they?"

"Billy Barker's paying. He says he has the gold and there's no better way to spend it than drink, women, or helping a friend." Theo smiled fondly. "He's quite the character.

Anyway, the barrister's name is Mr. Fitzgerald, and he thinks they'll have a hard time convicting me on McKenna's watch alone. He calls it circumstantial evidence. Furthermore, it's Jackson's word against mine. He's going to talk to Judge Begbie as soon as he arrives here in Richfield. This case most likely will be thrown out, he says."

Zach felt like a huge burden was lifted from his shoulders. "That's great!"

"Are you two all chatted out?" Beedy asked.

There was a knock on the door. It opened before Beedy had time to respond. Miss Mulligan, dressed in a green dress with a billowing skirt, came into the room. She closed the door softly behind her with a long slender hand encased in a white glove.

Beedy had scrambled to his feet and was now standing next to his desk, face flushed, a sheepish grin showing through the beard. "Ma'am, what a pleathure."

Miss Mulligan turned to him with a self-assured smile. "Well, good-day again, Mr. Beedy. What wonderful weather out there today."

"Tho it is. Tho it is."

"So how's our good Mr. Cox doing?" she asked Beedy in a coy voice. She winked at Theo.

"Quite well, Mith Mulligan." Beedy allowed himself a smile. "Driveth me mad with all that complainin' though." His lisp had become more pronounced.

Miss Mulligan looked coquettishly at Beedy, which made

him twirl his moustache nervously between his sausage fingers. "I better set him straight, don't you think, Mr. Beedy? Let me have a word with him."

Zach turned to Theo and noticed the look of rapture in his eyes as he stared at the newcomer. "I better be going," Zach told him.

Theo didn't even hear him. His eyes were riveted on Miss Mulligan.

Zach raised his voice. "I'll see you in a couple of days, Mr. Cox, if they haven't already let you go, that is."

Theo nodded distractedly. "Looking forward to it, lad." Zach smiled at Miss Mulligan as he left the room, and was rewarded with a glorious smile in return.

It was only when he was almost back in Barkerville that he realized he had forgotten to get his nail clipper back from Constable Beedy.

Chapter 34

THE DAY JUDGE BEGBIE was scheduled to arrive in Barkerville was like the homecoming of a favourite sports hero. The town was throbbing with energy. It was like an electric current that jolted even the most sedate person into frantic action. People ran about everywhere. The raised boardwalks were filled to capacity. More than one unlucky person was pushed into the street, which was muddy and full of puddles after two days of heavy rain.

Madame Pond breezed into the kitchen where Zach sat nursing a cup of tea, compliments of Miss Combs, who for some reason had suddenly taken a liking to him. "You can come and visit me anytime, just as long as you don't bring that whelp of a brother, you have," she had told him. He didn't know what she meant by whelp, but judging from her expression it couldn't be anything charming.

"Monsieur Begbie is just about to arrive in Barkerville." Madame Pond was so excited she could hardly stand still. "You should see the crowd out there."

Miss Combs, who was busy washing a huge stack of dishes, turned and looked in annoyance at Madame Pond, her face flushed from the hot water. "The way people carry on you should think it was the second coming of Christ."

Zach pushed the cup aside and jumped up. "I have to go," he told Madame Pond as he ran past her out of the kitchen. His heart was soaring. Now the judge had finally arrived, Theo would be out of jail before the end of the day. Miss Reid had taken Zach to meet Theo's lawyer, Oliver Fitzgerald, a pedantic man with thin dark hair and sad blue eyes behind thick glasses, and he had told them that this would very likely be the scenario. The lawyer didn't think the prosecution had a leg to stand on. If Theo said he had found McKenna's watch on the ground, then no one could dispute that.

He ran out the door of the hotel, nearly colliding with Miss Reid, who was standing just outside. "The judge is on his way here," she told him excitedly.

Zach took hold of her arm. "Come on." he said to her. They pushed their way through the crowd until they balanced precariously on the very edge of the boardwalk.

A tall man standing next to them pointed excitedly down the street. "There he is," he yelled.

Zach stretched his neck and there, finally, he caught sight of the much-talked-about judge. He was followed by three other men, also on horseback. Judge Begbie sat in his saddle, his back straight and his head held high. Now and then he waved at the cheering people crowding the boardwalks. Zach thought he looked quite dignified with his long grey goatee and dark moustache. He sort of reminded him of his own Uncle Grant, who was a CIBC banker. "You don't screw with your Uncle Grant," Zach's father had once told him. He had a feeling you didn't screw with Judge Begbie either.

"Hopefully, Mr. Fitzgerald will be able to speak to the judge right away," Zach shouted to Miss Reid over the din of voices.

"Maybe Theo will be out of jail before the day is over." There was pure joy in her voice.

"He will," Zach said firmly, fully believing it.

Miss Reid put a hand on his shoulder and squeezed lightly before she let go. "I'll see you at the hotel at dinner time then."

Zach watched her fight her way through the crowd back to the hotel. When she had disappeared from view, he turned his attention to what was happening on the street again. His breath caught in his throat when he found Jackson staring at him from the opposite boardwalk. He forced himself to meet his gaze. A shrewd smile crossed Jackson's narrow lips, before he turned around and disappeared in the throng of people, leaving Zach with a nagging feeling in the pit of his stomach.

Chapter 35

⌒⌒

"WHY HAVEN'T THEY released Mr. Cox yet?" Miss Reid asked Fitzgerald. "You said, even assured us, that the case against him would be thrown out by Judge Begbie." She wrung her hands as she anxiously waited for the barrister to respond. He was standing at the only window in the crammed office, looking out at the people hustling by on the boardwalk.

At long last, Fitzgerald turned around and faced her and Zach, who were each occupying the two leather chairs reserved for visitors in the room. His eyes behind the spectacles were so full of misery, Zach couldn't even be mad at him, though he wanted to. He badly needed to vent his anger and disappointment at someone.

"I know I did, Ma'am," the barrister said. "Believe me, I wouldn't have given you such hope if it wasn't for the fact that I was quite certain the judge would dismiss the case." He walked over to his desk, pulled out his chair and sank down on the seat. With a deep sigh, he looked at Miss Reid across the marred desktop. "Judge Begbie has talked to two of Dan McKenna's friends in Quesnellemouth and they insist that Mr. McKenna would never have been so careless as to lose his watch. It was his pride and joy, and apparently he guarded it scrupulously, and Mr. Jackson now says he heard Mr. Theo Cox and Dan McKenna have quite the row before he went to sleep."

This piece of news took Zach by surprise. "I didn't hear them argue." His gaze sought Miss Reid. "Did you?"

She shook her head. "Jackson's obviously lying to make Theo look bad."

Fitzgerald leaned forward. Resting his elbows on the desk, he steepled his fingers and regarded Miss Reid and Zach solemnly. "Mr. Jackson claims that everyone else was asleep when said quarrel took place."

"How convenient!" Despair was beginning to intermingle with Zach's anger.

Miss Reid looked closely at the lawyer. "That too must be circumstantial evidence, since Jackson was the only person who supposedly heard the quarrel." She sat back in the chair, and stared out the window. "This is a nightmare," she said after a while. Turning her attention to the barrister again,

Miss Reid noticed how he was fidgeting in his seat. "Mr. Fitzgerald, is there something else you haven't told us?"

The barrister hesitated for a moment before he answered. "It appears the prosecution has more than that on Mr. Cox. When a constable searched the cabin where Mr. Cox stays, he came across a small pouch containing gold nuggets hidden underneath the mattress of his bed. Mr. Jackson also claims that Mr. McKenna was boasting about his gold find that night at camp."

Zach jumped up from the chair. Bending over the desk, he slapped his palm down hard in front of the lawyer, giving him a start. "That's a lie for sure. Mr. McKenna said nothing of the kind."

Miss Reid put a hand on his arm. "Calm down, Zachary."

He turned to her. "Mr. McKenna never said anything about bringing gold with him, you know that", he shouted. "At least not when we were there . . ." his voice trailed as he fell back into his chair. He viewed Fitzgerald with apprehension. "Don't tell me, Jackson claims McKenna also said this when we had already gone to sleep."

The barrister gave him a cheerless smile.

"So what to do now?" Miss Reid said more to herself than anyone else.

Zach's mind was working full speed, trying to find a solution. "Why don't we get hold of Enos." He looked excitedly at Miss Reid. "Maybe he can help?"

She gave him a wry smile. "How are we supposed to do

that? Call him on my cellphone perhaps?"

"No, of course not," Zach snapped. "No need to be sarcastic. It was just an idea."

Fitzgerald darted a glance at first Zach then Miss Reid. "Cellphone?" he asked. "Who's Enos?" he inquired, instead, when neither of them responded to his question.

Miss Reid pulled a handkerchief out from behind her dress sleeve and wiped perspiration from her brow. It was sweltering hot in the small office. "He's the brother of Mr. Cox." She tucked the handkerchief back behind the sleeve. "Enos is his name, and he drives freight wagons between Fort Yale and Barkerville. He was also present when Mr. McKenna showed up in our camp."

"Do any of you have an idea where he is now?" Fitzgerald asked.

Miss Reid bit her lip and looked at Zach, who answered for them. "He's bringing more goods up to Barkerville this summer, but I don't know when he'll be arriving. Most likely, he's somewhere between here and Fort Yale."

Twiddling his thumbs in his lap, Fitzgerald sat for a while considering this new information. "I could get in contact with the Chief Constable," he finally said looking at Miss Reid. "Maybe he can spare a man to travel the Cariboo Road to try to get hold of Enos, but I highly doubt he would even make it here in time."

Zach exchanged a quick worried glance with Miss Reid. "What do you mean make it in time?" he asked the barrister. "In time for what?"

"I'm afraid there'll be a trial." Looking uncomfortable, Fitzgerald cleared his voice before he spoke again. "I was informed about it this morning."

Miss Reid stared at him in disbelief. "But I thought . . ." she swallowed hard.

"So did I," Fitzgerald said. "I never dreamed this case would proceed to trial, but that's what Judge Begbie has decided. Since he has another trial in Quesnellemouth at the end of the month, he has set a date for Mr. Cox's trial to commence on . . ." he paused before he continued, "on Monday."

"This Monday?" Miss Reid gasped.

"But that's in five days." Zach shook his head at the barrister. "How's that going to happen? I mean, I've seen enough episodes of *Law & Order* to know it takes time to interview witnesses and finish briefs."

Fitzgerald gave him a puzzled expression. "*Law & Order?*"

Zach realized his blunder, and quickly asked the barrister: "It takes time to prepare a case, which you don't have?"

"Of course, I wish I had more time, but I'll certain be able to prepare a good defence for Mr. Cox in the time allotted." His confidence made Zach feel a little better.

Miss Reid, who had sat quietly during the exchange, trying to process this new development, gave Fitzgerald a determined look. "I want to be one of your witnesses," she said. "I can speak to Mr. Cox's good character, and I can let Judge Begbie know that I certainly didn't hear this alleged fight between Mr. McKenna and Mr. Cox, and I would have." She gave the barrister a look that allowed for no objection. "You see, I'm a very light sleeper. And by the way, those gold nuggets found under his mattress? Mr. Cox could have won them in a card game, or Jackson might even have placed them there."

"Miss Reid, if you're going on the witness stand," Fitzgerald said, "I want you to answer only the questions directed at you." His expression became stern. "With that I mean, no conjecture, because people will then view you as unreliable and overwrought. I've seen that happen far too often."

Miss Reid leaned forward in her seat and tapped her finger on the desk. "Well, I happen to think that people should know what a conniving, despicable creature Mr. Jackson really is."

"Miss Reid, that's what you leave me to prove." His voice was rising. "Vilifying someone almost never works, but punching holes in Mr. Jackson's testimony will." He squared his shoulders. "I'm a very experienced barrister."

Grudgingly, she nodded and got up from her chair. "I'm putting my faith in you, Mr. Fitzgerald," she said as she extended a hand to him. "You know where to find me if you need me. Keep me posted on any new developments."

Fitzgerald scrambled to his feet and stared at her hand, maybe wondering if he should kiss it. He settled on what Miss Reid later described as a rather limp handshake.

Chapter 36

ZACH LOOKED AROUND the packed courtroom. The spectators, who had been lucky enough to make it inside, were now filling the seats. They were talking animatedly among each other, and would now and then stretch their necks to catch a glimpse of Theo. He sat in the prisoner's box, pale and stoic, his hands clasping the wooden railing in front of him. When Zach had visited him in jail a couple of days ago, Theo had still been in a state of shock about the upcoming trial.

"I never imagined it would come to this," he had admitted.

"Me and you both," Zach had answered. He explained that when Fitzgerald had pressed Judge Begbie about the need for a trial, he had been told by the judge that there were enough weeds in the garden to warrant calling in the gardener.

"Damnation! Git out. There's no more space to be had in here, I told you." The constable guarding the door was trying to push a throng of people back out into the humid warm summer morning.

"Well, there's still space," a portly man yelled while pushing against the constable's big bulk, his pockmarked face flushed from anger. "People only have to squeeze together more."

They were all startled by a loud thud. Zach spun around in his seat, and saw that Matthew Baillie Begbie had come through a back door and was now standing behind the bench. A tall stack of books he had just dumped on top teetered for a moment before it fell over, scattering books all over the desk. "Out," he roared, pointing a finger at the people in the doorway as if he was a doomsday prophet. First, there was a stunned silence, then a scurry of activity as people bumped into each other to escape his wrath. The constable closed the door firmly after them, and placed himself against it, arms folded over his chest.

Grumbling something that sounded very much like swearing, Judge Begbie gathered his books into two piles, which he pushed to a corner of the bench. He was formally dressed in judge's robes and with a grey wig on his head.

"What the heck is that thing on his head?" Kyle whispered. He was sitting between Zach and Miss Reid.

"It's a wig," Miss Reid informed him. "British judges still wear those. It's a symbol of their office."

Kyle didn't seem too impressed. "It looks like a dead sheep."

Zach leaned close to Kyle. "Better keep it down," he said. "You're only going to get us into trouble with comments like that."

With his piercing blue eyes, Judge Begbie surveyed the people in the courtroom. It was so quiet that only the buzzing of flies could be heard. He cleared his throat. "I tolerate no rowdiness or speaking out of turn from any spectators who have been so blessed as to secure space in my courtroom. Any transgression will result in an immediate expulsion." He exuded the confidence of someone who knew he deserved respect from everyone in the room, whether they liked him or not. "Constable Franklin, standing there at the door, will be more than happy to facilitate your hasty departure."

Constable Franklin smiled grimly at the faces turning to him.

The judge's gaze moved to the barristers standing at the two desks positioned between the bench and the spectators behind. "I would like to welcome counsel for the prosecution, Mr. Riddell, and counsel for the defence, Mr. Fitzgerald, to my court with a wish for a speedy trial. I have an important court date in Quesnellemouth in a couple of weeks." It sounded like the order it was intended to be.

"Good morning, Your Honour," both barristers said in unison. Mr. Riddell was a short, skinny man with thin greying hair and a nervous tic which frequently made his head jerk.

Judge Begbie sat down in his high-backed chair, opened a drawer and brought out a gavel, which he placed on top of the bench within easy reach. He gave Fitzgerald a penetrating look. "Yesterday the accused, Mr. Theodore Joseph Cox, pleaded not guilty to the charge brought against him. Is that still his plea?"

Fitzgerald nodded with a sombre expression on his face. "Yes, Your Honour."

Zach looked over at Theo. He seemed lost in thought as if everything going on around him had nothing to do with him. He wished he had been there yesterday afternoon to give moral support for Theo when he had entered his plea, but Johnny Knott had needed both him and Kyle to finish some doors in Barkerville's most recent saloon addition. Zach smiled encouragingly at Theo when the latter looked up and caught sight of him. He didn't smile back.

Judge Begbie surveyed the jurors, who were seated in the jury box next to the witness stand.

"I see you have only eleven jurors." He turned his attention to the barristers. "Why is that?"

"Well, Mr. Riddell rejected the two alternates." Mr. Fitzgerald directed a pointed look at Mr. Riddell, who sat fidgeting in his seat.

"Well, you refused our twelfth juror," Riddell said.

Fitzgerald sighed. "With good reason. It's a well-known fact around here that Mr. Montgomery is half deaf." He turned his attention to the judge. "It's only because I wouldn't accept Mr. Montgomery as a juror that Mr. Riddell rejected the two alternates."

Riddell moved from behind his desk and approached Fitzgerald. "That's outrageous. I had valid reasons to dismiss the alternates."

"Gentlemen, kindly shut up," Judge Begbie shouted. He picked up his gavel and pointed it at Riddell. "Go back behind your desk, counsel." Blushing, Riddell did as he was told. With a disgusted look on his face, Judge Begbie reclined in his chair. "Jesus, almighty God! You two sound like grand-mothers bickering over who's better at knitting." He put the gavel down. "So we have no alternates?" the judge asked Fitz-gerald, who shook his head.

The judge's gaze wandered over the courtroom. He pointed at a spectator in one of the front rows. "You, Sir, stand up."

The man he indicated scrambled to his feet. He was a middle-aged man with watery eyes behind thick glasses.

"Me?"

The judge gave an impatient nod. "I pointed at you, didn't I? What's your name?"

"George Milton, Sir, Judge, Your Honour." The man smiled nervously at the people seated around him.

"Residence?" Judge Begbie barked.

"Sir, Your Honour, I . . . I'm not sure," Milton stammered.

"Blood and ashes, Mr. Milton, where do you live?"

Zach couldn't believe the way Judge Begbie spoke in court. Weren't there any rules concerning courtroom decorum?

"I . . . I live in Barkerville, Sir, Your Honour." Milton's face was beet-red and big droplets of perspiration had appeared on his high forehead. "I'm . . . I'm a dentist." He twirled his hat nervously in his hands. "Judge, Sir."

"Any criminal record, Mr. Milton?"

The dentist looked shocked by this suggestion. "No, Sir, Your Honour, of course not. I'm a law-abiding man."

"Are any of the people involved in this case either a relative or a friend?" Judge Begbie pulled a pocket watch out from behind his robes, and cast a quick glance at it, before he put it down next to the books.

He looked up in time to see Milton shake his head fervently. "No, Your Honour, Sir."

The judge got up from the chair, leaned over the desk and pulled a thick book from the middle of one of the stacks without toppling the rest. "Come up here, Mr. Milton," he ordered, holding up the book.

The dentist gave the middle-aged, frumpy-looking woman sitting next to him a disconcerted look. She put a hand on his arm and nodded toward the judge, forming the word, go, with her narrow lips. Hand shaking, Milton gave her his hat to hold and crawled over legs, apologizing profusely to the spectators as he did so. Fearfully, he approached the judge who had come around the bench, and now stood in front of it waiting, the thick book resting on his hand.

"Mr. Milton, put your left hand on this Bible and raise your right." Judge Begbie said as the dentist came to a stop in front of him.

The dentist glanced back at the woman from before. She nodded again and he did as Judge Begbie had requested.

"Now repeat after me," the judge told him.

"Sir, I mean Your Honour, I don't think . . ." Milton gave the judge a miserable look.

"What?" Judge Begbie yelled, shaking his head in frustration. "Hell's bells, man, you pull rotten teeth out of people's mouths all day. What can be so hard about doing what I tell you to do?"

The dentist lips' began quivering, and for one cringe-worthy moment Zach thought he would start bawling.

The judge's look softened. "Listen Mr. Milton, pull yourself together and repeat after me: "I, state your full name . . .""

"I, state your full name," Milton said in a thin voice.

The judge had a sharp intake of air. "No, you fool, state your own name."

When Kyle sputtered with laughter next to him, Zach gave him a warning poke with his elbow. Even Kyle would be no match for Judge Begbie. Fortunately, the judge was too busy with the dentist to notice him.

Milton's voice trembled when he spoke again. "I, George Emmanuel Milton."

Judge Begbie nodded with satisfaction, ". . . do solemnly swear to listen to all the testimony of this court . . ."

The dentist repeated the words, handling them in his mouth as if they were hot potatoes.

". . . without bias, weigh the facts as they are presented and from those facts render a just verdict."

Milton repeated the words.

Judge Begbie smiled broadly. "My good man, you've now become the twelfth juror in this trial. You may take your seat with the others."

Milton quickly tried to collect himself. "But that's what I was trying to tell you, Sir, Your Honour. I . . . I can't possibly be a juror, since I've patients this afternoon."

The judge's eyes narrowed. "Are you challenging the order of this court?"

"No, he be not," the woman from before had gotten up from her seat. "George, you heard the judge."

Milton pulled out a handkerchief from his jacket pocket and wiped his brow with a trembling hand. "Mildred, I can't possibly . . ." he pleaded.

Mildred eyes blazed at him. "Yes, of course, you can."

The dentist swallowed hard and looked at the judge again. "It'll be an honour, Your Honour."

Chapter 37

JUDGE BEGBIE LOOKED at Riddell. "Are you ready to proceed, Counsel?"

"I am indeed, Your Honour." Riddell stood up and came around his desk. Clutching a paper with densely scribbled notes in his hand, he walked with a purposeful stride to the jury, all twelve of them men. The dentist still looked rather confused. Riddell began pacing in front of the jury box, his brow furrowed in concentration.

"I'm getting dizzy," Judge Begbie announced from the bench.

The barrister's head jerked in the judge's direction. "Oh, sorry, Your Honour. I was just collecting my thoughts."

Judge Begbie raised an eyebrow at him. "Collect them a little faster, would you please? We don't have all day."

Zach heard Kyle chuckle next to him. "That judge is freaking awesome," he whispered to Zach.

Miss Reid gave him sharp glance. "Keep it down, Kyle."

Riddell now stood facing the jurors. He glanced quickly at the paper in his hand. "On June second of this year," he began, "a miner named Matthew Phillips, was setting up camp north of Clinton." He began rolling so vigorously on his feet that he set his whole skinny body in motion. Zach was getting seasick from just watching him. "As he was gathering kindling for his fire," the barrister continued, "he came upon a grisly sight." He stopped his rocking motion and walked up to Milton, leaning in close. "A sight that haunts him to this very day giving him debilitating nightmares."

The dentist gulped, his eyes riveted to the barrister's face.

"Mr. Riddell!" Judge Begbie yelled at the barrister, looking at him as if he was a wayward child. "This is not a Shakespearian tragedy, for chrissake. Stick to the facts."

Riddell, his impetus broken, was momentarily thrown off balance, but he quickly pulled himself together again. With a determined look in his eyes, he straightened his shoulders and bravely met the judge's piercing look. "Your Honour, I was merely attempting to set the scene, so the jury would understand . . ." he began, but was interrupted by Judge Begbie. "I appreciate that fact, but set it with fewer adjectives."

"Certainly, Your Honour." Riddell turned to the jurors

again. "Matthew Phillips saw a lifeless hand, sticking up through the ground, fingers half-eaten by scavenging animals, exposing the white of the bone."

A collective gasp rose from the people in the courtroom.

This time the judge grabbed his gavel and made vigorous use of it. "Mr. Riddell!"

The barrister gave the judge a quick apologetic smile. "Sorry, Your Honour, but the description Matthew Phillips gave was rather gruesome. I only gave an abbreviated account."

"In that case, I don't think I would much like to hear the original version," Judge Begbie said with a wry smile. He nodded at the barrister. "Please do continue, Mr. Riddell."

The barrister turned his attention to the jurors again. "Matthew Phillips promptly alerted the law in the next town." He glanced at the notes in his hand again. "Constable Whiteford was dispatched to investigate," he said, lowering the paper. "He uncovered the victim from a shallow grave, a man in his mid-to-late-thirties, a miner from the look of his clothes." He made a dramatic pause. "Constable Whiteford quickly ascertained that the miner had most likely died from trauma to his head caused by some type of sharp edged implement."

Zach cast a glance at the prison box where Theo sat with his hands folded in his lap, a grim expression on his face.

"From a mining certificate found in the pocket of the deceased," Riddell continued, "Constable Whiteford established that said miner's name was Dan Philip McKenna." The barrister strolled to the other end of the jury box and now fixed a corpulent middle-aged man with his gaze. "The constable investigated the perimeter of the crime scene and found a linen travel bag torn apart by wild animals. It still contained some clothes and essentials such as a compass, razor and flint." Riddell paused again as he moved to the next juror in line.

"Constable Whiteford concluded the bag most likely belonged to the deceased. The body was taken to Quesnellemouth where Doctor James Crawford confirmed Constable Whiteford's findings that Dan McKenna did indeed die from a cracked skull." He again glanced down at the paper he was holding in his hand. "He also suffered a broken nose, several broken facial bones and deep cuts that caused significant blood loss."

This information produced another gasp from the courtroom, a fact that brought a pleased smile to the barrister's lips. He was obviously milking his talent for theatrics for all it was worth. "Asking around in Quesnellemouth," he continued, "Constable Whiteford located two of Dan McKenna's friends." He glanced at his notes again. "Mr. George Boyd and Mr. Nick Browne."

It was getting very hot and stuffy in the court room, and a pesky fly kept buzzing around Zach's head. For the umpteenth time he swatted it away, but with no luck. The fly kept coming after him.

Riddell cleared his throat. "George Boyd and Nick Browne told Constable Whiteford that Dan McKenna was going to Victoria to deposit gold in a bank there, so he could send money home to his family in England. They were apparently going to buy a farm there."

It gave Zach a certain personal satisfaction to know that he had been right in his assumption that McKenna was travelling with gold, and a lot of it too, it sounded like, since it was meant to buy a property.

"Upon hearing that Mr. McKenna had met with foul play," Riddell continued, "Nick Browne straight away asked about two saddlebags containing Mr. McKenna's gold. He had warned his friend about travelling to Victoria alone, carrying it, but Mr. McKenna didn't trust the banks in Barkerville, so there was no dissuading him." The barrister walked down the line of jurors, looking at them in turn as he continued speaking. "The conclusion Constable Whiteford finally came to was that Mr. Dan McKenna was brutally murdered out of greed and an utter disregard for precious human life."

Judge Begbie's gavel hit the tabletop again. "Mr. Riddell!"

The barrister turned his head to the judge with a self-satisfied smirk touching his lips. "All I'm trying to do is to establish the callous nature . . ."

"We can draw our own conclusions, Counsel." The Judge's gaze was darkening.

"Certainly, Your Honour," Riddell agreed hurriedly.

Zach sat wondering why Fitzgerald wasn't objecting to

some of the things Riddell had said. Lawyers did that all the time on TV shows, or were they not allowed to during opening statements? He couldn't remember. Zach glanced over at Fitzgerald, who sat with hands folded on top of his table, a scowl on his face.

Riddell turned his attention to the jurors again. "Nick Browne also asked if Constable Whiteford had found a pocket watch at the crime scene that bore the initials 'W.M.', and which had belonged to Mr. McKenna's father. Nick Browne, very kindly I may add, wanted to send the watch to Mr. McKenna's family in England." He paused as his gaze wandered over the jurors' faces. "Constable Whiteford had to disappoint Nick Browne on that point. No pocket watch had been found in the vicinity."

Riddell took a deep breath before continuing. "Making inquiries on his way, Constable Whiteford continued on to Barkerville where Mr. McKenna had spent the last year or so mining. When he carried on his investigation in Barkerville itself, he was approached by a miner, Mr. Julius Jackson."

Someone sitting in a back row of the courtroom sniggered at the mention of the name. The offender, an older bald man dressed in a suit much too small for his corpulent frame, drew an instant reprimanding look from both the judge and Riddell. His beefy face turned red as he pulled it down into his shirt collar, resting his chin on his chest, while watching the judge apprehensively.

"Mr. Jackson had heard about the investigation into Dan

McKenna's murder through a friend," Riddell went on. "He told the constable that one Theodore Cox, a notorious gambler, was in the possession of Mr. McKenna's watch." Riddell cast a hasty glance at Judge Begbie probably expecting another rebuke, but the judge had ink and a feather pen out, and was busy writing in a leather-bound notebook.

Riddell hastily continued his account. "Mr. Jackson told Constable Whiteford that when he, the accused, and the brother of the accused, Enos Cox, had driven freight from Fort Yale to Barkerville, Dan McKenna had stopped at their camp on his way to Victoria. Mr. McKenna decided to stay with the group overnight." He again walked down the row of jurors. "Upon awakening at daybreak, Mr. Jackson was surprised to discover that Mr. McKenna had already left camp." Riddell paused.

Miss Reid leaned towards Kyle and Zach. "The jury is completely under his spell," she whispered. "Just look at them." She was right. The jurors were hanging onto Riddell's every word. Zach would never have imagined that this nervous, unassuming man could be such a powerful speaker. He cast a glance at Fitzgerald again and found him busy pulling at the sleeves of his jacket, his expression one of determination. I sure hope you're as good as this guy, Mr. hotshot Barkerville defence attorney, Zach thought glumly.

"Mr. Julius Jackson found it odd, yes, very odd indeed, that Dan McKenna would take off before daybreak," Riddell carried on, "especially," the barrister held up his index finger for emphasis, "especially because he had imbibed heavily the evening before. Later that same morning, Theodore Cox showed a watch to Julius Jackson, which Mr. Jackson recognized as belonging to Dan McKenna. Mr. Cox stated to him that he had found it lying on the ground, an assertion, which Mr. Jackson found highly suspicious. Mr. Cox then made a show of riding out searching for Dan McKenna to give the watch back to him, but of course, he didn't find him. We now know why."

Judge Begbie put the pen down, pushed the notebook aside, and sat back in his chair, an incensed look on his face. "Mr. Riddell!" he roared.

The barrister tried hard to look unfazed by the judge's wrath, but he wasn't able to suppress his nervous tick. "Well, we now know that Mr. McKenna was already dead." His head jerked. "And so did Mr. Cox."

"Mr. Riddell, don't you dare embellish your opening statement with your own musings and opinions." Judge Begbie looked sternly at the jury. "You are to disregard Mr. Riddell's last inflammatory comments."

"Go on," Judge Begbie told the barrister. "Know that I'm watching you closely."

Riddell, his cheeks burning, cleared his throat. "As already mentioned, Mr. Jackson found it suspicious that Mr. McKenna's watch had been found so carelessly abandoned, because Dan McKenna had told him how dear the watch was to him, and that he guarded it with his life. Those were his exact words: guarded it with his life."

"Let Mr. Jackson tell what Mr. McKenna's exact words were when he is on the witness stand." Judge Begbie shook his head at Riddell, while Fitzgerald quickly covered a smile with his hand.

Riddell cleared his throat. "Instead of turning the watch over to the local constabulary, Mr. Cox decided to keep it, his contention being that he would give it back to Mr. McKenna when the miner returned to Barkerville." Riddell raised his eyebrows in disdain, a gesture Judge Begbie didn't catch.

Zach's hands clenched into fists. The barrister was painting a picture of Theo as a scheming, heartless individual. He looked toward the prisoner box again, wondering what might be going through Theo's mind right now as he sat there, eyes downcast. Feeling Zach's gaze upon him, Theo lifted his head and gave him a reassuring smile, but there was an uncertainty in his gaze, which didn't go unnoticed by Zach.

At that point, the thought that Theo might be convicted crossed Zach's mind, but he promptly pushed it aside again. He looked at Fitzgerald, who sat fidgeting in his seat, his expression changing along with Riddell's statements, from disbelief to anger and frustration, and back again. The sight encouraged Zach and he began relaxing, turning his attention to Riddell again, who was presently describing a quarrel Jackson had heard between Theo and McKenna.

"Oh, he's such a despicable liar," Miss Reid muttered through clenched teeth.

"Quiet," Judge Begbie yelled in her direction. Miss Reid blushed crimson.

Riddell, who was beginning to sound hoarse, went to his desk and drank some water. Hands clasped behind his back, he walked back to the jurors. "Constable Whiteford together with another constable went to seek out Mr. Cox, and not surprisingly found him in a place of ill repute."

The sound of the gavel reverberated through the room. "You're now in contempt, Mr. Riddell. Twenty dollars payable by tomorrow morning," Judge Begbie yelled. "I warned you against using inflammatory language against the accused."

The strong sunlight coming through a window glinted in Riddell's eyeglasses. "Sorry, Your Honour." He straightened his shoulders and began pacing in front of jurors again. Zach thought he resembled a striding peacock.

"On Mr. Cox's person was found the watch described by Nick Browne and Mr. Jackson," Riddell continued. "On the back were the initials 'W. M.', William McKenna, Dan Mc-Kenna's father. The chain was broken. The rest of the chain was found still attached to the victim's vest. Did this chain break in the struggle between Mr. McKenna and his assail-ant? Possibly."

Riddell stopped his pacing and faced the jurors. "As I already mentioned, it was ascertained that Mr. McKenna was carrying a great deal of gold in two leather saddlebags, both gold dust and nuggets. Constable Whiteford decided to conduct a search of the cabin where Mr. Cox was residing. Underneath the mattress of his bed, a small pouch contain-ing gold nuggets was found." The jurors were hanging on his every word now.

"The nuggets were bright, angular and of great purity just like the gold taken out of the mine worked by Mr. McKenna and his partner, Vernon Davis, also deceased." He paused again. Silence hung like an already passed death sentence in the air. All eyes, including Fitzgerald's and Judge Begbie's, moved toward the prisoner box, where Theo sat stone-faced, hands still folded in his lap.

Zach was surprised to hear that there could be a difference in the appearance and pureness of gold. He looked at Fitzgerald. Was he aware of it, Zach thought as he watched the barrister nervously fingering the papers in front of him.

Riddell marched back to his desk, bent over and retrieved a small carpet bag from underneath it. "In here," he straightened up, holding the bag in his hand, "are the clothes and other belongings found by Constable Whiteford at the crime scene. It has been identified as belonging to Mr. McKenna. His friends in Quesnellemouth, Nick Browne and George Boyd, recognized them." He allowed himself a smile. "Apparently Mr. McKenna had a penchant for red." He opened up the bag and pulled out a shirt, an undershirt, socks, pants.

Fitzgerald jumped up from his seat. "Your Honour, I have not yet had the opportunity to view this evidence."

Riddell smiled disarmingly at the judge. "Your Honour, this was only delivered to me late last night. It was brought here as fast as it was possible." He shrugged. "No one had expected this trial to take place so soon."

"This is not the way we usually do things, Mr. Riddell," Judge Begbie snapped.

Riddell made a great effort to look contrite. "I know, Your Honour. Believe me, had I been able to, I would have shared this evidence with Mr. Fitzgerald."

Judge Begbie sat back in his chair and studied Riddell with skepticism. "Is there any other evidence you just received late last night?" His voice was dripping with sarcasm.

Unabashed, Riddell smiled at the judge. "A shovel was delivered with the personal belongings, still bearing traces of blood on the shaft. Constable Dennis Leary of Quesnellemouth, who brought this evidence to me, found the shovel when he was sent back to the crime scene.

According to Dr. Crawford it's inconclusive if this is indeed the murder weapon, but it might very well be." He spoke quickly, probably afraid that the judge would interrupt him.

Zach sat up straight. The shovel in Jackson's wagon that had so suddenly disappeared had been found.

Fitzgerald's face was flushed with anger. "Your Honour, this is absolutely preposterous!" he yelled.

"Quiet!" Judge Begbie glared first at Fitzgerald then Riddell. "Is Constable Dennis Leary of Quesnellemouth, present today in court?" he asked as he looked out over the assembled courtroom watchers.

"Yes he is, Your Honour," Riddell answered eagerly.

Judge Begbie ignored him. "Constable Leary, stand up!"

A tall broad-shouldered man rose from a seat in the back row. He twirled his hat nervously in his hands as he viewed the judge uncertainly.

"Is it true, Constable Leary, what Mr. Riddell just told the court, that this evidence only passed into his hands late last night?" Judge Begbie asked.

Constable Leary nodded. "Yes, Your Honour." He kept on twirling his hat. "I would have been here sooner, if it wasn't for the rains around Cottonwood House, which made the roads treacherous and slowed me down."

Judge Begbie regarded Riddell for a moment before he spoke. "Will either Nick Browne or George Boyd be at the trial to identify Mr. McKenna's belongings?"

Riddell shook his head. "Regrettably, they're on their way to Victoria as we speak, but Constable Leary has already obtained written signed and sworn statements from both of them, identifying these items as belonging to Mr. McKenna." He placed his hand possessively on top of the clothes.

Judge Begbie turned his gaze to Fitzgerald, who was still seething. "Mr. Fitzgerald, I'm going to allow this evidence to be entered into the trial." He held up a hand to stop Fitzgerald's protest. "Neither Constable Leary nor Mr. Riddell has any control over the weather and we all know that travel conditions from Cottonwood House to Barkerville can be difficult at best. I'm satisfied that Constable Leary was trying to get the evidence up here as speedily as possible." He looked at the Constable with a frown. "Isn't that so?"

Constable Leary's Adam's apple bobbed up and down as he swallowed hard. "Yes, Your Honour."

"You can have a seat, Constable," the judge told him.

"Yes, Your Honour." Leary slumped back in his chair, relief written on his face.

"Mr. Riddell should, at the very least, have shown me the evidence this morning before the trial began," Fitzgerald fumed.

Judge Begbie turned to Riddell. "Mr. Fitzgerald does have a valid point. Why was this not done?"

Riddell looked remorseful. "I'm sorry, Your Honour. I should have. I guess I got ahead of myself." Zach didn't think he looked sorry at all.

"I'm not going to allow you to take any more liberties in this trial, Mr. Riddell," Judge Begbie warned.

The barrister nodded. "No, Your Honour."

The judge looked at Fitzgerald as he got up from his chair. "I'll give you this afternoon to view the evidence, Mr. Fitzgerald." He collected his books. "Court is in recess until tomorrow morning at eight," he said as he got out from behind the bench. "I'll be at my residence here in Richfield all afternoon if anyone needs me."

He waved Constable Leary out of his chair. "Would you please stay in the courtroom and keep an eye on the evidence while Mr. Fitzgerald views it, and when he's finished, bring it to me."

Leary nodded.

As Judge Begbie strode across the floor toward the front door, he looked at the constable guarding Theo. "Escort the prisoner back to jail."

Constable Franklin held the door open for the judge.

"Don't worry, Theo," Miss Reid said as he and the constable passed by her. "Things will sort themselves out." Zach hoped she sounded more confident to Theo than she did to him.

"See you tomorrow morning, Mr. Fitzgerald," Riddell said sweetly as he followed Theo and the constable out the door. Fitzgerald's disdainful gaze followed him.

Chapter 38

FINALLY, IT WAS ONLY Fitzgerald, Constable Leary, Zach, Miss Reid and Kyle who were left in the stuffy room.

"Are we allowed to stay while you view the evidence?" Miss Reid asked Fitzgerald as she nodded discreetly at Constable Leary, who stood guard a few paces from them.

"Well, at least that decision still rests with me," Fitzgerald answered with a bitter look. He walked over to Riddell's desk where McKenna's personal belongings and the shovel had been left for his inspection. He glanced back at them. "You can come and have a look."

Zach approached the desk apprehensively.

Leary squared his shoulders, his expression one of great self-importance. "Careful now with the evidence."

"I'm not an idiot, Constable Leary," Fitzgerald said.

Leary crossed his arms over his chest. "No need to rake me over the coals, Mr. Fitzgerald. Just doin' my job is all."

The barrister turned to him. "I know that," he said. "Sorry to take my frustration out on you, Mr. Leary." The constable acknowledged his apology with a curt nod. Fitzgerald focused his attention on McKenna's clothing that lay piled on Riddell's desk.

"Mr. McKenna certainly did have a penchant for red," he commented with a wry smile at Miss Reid, who was standing right across from him at the desk. "I honestly am not sure what evidentiary value all this has. They found the body, and they established through other means that the body was that of Mr. McKenna." He sank into deep thoughts, while distractedly fingering a button on his jacket.

"Mr. Fitzgerald, are you certain you are all right?" Miss Reid asked after a while.

He tore himself away from his reverie. "Sorry," he said. "I was doing a little wool gathering there for a moment." He removed his glasses and massaged the bridge of his nose. "As you can probably guess from today, Riddell has a love for the dramatics," he said as he replaced his glasses, peering through the thick lenses at Miss Reid. "He's clearly an experienced barrister and certainly knows well how much of an emotional impact that seeing the personal belongings of a murder victim can have on a jury."

Kyle nodded eagerly. "Yeah, the clothes was bad enough," he said. "But when Mr. Riddell showed them the shovel, man that jury looked like they're ready to hang Cox."

"Why don't you just shut up, Kyle. It's not helping," Zach said.

Kyle shrugged. "Well, I'm just saying."

Fitzgerald came around the desk and put his hand on Kyle's shoulder. "Kyle, I'm afraid, is right," he said. "At that moment the jury went from a group of people seeking justice to one that wanted revenge." He let go of Kyle. "I've seen it happen often enough before."

"Yes, but Mr. Cox is not guilty." Miss Reid fixed Fitzgerald with her stare. "And it's up to you to show them that."

With his shoulders hunched, Fitzgerald went back to his place at Riddell's desk and spread Mr. McKenna's clothes out in front of him. "If only I'd had the chance to view this evidence before Judge Begbie did," he said with a sigh, "I would have had time to prepare a decisive argument against it being entered into the trial."

He stared forlornly down at McKenna's belongings. "But it's too late now." He straightened up, grabbed the carpet bag standing next to the clothes and went through it. Finally he stuffed everything inside the bag and picked up the shovel, wrapped in a piece of cloth. He flipped the cloth aside.

Zach winced when he again saw the shovel that had been part of so many of his nightmares since McKenna's disappearance. Fitzgerald bent over it and examined the worn wooden handle. He pointed. "Those dark stains in the deepest of the crevices must be what Riddell was referring to. The rain, of course, washed away any evidence left on the blade."

Fitzgerald straightened up, and resolve replaced the discouragement in his eyes. "According to Mr. Riddell, Dr. Crawford in Quesnellemouth could not say conclusively if this was the murder weapon." He bit his lip for a moment. "And even if it was, there's absolutely no proof that Mr. Cox was the one wielding it."

Only now did Fitzgerald take notice of the fact that Constable Leary, who was still standing only a few paces from them, was listening with great interest to what was being said. "Constable Leary, these good people and I would very much appreciate a little privacy." He pointed to a bench in the far end of the room. "Why don't you go and sit over there for a while. Rest your legs."

Judging from his expression, Leary did not take kindly to being ordered around by the barrister. "Judge Begbie told me to keep an eye on the evidence."

Fitzgerald turned to him. "You can still watch it from over there." He again pointed at the bench. For a good while, they had a stare down, as Miss Reid later referred to it, and the constable was the one who finally budged. "I guess I could do that," he relented.

"It would be very much appreciated," Fitzgerald said.

The constable moved the tooth pick he had been chewing to the corner of his mouth and retreated to the seat indicated by the barrister. From this perch he kept a keen eye on them.

Fitzgerald turned his attention to Miss Reid again. "I won't lie to you, Ma'am." He spoke hurriedly, lowering his voice as he went on. "This case is more challenging than I originally thought. The evidence is mounting, but my strategy will still be to emphasize its circumstantial nature." He cast a glance towards the constable, who wasn't even hiding the fact that he was trying to listen in to what Fitzgerald was saying. From his frustrated expression, Zach could tell that he wasn't having much luck.

"As you yourself mentioned once," the barrister continued, "Mr. Jackson had an intense dislike for Mr. Cox, so that in itself would be enough for him to try to get back at him this way." He gave them a reassuring smile. "All I really have to do is sow the seeds of doubt in the jurors' minds."

Miss Reid nodded eagerly. "Sounds like a plan, and don't forget Jackson probably also planted that gold pouch underneath Mr. Cox's mattress."

"I wouldn't put it past that scumbag," Kyle said, nodding his agreement.

"And furthermore," Fitzgerald said, "where's the rest of McKenna's gold? The cabin Mr. Cox stayed in was thoroughly searched, but still they found nothing else but just that small pouch."

"So what you're telling us is that Mr. Cox will go free?" Zach searched Fitzgerald's face to see if he detected any doubt whatsoever.

The barrister's gaze was firm. "Yes, he will."

Chapter 39

"SO WHAT DO YOU THINK?" Zach asked Miss Reid a while later as they walked away from the courthouse.

She stopped and turned to him. "I have every confidence Mr. Fitzgerald will turn this whole thing around."

"You certainly had your doubts in there." He nodded toward the courthouse, where Fitzgerald was presently preparing his defence strategy for Theo. "While it's still fresh in my mind," he had told them as they left.

Miss Reid draped a light shawl around her shoulders. A brisk breeze had kicked up and it was now markedly cooler than when they had arrived for the trial that morning. "Well, for a while I was rather discouraged," she admitted, "but I'm definitely more hopeful now."

"So what now?" Kyle asked.

Everyone attending the trial had dispersed, but the excitement still lingered in the air, making it hard for Zach to relax.

"Let's go and have some lunch somewhere," Miss Reid's hand found its way through her voluminous tartan skirt, and extracted some coins. "One of our guests in the hotel, an older gentleman, gave me a very generous tip when he left."

"Hurrah." Zach gave her a lacklustre thumbs up. Fitzgerald's and Miss Reid's new-found confidence had not at all eased his worries about the trial. The prosecution had already shown how cunning they were, and they were not going to leave a stone unturned in their quest to get Theo convicted.

"Do we find a restaurant here in Richfield, or do we wait until we get back to Barkerville?" Kyle asked eagerly. Obviously, he was relishing the prospect of eating out. "I for one could really use a beer."

Miss Reid frowned at him as she straightened her skirt. "If you think I'm going to spend my hard-earned money on beer, you're sadly mistaken."

"Let's just find a place in Barkerville," Zach said. "We have to go back there anyway."

Miss Reid gave Zach a sidelong glance as the three of them walked toward the road. "Stop looking so gloomy," she told him. "It's important to stay positive, especially for Theo's sake."

"I know that," Zach said with a sigh.

Kyle, who was trudging behind them, was the one who broke the silence. "I'd pay for a beer myself, Miss E., only I don't get paid before Friday."

Miss Reid stopped and turned to him. "No Kyle."

"It would only be a loan."

"Oh, give it a rest," she snapped.

. . .

When they reached Barkerville, another blister on Zach's heel, which had begun developing on his walk to Richfield that morning, had now opened up, and was giving him great pain. He owned only one pair of socks and by now they were in tatters, so they weren't much help cushioning his feet against the hard leather of the boots. Zach eyed Miss Reid, wondering if it would be okay to ask her later to buy him a new pair of socks, since he had no more money of his own.

Even before they passed The Parlour, Zach heard Billy Barker's hallmark song:

"I'm English Bill
Never worked an' never will.
Get away girls,
Or I'll tousle your curls."

Miss Reid wrinkled her nose upon hearing the ditty. "Doesn't he do anything else than drink?"

"Well, at least he gets to drink," Kyle grumbled as they trudged past the saloon.

Zach slowed down. "Wait!" he told Miss Reid and Kyle. They turned to him with puzzled looks on their faces. "I think I'm going to have a word with Billy Barker," he said. "You two just go ahead. I'll join you later."

"We haven't even decided where to go," Miss Reid protested.

"Just go to the Wake Up Jake." Zach pointed down the street. "We'll meet there in a moment, okay?"

Without waiting for the others' consent, he turned and headed to the saloon.

Inside the muted light of the Parlour, peels of laughter drew Zach's attention to the far corner of the room, where he spotted Barker sitting at a small table next to a woman with the reddest hair he had ever seen.

Zach passed by the only other people in the saloon, a group of four men so inebriated they had to hold onto each other to stand upright. Zach stopped in front of Barker, who was leaning his head close to the woman, saying something to her that made her laugh out loud.

"Could I talk to you for a moment?" Zach asked.

Barker's boozy eyes met Zach's. "Oh it's you, lad." His voice turned serious. "How . . . how's the trial gittin' on? Would have gone meself, you see, but I got otherwise engaged." He smiled at the woman, who sat glaring at Zach. She was obviously not too happy about the interruption.

"Can we talk in private, Mr. Barker?" Zach asked.

"Certainly." Barker winked at the woman. "Be a good girl now and git yourself a dram on me." He patted her behind as she reluctantly got up from her chair. "Tell Floyd over there to put it on the tab." His head bobbed in the direction of the bar, where a tall skinny guy had appeared and was busy rearranging bottles on the shelves.

Shooting Zach another cross look from behind her untamed red tresses, the woman sauntered up to the bar counter.

Zach sat down across from Barker at the table. Since the woman kept watching them keenly from the bar, he lowered his voice. It was more instinctive than anything, since there wasn't much of a chance she might overhear what was being said. "To be honest with you, Mr. Barker, the trial has hit a few snags."

Holding his hand behind his ear, Barker leaned forward. "I've trouble hearin' you."

Zach got up from behind the table. "Could we maybe go outside and talk?" he asked. "It's noisy in here." He nodded at the four men who were getting increasingly louder.

"Outside? Well, certainly we can." Barker staggered to his feet, and for a moment had to hold onto the chair's backrest for support.

"Where you off to, Billy?" The woman at the bar whined as they passed by her.

Barker's eyes swam towards her. "Back in a moment, my

sweet." A young woman standing in the doorway squealed when Barker, squeezing by her, pinched her in the rear.

"Billy!" She swatted at him with her hand, but didn't seem too unhappy.

"Drinks on me," Barker yelled at Floyd. Cheers followed him outside. Zach was beginning to wonder if it was a mistake to have a serious discussion with Barker right now, considering how drunk he was.

Out on the boardwalk, Barker stopped and turned to Zach. "So . . . so what's it you told me in there, lad?" He nodded towards the open door into the saloon.

"That the trial isn't going as smoothly as it could."

"How's that?" Barker leaned so close to Zach, his face nearly touched his. "Fitzgerald promised he would git Theo off, no problem." Barker flicked his fingers in the air. "Just as easy as that." He squinted at him. "I surely hope that petti-fogger's doin' his job."

Zach took a step back from Barker to escape his alcohol breath. "Mr. Fitzgerald's doing a good job — so far," he added cautiously. After all, he hadn't yet seen the barrister in court-room action.

Barker folded his arms over his chest and gave a wobbly nod. "Good."

"It's just that some incriminating new evidence has been brought into the case." Zach thought he was beginning to sound like a lawyer himself. "All of it circumstantial, of course, but a jury might look at it and . . ." He shrugged.

"Would sure be nice to know if the prosecution has more curve balls they're going to throw our way."

Barker scratched his beard. "Curve balls?"

Zach nodded. "Yeah, surprises." He hesitated before he continued. "You happen to know Jackson?"

Barker snorted. "Of cours' I know Jackson. Lately he's makin' a right nuisance of hisself with all his braggin' about that stinkin' gold mine of his and Archie's." Barker's attention was drawn to a group of men who, singing loudly and with arms around each other's shoulders, came lurching across the street. One of them tripped in one of the road's many potholes and fell flat on his face, a sight that made Barker chuckle in his beard.

"I want to ask you a favour." Since Zach needed Barker as an ally, he saw no reason to hide the truth from him. "I think Mr. Jackson is the one who really killed Dan McKenna to steal his gold, and now he's trying to frame Mr. Cox to draw suspicion away from himself. Mining that claim of his is a perfect ruse to pass off McKenna's gold as his own."

Barker nodded. "Jackson's a sneaky feller, no doubt."

"He might be sneaky all right, but as you already know he also likes to brag," Zach continued.

Barker jutted out his chin. "Sure does."

"And sooner or later, he's going to say something incriminating."

Barker regarded Zach with admiration. "For a young lad you sure use scads of fancy words."

Zach gave him a wry smile. "Well, I've had quite a bit of experience with a great deal of lawyer talk lately." He paused for a moment before he went on. "I would spy on Jackson myself, but he has it in for me, so it would be neither safe, nor possible for me to do so, but you . . ." He smiled at Barker, figuring a little flattery wouldn't hurt. "You get along with everyone, and that's why I was hoping that you could sort of spy on Jackson for me. You know, hang out where he is, listen to what he says."

Barker's expression was one of confusion. "What would I have to listen for?"

"Incriminating stuff," Zach said. "Also, since the prosecuting attorney likes to spring surprises on Mr. Fitzgerald, finding out if any new evidence has come to light would be helpful."

Barker thought about what Zach had said. "Well, it wouldn't be difficult," he finally admitted. "It's true enough that I git along with most everyone." A smile spread over his face. "It might even be fun."

"There's no time to lose, Mr. Barker." Zach didn't want to sound as if he was begging, but he knew it came across that way.

Barker nodded. "Jackson's at the El Dorado as we speak. I'll git over there without delay."

Zach grabbed Barker's hand and pumped it up and down. "Thank you Mr. Barker. Thank you so much."

Chapter 40

ZACH LOOKED AROUND the courtroom, which again was filled to capacity. People talking in low voices sounded like bees buzzing around a honeycomb. Outside, someone would now and again hammer on the door with their fists, hoping to gain access to the trial, but Constable Franklin was as vigilant as ever. Once in a while he would open the door a crack and yell outside, "No more people allowed in here, I said. Now git goin', the lot of you." Each time his reprimand would elicit a collective cry of disappointment.

Zach noticed that the enchanting Miss Mulligan was there today, clad in a pretty light-blue dress with a matching bonnet. She looked as if she hadn't slept much, judging from the dark circles under her eyes. He caught the look of apprehension, which passed between her and Theo, who was already seated in the prisoner box, his posture rigid, and features tense.

Yet again someone banged on the door. This time when Constable Franklin opened it, he let the person inside.

Zach gave a start when he saw who it was. He leaned towards Miss Reid who was sitting next to him. "Jackson's here," he whispered as he watched Jackson scurry to an empty seat behind Riddell. Now Zach knew why Riddell had insisted no one sit in that space.

Miss Reid craned her neck to look. "Oh, I would so love to wipe that smirk off his face," she said through clenched teeth.

"Whose face?" Kyle asked her.

"Jackson's," she answered.

The judge, who sat scribbling something in his notebook, looked up at defence counsel. "Mr. Riddell, now that Mr. Fitzgerald has had an opportunity to go over the new evidence, why don't you continue where you left off yesterday?"

"Certainly, Your Honour." The barrister got up from behind his desk, and with a spring to his step went to the jurors, the carpetbag containing McKenna's belongings in his hand.

"Isn't he all chipper?" Miss Reid whispered to Zach. Her voice, which she probably intended to sound sarcastic, came across weighed down by worry. She was nervously clenching and unclenching her hands in her lap. Evidently, her newfound confidence from yesterday had waned overnight.

Zach put his hand over hers and squeezed. "Everything will turn out fine." He couldn't help thinking how ironic it was that he was now the one reassuring her, but he figured it served no purpose to feed her fears with his own.

"This bag," Riddell informed the jurors as he pulled the carpetbag open, "contains Mr. McKenna's earthly belongings. They were found in the vicinity of his makeshift grave." He pulled out pieces of clothing and handed them to the nearest juror, together with the knife, compass and flint.

The juror, an older man with watery blue eyes, looked uncertainly at Riddell. "What am I to do with this here stuff?" he asked.

Riddell gave him a kindly smile. "Pass it on to your fellow jurors, my good man. Let them also have a look at it."

It had been a while since Zach had last seen the lawyer's irritating habit of allowing a tic to jerk his head up and down.

Now as the prosecution's case gained momentum, the barrister was becoming more and more confident, and there were fewer tics.

"Where are the two saddlebags Mr. McKenna also brought with him?" Riddell continued. "They were not found with the body. A great deal of gold was inside those bags. For many, a fortune, especially for a struggling gambler like Mr. Cox, who was living from one win to the next." He winked at the jurors. "Or rather from one loss to the next."

"Mr. Riddell," Judge Begbie's gavel hit the bench so hard that the head broke off the handle and flew across the courtroom. Riddell jumped in surprise when it landed with a heavy thud right next to him.

"Sorry, I missed," the judge commented wryly, causing some of the jurors to break out in nervous laughter. He put what was left of the gavel down on the bench, and glared at Riddell, who was still trying to recover from the shock of the near miss. "You're again in contempt of court, Mr. Riddell, which will be another twenty dollars fine," the judge said. "Moreover, I don't want to hear any further derogatory characterizations of the defendant, or for that matter of any of the witnesses."

Riddell's head jerked. "I-I could have been killed, Your Honour."

"We all run the risk of dying every day, Mr. Riddell." Judge Begbie dipped his pen in ink and wrote something in his notebook. He looked up. "Mr. Riddell I want to remind you that you've not yet paid the fine from yesterday. I expect you to pay both fines today."

Riddell nodded. "Yes, Your Honour."

The Judge put his pen down. "Mr. Riddell, please continue, without undue comments of course," he added.

Zach watched Riddell keenly. The barrister seemed nervous now, off track. He hoped it was going to affect the rest of his statement. Personally, he wished the gavel *had* knocked Riddell out to the point that he would be unable to continue in the trial. The barrister had so far done too good a job.

Riddell, however, quickly recovered from the upset, and again had the jurors' undivided attention as he finished describing how Nick Browne, McKenna's friend, had sobbed as he had identified the unlucky miner's personal effects. Riddell leaned close to one of the jurors, a small shrunken man with shrewd eyes and an enormous handlebar moustache. "Remember how I told you that a small pouch, containing gold nuggets was discovered underneath Mr. Cox's mattress and that the gold was the same shape and consistency as the gold taken out of Mr. McKenna's mine."

It was as if the barrister was only talking to that one juror, making him party to a great revelation. He even lowered his voice, giving it a conspiratorial tone. "Same shape and consistency as the gold Mr. McKenna was taking to Victoria in those two missing saddlebags."

Riddell strode to his desk and carefully unwrapped the shovel. He returned to the jurors again, holding the shovel on his outstretched hands like an offering. "Gentlemen, I have here the murder weapon," he said in a loud clear voice. The spectators in the courtroom craned their necks to have a look. The jurors leaned forward, their faces eager.

Judge Begbie fixed the lawyer with a glare. "Alleged murder weapon, Mr. Riddell!"

"Yes, yes, of course, Your Honour. Slip of the tongue." The barrister gave the judge an appeasing smile and turned to the jurors again. "Gentlemen of the jury, this shovel was found close to the crime scene." He paused. "Mr. McKenna was brutally killed, because he carried with him a fortune in gold. All evidence points to this man, sitting there in the prisoner box as being the guilty party." He pointed at Cox. "Mr. Theodore Joseph Cox, a notorious gambler, turned murderer."

Judge Begbie groaned as he fell back in his chair.

"Thank you gentlemen of the jury," Riddell added quickly and then bowed his head at Judge Begbie. "Your Honour." He turned, and carrying the shovel with him, went back to his desk where he rewrapped it in the cloth and sank down in his seat. Zach would gladly have wiped the triumphant expression off Riddell's face.

Judge Begbie fixed the barrister with a stare. "Thank you so much, Mr. Riddell, for your unbiased take on events surrounding Mr. McKenna's demise."

Riddell, looking confused, searched Judge Begbie's face, clearly waiting for him to elaborate on his statement, but when it was clear nothing more was forthcoming from the judge, Riddell cleared his throat. "You're very welcome, Your Honour," he said. His head jerked not once, but twice in quick succession.

Judge Begbie turned to Fitzgerald. "Your opening statement, Mr. Fitzgerald. I assume you've had sufficient time to view the evidence?"

All through Riddell's presentation, Fitzgerald had frequently been smoothing his thinning hair with the palm of his hand as if he thought that a single hair out of place would jinx the trial's outcome. As he now stood up, he tried to hide his nervousness by clasping his trembling hands in front of him.

"He seems awfully jittery to me," Miss Reid whispered·to Zach, who nodded.

"You may begin, Mr. Fitzgerald," Judge Begbie said.

The barrister cleared his throat. "Thank you, Your Honour." He walked up to the jurors. "Gentlemen of the jury. You see here," he turned and pointed at Theo, "a man accused of a crime he didn't commit, an innocent man." The words hung suspended in the warm stuffy room. "Yes, but what about all that evidence, you ask," Fitzgerald continued. "All that evidence Mr. Riddell in a rather ostentatious fashion kept piling up in front of you?"

"Mr. Fitzgerald!" Judge Begbie warned. "Don't you start down that path too. Stick to the facts."

"Of course, Your Honour." Fitzgerald seemed to have overcome his nervousness now as he again turned to the jurors. "Circumstantial," he yelled, startling every one of them. Mr. Milton even jumped in his seat. The barrister studied the jurors' disconcerted faces, one by one. "Yes, gentlemen, every single piece of evidence so carefully presented by Mr. Riddell is just that. Circumstantial." With a skeptical expression, he shook his head as if by that single gesture he could dismiss all Riddell's reasonings as pure speculation. "True enough, the pocket watch that was found on Mr. Cox's person at the time of his arrest belonged to Mr. McKenna, but there was certainly no foul play involved." He took a moment before he continued. "Mr. Cox had simply found the watch lying on the ground the day Mr. McKenna disappeared, and had then carried it on his person so he could give it back to him, when Dan McKenna returned to Barkerville as he had indicated the night before he would." Fitzgerald nodded in the direction of Theo, who was sitting in the prisoner box, watching the barrister keenly. "Mr. Cox even spent the better part of that day, searching for Mr. McKenna, because he knew how dear the watch was to him." Fitzgerald turned his attention to the jurors again. "The only thing, which Mr. Cox can be accused of, is the fact that he's imbued with a sense of honour and duty."

"Mr. Fitzgerald." Judge Begbie crossed his arms over his chest. "Stop postulating."

The barrister shrugged at the judge. "I just want people to understand that Mr. Cox is a gentleman in every sense of the word."

"Which you've now done ad nauseam." Judge Begbie waved impatiently at the barrister. "Continue," he said. "Without undue commentary, of course," he quickly added.

Fitzgerald cleared his throat as he faced the jurors again. "Nick Browne, Dan McKenna's friend, told Constable Whiteford that Mr. McKenna had carried a great deal of gold with him in two saddlebags. It's alleged that some of this gold was found in a small pouch underneath Mr. Cox's mattress."

"Not alleged, Mr. Fitzgerald!" Judge Begbie interrupted, "Constable Whiteford will later testify to the discovery of said gold and the conclusions drawn from this. Tread ever so lightly."

"Your Honour," Mr. Fitzgerald said, bravely meeting the judge's glare. "I only want to establish that the prosecution is basing this hypothesis on the fact that the gold in the pouch is of a similar appearance to that taken out of Mr. McKenna's mine." He shrugged at the judge. "Similar, your Honour, is an inconclusive term, and clearly used by Mr. Riddell, because he doesn't know for a fact if the gold is, or isn't from Mr. McKenna's mine."

"I'll grant you that, Mr. Fitzgerald," Judge Begbie allowed grudgingly.

Mr. Fitzgerald made no effort to hide his triumphant smile as he turned from the judge and, hands clasped behind his back, walked to the other end of the jury box where he stopped in front of the dentist. "Don't tell me that other mines throughout this vast area, all of the Cariboo district couldn't produce gold of similar shape and consistency as the gold from McKenna's mine." He emphasized the word *similar*.

Eagerly, Milton nodded his agreement.

Wedging his thumbs in the armholes of his waistcoat, Fitzgerald strode away from the dentist and again stopped, this time in front of the juror with the impressive handle-bar moustache. "According to Mr. Wilson, who owns the cabin, where Mr. Cox is staying, the door was never locked." He paused. "Anyone, absolutely anyone, could have walked into that cabin and placed the pouch containing the gold under Mr. Cox' mattress."

Fitzgerald walked down the line of jurors once more. "Circumstantial evidence, gentlemen, is woven like a thread throughout this whole case." He stopped and turned to the jurors again. "Now let's turn to the shovel, the *alleged* murder weapon." Fitzgerald headed to his desk, where Riddell a moment before on Judge Begbie's urgings, had placed the shovel. He flipped the cloth covering the shovel aside, and carefully picked it up. Resting the shovel on the palms of his hands, he brought it over to the jurors.

It was dead quiet in the room now. The jurors' eyes were riveted on the shovel as Fitzgerald turned it over in his hands.

"As you can see, this is a standard shovel that you can buy at any general store. In short, it could have belonged to anyone who's travelled the Cariboo Road in the last couple of months." His gaze stopped at Mr. Milton, who sat gaping at him. The dentist quickly closed his mouth.

"The dark areas you see imbedded in the cracks of the wooden handle, Mr. Riddell has asserted is that of blood." Fitzgerald pointed to one of the spots on the handle. "It might well be blood, but how would we know if it's human in origin. It could be the blood of an animal: a coyote, a bear. No way of knowing. Here again we have circumstantial evidence."

He looked up at the jurors. "And that, gentlemen of the jury, is what this whole case is built upon. Keep that in mind when you finally go to deliberate." He nodded to the jurors and returned to his desk with the shovel.

"He did very well, I think," Miss Reid whispered to Zach as she watched Fitzgerald rewrap the shovel in the cloth.

Judge Begbie glanced up from his notebook at Riddell, who had stood up from behind his desk. "You may call your first witness, Mr. Riddell."

With an air of great confidence, the barrister nodded. He didn't seem in the least deterred by Fitzgerald's opening statement, a fact which filled Zach with apprehension.

"I call Mr. Julius Jackson to the stand."

Chapter 41

❧

ALL EYES WERE ON JACKSON as he got up from his seat and with a swagger walked across the floor. He was wearing a brand-new suit and new leather boots that shone in the sunlight streaming through the windows. It looked like he had even found time to visit the barber. His hair was newly trimmed and his face clean-shaven.

Jackson took the stand and put his left hand on the Bible Judge Begbie held out to him. "I swear to speak the truth . . ." His hated squeaky voice droned on in Zach's ears.

When he was finished and had seated himself, Riddell moved out from behind his desk. "State your full name for the court."

"Julius Albert Jackson." Jackson grinned at Judge Begbie, who ignored him.

"Where do you know the accused from, Mr. Jackson?" Riddell asked, pointing to Theo.

"I'm a friend of his brother, Enos Cox." He pulled at the collar of his shirt to loosen it. "I was hired on by Enos to drive one of his wagons."

Riddell approached Jackson. "Can you elaborate?"

Jackson appeared confused. "Elaborate?"

Riddell nodded with a patient smile as he came to a stop in front of the witness stand. "Yes, tell us Mr. Jackson, what is Enos Cox's line of business?"

Understanding flooded Jackson's eyes. "Oh, you mean what he be doin' for work. He brings goods from Fort Yale up to Barkerville durin' spring and summertime. I drive one of the wagons he owns."

Riddell held his jacket by the lapels, while rocking on the balls of his feet. "Have you known Enos Cox for a long time?"

Jackson shrugged. "Three years, or there about. Met him at a hotel in Fort Yale after I come up from the Californias. Gold down there was run out." He grinned once again at Judge Begbie. "Now I mine up here with my partner, Archie, and we . . ."

"Limit yourself to answering the questions put to you by Counsel, Mr. Jackson," the judge interrupted him as he leaned back in his seat and regarded him with irritation.

Jackson nodded eagerly. "Yes of cours', of cours'."

Riddell cleared his throat and looked toward the prisoner box. "Did the accused, Mr. Theodore Cox, accompany you and his brother on any of your wagon trips?"

Jackson nodded eagerly. "He usually travels with us on our first haul from Fort Yale to Barkerville. Sometime mid-April or so. This year we were late, becaus' Enos didn't show up in Fort Yale before April was near over. He usually . . ."

"Mr. Jackson," Judge Begbie interrupted. "Don't tell us everyone's life story please. You'll only put us to sleep."

People in the courtroom chuckled.

Jackson's face reddened. "I was just tryin' to provide the particulars, is all."

Judge Begbie stared hard at Riddell. "Have your witness stick to the facts."

Zach exchanged a pleased smile with Miss Reid. It was great to see Judge Begbie put Jackson in his place. Even Theo was smiling.

"Mr. Theodore Cox would then stay on in Barkerville?" Riddell asked.

Jackson wiped his nose with the back of his hand. "Yeah, he's a gambler, you see. Enos too until he was caught cheatin' that is." He ignored Riddell's hand gesture, imploring him to stop talking. "That's how come he's in the freight business now. He's banned from gamblin' and . . ."

"So Mr. Theodore Cox stays in Barkerville all summer?" Riddell quickly cut in.

Jackson looked offended by the interruption. "Yes, he does."

Riddell crossed his arms over his chest and looked keenly at Jackson. "Did anything unusual happen this year on your trip up here to Barkerville?"

Jackson's expression brightened. "Oh yeah. First Mr. Cox . . ."

"With that you mean Mr. Theodore Cox," Riddell corrected. "Please refer to the defendant as Theodore Cox to avoid confusion with his brother."

"Yes, of cours'. First, Mr. Theodore Cox talked Enos into bringin' her," he pointed at Miss Reid, "and those two lads along." He pointed in turn at Zach and Kyle. "They supposedly found themselves stranded in Fort Yale." He snorted in disdain. "I didn't trust them one bit. They were all dressed up in this strange garb, and the woman strutted around like a harlot, she did, even though she ain't . . ."

"Mr. Jackson, watch your language," Judge Begbie warned.

Miss Reid, who was blushing crimson, sank down in her seat when people in the courtroom craned their necks to get a better look at her.

Jackson leaned forward, turning his head so he could look at the jurors. "I warned Enos about them, but he brought them along regardless." He grimaced in disgust. "Worst drive I ever had. The grub that woman served wasn't fit for humans — and those lads, they were a constant pain in the . . ."

"Mr. Jackson!" Judge Begbie's fingers were reaching for the gavel, but suddenly recalling its shattered state, he quickly retracted his hand. "Don't you dare use profanity in my court," he roared instead.

Jackson sat back in his seat. "But I didn't, Your Honour!" he said, looking genuinely offended.

The judge's eyebrows knitted together. "Only because I stopped you in time." He gave a deep exasperated sigh as he scrutinized Jackson. "You seem to insist on getting on my nerves, don't you?"

Jackson scratched in his hair. "Your Honour, I surely don't mean to."

Judge Begbie raised an eyebrow at Riddell. "Mr. Riddell, we don't have all year. Please keep your witness focused."

"Yes, Your Honour." Riddell shot Jackson a warning look, before he continued. "Mr. Jackson, what transpired on the eve of May the twentieth of this year?"

"Well, Dan McKenna showed up." He wiped his palms on his thighs. "On his way to Victoria he was, and Enos invited him to stay the night in camp." He glanced at the judge, who was scribbling in his notebook. "It was gittin' dark so it only made sense, he would stay until mornin'," he explained for the Judge's benefit, who again ignored him and continued writing.

Riddell walked over to the jurors where he turned to Jackson, arms folded across his chest. "According to your recollection what happened that night?"

Jackson chuckled. "Well, we began drinkin' is what we did. It's a long haul from Fort Yale to Barkerville, and it's not often you run into good company, and Dan McKenna was that . . . good company, I mean."

Riddell's gaze moved across the juror's faces. "You all drank then?"

Jackson shrugged. "Well, yes we did." A mocking smile crossed his lips. "Even that woman partook." He nodded at Miss Reid. "Not very ladylike if you ask my opinion. No doubt, she's . . ."

"Then what happened, Mr. Jackson?" Riddell interrupted quickly as he strode over to Jackson and planted himself in front of him, blocking his view of Miss Reid. "Then what happened, Mr. Jackson?" he repeated when Jackson didn't answer right away.

Jackson leaned to the side in an effort to look around the barrister. "Mr. Jackson?" Riddell was beginning to sound angry.

"Well, the lads and that . . . that mad woman." He again tried to look around the barrister to where Miss Reid was sitting, but Riddell quickly took a step to the side to again obstruct his view of her. With a grumble, Jackson gave up and fell back in his seat. "The three of them went to sleep, and after a while me and Enos called it a night too."

"What about Theodore Cox and Mr. McKenna?" Riddell asked.

Jackson shrugged and looked down at his hands, which lay folded in his lap. "Well, they continued drinkin' and talkin'." He looked up at the barrister. "Before long I was fast asleep beside the fire."

"And you didn't wake up again until dawn?"

"Well, not exactly." Jackson turned his attention to the jurors. "I did wake up once because the two of them were so loud."

Riddell leaned close. "Who were loud, Mr. Jackson?"

Jackson pointed toward the prisoner box where Theo sat watching him with a frown. "Him over there was standin' over Mr. McKenna yellin' at him somethin' awful," he said. "I told them both to pipe down. It worked a while, but then Theodore Cox started in on poor Mr. McKenna again." With eyes narrowed and face flushed, Theo had risen halfway from his seat, before he was pushed back down by the constable standing next to him.

"Did you make any attempt to intervene?" Riddell asked.

Jackson gave the barrister a sheepish grin. "To be truthful, Mr. Riddell, I had swilled far too much Scotch that eve'ing, so I kind of dozed off again, and didn't wake up until day-break." He looked distraught all of sudden, his eyes tormented by guilt. "Had I only said somthin', Theodore Cox might not have killed McKenna."

The urge to run up and punch Jackson in the face was so great that Zach had to grab onto the seat of the bench he was sitting on with both hands.

"Mr. Jackson," Judge Begbie interjected sternly. "We're here to determine whether Mr. Theodore Cox committed this murder or not, so unless you saw him outright kill Mr. McKenna keep your personal conclusions to yourself, or I'll strike your whole testimony. Am I understood?"

Jackson quickly hid the sly smile curling his lips. "Absolutely, Your Honour."

Judge Begbie straightened his back and regarded the jurors with a severe look. "Disregard the last statement of this witness," he ordered them.

"How can we?" Mr. Milton blurted out. "He already said it, so it's too late." His face reddened under the judge's glare.

"Disregard that last statement in your deliberations. Is that clear, Mr. Milton?"

The dentist retracted his head between his narrow shoulders. "Certainly sir, Your Honour."

At that moment Zach thought he looked very much like an anorexic turtle.

Riddell turned his attention to Jackson again. "So when you next woke up it was daybreak?"

This time Jackson wiped his nose in his jacket sleeve. "Yeah, like I just told you," he said with irritation. "Theodore Cox usually has the last watch of the night, but he wasn't there, and the fire was almost out, so I went ahead and threw some kindlin' on it."

He was looking at the jurors now with the demeanour of someone eager to tell a truth he had been forced to keep secret for far too long. "I waited for everyone to wake up. Enos was first. He asked if I had seen Dan McKenna and his brother, Theo, which, of cours' I hadn't."

He cleared his throat. "We noticed then that Dan McKenna's mule was gone, so we figured he had already left." He turned his head to the judge. "He was a friendly feller, so we, me and Enos that is, couldn't help wonderin', why he would take off without so much as a goodbye to us."

Miss Reid's hands clenched into fists as she leaned toward Zach. "That's not at all what happened that morning," she whispered.

"So did you eventually find Theodore Cox?" Riddell continued.

"Well, it turned out he was sleepin' soundly behind one of the wagons like he didn't have a care in the world." He gave the jurors a knowing smile. "Like he had done nothin' wrong at all."

"You heard what the honourable judge said, no personal comments," Riddell warned. He smiled apologetically at Judge Begbie, whose gaze was quickly darkening. The barrister turned, walked to his desk where he opened a small leather pouch, and shook an object out into the palm of his hand. He returned to Jackson, dangling the silver watch by the chain. "Have you seen this watch before, Mr. Jackson?"

With an expression of great importance, Jackson took the watch from the barrister. He turned it over in his hand, opened it and studied its face for a while, then closed it again. He looked up at Riddell. "It's the watch Dan McKenna showed to us that evenin' in camp." Jackson smirked. "Of cours' the chain wasn't broken then."

"Is there anything in particular about the watch that would cause you to recognize it as Mr. McKenna's?" Riddell asked.

Jackson turned the watch over in his hands again, almost dropping it in the process. He pointed to the back. "See them initials, W.M." He held the watch up, so Riddell could have a look. "They stand for William McKenna, Dan McKenna's father."

Riddell held out his hand and Jackson returned the watch to him. "McKenna was very fond of this watch, wasn't he?"

Jackson nodded eagerly. "Sure was. He even said he guarded it with his life. 'I guard it with my life'. Those were his exact words."

Riddell turned to the jurors. "Mr. Jackson just mentioned the fact that the chain on the watch was broken. The rest of the chain, as I stated before, was found still attached to the victim's vest." His voice rose. "This watch, you see here in my hand, Mr. McKenna's watch, was found on the person of the notorious gambler and womanizer, Mr. Theodore Cox."

"Mr. Riddell!" Judge Begbie yelled, halfway out of his seat.

The barrister looked contrite. "Sorry, Your Honour. I forgot myself."

"Womanizer!" Zach heard Miss Reid exclaim beside him. "How dare he?"

Judge Begbie's gaze jumped in her direction. "Ma'am, one more outburst from you and you'll be banished from this court for the duration of the trial. Am I understood?" he asked when he didn't get a response.

Poking his elbow in Miss Reid's ribs, Zach prompted her to answer. She swallowed hard and in a trembling voice muttered, "Yes, Your Honour."

The judge turned his attention to Riddell again. "Go on."

"This watch, Your Honour, found on Mr. Theodore Cox's person," Riddell held the watch toward the judge, "and belonging to Mr. McKenna, is hereby entered into evidence."

Judge Begbie shook his head in exasperation. "Let the jurors examine it first, Mr. Riddell. That's the way things are usually done."

The barrister was momentarily flustered. "Yes of course, Your Honour." He quickly walked over to the jurors and handed the evidence over to the man with the handlebar moustache, who received the watch with an expression of great reverence. When he had finished inspecting it carefully, he handed it over to the next juror.

One by one, the jurors examined the watch, turning it over and bringing it close to their faces so they could make out the initials. Some of them nodded with solemn expressions on their faces while doing so.

The last juror, Mr. Milton, returned the watch to a waiting Riddell. The barrister walked it to the bench and passed it on to Judge Begbie, who dipped his pen into a bottle of ink and started scribbling in his notebook.

Riddell turned to Jackson again. "Did anything unusual happen that morning Mr. McKenna disappeared?"

Jackson made a show of studying his nails. "Well, I did notice that shovel you now have in your keep."

A collective gasp went through the courtroom.

Jackson looked up at Riddell. "It was inside the wagon I

drove, only it had blood on the blade then too." Judge Begbie's pen hovered over his notebook as he stared at Jackson.

"Are you quite sure it's the same shovel?" There was a breathless quality to Riddell's voice, which led Zach to believe this was the first time the lawyer had heard about this too.

"Yes, I'm quite certain, Mr. Riddell, even though I only had a brief look at it to be sure." Jackson turned to the jurors again. "You see, when I came back later to have another look, the shovel was all gone." His gaze moved to Theo. "Someone tossed it out."

Miss Reid inhaled sharply. "He's turning everything around," she muttered.

"One may ask, why you didn't inform the authorities as soon as possible?" Riddell asked Jackson tentatively.

Zach was surprised to see fear in Jackson's eyes.

"I'm not proud of this fact, but I'm right scared of Theodore Cox." Jackson's voice trembled. "He has somethin' of a fierce temper, so I was fearful of him killin' me with that shovel like he . . ."

"Mr. Jackson!" Judge Begbie dropped the pen down on the notebook and leaned towards him with a scowl. "Don't you even think of finishing that sentence."

This time Jackson appeared unfazed by the judge's anger. "But it's true, your Honour," he said. "I was scared for my life. Dead scared."

"Still you came forward in the end," Riddell quickly cut in

before Judge Begbie could respond to Jackson's statement.

"I'm a God-fearin' feller," Jackson said with a solemn expression. "I finally couldn't live with meself any longer, no matter the consequences." He shook his head. "It ain't right that someone should lose his life because he'd found hisself some gold," he said to the jurors. "It just ain't right."

Some of the men in the jury nodded sympathetically.

"Thank you, Mr. Jackson," Riddell said with a pleased expression and went back to his seat.

Judge Begbie eyed Fitzgerald. "Do you have any questions for this witness, counsel?"

Fitzgerald nodded. "Yes, I certainly do, your Honour." He got up from behind his desk and strode over to Jackson. "Mr. Jackson, if you, as you just stated, were so deathly afraid of Mr. Theodore Cox, why did you continue driving freight for his brother, when you knew you would then also be travelling with Theodore Cox?" He folded his hands in front of him and fixed Jackson with a stare. "Was it that the pay you got from Enos Cox was so vastly superior to what others offered that this overrode this debilitating fear you apparently had for his brother?"

Jackson averted his eyes from the barrister. "Me and Enos are friends," he answered evasively.

Fitzgerald put a hand on the wooden bannister surrounding the witness stand, and leaned toward Jackson. "So your working for Enos Cox was more like a favour?"

Jackson studied his nails. "As I just said, we're friends."

Fitzgerald let go of the bannister and turned to the jurors. "So, Mr. Jackson, since you're such good friends would it be a fair statement to say that you trust Enos Cox implicitly?"

The jurors' eyes were riveted on Jackson, afraid to miss a single word of what was being said.

There was confusion in Jackson's eyes. "Of cours' . . . of cours' I do."

Fitzgerald looked at him again. "So you were used to confiding in each other . . . you and Enos Cox, weren't you?"

There was a momentary hesitation in Jackson's voice. "I would say so, yes."

"So when you *allegedly* found that shovel, you, of course, told Enos Cox about it?" he said in a loud and clear voice.

Jackson shook his head. "No, no I didn't."

"So you deemed that Enos Cox, your friend and a person you trusted implicitly, shouldn't know about the bloody shovel, and your suspicions concerning his own brother?" Fitzgerald smiled sweetly at Jackson, who sat biting his lip.

"You're tryin' to confuse me," he answered with sullen look at the barrister.

"No, my good man, I'm only trying to understand you." Fitzgerald turned to Judge Begbie. "That's all, your Honour." He walked back to his desk and sat down.

The judge looked at Jackson. "You can take your seat."

"How do you think Mr. Fitzgerald did?" Miss Reid whispered to Zach as they watched Jackson scurry back to his place behind Riddell.

He shrugged. "Fine," he said even though he thought Fitz-gerald's cross examination of Jackson had been rather unimaginative and lacklustre compared to his spirited opening statement.

Judge Begbie rose from behind the bench. "Court is in recess for an hour," he said as he grabbed his notebook and hurried to the front door, which was held open for him by Constable Franklin. People in the courtroom quickly followed him, milling out in the sunshine of a beautiful balmy July day.

The constable guarding Theo, walked by, pushing his charge in front of him.

Miss Reid, who had gotten up from her seat, leaned over and touched Theo's arm. She gave him an encouraging smile when he turned to her. "Everything will turn out fine. You'll see," she said.

He smiled hesitantly back. "I hope so, Eliza."

"Psst, lad, over here." Zach turned his head and noticed that Billy Barker was standing in the doorway, nervously fingering the brim of his hat. He too looked newly washed and shaven. "Can I have a word with you?" Barker quickly stepped aside to let Theo and the constable by.

Zach got up from the bench. "I'll be outside for a moment," he told Miss Reid.

She nodded distractedly at him. "Sure."

"I'm coming with you," Kyle told him.

The two of them hurried outside and spotted Barker

standing underneath a tree, a distance away from the other groups of people, who were congregating just outside the courthouse.

"I meant to be at the trial today," Barker said with a sheepish grin at Zach, when he and Kyle reached him. "It's only I had a busy night."

"So did you find out anything?" Zach asked expectantly.

Barker pressed his short-brimmed hat down on his head. It looked too small, and sure enough it popped right back up again. He pushed it down harder, and this time it stayed in place. He leaned close to Zach. "I did what you asked of me. Found Jackson in the Eldorado." Barker winked at him. "I acted real friendly like to him, but he sure wasn't keen on givin' up any particulars." With a sigh, he shook his head, again dislodging the hat, which would have gone flying had he not prevented its launch with a quick maneuver of his hand. "No, Jackson, he just was sittin' there across from me at the table, braggin' about the strike he and Archie had just made in their goldmine."

Zach's heart gave a jolt. "A strike!"

Barker nodded eagerly, holding on to his hat. "Yeah, quite a big one apparently."

"Some people have all the luck," Kyle said with a sigh.

Barker nodded toward the courthouse. "How's the trial goin'?"

"Not really that great," Kyle said with a shrug. "Riddell, the defence lawyer, is killing them."

Zach, who's mind had been working full speed, since Barker had told him about the gold strike in Jackson's mine, took hold of Kyle's arm. "I'm going back inside for a moment. You just stay right here with Mr. Barker. I have something I need to talk to Mr. Fitzgerald about."

Fitzgerald and Miss Reid were the only ones left in the courtroom when Zach burst inside. In his haste he bumped into a chair, standing next to the door. It fell over and struck the floor with a loud bang, which made both of them spin around.

"What in the world is going on?" Miss Reid asked him with a startled expression.

Zach quickly righted the chair and hurried over to the barrister. "Mr. Fitzgerald, I . . . I just found out something that's important to this case." He gulped some of the courtroom's stale air into his lungs. "Jackson just made a strike in his goldmine!" Zach looked eagerly from Miss Reid to Fitzgerald and back again, and with dismay noticed the blank looks they were giving him. "Don't you get it?" he blurted out, wanting to shake them both. "It's a perfect ruse for passing off McKenna's gold as his own."

"As I mentioned before, Mr. Fitzgerald, Zachary's convinced Jackson is the one who killed poor Mr. McKenna," Miss Reid explained to the lawyer, who was contemplating Zach from underneath knitted eyebrows. "And quite frankly so do I."

"This is pure and utter speculation." Fitzgerald glared at both of them in turn. "I'll hear no more of this nonsense."

Zach bravely faced Fitzgerald's ire. "Mr. Riddell himself compared the gold from the pouch found in Mr. Cox' cabin to McKenna's gold, saying that it was also bright, angular and of great purity. Compare the gold in the pouch to what Jackson has supposedly taken out of his mine and if it's the same . . ."

"Enough!" Papers scattered on the ground as Fitzgerald in frustration slapped the palm of his hand hard down on his desk. His face contorted in pain. "Jesus almighty that hurt!" he exclaimed, shaking his hand.

"So you won't do it?" Zach asked, ignoring Miss Reid's warning glance.

Fitzgerald took a deep breath to calm himself. "No, I certainly will not. I would look a fool to Judge Begbie, especially since I myself argued that there was no guarantee that the gold in that pouch couldn't have come from another mine in the Cariboo district." Silence fell over the room. Zach was the one to break it as he made a quick decision.

"I'm the one who discovered Mr. McKenna's watch lying on the ground," he said. "I gave it to Theo Cox, who then went in search of him." He took a deep breath. "And that shovel Mr. Riddell showed to the jurors, I'm also the one who found that in Jackson's wagon. Jackson lied when he said there was blood on the blade," he added quickly "It was only on the handle. When I told Mr. Cox about the shovel he confronted Jackson who claimed that the blood was there because he had killed a racoon with it."

At first Fitzgerald was too stunned to say anything. Then

he turned to Miss Reid, eyes blazing. "Ma'am, did you know about this?"

Miss Reid fidgeted. "Yes."

He kept looking at her. "And you didn't think to tell me?"

"You're right, Mr. Fitzgerald, I should have," she admitted in a subdued voice.

"The day Mr. Cox was arrested, I tried to tell Constable Stevenson at the Barkerville jail that they had the wrong man," Zach informed Fitzgerald. "That Jackson was the one who had killed Mr. McKenna, but he didn't believe me." He gave a resigned shrug. "He just thought I was lying to save Mr. Cox so I figured no one else would believe me either. That it would all come down to my word against Jackson's."

"Well, the constable is right about that." Fitzgerald bit his lip as he watched people begin to file into the courtroom after the break. "Let's see what happens this afternoon."

During the next couple of hours, Riddell presented the rest of the witnesses for the prosecution. First Constable Whiteford, who had uncovered McKenna's body from its shallow grave described the brutal way with which the miner had been killed. "Scavenging animals had been feasting on his remains, hands, nose, ears nearly gone," he ended his description, a sorrowful expression on his hangdog face. A woman among the spectators had promptly fainted, and it took a while to revive her.

Following Constable Whiteford's testimony, it was James Crawford's turn, the doctor from Quesnellemouth who had examined McKenna's body. He testified that the shovel found at the scene might have inflicted the victim's terrible head wounds. No matter how hard Riddell pressed this witness, a short wizened man with a huge head, he was not able to extract a more definitive answer from the doctor.

At last the written testimonies from Dan McKenna's friends, Nick Browne and George Boyd were read out loud by Riddell.

The court was now in recess for the day and would resume the next morning at eight o'clock. Only Zach, Miss Reid, and Fitzgerald were again left in the courtroom, where the sour stink of too many people pressed together for too long still lingered.

"That was powerful stuff," Miss Reid commented to Fitzgerald as she watched him buttoning his jacket.

"It was," he said. "Constable Whiteford, especially, made quite an impression on the jury."

Miss Reid nodded and got up from the bench. She stretched her arms out and laced her fingers together in order to get rid of the kinks from having sat in the same spot for too long. "He came across with such gravitas."

Fitzgerald nodded at her. "He did give a compelling testimony." he admitted.

Kyle appeared in the doorway to the courthouse puffing vigorously on a cigar he had bummed from Barker earlier. "It looks even worse for Cox now, doesn't it?" he asked as he leaned against the doorjamb. They all ignored him.

"So what now?" Miss Reid sounded utterly spent. Zach knew she tried to catch up on her chores at the hotel the best she could when she was not at the trial. Madame Pond was understanding but still expected most of the work to be done. He doubted the teacher got much more than a couple of hours sleep a night. Johnny had been far more generous, giving Kyle and Zach the time off to attend the trial without demands. "Just do what you can to keep Theo's spirits up," he had said.

"We go ahead and present our case," Fitzgerald said in response to the question just asked by Miss Reid. "First, you Ma'am, you'll tell your version."

"Isn't Theo going to go first?" she asked.

Fitzgerald brushed some lint from the front of his jacket and looked inquiringly at her. "Go first with what?"

She searched his face. "His testimony, of course."

"Whatever gave you the idea he was going to testify?"

"Well, why on earth wouldn't he?" Miss Reid sounded annoyed with Fitzgerald. "He's such a likeable man and can only help in his own defence."

"Ma'am, that's not the ways things are done." Fitzgerald pushed his chair underneath the desk.

Miss Reid crossed her arms over her chest. "And why not, Mr. Fitzgerald?"

"Because Mr. Cox is the defendant." He sounded testy now. "Clearly, you must know that."

Zach finally understood what the barrister was trying to tell them. "You don't do that in . . ." He was about to say 1866, but quickly changed it to: "You don't usually do that? I mean put the defendant on the stand?"

Fitzgerald looked offended. "No, of course not. No barrister worth his salt would even suggest that."

Miss Reid pointed a defiant chin at him. "You wouldn't be worth your salt if you didn't do it."

Fitzgerald's face reddened. "Ma'am, I don't think you understand. The law says I can't." He spoke slowly as if he was addressing someone hard of hearing. "Mr. Cox will only be allowed to make an unsworn statement at the end of the trial, if he so chooses."

"That's the way it's done *these* days, Miss Reid," Zach quickly interjected before she had a chance to really tear into Fitzgerald.

At last the truth dawned on her, and her hands fell heavily to her sides. "But that's unfair."

"So who testifies after Miss Reid, I mean my aunt?" Zach asked of Fitzgerald.

"You do," he answered as he neatly stacked the papers on his desk, and wedged them under his arm. "When you're on that stand you tell everything, including the discovery of the watch and the shovel inside Mr. Jackson's wagon." Fitzgerald looked sternly at him. "And I mean everything."

Zach nodded. "Of course."

"Hopefully, that way we'll be able to cast some doubts on the prosecution's version of events, taking place that evening in camp." Fitzgerald brought out his pocket watch and glanced at it. "I have to go to my office so I can prepare for tomorrow," he said as he dropped the watch back into his vest pocket. "See you here in court in the morning." He nodded at Miss Reid and Zach and left the courtroom. Kyle stepped away from the doorway to let him by. "See you tomorrow Mr. Fitzgerald," he said.

Miss Reid leaned over and grabbed her shawl from the bench behind her. "This is incredibly disappointing," she said through clenched teeth. "The prosecution is clearly being shown favouritism." She wrapped the shawl around her shoulders. "I'm sure glad I don't live in 1866."

You do live in 1866, Zach was about to say, but kept quiet. He watched as Miss Reid walked to the door. "So are we going back to Barkerville now?" he asked her.

She turned to him. "I'm dropping in on Theo. He needs some cheering up, I'm sure. After all he's spending most of his time in that awful jail cell. If one of you could stop by the hotel and tell Madame Pond I'll be there soon, it would be appreciated?"

"Why don't we just wait for you outside" Zach suggested. "That way we can walk back together."

"I'll make it short." Miss Reid promised as she hurried to the doorway. She pushed Kyle out of the way so she could get by. "For heaven's sake, throw that vile thing away," she said, nodding at the cigar.

"I'm not about to throw a perfectly good cigar away," Kyle protested. "I'll save it for later."

"It's only going to make you sick." Miss Reid snapped. "And besides it's a nasty habit."

"She treats me like I'm five years old," Kyle said when Zach joined him outside.

"She's only concerned about you," Zach said as he watched Miss Reid stride towards the jail.

He turned his head when he heard heavy steps approach and saw Constable Franklin come around the corner of the building. Franklin stopped abruptly, and looked at Kyle with a grin. "Are you certain you can handle that?" He nodded at the cigar in Kyle's hand. "You look a little green."

"I can handle it just fine," Kyle told him. Constable Franklin chuckled as he passed by and walked through the open door into the courtroom. They heard his heavy footfall across the floor inside.

"Everyone's a critic," Kyle mumbled as he extinguished the cigar against the sole of the boot and stuck it in his jacket pocket. Constable Franklin came outside again, closed the door to the courthouse and locked it. He walked past them with a curt nod and headed for the jail.

"Cox already has himself a woman, you know," Kyle said when the constable had gone inside the jail and closed the door. "The way Miss E. fawns over him, I'm pretty sure she doesn't have a clue."

Zach gave him a surprised look. "You know about Miss Mulligan?"

Kyle smiled wryly at him. "Well, you obviously do too. It's not like it's a secret around here." He kicked at the dirt with the nose of his boot. "Love is blind, I guess."

"You don't have to act so pleased about it!" Zach said. "She really likes him, and it's going to hurt when she finds out. What do you know about love anyways?" he scoffed.

"Jeez, like I haven't done it."

"I'm talking about love, not sex." Zach knew he was being overbearing, but he couldn't help it.

"What's the difference?"

There was a guardedness in Kyle's eyes that aroused Zach's curiosity. "You don't really mean that, do you?" Kyle didn't answer. "Nothing wrong in talking about stuff, you know," Zach said when the silence between them became awkward.

Kyle spat on the ground. "What are you, freakin' Oprah Winfrey now?"

"No, I'm just Zach, and I hope your friend."

Kyle averted his gaze. "My mom's a drunk," he said. "She's on her third marriage, or is it the fourth? I've lost count." He cleared his throat and looked at Zach. "Anyway, the one she's married to now is a total loser. I have two older sisters. The oldest one is working on her third kid, each with a different jerk for a father, and we all live squeezed together in a three-bedroom apartment. Just one big happy family." Hostility ran deep in his voice. "Satisfied?"

"No, not really," Zach answered, "but I'm glad you told me."

Chapter 42

THE NEXT MORNING started with a sudden cloudburst that turned the roads muddy and the hillsides slippery. The walk from Barkerville to the Richfield courthouse was an ordeal.

"What I wouldn't give to have an umbrella right now," Miss Reid lamented as she straddled a puddle, hitching up her skirt to just above her knees. She didn't quite make it over the puddle and one of her boots slipped into the water.

Angrily, she jerked her foot out. "Look my boot is all covered in mud." She pulled the cloak Madame Pond had loaned her tighter around her tall frame, and sighed. "Oh, what does it really matter? I'm soaked anyway."

So was Zach. The jacket he had borrowed from Johnny

Knott wasn't much help in a downpour like this and he could feel his wet shirt clinging to his back. He looked with envy at Kyle whose leather jacket was still intact. Only one of the metal snap buttons had popped off.

They were among the first ones to arrive at the courthouse and managed to secure seats in the middle row behind Fitzgerald, who was already sitting at his desk looking tense, his eyes focused on the witness stand as if someone was already sitting there. Riddell, who arrived right after them gave them a curt nod as he walked to his desk. Soon the courtroom filled up.

Judge Begbie marched inside through the front door. The heavy coat, draped over his judge's robes, dripped water across the floor. "Devilish weather out there," he said as he removed the coat and his hat and hung them from a peg in the back of the courtroom. He went up to the bench and seated himself. Pulling out a drawer, he retrieved a replacement for the gavel he had broken the day before and placed it in front of him. He put his wig on and looked at Fitzgerald. "Ready to proceed, Counsel?"

Fitzgerald pulled nervously at his jacket sleeves. "The defence calls Miss Eliza Reid to the stand."

"Here goes nothing," Miss Reid said to Zach and Kyle as she got up. She excused herself as she navigated her way between benches. Judging from startled outbursts, she had managed to step on a few toes with the men's boots she had taken up wearing. She found the women's boots of the time to be too dainty for her twenty-first century double-D feet.

With her head held high, she marched up to the bench where she was quickly sworn in by Judge Begbie. She then took her seat.

Fitzgerald walked up to her. "State your full name for the court."

"Eliza Jane Reid," she said in a loud clear voice.

"How are you acquainted with Mr. Theodore Cox?"

A smile brightened her lips. "We met earlier in the year. He helped me and my nephews when we found ourselves, eh-um, stranded in Fort Yale." She turned her head and looked at Theo. "He's a real gentleman. Very kind and helpful."

She turned her attention to Fitzgerald again. "He persuaded his brother to bring us along with them to Barkerville."

"It was on this trip that you met Mr. Julius Jackson?"

Her face darkened. "It sure was. I took an instant dislike to him. His appearance alone . . ." She shuddered. "Yes, right now he looks all clean with new clothes on, but back then he was dirty and unkempt, and did he ever smell." She rolled her eyes.

People in the courtroom sniggered and craned their necks to get a glimpse of Jackson, whose face had turned red.

"I think we can appreciate your insight, Ma'am," Judge Begbie said with a hint of amusement. "Please move on."

"How did you find Mr. Jackson as a travelling companion?" Fitzgerald asked.

Miss Reid shook her head, contempt in her eyes. "He was

a very disagreeable man. Complained about everything and was nasty and mean to my nephews, and he continuously tried to poison Enos' mind against us."

"You're talking about Mr. Enos Cox?" Fitzgerald asked with a quick look at the jurors.

"Yes. Mr. Jackson kept telling him we were useless, and that Enos would be better off dumping us on the side of the road." She frowned at Jackson, who was sitting in one of the back rows shoulders hunched, scowling at her. "If it hadn't been for Mr. Theodore Cox it would have been quite unbearable for the three of us. He was so kind and considerate." She smiled brightly at Theo. "An absolute gentleman."

Zach slumped down in his seat. Her praise for Theo was becoming quite nauseating. He exchanged an embarrassed glance with Kyle.

To his relief, Judge Begbie interrupted her before she had time to rave further about Theo. "Please proceed, Mr. Fitzgerald."

"Certainly, Your Honour." The barrister cleared his throat again. "Miss Reid, what is your recollection of the events taking place on the eve of May the twentieth?"

She crossed her legs and discreetly tried to wipe away one of the many dried mud stains on her dress. "Well, Mr. McKenna arrived in camp. He was a miner on his way to Victoria." She gave up on the stain and looked straight at Mr. Fitzgerald. "He turned out to be a very pleasant, very polite, carefree sort of individual. The only time he turned sad was when he talked about his partner, Vernon, who died from the typhoid." She straightened her back. "You probably know it better by the name of Mountain Fever, but I talked to a doctor here and we're definitely talking about typhoid." She sounded quite pleased with her new-found knowledge.

Fitzgerald didn't comment on her medical acumen, but instead walked over to the jurors. He faced them "Did Mr. McKenna say anything about why he was going to Victoria?"

Miss Reid shook her head. "No, not as far as I know. To be honest, I really didn't pay much attention." She uncrossed her legs and leaned back in the chair, folding her hands in her lap. "It had been a long day and I was bushed. All I wanted to do was go to sleep."

Fitzgerald came over to her again. "What about Mr. Jackson, was he curious about why McKenna was going to Victoria?"

"He most assuredly was. As soon as he heard that Mr. McKenna had struck gold around Williams Creek, he wanted to know if he was bringing any of it to Victoria with him." She smiled fondly at Theo again. "Mr. Theodore Cox, however, wouldn't have any of that. He told Jackson that Mr. McKenna was our guest and shouldn't be bothered with such questions."

"If she says something about him being such a gentleman, I'm going to barf," Kyle whispered hurriedly to Zach.

"He's such a . . ." Miss Reid began, but was cut short by Fitzgerald.

"Did the men start drinking at one point?" he asked her.

Momentarily flustered by the interruption, it took her a while to respond. "Yes, Enos brought out a bottle of Scotch," she finally answered.

"So did they all get drunk?" Fitzgerald asked.

"I guess you can say that. I know Enos still had a couple of bottles stashed away." She shook her head. "I don't know if they drank all of it, because I called it an early night."

Fitzgerald went back to his desk to glance at his notes. He faced Miss Reid again. "At any time during the night were you awakened by a loud quarrel between Mr. Theodore Cox and Dan McKenna?"

She made a point at looking squarely at Jackson. "No, I certainly wasn't. Had this quarrel taken place, rest assured, I would have woken up." Her jaw tightened. "I'm an extremely light sleeper."

"What happened the next morning?" Fitzgerald asked her.

Miss Reid turned her attention to him again. "When I woke up Mr. McKenna had already left. Later, Mr. Theodore Cox told us Mr. McKenna's watch had been found, and he took one of the horses and rode out in search of him, so he could return the watch."

Fitzgerald walked back to the witness stand. "Ma'am, when did Mr. Theodore Cox return to camp?"

"A couple of hours later." She frowned as she thought back. "He was quite frustrated by the fact that he hadn't been able to locate Mr. McKenna, and he told us he would keep the watch so he could return it to Mr. McKenna when he came back to Barkerville. That's why he had the watch on his person."

Fitzgerald began pacing in front of her, then stopped again. "Ma'am, after Mr. McKenna disappeared, did you at any point see the shovel, now in evidence?"

She shook her head. "No, only Zachary, my nephew did, but the only one he told was Mr. Theodore Cox." Her gaze sought Zach's. "My nephew apparently didn't want to worry me, so I didn't know about it until weeks later." Her voice still bore traces of the hurt she felt over the fact that Zach hadn't confided in her right away.

Fitzgerald clutched his hands behind his back. "Ma'am, do you think, Mr. Theodore Cox would be capable of murder for profit?"

For a moment, Miss Reid was taken aback by the barrister's bluntness, but quickly recovered, shaking her head emphatically. "Absolutely not. No way."

"That's all I have for this witness," Fitzgerald said, looking at Judge Begbie.

Zach's attention was on the twelve jurors. Did they think Theo was guilty? He saw nothing in their faces to give him any indication one way or the other. A phrase suddenly jumped to his mind: Innocent until proven guilty. Guilty until proven innocent, he thought seemed more appropriate in this case.

"Mr. Riddell, your witness," the judge said.

Riddell dismissed Miss Reid with a wave of his hand as if she was of no importance to him. "I have no questions for this witness."

"No questions?" Miss Reid said as she looked at Judge Begbie. She looked rather put out by the fact.

The judge smiled kindly at her. "As you've heard, the prosecution has no questions for you, Ma'am. You can take your seat."

"Please, Miss Reid," Fitzgerald said with a quick look at the judge. "You're dismissed."

Miss Reid got up. "Well, if that's the case."

"That's odd," she whispered later to Zach when she sat down next to him on the bench.

Chapter 43

∾

FITZGERALD PICKED UP a notebook from his desk and opened it. "I call Zachary Stillman to the stand," he said after a brief look at one of the pages.

Zach's legs were shaking as he made his way up to the bench, where he too was sworn in by Judge Begbie. He took his seat in the witness stand. Fitzgerald walked up to him. "State your full name for the court."

Zach cleared his throat. "Zachary . . ."

"Speak up, lad," Judge Begbie said. "People can't hear you."

"Zachary Alexander Stillman," he yelled, startling Fitzgerald so much he dropped the notebook in his hand. With an apology to the judge, he picked it up, walked back to his desk and placed it there. He returned to the witness stand.

Zach was so nervous he had a hard time collecting his thoughts. He wiped his sweaty palms on his pants and took a deep breath. It was important he stay calm. Fitzgerald had told him his testimony was crucial to the case. He looked toward Miss Reid who gave him a reassuring smile. Kyle was giving him the thumbs up.

Fitzgerald glanced at Theo. "What's your impression of Mr. Theodore Cox?"

Zach tried again to swallow the lump in his throat, but it was as though it was attached to a rubber band, because it jumped right back up. "He's a real great guy," he said hoarsely.

Fitzgerald couldn't help smiling. "Could you maybe elaborate a little?"

Elaborate. In a moment of panic Zach had forgotten what the word meant.

Judge Begbie leaned across bench towards him. "Do you need a glass of water?" he asked in a such a kindly voice it was difficult to associate it with the usually stern judge.

Zach nodded gratefully, and Fitzgerald went to pour him some water. He almost dropped the glass when the barrister handed it to him. Jeez, get a grip, he admonished himself. Why was he so doggone nervous? His eyes met Jackson's hateful gaze. He drained all the water in big gulps and returned the empty glass to Fitzgerald.

"Was Mr. Theodore Cox honest and friendly in his dealings with you and your aunt?" Fitzgerald asked after he had returned the empty glass to his desk.

Zach nodded. "Oh yeah, I frankly don't know what would have become of us if he hadn't stepped in and helped us out."

"So you would also describe him as a compassionate man?" the barrister continued.

Judge Begbie looked up from his notes. "Mr. Fitzgerald, stop putting words in his mouth."

"I'm only trying to help him along, Your Honour." The barrister gave the judge a conciliatory smile. "As you can see he's very nervous."

The judge leaned back in his chair. "I understand that, but you're still not allowed to lead your witness," he said with irritation. "The jurors want to hear his testimony, not yours. I would highly recommend you cease with this approach before it really starts annoying me."

"Certainly, Your Honour. Of course." Fitzgerald turned his attention to Zach again. "Do you consider Mr. Theodore Cox a friend?" he asked.

"I do," Zach said firmly.

"Tell us about the events taking place on the eve of May the twentieth when Mr. McKenna arrived in camp. In your own words of course," he added with a pointed look at the judge.

Zach wiped his forehead with his hand. With all the people assembled, it was hot and stuffy in the room and perspiration kept trickling from his hairline. "Mr. McKenna came to our camp, which was great because it could usually get boring in the evening." He shrugged. "Sometimes Mr. Cox, Theodore Cox, would play cards with me and Kyle, but most of the time we would just hang around the fire and do nothing until we had to go to sleep." I'm rambling, he thought.

"You liked Mr. McKenna?" Fitzgerald asked.

Zach nodded.

"Speak up," Judge Begbie said with a sidelong glance at him. "The jurors need to hear."

"Yeah, I liked him." He leaned forward and glanced at the jurors. "He was a fun guy to be with. He really was." Some of the men smiled at him.

"At any point did Mr. McKenna say he was bringing gold to Victoria?" Fitzgerald asked.

Zach shook his head. "No. Mr. Jackson asked him about that at one point, but Theodore Cox said he was being impolite."

"Did the men get drunk that evening?" Fitzgerald asked.

Zach glanced at Jackson. "Yeah, they did, except Mr. Jackson. He was hardly drinking anything."

The barrister was watching him keenly. "Was that unusual for him?"

"Sure was. He likes to get wasted." Zach heard some of the jurors chuckle.

"So what do you think was the reason Mr. Jackson was not drinking?"

"Refrain from speculations, Mr. Fitzgerald," Judge Begbie admonished him. "Stick to the facts."

Fitzgerald smiled affably at the judge. "Of course, Your Honour." He turned to Zach again.

"At any time during the day, or that evening had Mr. Jackson complained of any ailment that might have prevented him from imbibing as was his usual wont, such as a stomach affliction?"

Zach shook his head. "No. Personally, I think Mr. Jackson suspected that Dan McKenna had gold in the two saddlebags his mule was carrying." He turned and faced the jurors again. "He probably wanted to keep a clear head so he could figure out a way to steal it later."

"Mr. Fitzgerald!" The judge brought his new gavel down on the bench. "This is pure and utter conjecture." He gave the jurors a fierce look. "Ignore that last statement of this witness." This time they all nodded obediently. "Kindly continue, Mr. Fitzgerald."

"Certainly, Your Honour." The barrister didn't look too terribly concerned about Judge Begbie's reprimand. As a matter of fact he appeared rather pleased. He gave Zach a quick encouraging smile. "So the men, except Jackson, all got drunk?"

Zach nodded. "Yeah, when I went to bed they were getting real loud."

"Loud, but not quarrelling?" Again the intense stare from Fitzgerald.

"No, they were just laughing and joking, that's all," he said with a shrug.

Hands clasped behind his back, Fitzgerald walked all the

way up to Zach and leaned towards him. So close was the barrister's face that Zach could see the pores on his nose. "At any time during the night did you hear Mr. Theodore Cox and Dan McKenna quarrel?"

It made Zach nervous to have the barrister's presence loom over him like that, and he slumped down in his seat to create some distance between them. "No, I only woke up once during the night, and saw Mr. Jackson and Enos Cox sit at the fire. They were in a heated discussion and Jackson was telling Enos to keep his voice down."

He cleared his throat. "When I woke up again it was morning, and Mr. Jackson and Theodore Cox were discussing Dan McKenna being gone without having said goodbye to them. Later Enos Cox woke up and joined them."

Fitzgerald gave Zach a penetrating look. "So Enos Cox was not the first one joining Mr. Jackson at the fire that morning as indicated by Mr. Jackson in his testimony?"

"No, Theodore Cox was the first one," Zach said firmly.

"So what happened next?" Fitzgerald inquired.

"I found Mr. McKenna's watch. It was lying on the ground after I went . . ." he blushed as he searched for the right words, "after I answered the call of nature," he blurted out, drawing chuckles, even from Judge Begbie.

"Did you notice something different about the watch?" Fitzgerald asked.

Zach nodded. "Yeah, the chain was broken."

"What did you do with the watch?"

Zach looked towards the prisoner box. Theo smiled encouragingly at him. He turned his attention to the Fitzgerald again. "I gave it to Theodore Cox. He then borrowed one of the horses and went in search of Mr. McKenna so he could return the watch to him. Only he couldn't find him."

One of the jurors started coughing, and Fitzgerald waited impatiently for him to stop before continuing his questioning. "Did you find anything else?"

To create some further distance between him and Fitzgerald's hovering presence, Zach leaned as far back in his seat as he possibly could, an unnatural position, which made his tailbone ache.

"Mr. Fitzgerald, the witness is clearly not comfortable having you stand so close to him."

Fitzgerald straightened up and gave the judge a flustered look. "Your Honour?"

With his hand the judge gestured at the barrister to back up from the stand. "Give the witness room to breathe, Mr. Fitzgerald."

"Certainly." To Zach's relief Fitzgerald moved away from him, and he quickly shifted into a more comfortable position on the hard wooden chair. So great was the relief that he didn't pay attention to the barrister's next question.

"I'm sorry, what was that?" Zach asked.

By the way Fitzgerald's eyebrows knitted together, he clearly did not like Zach's inattention. "Did you find anything else?" His voice was brusque.

Zach's gaze moved past the barrister towards Jackson. He pointed at him. "I discovered a dirty shovel inside the wagon *he* drove. It had blood on the handle."

Fitzgerald turned and looked at Jackson. "Let the record reflect that the witness identified Mr. Julius Jackson." He turned at Zach again. "Did you tell anyone?"

Zach was gratified to see Jackson squirm in his seat. "I told Theodore Cox, and he went and got the shovel, showing it to Mr. Jackson, who said he had killed a racoon with it the night before, which accounted for the blood and dirt." He swallowed hard. This time the lump in his throat stayed down. "Even though Theodore Cox bought the story, I didn't."

Jackson's eyes blazed at him, but Zach didn't care. He wanted the truth to come out. "I figured he had killed Mr. McKenna and then hidden his gold somewhere in the wagon, and I searched for it when I had a chance, but I couldn't find it. The weird thing was that suddenly the shovel was gone. Mr. Jackson must have tossed it out after Theodore Cox confronted him."

Zach was so caught up in his narrative, he barely registered that Judge Begbie was objecting like crazy to his testimony. Only when the gavel hit the table hard did he realize that the judge was livid. It was, however, not him the judge's ire was directed at, but rather Fitzgerald.

"This is pure and utter speculation," the judge yelled at the barrister, his face flushed from anger. "Don't you know how to control your witness."

"I'm sorry, Your Honour," Fitzgerald apologized. "As you well saw, I was trying to signal to the witness that he had to stop, but he was so caught up in his narrative that he didn't take notice." Vaguely, Zach now remembered that the barrister had been waving a hand in front of him.

"Jackson tried to kill me too." Zach didn't know what had gotten into him, except that he wanted everything out in the open now.

A hush went through the courtroom. Zach looked at the faces around him. "It's true. On the steamer from Soda Creek to Quesnellemouth, Mr. Jackson fired a gun, scaring the horses I was tending. Had it not been for Theodore Cox grabbing Prancer, I mean one of the horses, I would have been trampled to death." He hesitated. "Well, I didn't exactly see Jackson do it, since I was inside the ship's hold and he discharged the gun outside on the deck, but yes I'm sure it was him."

"Thank you, Zachary. That's all the questions I have," Fitzgerald said quickly before Judge Begbie had time to protest.

The judge shook his head at the barrister while emitting a frustrated sigh. He looked at Riddell. "Your turn, Mr. Riddell" he said as Fitzgerald returned to his seat.

Zach hoped Riddell would leave him alone as he had Miss Reid. His heart sank when the barrister got up. The click of his hard heels on the wooden floor echoed through the quiet courtroom as he walked up to Zach.

"You don't like Mr. Jackson much do you?"

"Honestly, I doubt anyone does." The statement flew out of Zach's mouth before he had time to stop himself. He heard laughter sputter from the courtroom. "What I'm trying to say is that he isn't exactly pleasant to be around. He always bellyaches about something and . . ."

"Enough," Judge Begbie glared at Riddell. "What do you hope to achieve with these kind of idiotic questions?"

Riddell tried to appear unruffled, and was doing a fairly good job at it, except that he wasn't able to suppress his nervous tick. His eyes opened and closed rapidly as he answered. "I was only trying to establish that Mr. Stillman's deep dislike for Mr. Jackson might have motivated him to try framing him."

The judge leaned back in his chair with a groan. "Might have!" He closed his eyes as he said it, shaking his head.

"Your Honour, if you would let me continue with my line of inquiry, I . . ." Riddell began.

Judge Begbie was already halfway out of his seat. "No, I will not let you continue with this hogwash." He slumped back in his seat again. "Do you have any other questions for this witness?"

Zach had to give it to Riddell. He was not easily defeated.

Squaring his shoulders, Riddell looked bravely at the judge. "Yes, I do."

He turned to Zach giving him a penetrating look. "You stated earlier that you didn't know what would have become of you had it not been for Mr. Theodore Cox, isn't that true?"

Warily, Zach nodded. "Yeah, he has helped us out a lot."

Riddell smiled sweetly at him. "Would it be erroneous to say that you owe Theodore Cox a great debt?"

Zach wondered where the barrister was headed with all this, and hoped Judge Begbie would object again, but one look at his placid expression told him no help could be expected from there. "Yes," he answered tentatively.

"You would do anything to help him, wouldn't you?" Riddell said with a wry smile.

Zach felt trapped. "Anything in my power, yes."

Riddell turned to the jurors. "Even trying to frame someone else for a crime Theodore Cox committed," he said loud and clear.

This time Judge Begbie didn't stay quiet. "That's enough Mr. Riddell," he yelled, using his gavel energetically to underscore his words.

Chapter 44

"HOW LONG IS THIS GOING TO TAKE?" Miss Reid asked more to herself than Zach and Kyle, who stood underneath a tree, watching her pace back and forth. She stopped and glanced up at the courthouse. "How long can it possibly take for the jury to figure out that Theo is innocent."

The sun came out from behind the heavy clouds, which had covered the sky like a grey blanket all morning. The sudden bright light emphasized the lines of worry radiating from Miss Reid's eyes. Zach thought she looked as if she had aged ten years but of course he was not about to point that out to her.

Kyle spotted a small twig on the ground and bent over to

pick it up. He stuck it between his teeth and began chewing on it. Zach wondered how many people might have stepped on that twig throughout the morning, but he didn't mention that either.

"Riddell was really good wasn't he?" Kyle said around the twig as he nodded at the closed door to the courthouse.

Kyle was right, Zach reluctantly admitted to himself. In their testimonies, Kyle, Johnny Knott, Mr. Wilson, the guy who owned the cabin Theo stayed in, and a few more of Theo's friends, hadn't really added significantly to his defence, other than that he was basically a good guy.

Zach, himself, had been mortified after he had finished with his testimony. He felt he had done a terrible job, and Riddell's questions and his own clumsy responses kept going through his mind. Miss Reid kept reassuring him that he had held up well under very difficult circumstances, but he suspected she just said it so he wouldn't feel bad.

"Hey, are you even listening?" Kyle asked Zach when he didn't respond to his statement.

"Yeah, I heard you." Zach said with a sigh.

Kyle chewed for a while on the twig. "Honestly, I'm really disappointed in Fitzgerald," he said. "Billy Barker sure wasted his money on that loser." He spat the twig out.

"Did you two notice how carefully Mr. Riddell tied up all the loose ends in his closing argument?" Miss Reid looked like she was ready to cry.

Kyle removed the cap he had taken to wearing lately, and

wiped his forehead with the back of his hand. "Why don't we face it, Riddell killed it in there" he said with a sigh. "And Fitzgerald was pathetic."

Zach looked dismally at the people standing outside the courthouse, most of them huddled together in small groups, their excited voices a steady hum, while Theo was awaiting his fate in jail with Fitzgerald to keep him company. He spotted Miss Mulligan. She was accompanied by a tall middle-aged angular-looking man, who looked acutely uncomfortable in a suit, and an older rotund woman with a red puffy face.

"I so wish Theo would have given a statement." Miss Reid was doing her utmost to pull the handkerchief she was holding in her hands to shreds. "I mean, he's so personable. People can't help liking him." She had been very upset when Theo had refused to give an unsworn statement at the end of the trial as Fitzgerald had said he was allowed to do. Everything there is to say has already been said, he had told Miss Reid. Now it's up to the jurors. No amount of coaxing from her had been able to change his mind.

"How long has it been now?" Miss Reid asked.

Zach shrugged. "I've no idea. Maybe an hour." He began biting his nails.

"It feels longer." She began pacing again, but stopped abruptly when Constable Franklin emerged from the courtroom.

"A verdict has been reached," the constable announced in a loud and clear voice.

The groups rapidly broke up as people rushed to the door, pushing and shoving each other to get inside first.

"Ladies, Gentlemen," Constable Franklin yelled, spreading out his arms to bar their way. "Enter in an orderly fashion."

Five minutes later they were all seated in the courtroom. Zach tried to read the jurors' faces. The dentist, Mr. Milton, fidgeted in his seat and constantly wiped his palms on his pants.

Miss Reid leaned towards Zach. "What do you think?" she whispered.

He bit his lip. "I don't know. I just don't know."

Judge Begbie took his seat. "Where's the accused?" The question was barely out of his mouth when the door to the courtroom opened, and Theo walked inside, followed by a constable. He gave Miss Mulligan an apprehensive smile as he proceeded to the prisoner box. He didn't take a seat this time, but stood staring at the jurors, his hands clasped in front.

Judge Begbie looked at the twelve men in the jury. "Gentlemen, have you reached a decision?"

The man with the handlebar moustache stood up, clearing his throat. "We have, Your Honour." He looked confident and spoke without a hint of hesitation.

"What is your verdict?" Judge Begbie asked.

"Guilty, Your Honour."

A collective gasp went through the courtroom.

Miss Reid gripped Zach's hand, squeezing it so hard it sent a wave of pain through his arm "Oh, good God, this can't be."

Zach, too stunned to react, just sat staring at the jury.

Kyle patted Miss Reid awkwardly on the shoulder. "Don't worry, Miss E.," he said. "We'll find a way to break him out of jail."

Judge Begbie stood up as he used his gavel with zeal. "Order in the court," he yelled. Gradually people settled down.

The judge turned to Theo. "Mr. Theodore Joseph Cox, by a group of your peers, you've been found guilty of the murder of Mr. Dan Philip McKenna. Sentencing will take place the day after tomorrow at noon." He used the gavel again. "Court will be in recess until then."

Looking grim, Fitzgerald returned to his desk in the courtroom. Immediately, Miss Reid descended on him. "Do something, Mr. Fitzgerald." Seizing his shoulder she bent over so she could look him straight in the face. "Listen, that jury clearly didn't know what they were doing. You only have to look at that dentist to see he's an idiot!"

Fitzgerald got up from his chair and gathered his papers and notebook. "Ma'am, Mr. Cox was convicted by a jury of his peers, and we have to accept their verdict. All that is left for me now," he said with a sigh as he faced Miss Reid, "is to try to appeal to Judge Begbie's sense of compassion, so Mr. Cox goes to jail and doesn't end up hanging."

"What's the chance he'll hang?" Zach asked with dread. Kyle stood so close behind him, he could feel his breath on his neck. The only answer they got from Fitzgerald was a quick shrug, before he turned around and hurried out the door.

Chapter 45

ONLY A COUPLE OF THE tables were occupied in the lobby of the Hôtel de France when Zach walked inside. He closed the door after himself just as Sinclair, busy straightening the collar of his jacket, came down the stairs from the first floor. Madame Pond now insisted he wear a jacket inside the hotel, and always buttoned all the way up. The way Sinclair constantly adjusted it and pulled at the sleeves, it was clear he would prefer to be rid of it. "You're up early," he told Zach. "As you can see, people are only now arrivin' for their *petit déjeuner*." The French term for breakfast had been drilled into Sinclair's head by Madame Pond until it had become second nature to him.

"I couldn't sleep," Zach said as he followed Sinclair over to the hotel counter. "Is my aunt in the kitchen?"

Sinclair turned to him, giving him a strange look. "Of course she is. You know very well that she always helps Miss Combs in the mornin'."

Zach now remembered Miss Reid telling him earlier that her duties were also going to include serving breakfast for the guests. "Oh yeah, that's right."

Sinclair shook his head at him. "So young, and already a memory like a sieve."

It was a good-natured jab and Zach couldn't help smiling. "Very funny." He nodded towards the back door. "So can I go see her?"

"You know this is a busy time, and your aunt . . ." Sinclair stopped mid-sentence when a tall man, came hurrying down the stairs, still buttoning his single-breasted vest, and with a jacket slung over his arm. "Mr. Sinclair, breakfast right away," he said as he hurried to the nearest empty table.

"Go tell you aunt that Mr. Briggs wants his *petit déjeuner*." Sinclair pushed Zach toward the back door. "Promptly. Coffee, scrambled eggs, ham and brown bread."

. . .

Zach found both Miss Reid and the cook busy at work in the kitchen. The smell of frying bacon and eggs made his mouth water. He hadn't had anything that morning, except a glass of water before he set out from Johnny Knott's cabin.

"Watch them potatoes, they don't turn to a crisp," Miss Combs told Miss Reid, who was overseeing the four frying pans they had going on the stove.

"I've everything under control, Agatha." Miss Reid shook the pan with the potatoes, while the cook resumed cutting thick slices from a large bread loaf.

"Mr. Sinclair asked me to tell you that Mr. Briggs wants his breakfast right away," Zach said as he walked over the threshold to the kitchen.

Miss Reid turned around in surprise, spatula in hand. "Zachary, when did you arrive?"

"You're dripping fat on the floor," Agatha cautioned, nodding at the spatula. "I don't much want to land on my arse steppin' in that."

Miss Reid quickly returned the spatula to the stove. "Mr. Briggs, you said?" She shook her head in frustration. "Everything with him always has to be at once. I wish he would leave soon. Find another hotel's staff to drive crazy."

"Madame Pond better not hear you talk that way," Miss Combs grumbled. "She's forever goin' on about the guests always bein' right." She tossed the piece of bread she had just cut on a plate. "Balderdash, if you ask me. Why should I pretend they're right if they're clearly not. I sure hope the owners of this hotel will make it back from Quebec soon," she said as she wiped perspiration from her forehead with the back of her hand.

"So what does Mr. Briggs want for breakfast?" Miss Reid asked.

"Coffee, scrambled eggs, ham and bread . . . brown bread," Zach answered.

Miss Reid turned to the cook. "Agatha, hand me a plate with some bread . . . please," she added quickly when she noticed Miss Combs' raised eyebrow.

"Can I do anything to help?" Zach asked, seeing how frazzled Miss Reid looked.

"Oh, if you could help me serve the guests later that would be great." She took the plate from Miss Combs' hand, and spooned scrambled eggs down next to the bread.

Zach walked up to the stove. "Did you hear from Mr. Fitzgerald?" he whispered to Miss Reid.

She skewered a piece of ham from one of the pans and placed it next to the eggs on the plate. "We'll talk after breakfast is over, okay?" she said, nodding at Miss Combs' broad back.

"*Petit déjeuner*," the cook corrected her with a derisive snort. "Don't let Madame Pond hear you call it breakfast." She sniffed in the air. "Them potatoes are burning."

. . .

About an hour later, after the last guests had been taken care of, Miss Reid came back into the kitchen where Zach was sitting at the table, drinking strong coffee, and making short work of the bacon and eggs served to him by Miss Combs. Miss Reid sank down on a chair across from him at the table.

She looked pale and the skin around her eyes were puffy and red from lack of sleep, and too much crying.

"Edna will be comin' at eleven to help you with the wash." Miss Combs reminded Miss Reid.

"Who's Edna?" Zach asked as he wiped his plate clean with a piece of bread, and stuffed it in his mouth.

Miss Reid gave him a tired smile. "I had way too much to do, so Madame Pond finally broke down and hired a young woman to help me on laundry days." She gave a deep sigh. "I wish she would just send the hotel laundry out to the Chinese laundries like everyone else."

Miss Combs put the pan she had just scrubbed back on the stove. "I was the one who gave Madame Pond a good talkin' to, tellin' her how she was workin' us all to the bone." She dried her hands on her apron, while nodding at Miss Reid. "I mean look at your aunt, she's becomin' skin and bones right in front of our eyes, and certainly this whole sorry affair with that gambler isn't helpin' matters." She pulled the apron over her head. "Well, I'll be goin' down to the butcher to see if he has corned beef I can serve up for supper."

"*Dîner*," Miss Reid said with a yawn. Miss Combs frowned at her. "Remember, Madame Pond wants us to call it *Dîner*, not supper, Agatha."

"Oh, her, and her uppity ways," Miss Combs scoffed as she marched over and hung the apron on a peg next to the door. She turned to Miss Reid. "There's still coffee left in the pot. I suggest you drink some, so you can stay awake."

"Will do," Miss Reid told her.

"So did you talk to Mr. Fitzgerald?" Zach asked as soon as the backdoor slammed shut after the cook.

Miss Reid nodded. "I did."

"And?" he prompted when she hesitated.

"Mr. Fitzgerald, as you know, had promised to come to the hotel right after he talked with Judge Begbie." She flicked some bread crumbs off the table with her hand. "I waited and waited, but he didn't show up. Finally, I went to his office, and there he was — trying to hide from me most likely." She gave Zach a wry smile. "Not a very imaginative place if you ask me."

Zach pushed his empty plate away and leaned forward. "So what did he say?" He paused, eyeing her suspiciously. "Are you trying to tell me that Mr. Fitzgerald didn't even speak with the judge?"

"No, no he did." Miss Reid sat back in the chair, crossing her arms over her chest. "He said he tried to reason with the judge for a long time. Argued his case for leniency from all angles, he could think of, but all his rationales seemed to fall on death ears."

Miss Reid's lips began quivering. "Mr. Fitzgerald got a strong sense that Judge Begbie is leaning toward a death sentence. That's why he was delaying coming to the hotel to tell me." She began sobbing while wrapping her arms tightly around herself. "This is really going to happen, isn't it?"

Chapter 46

ZACH LEFT THE HOTEL feeling wretched. Sitting there across from Miss Reid at the table, watching her misery had been gut-wrenching. He had tried to tell her that it was not a foregone conclusion that Judge Begbie would condemn Theo to death tomorrow morning, but that only made her sob even harder. And it was tough to sound convincing, when he himself felt so fearful and uncertain, and his words came across exactly what they were. Empty.

When Miss Combs had again walked into the kitchen, carrying a package containing the coveted corned beef, a fact she proudly announced as soon as she stepped over the threshold, Zach had seen his chance to leave.

He looked up at the sky. It was covered in heavy grey clouds, and perfectly matched his mood. He was grateful now for the loan of Johnny's jacket because the early morning chill was still in the air. He figured he better head to the workshop to tell Kyle about Miss Reid's meeting with Mr. Fitzgerald and see if the carpenter had some work for him.

He was halfway to the workshop when a thought struck him. What if he sought out Judge Begbie and tried to talk with him. Maybe someone other than a lawyer would stand a better chance. Someone like Zach, who recently in Mr. Youtz' Social Studies class, together with twenty plus students, had discussed issues surrounding the death penalty in the United States. If Judge Begbie, as Fitzgerald claimed, already had made up his mind about condemning Theo to hang, what did Zach or, more importantly, Theo, really have to lose by his doing so.

Zach knew that Judge Begbie stayed at his cabin in Richfield when he presided over a case in the area. There was a good chance he would find him there. Determined, he headed in the direction of Richfield, already thinking of what sort of arguments to use with a shrewd judge, who had years of law experience behind him.

. . .

Asking for directions, Zach located Judge Begbie's cabin easily enough, since it turned out it was situated in close proximity to the courthouse. He had expected a man of

Judge Begbie's stature to live in grander accommodations, but to his surprise he found himself standing in front of what could best be termed a shack. Constructed from rough-hewn logs, the cabin was built up a hill, and in front was a worn fence marking the boundary of the property. Underneath a shuttered window stood a well-worn chair.

Before he had time to lose his nerve, Zach walked resolutely up to the closed front door and rapped hard on it with his knuckles. From inside the cabin, he heard quick footsteps across the floor. The door opened and a tall skinny woman dressed all in black, stared out at him. She probably wasn't much more than thirty, but her gaunt face made her look much older. Her brown hair was twisted into a tight bun, which was fastened at the nape of her neck.

"Hello, Mrs. Begbie," Zach said tentatively, not knowing if the judge was married, or not.

The corners of her tight lips pulled up slightly as if she wanted to smile, but didn't quite know how to go about it. "I'm certainly not Mrs. Begbie."

"Who is it, Mrs. Garrick?" Judge Begbie asked from inside the cabin.

"It's a young lad," she said over her shoulder. "What do you want with the judge?" she asked, turning her attention to Zach again.

He cleared his throat. "I would like to talk to Judge Begbie. It's urgent," he added, so she was less likely to dismiss him.

"Tell him to wait for me outside," the judge said. "I'll be

with him momentarily." He didn't sound too happy about being interrupted.

"You heard the judge," Mrs. Garrick told Zach and promptly shut the door in his face.

A couple of minutes later the judge walked outside.

Pulling on his jacket, he viewed Zach with irritation. "Mr. Zachary Stillman," he said, closing the door firmly behind him. "I thought I recognized your voice."

Zach nodded towards the cabin. "Sorry, I really thought she was your wife."

"Good heavens no. Mrs. Garrick works at one of the restaurants in Richfield. She brings food up and prepares my meals when I'm here." Judge Begbie looked up in the sky. "Looks like rain soon." He went over to the chair and sat down on it. Crossing his legs and folding his arms across his chest, he fixed Zach with his gaze. "I know you're here to plead for Mr. Cox," he said. "Mr. Fitzgerald came here to do the same."

"I am," Zach said. They kept staring at each other for a while, until finally the judge gave a deep sigh and looked down as his crossed legs. "Listen, all of you, every single one of you was given the opportunity to testify, to present your version of events, but still the jury, after a long deliberation, I may add, and weighing all the facts presented to them, came back with a verdict of guilty." He met Zach's gaze again. "The jury has spoken."

Zach nodded. "I don't agree with their verdict, but I didn't come here because I wanted to dispute it." He bit his lip. "I'm here to ask you to spare his life, and give me and his other friends a chance to prove his innocence. If you hang him . . ." He fought back tears.

Judge Begbie shifted on his seat. "My first and foremost responsibility as a Justice of the Crown Colony of British Columbia is to uphold order in a vast area where the lure of gold attracts people of often questionable character. It's a daunting job, but I happen to be good at it." He unfolded his arms and leaned forward. "I can't be seen as weak and . . ."

"What about *just*." Zach couldn't help interrupting, even though he knew he might make the judge angry. "That's what they also call you. A *just* person."

Judge Begbie got up from the chair. "I am being just," he said quietly, "because I happen to agree with the jury."

Zach stood staring at the judge. "And I happen to know Mr. Cox is innocent."

Turning his back on Zach, Judge Begbie walked over to the low fence and looked out over the tree and grass-covered hills. "I know that you sincerely believe he is," he said after a while, "but there's too much evidence, pointing to his guilt and the jury recognized that, and so did I."

Zach's hands clenched. "Even though the evidence is stacked against him doesn't mean he's guilty."

Judge Begbie turned to him. "In some cases that might be true, but I'm afraid not in this one. It was not lost on me in court how much you cared for him." He sighed. "Listen, lad, often the dark corners of the soul can be well-hidden from the people closest to you."

"Four percent," Zach said, holding up four fingers. "It's a proven fact that four percent of people executed are innocent. The Innocence Project . . ." He stopped abruptly, realizing his blunder.

Judge Begbie frowned. "The Innocence Project?" he asked.

"It's . . . it's a legal organization in the States studying the death penalty," Zach said, trying to think of a way to extract himself from the hole he was digging himself into. "As I said, they discovered that four percent of people executed are innocent. That's four out of every one hundred."

Judge Begbie was still trying to get his head around the information Zach had just given him. "How could they possibly back up that claim?" he said. "I read any and all legal journals and books I can get my hands on, and I've never heard of this . . . this Innocence Project."

Zach figured that since he had already stepped into it, he could just as well continue his twenty-first century arguments. "When you think about it, executing a person, who has killed someone, makes us, society, killers too, and I for one don't want to be part of organized killing."

Judge Begbie's face reddened and his eyes narrowed. "There has to be consequences for evil acts, otherwise how can society function? It would be anarchy."

"No, it wouldn't." Zach was determined to stand his ground. "Don't you see, Judge Begbie, that capital punishment clearly isn't working, because people still keep on killing one another. Besides, seven percent of all executions are botched." Zach didn't care that this number was connected to executions by lethal injections in the US. He was sure there were botched hangings here too. Billy Barker once mentioned that he had witnessed an incident where the head had snapped off the condemned.

The anger in the judge's eyes dissipated and gave way to something resembling respect. "How old are you?" he asked.

"Fifteen," Zach answered.

The judge nodded. "You're an usual young man, I'll grant you that."

They were interrupted when the door to the cabin was opened, and Mrs. Garrick stuck her head out. "Judge, remember that Mr. Bowron will be here any moment now," she said. "Do you want me to make tea with the meal?"

Judge Begbie smiled at her. "That would be wonderful, Mrs. Garrick."

She gave a curt nod and disappeared into the cabin again, closing the door.

Judge Begbie looked at Zach. "Well, duty calls." He paused for a moment before he continued. "Despite our discussion being rather unsettling, I did appreciate it."

"Me too." Zach watched the judge walk toward the cabin, hands clasped behind his back. "Judge Begbie," he called out. The judge turned around. "Mr. Cox does belong to those four percent I was talking about."

"I'll see you at the sentencing, lad," Judge Begbie answered. He opened the door to the cabin and walked inside.

Zach stood staring at the closed door for a while. He hadn't been able to tell if he had made any headway with the judge, but he sure hoped so. Zach turned around and headed for the road. When he walked through the town of Richfield, big fat raindrops began falling around him, and when he made it back to Barkerville, he was soaked.

Chapter 47

"WHERE WERE YOU TODAY?" Kyle asked Zach, who was absentmindedly chasing a piece of carrot around on his plate. The two of them were sitting across from each other at the table in Johnny Knott's cabin, eating their dinner of leftover beef stew. The carpenter was negotiating a contract with a new client, and hadn't yet made it home.

Zach met his friend's gaze. "I was worried about Miss Reid, so I wanted to see how she was doing."

Kyle shrugged. "Well, this whole thing with Cox has been stressful on all of us." He pushed his half-filled plate away. "I don't even have any appetite." He leaned back in the chair and wedged his thumbs behind his belt. "So how's Miss E.?"

Zach put his spoon down. "She honestly looks like death warmed over. I don't think she sleeps much, if at all."

"Did she speak to Fitzgerald yesterday after his meeting with the judge?"

Zach pointed at the water jug, standing close to Kyle. "Could I have some water?" Kyle pushed the jug across the table to him.

"Yes, she did speak to him," Zach said in answer to Kyle's question as he poured himself a glass of water, "but Mr. Fitzgerald wasn't exactly encouraging. He felt that Judge Begbie already had made up his mind."

"You mean he's leaning toward hanging Cox?"

Zach took a sip of water and nodded. "Yeah, and that was why I decided to go and have a talk with Judge Begbie myself." He shrugged. "I figured I had nothing to lose."

Kyle leaned forward and stared at Zach with awe. "Wow, you're braver than I thought. How did that go?"

Zach drank some more water and wiped his mouth with his shirtsleeve. "Hard to say if it had any impact at all." He put the glass down next to his plate. "I really stepped into it," he said after a pause. "For a moment there I forgot it was 1866 and brought up the Innocence Project." Kyle stared blankly at him. "You know that legal organization in the States that Mr. Youtz once talked about in class. The one that helps clear wrongly convicted people with the use of DNA analysis."

Kyle raised his eyebrows at Zach. "Ouch, how did you extricate yourself from that one?"

Zach smiled wryly at him. "With a combination of audacity and lying."

The door to the cabin opened, and Johnny breezed inside with his usual air of efficiency, slamming the door shut behind him with his foot. "I hope you lads didn't eat all the grub. I'm starvin.'" He pulled his jacket off and hung it on the peg next to the door.

"No, there's plenty left." Zach got up from his chair and went over to the stove. "Just sit down, and I'll get some stew for you."

"Well, thank you," Johnny walked over to the table, pulled a chair out and sank down on it.

From the pot, which stood simmering on the stove, Zach ladled a generous portion of stew onto a plate. He brought the food over to the table and placed it in front of Johnny. Zach sat down on his chair. The carpenter dipped his spoon into the piping hot stew. He blew impatiently on the spoonful to cool it down enough for him to eat it.

Twilight had descended outside, and its muted light filtered through the cabin's only window, cloaking the interior in a greyness that perfectly matched Zach's morose mood. "What if Judge Begbie decides tomorrow that Mr. Cox should not hang, how many years do you think he'll get?" Zach asked the carpenter.

Johnny swallowed his mouthful of stew. "Life sentence, no doubt." He glanced across the table at Kyle. "Could you light the lantern, please?"

"With no chance of parole?" Zach asked as he watched

Kyle get up, grab the kerosene lamp and walk over to the stove.

When Zach turned his attention to the carpenter again he found him shaking his head. "Parole? I'm not sure what you mean by that?"

"You know time off for good behaviour."

Johnny pushed his plate away. "What an odd notion. No, you can be certain that a life sentence is just that. For life."

Kyle came back with the lit lantern and put it at the end of the table. "So Cox either hangs, or he spends his life in a hole somewhere?" Kyle sat down with a grunt and dismally viewed the leftovers on his plate. "What a choice," he added. He looked up at Johnny. "I say we assemble a group of men and break him out of jail." He nodded at the shotgun hanging on the wall over the carpenter's bed. "You already have a gun and I'm sure others do too."

Johnny got up from the table and walked over to his jacket, where he fished out his meerschaum pipe from one of the pockets, together with the small leather pouch he kept his tobacco in. "So let's say, Kyle, that you succeed in breakin' Theo out of jail," he said. "What then?"

Kyle shrugged. "We get ourselves some horses and escape."

"We would have a posse after us, the likes of which has never been seen in all of the Cariboo." Johnny came back to the table and sat down. "No, believe me, it's all in Judge Begbie's hands now." He opened the tobacco pouch and filled the chamber of his pipe with it. "I pray he'll show enough mercy not to let poor Theo hang. That's all we can really hope for." He stared hard at Kyle as he tamped the tobacco down in the pipe chamber with his thumb. "And I'll listen no more to foolish notions like this."

Chapter 48

ℴ

"THEY WOULDN'T LET ME go and see him at the jail yesterday," Miss Reid said to Zach, who was sitting next to her in the filled courtroom. Her eyes were puffy from crying, and her nose shone like a big red beacon on her pale face. "They only allowed Mr. Fitzgerald to stay with him." She cast a glance at Theo, who was sitting stone-faced in the prisoner box. The sight brought more tears to her eyes. "Poor man. He's obviously still in shock."

Zach hadn't slept much last night, and the constant drone of voices in the packed courtroom threatened to lull him to sleep. Every time his eyelids began to close, he pinched himself on the arm to stay awake.

Zach's eyes flew open when the door to the courtroom opened. This time he hadn't needed to pinch himself. Judge Begbie strode inside. When he sat down at the bench, he solemnly surveyed the people assembled. "I want absolute quiet when I pass sentence. No outbursts, no comments." He looked at the prisoner. "Mr. Theodore Joseph Cox, please rise for sentencing."

Theo obeyed. His expression reminded Zach of the stunned look of the deer once caught in the headlight of his grandfather's big truck just before it was hit. It had happened nearly five years ago when Zach had visited with his grandparents, but he still had nightmares about it: the shudder of the truck when the deer bounced off the bumper, and finally the numb, helpless feeling of knowing that a life had been taken, and there was nothing he could do about it.

The judge cleared his throat. "Over the past two days," he said, "I've spent all my time weighing the evidence, and taking into consideration the heinous nature of this crime. What appears to have been, from all accounts, an honest and hardworking man was taken from this world in the prime of his life, only because through hard toil he came into some wealth.

It was a murder committed out of greed, and to me this is the most grievous of crimes." He paused for a moment. "Last night as I carefully went over my notes one last time, and thought of the testimonies I had sat through, I realized there were still areas I felt ambiguous about."

He looked at the jury, who sat watching him keenly. "You as a jury did your duty and I commend you for that. I know well what a weighty responsibility it is to hold someone else's fate in your hands. In your minds the facts presented to you in this case were clear enough for you to come back with a guilty verdict."

His gaze moved across the courtroom until it settled on Zach. "I, however, find that I cannot in good conscience pass the ultimate sentence in this case."

A murmur went through the courtroom.

"He's going to live," Miss Reid's whispered. "He's going to live," she repeated.

The Judge looked at Theo. "Mr. Theodore Joseph Cox, it's the order of this court of the District of British Columbia, which I represent, that you'll spend the remainder of your life in the Victoria Gaol."

. . .

"This is so wrecked," Kyle said through clenched teeth as they stood outside the courthouse, staring after Theo, who was being marched off to jail by two constables, each of them with a firm hold on his arms.

"Well, right now I'm just grateful, he was spared the death sentence." Miss Reid wiped her eyes with her handkerchief.

"Instead he can sit and rot in jail for something he didn't do." Kyle kicked at a small rock. It bounced down the hill before it came to a rest. He glanced at Miss Reid. "When are they taking him to Victoria?"

"Three days, Mr. Fitzgerald told me." She hesitated. "I'm actually thinking about going to Victoria myself. That way I can visit him in jail, as often as they'll let me, of course."

Zach couldn't believe his ears. "Miss Reid, that's a terrible idea. You've work and a place to stay here in Barkerville. There are no guarantees you'll find that in Victoria." He looked at Kyle. "Tell her it's a bad idea."

Kyle nodded. "Zach is right, Miss E. To begin with, how are you going to get down there without money?" he asked. "It's not likely they'll let you travel with Cox."

Miss Reid's face fell. "I know. I know." She blew her nose. "It's only that I feel so powerless."

Zach hooked his arm through hers and she leaned her head against his shoulder. He watched as people around them began dispersing to head for home and carry on with their business.

Miss Reid sighed. "Theo's the kindest, most decent man I know, and I have no way of helping him." She lifted her head from Zach's shoulder. "That jury's verdict is an outright travesty of justice."

"Exactly," Kyle said as he looked towards the jail where the door had just closed after Theo and his jailers. "That's why we should break him out of jail." He lowered his voice. "I know where I can get another gun. Add that to Johnny's and we have ourselves some real firepower."

Zach shook his head at him. "Don't start that again, Kyle."

"No, no, listen for a moment," Kyle said. "I'm pretty sure I can also smuggle out a couple of horses from one of the livery stables in Barkerville. Mr. Farley who owns the bar next to the stable says the guy who guards it at night is asleep half the time." He looked eagerly at Miss Reid. "We free Theo, and we all escape." He snapped his fingers. "Just like that."

"You heard what Mr. Knott said last night," Zach warned him. "They'll hunt us down. What do you think is going to happen then?" He stared hard at Kyle, who gave a shrug.

"Well, it can hardly get any worse for Cox," he said.

"Kyle, when I said what do you think is going to happen, that also included *us*." He gave a sigh when he saw the confusion in Kyle's eyes. "Come on now, do you think they would let us get away scot free if we pulled a stunt like that?"

"Zach is right, Kyle," Miss Reid said. "We could all end up in jail or maybe even worse." She pulled open the small crocheted drawstring purse that Madame Pond had given her as a gift. "Theo would never let us risk our lives like that." Miss Reid stuffed her handkerchief down in the purse. "He would simply refuse to go with us."

"You two are just going to throw in the towel without a fight, aren't you?" Kyle stared at both of them in disgust. "This is so pathetic," he said before he spun around and marched down the hill toward the road.

"Where are you going?" Zach yelled after him.

"Work," Kyle answered.

"Let him be," Miss Reid said. "He just needs to simmer down a bit." They watched as Kyle turned onto the road and headed in the direction of Barkerville. "Are we pathetic?" Miss Reid sounded subdued. "Are we really doing everything we can?" she asked when Zach looked at her.

He thought about his visit to Judge Begbie the day before. "I honestly don't know what else we can do right now," he answered her.

Chapter 49

∽

ZACH CLOSED THE DOOR to Johnny Knott's cabin, and headed out in the rain. It had been raining for two solid days now. Because the hills around Barkerville had been clear-cut to provide lumber for houses and mine shafts, flash floods occurred at times, which Zach was very mindful of as he made his way through the mining fields toward Barkerville. Just yesterday a flash flood had buried two cabins. Fortunately it had been in the middle of day and nobody had been at home. He could only hope he would be fast enough to get out of the way if one did happen.

When Zach finally arrived at Johnny's workshop in Barkerville no one was there. Not particularly keen about going out in the rain again to look for them, he decided to stay and wait for their return. He sat down on a stool next to the workbench and listened to the rain pounding on the roof.

"Oh, here you are, Zach," Johnny said as he entered the workshop and leaned a plank of pinewood up against the wall. He pulled his cap off and with the back of his hand wiped rain from his face. "I have a few things to do here. Kyle is working on the shelves and counter at Mr. Farley's new bar next to the livery stable." He removed his jacket and hung it together with his cap on a peg next to the door. "Why don't you go and help him," he told Zach. "I'll come by later to see how you two are doing."

"Okay," Zach trudged outside in the rain again. Dodging big pools of water in front of the workshop, he made his way up to the boardwalk. At least here the buildings had the occasional overhang he could walk underneath.

. . .

Only one person was in the bar, when Zach arrived. A middle-aged short bald man with a huge beard. "Mr. Farley?" Zach asked, figuring he must be the bar's owner. At least he matched the description Kyle had given of him.

The man who was busy placing liquor bottles on the brand-new shelves that had been put up on the wall behind the counter, turned abruptly around. "I'm looking for Kyle," Zach said. "I work for Johnny Knott."

Mr. Farley furrowed his meaty forehead, and his small eyes glared at Zach. "Heaven only knows where he took hisself off to. Told me he had to go to the privy, and that's nigh . . ." He pulled his pocket watch out, flipped the cover open and glanced at it, "an hour ago." He looked up at Zach again. "Sure enough when I just went to check, he wasn't even there." Mr. Farley placed his hand on top of the un- finished counter. "I need this done today, so I can open for business tomorrow, and that's no more than what Johnny promised me." He slapped the palm of his hand down on the counter. "I need Johnny here, and soon."

Zach saw no reason to argue and nodded. "I'll go and get him." He turned around and left through the open door. He stood for a while underneath the bar's overhang, looking into the driving rain. Where could Kyle have gone? He looked up and down the boardwalk, but saw no sign of him. Stick- ing his hands in his pockets, he headed for the workshop. Hopefully, Johnny was still there so he could deal with Mr. Farley right away.

. . .

Johnny was busy sawing a piece of wood in half when Zach walked over the threshold to the workshop. "Mr. Knott," he said loudly, so he could be heard over the noise.

The carpenter stopped sawing and turned to Zach. "You need some materials for the bar?" he asked.

Zach shook his head. "No, it's not that. Kyle wasn't there."

"What do you mean he wasn't there?" Johnny asked, frowning. "I left him there with clear instructions to finish up."

Zach shrugged. "He told Mr. Farley that he was going to the privy, but he just never came back."

Johnny put the saw down on top of the wood. "Well, that's mighty odd. Kyle's hard to motivate at times, but he's never taken off from his work."

"Well, Mr. Farley is ticked off," Zach said. "And he wants you to come and finish up, so he can open the bar tomorrow."

The carpenter went over and grabbed his hat and jacket from the hook. "This is ill-timed with all I have to do today." He fought to get his arms into the sleeves of the still wet jacket. "Why don't you go and look for Kyle, while I appease Mr. Farley?" As he turned around to leave, he nearly collided with a tall man who came rushing through the doorway. He was clad in an oversized coat and with a broad brimmed hat pulled down over his eyes.

"Evan," Johnny said in surprise.

Evan pulled off his hat, and slapped it against a knee to shake the water from it. "Someone stole your horse, Johnny." Zach knew that the carpenter stabled his horse, Ace, at the stable located next to Farley's bar.

Johnny stood staring at him. "Someone took Ace?"

Evan nodded. "Yeah, Stuart, my stablehand, had gone

outside for a smoke, and ran into Neil, one of the coach drivers for Barnard's Express. They stood talking for a while, and when Stuart came back and checked on the horses, he noticed Ace was gone." He pushed his hat down on his head again. "Whoever took it managed to sneak it out the back way without Stuart or Neil noticing." He put his hand on Johnny's shoulder. "I'll go and inform the law. If there's one thing that's not tolerated around here it's horse thieves."

"All I really care about is getting Ace back unharmed," the carpenter said.

Evan patted his shoulder. "I'll make sure of that."

"Wait," Zach blurted out when Evan was about to leave. Both men turned to him with a startled look. "It's just that Kyle was working next door to the stable. I think there's a possibility that he *borrowed* Ace," Zach said, emphasizing the word borrowed.

Johnny shook his head at him. "Why take my horse without asking me?"

Zach shrugged. "I have no idea, but it has to have been something urgent."

"Don't alert the law just yet," the carpenter told Evan who stood fidgeting in the doorway.

Evan nodded. "If that's what you want." He flipped up the collar of his coat and headed out into the rain again.

"How foolish of Kyle to ride out in this weather," Johnny said as he buttoned his jacket. Zach was not about to point out that as far as he knew, Kyle had never ridden a horse before. The carpenter sighed. "Well, I'll have to go appease Mr. Farley. Do you want to stay here?"

Zach shook his head. "If it's okay, I would like to go and see my aunt at the hotel."

Johnny pulled his cap on. "You do that. Maybe she knows something about why Kyle might have taken Ace."

Zach doubted it. Kyle's actions seemed more like a spur of the moment decision. "Maybe," he answered.

. . .

The hotel was relatively quiet when Zach arrived. A group of men were playing cards at a corner table, and Sinclair was checking in a guest at the counter, an older man clad in mud-splattered pants and a long rumpled coat. "Devilish weather out there," Zach heard the man say. "The stagecoach from Cottonwood to here took double the time it normally does with those muddy roads."

Sinclair who had been busy writing in the hotel ledger, looked up. "Yeah, I've heard that travel is near impossible right now," he said. "I don't remember ever havin' seen so much rain at this time off year." Sinclair caught sight of Zach. "Your aunt is out back," he told him.

Zach found Miss Reid in the kitchen, where she was busy packing food into a wicker basket.

"You can take along some of the mutton too, Eliza." Leaning her back against the kitchen counter and with her arms folded over her ample chest, Miss Combs was busy surveying Miss Reid's efforts. "I don't know why you're venturin' out in that foul weather. It's a long way to Richfield. Why not wait until tomorrow?"

"You haven't heard yet," Miss Reid said, looking up at her. Her voice sounded frantic. "They're taking poor Theo to Victoria a day earlier than planned. Someone told Sinclair when he went to the bank."

Miss Combs saw Zach standing in the doorway. "You look like a drowned rat." She pushed herself away from the counter. "I still have coffee on the stove."

Zach nodded. "Thanks, I could really use that."

Miss Reid turned to him. "You heard about Theo, too?" She asked when she noticed his troubled expression.

"No, no I didn't," he said as he walked over to the stove where Miss Combs was pouring him a mug of coffee from the blue coffee enamel pot. "I'm here because Kyle has disappeared."

"That whelp's always trouble," Miss Combs said as she handed Zach the mug.

Miss Reid had stopped what she was doing, and stood staring at Zach, holding three hardboiled eggs in her hand. "Disappeared?"

He took a quick sip of his coffee, burning his tongue. "He borrowed Mr. Knott's horse without asking, and took off. You don't know anything, do you?"

Miss Reid put the eggs into the basket. "No, I don't." She looked up at Miss Combs. "Do you?"

The cook snorted. "No, I certainly don't."

Miss Reid closed the lid on the basket. "I wouldn't even know where to start searching for him." She shook her head in frustration. "Why would he go and pull a stupid stunt like that?"

"Because he's Kyle," Zach said with a shrug. "So why are they taking Mr. Cox to Victoria early?"

"Who knows." Miss Reid bit her lower lip to keep from crying. "He leaves tomorrow morning apparently, and this . . ." She couldn't keep the tears at bay anymore, "this might be the last time I see him."

"Here she goes with the waterworks again." Miss Combs pulled a handkerchief out of her apron pocket and handed it to Miss Reid.

"Thank you, Agatha." Miss Reid sniffled as she dabbed her eyes with the handkerchief. "Zach, can you go with me to visit Theo?"

"Of course he can, Eliza," Miss Combs said, patting Zach's arm. "The state you're in, someone has to keep an eye on you. That way he can also carry that basket of yours."

"If Mr. Knott agrees, I'll go with you," Zach promised Miss Reid.

Chapter 50

AS IT TURNED OUT Johnny Knott was only too willing to
help. He had a friend who was delivering some goods to a
store in Richfield, and Zach and Miss Reid were able to hitch
a ride with Nels, as he was called, a Swede of few words and
even fewer facial expressions. Fortunately, the rain tapered
off on their way, putting an end to the two days of solid rain.
It was a relief to look up into the sky and see glimpses of blue
among the grey clouds.

Nels dropped them of at the store where he had to deliver
his goods, and Zach and Miss Reid, after having thanked him
profusely, walked the last distance up to the courthouse and

jail, Zach lugging the basket of food, which was certainly by no means light.

As Miss Reid knocked on the door to the jail, the sun peeked out from behind the cloud-cover. Its light reflected in the raindrops still hanging onto the grass leaves and flowers, and it was as if the ground was covered with diamonds.

They heard the scraping of a chair and then heavy footfalls across the floor. The door was opened and a thickset man somewhere in his mid-thirties with a round plump face covered partly by a goatee, looked out at them. "Miss Reid," he said, stepping aside to let them by. Zach didn't remember having seen him before, but it was obvious Miss Reid had already met him.

"Thank you so much, Constable Allerton," Miss Reid said, entering the jail with Zach. Here they found Constable Franklin, sitting at the room's only desk, with a chess set in front of him. Evidently, Zach and Miss Reid had interrupted a game.

"I was losing anyways," Franklin said, smiling wryly. He sat back in his chair and wrapped his arm around the backrest. "Hello, Miss Reid. I take it you're here to see our favourite prisoner." He nodded at the picnic basket in Zach's hand. "Bringing him sustenance I see." He grinned at Allerton, who was closing the door to the jail. "Our prison grub ain't all that bad, is it, Brett?"

"It's atrocious," Theo commented from his cell. He stood up and wrapped his hands around two of the iron bars, smiling warmly out at Miss Reid. "So wonderful to see you, Eliza."

She hurried over to him. "I heard they were going to take you to Victoria tomorrow."

His expression turned serious. "I'm afraid so."

"Put that basket on the chair over there." Franklin told Zach and nodded at a chair standing underneath a window. Zach was only too happy to rid himself of the heavy basket and lugged it over to the chair, placing it on the wooden seat.

"Brett, can you please go through it?" Franklin asked Allerton.

Franklin glanced at Miss Reid, who had turned to him with a frown. "Not that I suspect you of hidin' a file or a weapon in there," he told her apologetically. "It's only procedure, that's all."

Zach glanced out the window, and gave a start when he saw a horse come galloping towards the jail. He pushed the chair aside, moving his face closer to the window so he could make out the rider. His warm breath fogged up the window, and he wiped the glass with his jacket sleeve. There was another horse following close behind the first one.

Allerton had noticed Zach's interest in what was going on outside. "What's afoot?" he asked as he pushed Zach aside to have a look himself. He turned to Franklin. "Two riders comin' our way, possibly armed."

Franklin jumped up from his chair so fast it fell over with a loud clatter. He turned and grabbed two rifles from the gun stand and threw one of them to Allerton, who barely caught it on time. "Let's go," he told him.

Miss Reid hurried over to the window and peered outside. "Is that who I think it is?" she asked Zach, who nodded. She turned to Theo. "It's Kyle and Enos."

The two constables had already torn the door open and rushed outside to face the riders. Zach and Miss Reid collided in the doorway as they scrambled out after them. Franklin held up a warning hand when he saw them. "Go inside again," he ordered.

"But we know them," Miss Reid protested. "It's Kyle, my . . . my nephew." She looked at Franklin. "Come on, you know Kyle from the trial, Constable."

"And the other one's Theo's brother, Enos," Zach said.

Despite Miss Reid's assurances, Allerton still kept his rifle trained on Enos, who looked the most threatening with his unkempt beard and dirty stringy hair. "You're Theo's brother?" he yelled when Enos reined in his horse in front of him. The constable probably had a hard time equating this brawny man in his mud splattered coat and pants with the slim usually impeccably dressed Theo.

Enos jumped down from his horse. "I am." He turned and handed the reins to Kyle, who had just dismounted Ace in a rather ungraceful manner. "I wanna see my brother," Enos said, trying to bypass Allerton, who was still pointing his rifle at him.

"It's all right, Brett," Constable Franklin said.

Enos gave Allerton a withering look as the latter stepped aside to let him by. Zach and Miss Reid received a curt nod from Enos before he hurried through the doorway into the jail with Allerton following him closely.

Miss Reid looked at Franklin. "Is it okay if I go in there too, Constable Franklin?" He nodded and she walked inside the jail with him.

Zach hurried over to Kyle, who was busy tying the reins of the two horses to a nearby tree. The horse Enos had ridden was Youtz. He turned his big head to Zach and whinnied softly in recognition.

Zach reached out his hand and stroked the animal's neck. "Where did you find Enos?" he asked Kyle.

Kyle arched his back, wincing along with pain of the movement. "I don't know what's most sore my back, my ass, or my thighs."

"Kyle, I asked you a question." Youtz pushed his nose into Zach's hand when he stopped stroking it.

Kyle patted Ace's flank. "I was working at Farley's bar next to the stable," he said, "the door stood open and I overheard the stablehand and Neil, one of the coach driver's for Barnard's Express, talk about how bad the roads were because of all the rain we've had."

He stopped patting Ace, folded his hands and stretched his arms over his head. Zach heard his knuckles crack. "Neil had apparently just made it back from Cottonwood House and he told the stablehand that the rain had turned the roads into a mess, and he had come across several freight wagons that couldn't make it and had had to stop."

"What does that have to do with Enos?" Zach asked as he continued stroking Youtz.

"I'm coming to that," Kyle said, lowering his arms. "Neil happened to mention he had spotted Enos on the side of the road about ten miles out from Barkerville," he said. "I had just heard from Mr. Farley that they were going to take Cox to Victoria tomorrow morning, so I figured if I could get Enos to Richfield in time, he could at least disprove some of Jackson's lies and that way cast some doubt on the rest of his testimony." He shrugged. "Maybe it's a long shot, but I couldn't just sit around and do nothing."

"So you took Ace."

Kyle nodded. "Yeah, even though I had never ridden a horse in my life, I couldn't think of any other way to get to Enos fast enough." He swatted a fly away that had settled on his cheek. "The back door to the stable was unlocked and sneaking Ace out was the easy part." He rolled his eyes. "Figuring out the tack was a different matter. Johnny once showed me how, but I tell you it was still a challenge."

"So it was easy enough to find Enos?" Zach asked.

Kyle nodded. "Yeah, he was where Neil had said he was. I found him dozing off inside his wagon." He grinned broadly at Zach. "He was so shocked when I woke him up that I honestly thought he was about to have a heart attack. Of course, true to form, he began calling me all sorts of names."

It was getting warm in the sun, and Kyle unbuttoned his mud-splattered jacket, pulled it off, and draped it over Ace's saddle.

Zach stopped patting Youtz, and the horse bent his head and began eating from the tall grass growing around the tree. Ace quickly followed suit. "Did Enos even know that his brother was on trial for McKenna's murder?" he asked Kyle as he watched the two horses tearing at the grass with their teeth.

Kyle shook his head. "He had no idea. He hadn't read a newspaper, or really talked to anyone on his way up from Fort Yale, he said."

Kyle rolled his shirtsleeves up. "Since Enos was unable to find another driver to replace Jackson, all he was intent on was bringing his freight up to Barkerville in a hurry, so he could get back to Yale again for the next load. Even during the sailing from Soda Creek to Quesnellemouth, Enos said he was so exhausted he pretty much slept most of the time."

"So what was his reaction when he heard about his brother's conviction?" Zach asked.

Kyle emitted a low whistling sound that made both horses turn their heads towards him. "Man, he was so furious when I told him about Jackson's lies that he right away saddled one of his horses, and we rode at breakneck speed to get here." He shook his head. "We were lucky to make it in one piece."

Zach saw Constable Franklin come out of the jail and head towards them. "Here comes Franklin," he whispered to

Kyle, who turned around and watched the constable intently as he approached. Franklin stopped in front of them and pointed to Judge Begbie's cabin in the distance. "Zach, could you go up and fetch the judge and tell him to meet us inside the courthouse?" There was a breathless quality to his voice. "He'll want to hear what Enos Cox has to say."

Chapter 51

ZACH AND JUDGE BEGBIE were the last ones to arrive at the courthouse. Enos sat on a bench up front, his head bent. A short distance away stood Miss Reid, together with Kyle and Constable Franklin. In the prisoner box, Constable Allerton was sitting with Theo, who looked pale and shaken. Judge Begbie, clearly irritated by having his dinner interrupted, had asked Zach questions about why the devil he was being summoned as the two of them covered the distance from the cabin to the courthouse. There wasn't much Zach could tell him, except that Theo's brother had arrived.

Franklin said something to Miss Reid and walked up to meet the judge.

Zach hurried over to her and Kyle. "What did Enos have to say?" he asked her as the judge and Franklin conferred in hushed voices.

"Oh, believe me he had plenty to tell," Miss Reid said, shaking her head. "Theo's still stunned by all his brother's admissions."

Before Zach had time to inquire further, Judge Begbie concluded his conversation with Franklin and strode up to where Enos was sitting. "I understand from Constable Franklin that you have a great deal to add to this case."

Enos looked up at him. "I do indeed," he said. "My brother is innocent of the crime he has been convicted of." His jaw tightened. "Oh, if I had Jackson here right now, I would . . ."

"Better not finish that sentence, Mr. Cox," the judge said. He stood thinking for a while, his brow wrinkled. "This is highly irregular, but since I'm off to Quesnellemouth early tomorrow on an urgent matter, I have no choice but to listen to what you have to say in this rather informal manner."

He turned and looked at the constables in turn. "You, Constable Franklin and you, Constable Allerton are my witnesses to what will be said here today." The two men nodded, their expressions solemn. Judge Begbie walked to the bench, picked up the Bible and returned to Enos with it.

"You're going to swear me in?" Enos asked. He sounded put out. "Believe me, I'll be tellin' the truth here today."

Judge Begbie raised his eyebrows at him. "If that's the case, then you'll have no trouble swearing to that on the Bible." He

Bitten Acherman

held the thick book out to Enos who put his left hand on the Bible and raised the right.

"Repeat this after me," Judge Begbie said. "I swear that the evidence that I shall give, shall be the truth, the whole truth and nothing but the truth, so help me God."

Enos repeated the sentence in a loud and clear voice.

Judge Begbie then returned the Bible to the bench and seated himself. He pointed to the witness stand. "Please take a seat, Mr. Cox."

Judge Begbie waited for Enos to do so. "I'm listening," he said as he folded his hands in front of him.

Enos suddenly looked very small to Zach as he sat there in the witness stand with his head pulled down between his hunched shoulders. "I so often wish Mr. McKenna had never shown up at our camp," Enos said. "I've honestly not had a moment's peace since that day." He gave a deep sigh as he looked at his brother, who viewed him with a stricken look. "But Mr. McKenna did show up," Enos said, "tellin' us about his gold mine and the riches he and his partner hauled out of there."

He turned his attention to the judge. "I've seen plenty of men try their luck in the Cariboo, sinkin' everythin' they own into their quest for gold, and most of them fail, and often turn into paupers overnight, and yet they can't stop." He shook his head. "Gold fever is indeed a heady thing and the ones afflicted will lie, steal and even kill to get their hands on it." He paused for a moment. "And here suddenly sat a man among us, who had succeeded where so many others had failed," he continued.

Judge Begbie leaned back in his seat. "What happened that night, Mr. Cox?" he prompted, clearly impatient with Enos' long lead-in. "The night Philip McKenna came to your camp."

"We all had too much to drink, especially Mr. McKenna," Enos said.

Yes, all except Jackson, Zach thought. Was he really the only one that night who had noticed?

"To be honest, I don't remember much from that night," Enos continued. "Don't even recall rollin' out my blankets to sleep, but that's where I found myself when I woke up again, flat on my back right next to Mr. McKenna, who was sawing wood louder than I'd ever heard it before."

He shrugged. "Maybe that was what woke me up. My brother was sleepin' soundly a bit away from us." Enos smiled at his brother. "The snorin' didn't seem to bother Theo one bit," he said. "Anyways, I was feeling a headache comin' on so I decided to find myself a more peaceful place to rest. It was when I was gatherin' my blankets that I realized Jackson was nowhere to be seen."

"Mr. Julius Jackson, who testified here in court?" Judge Begbie asked.

Enos nodded. "His blankets were rolled out next to me, but he wasn't sleepin' there. Since the fire was still burnin' strong it was clear that someone had recently thrown logs on it. That someone could only be Jackson since everyone else was fast asleep." He took a deep breath. "It angered me that Jackson, despite all my repeated warnings, had left the fire unattended, so I decided to give him a good talkin' to about it."

Zach leaned forward on the bench where he was sitting between Kyle and Miss Reid, afraid to miss a single word being said.

"I found Jackson a little ways from camp. It was a full moon that night and he stood outlined there in its bright light with a shovel in his hand, diggin'. Next to him lay the two saddlebags Mr. McKenna's mule had carried." Enos looked at the judge. "I've never seen someone jump like Jackson did when he turned and saw me. He dropped the shovel, and then began makin' some foolhardy excuse about suddenly rememberin' that no one had unloaded the saddlebags from the poor mule's back and that he couldn't stand the thought of the animal standin' there all night burdened down like that."

Enos snorted. "He must surely have taken me for a fool, so I asked straight out if he was plannin' to bury them bags in the hole he was diggin'?" Enos shook his head. "Of course he couldn't wiggle himself out of that one, since the evidence as to his intentions was in plain sight."

"Was the mule anywhere to be seen?" Judge Begbie asked.

"No, no it wasn't, so of course I asked him what he had done to the animal. Jackson finally had to admit that he had chased it away." Enos scratched his neck, a raspy sound easily heard in the eerily quiet courtroom. "He then told me that McKenna's saddlebags were indeed full of gold, and he proposed that we bury the bags together. The next morning we would tell Mr. McKenna that the mule had escaped from the tether and taken off with the gold." He bit his lower lip for a moment before he continued. "We would then come back later, dig up the gold and share it between us." He looked over at his brother again. "I admit it was temptin', Theo, but all I kept hearin' in my head was your voice, tellin' me: what would our mother think?"

Enos' gaze returned to the judge. "I told Jackson that he could count me out and that we were goin' to capture McKenna's mule, and put things right again, but then . . ." His hands clasped the railing in front of him, "but then suddenly there was McKenna standin' in front of us, still drunk, eyes wild. He was callin' us thieves and scoundrels, accusin' us of lurin' him to spend the night at camp, and get him drunk, so we could rob him." Enos shook his head. "I tried my best to reason with him tellin' him that Jackson had had a momentary lapse of judgement, but that I would put everythin' right again."

"As soon as I mentioned Jackson's name," Enos continued, "McKenna turned on him like a flash, punchin' Jackson so hard in the stomach that he staggered backwards and fell over the saddlebags. McKenna went after him again, kickin' him in the side over and over again as he lay there on the ground. I feared that McKenna would kill him, so I ran over, grabbed hold of his arm and pulled him away from Jackson." Enos let go of the railing. "I'm a strong man, but McKenna's fury made him so much stronger and I had to let go of him. As McKenna turned around, Jackson was standing there in front of him with the shovel raised over his head." Enos' voice trailed off.

Judge Begbie leaned forward. "Go on, Mr. Cox."

Enos swallowed hard. "Your Honour, I had been so intent on tryin' to restrain McKenna that I hadn't even noticed Jackson get up from the ground and pick up that shovel." He sank back in his chair. "Jackson hit McKenna over the head with all his might, and McKenna dropped to the ground without a sound." Enos stared in front of him. "My heart was in my mouth when I crouched down next to McKenna who was lying there so still. I felt the side of his neck for a pulse but didn't detect any. I looked up at Jackson, who still stood there holding the shovel with both hands while starin' down at McKenna. 'Is he dead?' he asked me. 'I think so,' I answered."

Enos turned his gaze to the judge. "Jackson pointed out to me that it was self-defence, which of course it was, but then he went on to say that most likely no one would believe us and that we could end up hangin' for murder." Enos paused for a moment. "What he said frightened me," he continued. "So, when he suggested we bury the body, get rid of his belongings and then tell the others the next mornin' that

McKenna had left camp early, I . . . I went along with it."

Enos averted his gaze from the judge. "We carried McKenna over to the hole that Jackson had already started diggin', but it wasn't big enough to hold his body. I jumped into the hole while Jackson went to get the shovel so I could lengthen the space. When he came back and was about to hand the shovel to me, Mr. McKenna all of a sudden groaned and lifted his head from the ground." Enos closed his eyes. His face was pale and his lips were trembling.

"Are you all right?" Judge Begbie asked.

Enos opened his eyes. "I'm okay, Your Honour." He took a deep breath to calm himself. "Jackson, he . . . he turned to McKenna and he began hitting him with the shovel. My eyes were seein' what was happenin' but my mind had trouble graspin' it." He was shaking his head as if he was trying to rid his mind of the image. "It was the smell of the blood that finally woke me from my stupor. I scrambled out of the hole and tore the shovel from Jackson's hands before . . ." Enos voice began shaking so hard he had trouble getting the words out . . . "before he had time to hit poor McKenna yet again."

Zach suddenly felt the need to breathe and he inhaled deeply.

Enos' hands clenched and unclenched. "Jackson didn't seem the least bit affected by what he had done. It had been necessary, he said. Had McKenna survived he would most assuredly have alerted the law and turned us both in for tryin' to steal his gold, and probably for assault too. I've been to jail before and I'm not about to get locked up again, he told me."

Enos shifted nervously in his seat. "What Jackson said next sent chills down my spine: 'We're the only ones who know what happened here and that's the way it's goin' to stay.' He then pointed down at McKenna's body. 'If you breathe a word about this, Enos, I'll just say you did it. Everyone knows that you have a hot temper, so I've no doubt people will believe me when I tell them how you went crazy on McKenna and killed him.'"

Tears welled up in Enos' eyes and he wiped them away with the back of his hand. "I'm sorry, Your Honour. It's just that I can't rid myself of the image of Mr. McKenna spread out there in front of me, his face smashed to a pulp and with his blood seepin' into he ground." Enos shuddered at the memory. "It was like your worst nightmare come to life."

"How did the pocket watch that figured so prominently in the trial end up on the ground among some bushes?" Judge Begbie asked as he leaned forward.

"Oh yes, the watch," Enos said, nodding. "It had slipped out of McKenna's vest pocket, probably when we carried him to the hole, and it was danglin' from its chain. The chain was attached to one of the buttonholes in the vest. I told Jackson to leave the watch be, but he wouldn't listen. He first tried to unhook the chain from the buttonhole, but havin' a hard time at it, he grew frustrated and ended up yankin' at it instead, breakin' the chain. 'Since you seem to like this watch so much, I'll let you have it,' he said, and gave it to me."

Enos held up his right hand, opened it and viewed his palm for a moment, then looked up at the judge. "Your Honour, it was as if that watch burned my hand and I hurled it as far away from me as I could. Jackson went lookin' for the watch later, but he couldn't find it." Enos' gaze returned to his palm. "It still burns at times where that watch touched my skin. It's God's punishment is what it is." Enos seemed to lose himself in thought as he kept staring at his palm.

"What happened then?" the judge asked after a while, bringing Enos back to reality.

Enos lowered his head. "I was still in shock over what had taken place and had trouble thinkin' straight." He shrugged. "I let Jackson take charge. He dug the hole bigger and pulled the body in there. Afterwards, he snuck back to camp to get McKenna's personal belongings which he threw on top of the body and . . ." Enos paused. "And he covered it all with dirt," he added, his voice breaking.

"What about the gold?" Judge Begbie asked as he contemplated Enos with a frown.

Enos wiped his nose with the back of his hand.

"We hid the bags with the gold in a flour sack, which we placed in the very back of the wagon I was drivin'."

Zach was hanging on Enos' every word. The narrative was not at all what he had expected. He hadn't even considered that anyone else but Jackson could have been involved in McKenna's disappearance.

Enos' eyes darkened. "Jackson's surely rotten to the core to think that I would sacrifice my brother to save my own hide." His voice shook from anger. "Had I known about Theo's trial I would have dropped everythin' and made haste up here, or gone to the local constabulary. Rest assured that no matter the consequences, I would have told them exactly what transpired that night."

He buried his face in his hands for a moment. When he looked up again, anguish had replaced the anger in his eyes. "To think that my brother could have been hanged without me knowin' it." He viewed Theo through tears. "I'm so terribly sorry for all the sufferin' you've had to go through, because of this." He wiped his nose with the back of his hand. "I hope you can see in your heart to forgive me."

There were also tears in Theo's eyes. "Of course, I forgive you, Enos."

"You're a good brother to me, Theo, and I appreciate that, even though I don't always show it," Enos said.

"I only want what's best for you." Theo smiled at him through his tears. "That's why I take you to task when I think you've done wrong."

"Mr. Cox," the judge said to Enos. "You'll have time to catch up with your brother later."

Enos turned his attention to the judge again. "I apologize, Your Honour." He massaged his neck. "I haven't been the same since that night of Mr. McKenna's passin'. Haunted as I am by nightmares, a peaceful night's sleep has become a thing of the past," he snorted. "And Jackson, who could certainly never be accused of bein' a friendly man even on his best days, became suspicious to the point of becomin' half mad." His gaze sought out Zach. "He was convinced that the lad, sittin' down there," he nodded at Zach, "had worked out what we'd done, and Jackson was forever pesterin' me about doin' away with him, before he made trouble for us. He wanted to make it look like an accident somehow."

He looked at the judge again. "Of course, Your Honour, I refused to take part in it." Enos shook his head. "But Jackson wouldn't let it go, and I soon began to fear for the lad's life. I made it my mission to watch over him as much as I possibly could." His jaw tightened. "The only time I wasn't payin' attention, Jackson nearly succeeded in killin' him."

"When I was with the horses on the steamship, and they panicked because of that rifle shot," Zach blurted out before he could stop himself.

Enos nodded. "Fortunately, my brother was there to protect you from bein' trampled by the horses." He nodded at his brother. "And for that I'm grateful, Theo. I couldn't bear havin' the lad's death on my conscience. When we finally arrived in Barkerville," he continued. "I'd had it with Jackson, and was tryin' to figure out a way to tell him that it was time for us to part ways, when he beat me to it, tellin' me that he wanted to partner up with his friend, Archie, on a goldmine venture."

"Do you still have Mr. McKenna's gold, Mr. Cox?" Judge Begbie asked.

Enos shook his head. "No, I don't," he said. "Truth is that when it came time to split the gold, I couldn't even bear to look at it, much less have it in my possession." He smiled wryly. "Believe me, Jackson was only too happy to take it all." Enos looked over at Theo. "And now, Your Honour, please let my brother go."

Chapter 52

∽

TALK AT THE OTHER tables ceased as soon as Theo, Miss Reid, Zach and Kyle arrived at the Wake Up Jake. People curiously watched the four of them as they made their way toward the very back of the restaurant where Theo had spotted an empty table.

One portly man with a full beard, whom Zach recognized as the owner of a local brewery, got up and seized Theo's hand, pumping it up and down. "So happy that you're free."

Still shaking Theo's hand, he looked at the three other men sitting at his table. "I kept tellin' you that he was innocent, didn't I?"

One of the men nodded. "You sure did, Joseph," he said with a wry smile.

Joseph looked at Theo again. "What was done to you was a travesty of justice," he said as he finally let go of Theo's hand. "That brother of yours was always a bit a scoundrel if you ask me."

Theo stiffened and took a step back from Joseph. "I'll not have you speak ill of Enos."

Joseph, momentarily thrown off balance, quickly regained his composure. "Of course not, Theo, after all he's your brother." He lifted his hat to Miss Reid. "Ma'am, I wish you a pleasant meal."

She nodded curtly at him and followed Theo to the table, where she seated herself across from him. Kyle grabbed the chair next to Theo, and Zach sat down next to Miss Reid. Before long, people stopped staring at them and resumed their conversations.

"Don't mind them, Theo," Miss Reid said. "They mean no harm."

Theo nodded. "I know that, but I'll not tolerate anyone speaking ill of my brother." He turned to Kyle. "I never properly thanked you for what you did, finding Enos, and getting him here in time."

Kyle shrugged. "Well, it was my chance to finally ride a horse." He shifted gingerly in his seat. "My hemorrhoids sure took a serious beating," he said with a grin.

Theo burst out laughing. "Oh, it feels so good to be free

and among friends." His expression turned serious again. "I had given up all hope and resigned myself to the fact that I was going to spend the rest of my days in jail."

Miss Reid stretched her hand across the white and red checkered table cloth and placed her hand on top of his. "Thank goodness everything turned out okay."

"I'll never take life for granted again," he said, looking into her eyes.

Zach's gaze moved from Theo to Miss Reid. Considering the way she acted around him, it was painfully obvious how much she was into him with all her adoring looks and the way she always found a reason to touch him. Zach made up his mind that if Theo didn't come clean about Miss Mulligan soon, he would tell Miss Reid about her.

"So do you think they're ever going to catch Jackson?" Kyle asked Theo. After Enos had come clean to Judge Begbie, the judge had dispatched two constables to arrest Jackson. As it turned out, he was not at his mine. His partner, Archie, hadn't been much help, telling the constables that he wasn't Jackson's keeper and had no idea where he was. All he knew was that Jackson had not shown up for work that morning. The constables had then tried the cabin Jackson and Archie shared, but that too was empty. It had now been two days and they still hadn't been able to locate him, which was a point of endless fascination to Kyle.

"Eventually, I'm sure they will," Theo said in answer to Kyle's question.

"When I ran into Constable Franklin, I told them to search all the mines," Kyle said with a grin. "After all, rats like to hide in the dark."

Theo pulled his hand from underneath Miss Reid's when the waiter arrived at their table. "Sorry, it took so long," the waiter said to Theo. "As you can see, we have quite the crowd today."

Twenty minutes later they had their meals in front of them, and Kyle right away attacked his plate with enthusiasm, cutting big pieces off his steak and stuffing them in his mouth, chewing with relish. "This is good grub," he said.

"Close your mouth when you chew," Miss Reid scolded him.

Kyle gave her the thumbs up. "Sure thing, Miss E."

When Kyle had finished his own food in record time, he began eying Zach's plate. "You're not going to eat that?" he asked pointing at the fried potatoes and beans still left there.

Zach, who didn't have much of an appetite, shook his head and pushed the plate over to Kyle, who right away dug into the potatoes.

"So where's Enos?" Miss Reid asked Theo as she put her fork down.

Theo, who had also finished his meal, pushed his plate aside and wiped his mouth with his napkin. "He's getting ready to go back to Fort Yale early tomorrow morning."

Miss Reid sat back in the chair. "He was incredibly lucky that Judge Begbie was so lenient."

Theo nodded as he put his napkin down on the table. "He knows that well." After Enos had come clean, Judge Begbie had told him how wrong it had been for him not to have come forward earlier, but that he also understood how intimidated Enos felt by Jackson's threats. We're all human, Mr. Cox, he had said. We make mistakes and to me it looks as if you have suffered enough. Enos had thanked him with tears in his eyes.

"Theo!"

The four of them hadn't noticed Miss Mulligan walk into the restaurant. She was now headed straight for their table.

Theo scrambled to his feet. "Charlotte!" Looking flustered, he turned to Miss Reid. "Eliza, this is Miss Mulligan."

The young woman smiled brightly at Miss Reid. "Call me Charlotte. I saw you at the trial all the time." She nodded in turn at Zach and Kyle. "You, and your nephews." Miss Mulligan looked great in her long-sleeved, small-checkered green and white dress with the only adornment being a white lace collar. Her long heavy blonde hair was pinned back from her forehead and cascaded down her back in ringlet curls. "I want to thank you, Miss Reid, or may I call you Eliza, for being such a good friend to poor Theo throughout his ordeal." Miss Mulligan came around the table and placed her grey gloved hands on Theo's arm. "I know how he appreciated it."

"We were only too happy to be of help," Miss Reid said with a strained smile.

"Won't you sit down, Charlotte," Theo asked, offering his own chair to her.

Miss Mulligan let go of his arm. "No, my aunt and uncle are expecting me, so I must take my leave." She looked at Miss Reid again. "I so much hope that you and your nephews, of course, will be able to come to my uncle's establishment tonight to celebrate."

Miss Reid looked in confusion from Theo to Miss Mulligan and back again. "Celebrate what?" Understanding filled her eyes. "Oh, you mean Theo's release."

Miss Mulligan looked up at Theo, eyes shining. "No, our engagement. Theo and I are to be married next month. See you later, Dear."

Theo cleared his throat. "Six o'clock, isn't it?"

Miss Mulligan nodded and left.

Zach snuck a glance at Miss Reid. She sat staring at Theo, her mouth half-open.

"Eliza, I meant to . . ." he began, but was interrupted when Miss Reid shot up from her chair and flung her napkin in his face.

"Well, I hope you'll be happy, Mr. Theodore Cox." She struggled to get out from behind the table. With a muffled cry, she ran from the restaurant. The slam of the front door reverberated through the room.

Theo looked stunned.

Zach shook his head at him as he got up from his chair. "How did you think she would react?" He looked over at Kyle. "Come on, we have to find her."

Theo began pulling his jacket on. "Maybe I should be the one . . ."

He was cut short by Zach. "No, I think it's best you let Kyle and me handle this."

Looking contrite, Theo nodded and sat down again. "When she feels ready, I would like to have a proper talk with her."

Too little too late, Zach thought. "I'll let her know. Hurry up, will you," he said, turning to Kyle.

Kyle threw his napkin on top of his plate and got up from his chair. "See you later, Theo," he said.

"Any idea where she might have gone?" Kyle asked Zach when they stood outside the restaurant.

Zach gave a shrug. "Probably she went back to the hotel to get some privacy." They headed in that direction.

Chapter 53

AS IT TURNED OUT, Miss Reid hadn't gone back to the hotel.

"When you find your aunt, you send her back here," Miss Combs told them when they asked her if she had seen her. "Madame Pond's in a right lather, becaus' we're gettin' a new guest shortly and she wants the rooms readied." She waved toward the door. "Go to it, instead of just standin' there."

Outside the hotel, they stood looking up and down the street, not sure where else to search for Miss Reid. At last Zach shrugged. "Let's just walk through town. Maybe someone saw her."

"Fine with me," Kyle said. "Johnny gave me the day off, so I have the time."

They hadn't gone very far, when Zach heard someone yell out his name.

Across the street, he saw Billy Barker wave at him from the opposite boardwalk. "You lookin' for your aunt?" he yelled.

Zach nodded. "Yes, we are." He and Kyle hurried down the steps from the boardwalk and ran across the street.

"Where is she?" Zach asked Barker as soon as they reached the other side.

Barker turned, and pointed. "Down there in The Gold Nugget."

"The Gold Nugget?" Zach asked.

Barker nodded. "Yeah, it's a new saloon. Just opened last week."

"Saloon!" Zach had a hard time believing that Miss Reid would willingly set foot in a place like that.

A stench of whiskey surrounded Zach when Barker burped. "Better git her out of there, lads. A lady shouldn't be in a place like that on her own."

Kyle patted Barker on the shoulder. "Thanks, man."

They found Miss Reid sitting alone at a table in the middle of the saloon, staring angrily at the middle-aged man serving drinks at the counter. The men occupying the other tables were clearly uncomfortable having her there, and they kept sending uncertain looks her way.

Zach and Kyle claimed a couple of chairs and sat down across from Miss Reid at the table.

Zach leaned toward her and touched her arm. "What are you doing here, Miss Reid?"

She turned in her seat and glared at both of them. "Leave me alone."

"Sorry, can't do," Kyle said, shaking his head at her. "Honestly, Miss E., I didn't take you for a boozer."

"I like the occasional Martini or glass of white wine, okay, but that . . . that . . ." She couldn't find the right word to describe the barkeep and instead pointed at him. "He refuses to serve me."

The barkeep, noticing her gesture, came around the counter, and hurried over to their table. He stared hard at Miss Reid. "Ma'am, I already told you that I would like you to leave."

She wrapped her arm around the backrest of the chair, pointing a defiant chin at him, "Why? My money is as good as any, and I would like a drink."

He grabbed the edge of the table and leaned toward her. "Ma'am, we don't serve unaccompanied women here."

Zach got up from his chair. "Come on, Miss Reid, we better go."

She waved at him to sit down again. "As you can see, I'm not unaccompanied," she told the barkeep as she indicated Kyle and Zach with a nod of her head. "So now can I have my drink? I'll even settle on a whiskey, or a brandy."

The barkeep straightened up, and gave Kyle and Zach the once over. "Those two are clearly minors." He pointed to the exit. "Now all of you, please leave. I don't want a scene in here."

"Fine," Miss Reid got up from behind the table. "I'll find myself a place more accommodating than this joint."

"You do that, Ma'am." The barkeep turned and marched back to the counter.

"Jerk," Miss Reid said through clenched teeth. She turned her attention to Zach. "Did you know about Theo and Miss Mulligan?"

Zach got up from his chair again and pushed it under the table. "Well, not about the engagement, but I did know he was seeing Miss Mulligan."

"And you didn't think to tell me." Tears welled up in her eyes. "I felt such a fool. You should have told me." She swiped angrily at her eyes with the back of her hand.

"You're not being fair," Zach said. "It was up to Mr. Cox to tell you, and he promised he would, but then he got arrested . . ."

"Would you two shut up." Kyle, who had remained in his seat, interrupted them. He was staring at something in the back of the room. "Take a look," he told Zach. "Is that who I think it is?" Zach looked in the direction Kyle was pointing. At one of the tables, hidden in shadows, sat a man who had his wide-brimmed hat pulled down low over his forehead. He was fingering a whiskey glass on the table.

Zach shook his head. "I don't know what you . . ."

"Look closely," Kyle insisted.

Zach studied the man carefully. There was something familiar about his chin. The breath caught in his throat. "No, he can't possibly be stupid enough to sit here in full view of everyone."

"And yet here he is, Mr. Piss-ant himself." Kyle shot up from his chair.

Miss Reid gave Kyle a disconcerted look across the table. "What's going on?" she asked.

"Jackson is over there." Zach indicated the table where Jackson was sitting, or rather had been sitting, because he wasn't there anymore.

"There he is," Kyle yelled, pointing out Jackson, who was disappearing through a door in the back of the saloon. Kyle began weaving his way between tables and chairs. "Come on, Zach," he yelled over his shoulder.

"I'll go with Kyle while you find a constable," Zach told Miss Reid. "Tell him we saw Jackson and that he most likely is somewhere out behind the saloon called The Gold Nugget."

Miss Reid shook her head firmly. "If you think I'm going to leave you two to do battle with Jackson alone, you're sadly mistaken." She turned and followed Kyle. "What are you standing here for?" she yelled at Zach over her shoulder.

Kyle was opening the door when the two of them reached him, and they followed him into a small room that was clearly used for storage. Their only light source, when the door to the saloon clicked shut behind them, came from two narrow windows placed close to the ceiling. To their left, there were floor-to-ceiling shelves jammed with baskets and boxes of all sizes, and to their right big crates and barrels were pushed up against the wall. Across from them was another closed door leading to the outside.

"Jackson probably ran out that way." Kyle indicated the door with a nod of his head.

"That surely must be locked considering all the goods that are stocked in here." Miss Reid looked anxiously around. "He could be hiding in here," she whispered. The thought made Zach's skin crawl.

"Well, let's find out if it's locked." Kyle hurried over to the door and tried the handle. "No, it's not," he said opening the door. He froze in the doorway.

"What's wrong?" Miss Reid asked.

Kyle turned and looked at them, his face pale. "You're not going to believe this."

Miss Reid and Zach rushed over to him and looked through the doorway.

"This can't be," Miss Reid gasped as she stared into the interior of a church, but not just any church.

Zach swallowed hard. "We're back in Yale!"

"Yup," was all Kyle said.

Miss Reid edged past Kyle through the doorway and walked tentatively into the church. She stopped in front of the altar and looked up at it for a moment, then turned to Zach and Kyle with disbelief written all over her face. "We went from Barkerville to Yale just like that." She snapped her fingers in the air. "Which means . . ."

Miss Reid didn't have time to finish the sentence when the

front door to the church opened and in walked a young woman dressed in a long blue-and-white checkered dress with a white shawl. She was followed by two older women and a young couple with three kids.

"The church of St. John the Divine was built in 1863," the young woman told the group. "And it went through a major restoration in 1953 . . ." Her voice trailed when she saw Miss Reid standing there in front of the altar. "Sorry, I didn't know anyone was in here," she said.

Miss Reid, who seemed mesmerized by the brightly striped ball, one of the three kids, a boy of about five, was holding in his hands, didn't answer. "Can I help you?" the young woman asked. "Well, you're welcome to join our group," she added hurriedly. "All of you," she said when she spotted Zach and Kyle still standing in the doorway.

Shaking his head, Zach walked over to Miss Reid. "No, that's okay," he told the young woman. "We were just leaving." He hooked his arm through Miss Reid's and began leading her down the aisle of the church. Zach heard the slam of a door, and then Kyle's heavy footsteps following them. Zach smiled at the guide and her group as they passed by them. "Have a nice day," he said, and continued out the front door and down the steps of the church.

At the base of the staircase, Zach stopped and let go of Miss Reid, who still looked shaken. The sun was shining brightly from a clear blue sky and from the road Zach heard a car speed by, tires squealing.

"I think we can all agree that this is obviously not 1866 anymore," Kyle said from the middle of the staircase where he stood, gazing around him.

Zach looked up at him. "No, obviously it's not." Another car drove by on the road as the two of them stood there staring at each other.

"So what now?" Kyle asked as he walked down the rest of the steps.

Miss Reid finally stirred into action. "Well, no use standing around here," she said with a shrug and walked down the pathway leading away from the church.

Zach didn't bring up something that had just occurred to him as he and Kyle trudged after her. *What if they hadn't returned to the same year they had left?*

When they reached the road, Miss Reid headed in the direction of the museum. Walking along the side of the road, Zach kept a keen eye on the cars driving by. He saw a Tesla, a Honda and a red Mini pass by in quick succession.

"There's the bus." Miss Reid pointed excitedly at the yellow school bus as they approached the museum's parking lot. "And there's the class."

She was right. Zach had already spotted Mr. Youtz among the group, but how could that be, since they had been in Barkerville for well over three months! This obviously had occurred to Kyle too when he said, "They can't still be here."

Derek was the first one to notice the three of them as they hurried across the parking lot towards the class. "There she is, Mr. Youtz," he yelled, pointing at Miss Reid. "And Kyle and Zach are there too." In his excitement, he began jumping up and down.

Mr. Youtz pushed his way through the throng of students. "Eliza, where've you been? We looked absolutely everywhere." Then the relief in his eyes turned to anger. "Why in the world didn't you answer my calls and..." He stopped mid-sentence as he now for the first time, noticed their clothes. His gaze jumped to Miss Reid's face. "Why are you dressed like that?"

"Yeah, why have you all changed into clothes from the gold rush period?" Susan piped up. Of course, she would be the one to know.

"So where were you?" Mr. Youtz asked again.

"In Barkerville," Miss Reid blurted out, before she could stop herself.

A hint of a smile crossed Mr. Youtz's lips. "Barkerville! Good one, Eliza. That's at least three hundred kilometres north of here. Even if you flew you couldn't make it there and back in an hour."

Zach thought he had heard wrong. "We've only been gone for an hour?"

Mr. Youtz looked at his watch. "Well, more like an hour and a half by now. We were quite worried. As a matter of fact we were just talking about calling the RCMP." He looked back at the two chaperones, who nodded in agreement.

Susan, who had sidled up next to Zach, fingered the sleeve

of his checkered shirt. "Whew, this stuff is scratchy. So why are you wearing it?" she asked.

Flustered, Zach looked down at his clothes. "We were . . . well, we were asked if we wanted to be extras in some movie they were shooting." He hesitated before he continued. "The movie takes place in the 1860s, we were told, so that's why we're dressed this way."

Mr. Youtz, who had overheard Zach, frowned. "A movie?" He shook his head at Miss Reid. "We didn't notice them filming any movie here."

"How much did they pay you?" Susan asked Zach.

"Eh nothing," he answered, wishing Susan would leave him alone. He turned his head and saw that Kyle was heading away from the bus toward the museum building. "I have to go," Zach told Susan and hurried after Kyle.

"What's going on?" he asked when he caught up with him. Kyle didn't answer as he continued up the steps to the front porch of the museum. Zach trailed after him.

Kyle stopped in front of the open door to the museum where he first peeked inside, then turned to Zach. "I just needed to get away. Too many questions I don't feel like answering right now."

After just having been set upon by Susan, Zach knew exactly how he felt. "Yeah, you're right about that." He hesitated before he asked Kyle his next question. "You really don't seem too happy about being back home."

Kyle stepped away from the door when some museum

goers wanted to leave. "Are you?" he asked Zach.

"I'm what you can call ambivalent," Zach admitted after having thought about it. "I mean, I can't wait to see my parents, family and friends, but at the same time I'm really going to miss the people I've met over the last couple of months, especially Mr. Cox," he added.

Kyle nodded. "What if I told you that I would rather be back in Barkerville than here?" Tears were glistening in his eyes. He swallowed hard. "I'm going to miss Johnny so much. He respected and treated me like an equal, which is more than I can say for my own family."

Kyle tried blinking the tears away, but to no avail. Wiping his eyes with the back of his hand, he turned and walked over to the porch railing. Zach followed him. They stood next to each other, looking out over the museum's adjoining yard where spring flowers bloomed in abundance. Zach glanced at Kyle's hands which rested on the wooden railing, noticing the callouses and scars he had acquired working for the carpenter. "Yeah, Johnny was . . . is a great guy," Zach said.

He heard the rustle of skirts behind him and turned around. Miss Reid was coming up the steps. "The bus will be leaving soon," she said as she walked up to them.

An older lady who had been following closely behind Miss Reid came over and tapped her on the shoulder. "Do you work here?" she asked with a very British accent as she glanced at Miss Reid's old-fashioned dress.

"No, I don't work here." Miss Reid pointed to the entrance

of the museum. "I'm sure they'll be glad to help you in there."

"Oh, okay." With a last flustered glance at the teacher's clothes, the other woman did as she was told.

Miss Reid turned her attention to Zach and Kyle again. "What were you two talking about?" she asked looking at them in turn.

Kyle shrugged. "About how much we're going to miss Barkerville and the people we left behind." He gave Miss Reid a crooked smile. "Of course we already know who you're going to miss the most."

"Kyle!" Zach warned, noticing how Miss Reid's lips had tightened. "I'm really sorry about what happened between you and Mr. Cox," he told her. "I realize now that I should have mentioned his relationship with Miss Mulligan."

"No, you were quite right when you said that it was not your responsibility," she said. "It wasn't anyone's fault really. I was only angry and upset." Tears welled up in her eyes. "You've no control with whom you fall in love with, and I'm not blaming Theo one bit." She took a deep breath. "He's a wonderful man and I wish him all the happiness in the world."

Kyle pulled a handkerchief which, surprisingly, looked fairly clean out of his jacket pocket. "Here you go."

Miss Reid gave him a surprised look as he handed it to her. "You actually carry around a handkerchief." She shook her head. "Miracles never cease," she said, wiping her eyes with the handkerchief.

"Eliza!"

The three of them had been so absorbed in their conversation that they hadn't noticed Mr. Youtz walk up the steps. Miss Reid quickly crumpled the handkerchief in her hand as she turned to him. Mr. Youtz waved impatiently at them to follow him. "Come on, we're all waiting for you." He hastened down the steps.

Miss Reid, Zach and Kyle hurried after him. The students had already boarded the bus. Susan, who had spotted them through the window as they crossed the parking lot, waved at them.

"So I guess we're now supposed to pick up our lives as if nothing happened," Zach said more to himself than the other two.

Kyle shrugged. "What choice do we have?" He grinned at Miss Reid. "Isn't that right, Miss E.?"

"You better drop that Miss E. now," she said frowning at him. "Now we're back, it'll be Miss Reid to you." She watched Mr. Youtz run up the steps to the entrance of the bus. "My belief is that our little time travel adventure was a one-time thing."

Mr. Youtz stuck his head out of the doorway of the bus. "You guys, we're waiting," he yelled. The bus roared to life.

Inside the bus, Miss Reid sat down next to Mr. Youtz. She gave Zach and Kyle a quick smile as they walked down the middle of the aisle on their way to their own assigned seats. They were followed by curious stares from their classmates.

Zach scooted to his window seat. Kyle slumped down next to him and stretched his arms over his head while yawning. "This has been a rather eventful twenty-four hours or should I say couple of months."

"That, Kyle, is the understatement of all time." Zach's foot hit something stowed underneath the seat in front of him. He now remembered he had stuffed his backpack in there when the class went to visit the museum that morning. As he bent over to retrieve it, Jenkins put the bus into gear. It started up with such a jerk that it sent Zach face-first into the back of the seat in front of him. "Ouch," he said.

"That didn't do your ugly mug any good," Kyle said.

Wrinkling his nose, which had taken the brunt of the impact, Zach dislodged his pack from underneath the seat and straightened up again. He placed the pack on his lap and unzipped it.

Inside was the bagged lunch his mother had handed to him that morning. He pulled the brown paper bag out and opened it. Instead of one sandwich there were two, both wrapped in cellophane. His mother had obviously thought that he might get hungry on the way home and therefore needed an extra sandwich. Zach couldn't help smiling since it was so like his mother to plan everything to the nth degree.

He held one of the wrapped sandwiches out to Kyle. "Hungry?" he asked. "Ham. It's the only sandwich meat I like," he added as an explanation. He had always been a picky eater. Probably not anymore, he couldn't help thinking. Not after the fare he had to get used to over the last couple of months.

Kyle took the sandwich from his hand. "You should know by now that I'm always hungry," he said as he unwrapped it and took a big bite.

"No eating or drinking on the bus," Jenkins, who had observed them in the rear-view mirror, yelled.

"No, Sir," Kyle said as he ducked down behind the seat in front of him and took another big bite from the sandwich. When Zach saw Mr. Youtz frown at him, he folded the top of the paper bag and dropped it back into his pack. It wasn't worth drawing the teacher's ire for a lousy ham sandwich.

Zach watched as Kyle continued eating and was struck by the thought that had he and Kyle not been thrown together by unforeseen circumstances they would most likely not have become friends.

Kyle looked at him. "What do you think happened to Jackson?"

With everything that had been going on, Zach had completely forgotten about his nemesis.

"If he ran out through the same door as we did," Kyle continued, "then he would have ended up inside the church too, wouldn't he?"

"Which means he's here in Yale right now and that's not what you would call a comforting thought." Zach looked out the window. The bus had left the museum's parking lot and they were driving past the Church of St. John the Divine. He saw no sign of Jackson.

Kyle chuckled next to him. "Can you imagine the culture shock he's in for."

Zach turned his head and looked at him. "Maybe the time warp only works for us and not him," he said hoping fervently that this was true.

Kyle shrugged. "Well, if that's the case he'll probably be shaking in his boots in front of Judge Begbie before long."

Zach directed his attention to the outside again watching as the bus headed for the town of Hope. Soon he heard soft snoring next to him. Kyle was asleep. He sat with his head leaning against the backrest, his mouth open.

Zach, too, was exhausted but knew that his mind wouldn't give him the rest he needed to follow his friend into dreamland. He was looking forward to seeing everyone at home again, especially after having thought for so long that this might never happen. At the same time, he didn't fully belong in that world anymore. There was a place from long ago where there were people Zach would miss, and who would in turn miss him.

Barkerville.

ABOUT THE AUTHOR

Bitten Acherman was born and grew up in Denmark. After completing a degree in Library Science from the Royal School of Library and Information Technology in Copenhagen, she married a Canadian and immigrated to Los Angeles, California, where she worked a number of years at a university library. In 1997 Bitten and her family moved to Canada and settled in Burnaby, British Columbia. She enrolled in a manuscript group at the Shadbolt Centre in Burnaby and began developing her ideas into creative fiction. She soon found herself enjoying writing for the young adult market. Today she writes mostly historical fiction because she loves the process of immersing herself in another time period. *Lost in Barkerville*, a time travel adventure for young readers, is the first installment in a series about life in Barkerville, British Columbia, during the 1860s Cariboo gold rush. In the past, Bitten has won prizes and honourable mentions in short story fiction. *Lost in Barkerville* is her first published novel. Visit her at www.bittenacherman.com.